Grif
A Story Of Australian Life

By

B. L. Farjeon

Double 9
BOOKS

Grif
A Story Of Australian Life
by B. L. Farjeon

Copyright © 2024

All Rights reserved.

ISBN: 978-93-61420-22-1

Published by

DOUBLE 9 BOOKS

2/13-B, Ansari Road
Daryaganj, New Delhi – 110002
info@double9books.com
www.double9books.com
Tel. 011-40042856

ABOUT THE AUTHOR

B. L. Farjeon, born Benjamin Leopold Farjeon (1838–1903), was a prolific British author and playwright known for his contributions to Victorian literature. Farjeon wrote throughout diverse genres, which include novels, performs, and poetry, with a penchant for growing attractive and emotionally resonant memories. One of his super works is "Basil and Annette," a singular that showcases Farjeon's storytelling prowess. Published in 1877, the narrative unfolds towards the backdrop of Victorian society, and Farjeon's eager observations capture the nuances of the time. "Basil and Annette" in all likelihood reflects the Victorian fascination with romantic topics, societal expectations, and ethical dilemmas. Farjeon's capability to craft characters with intensity and authenticity, coupled with a compelling plot, made his works famous among readers of his era. Though now not as widely remembered today as some of his contemporaries, B. L. Farjeon's literary legacy endures via his contributions to the rich tapestry of Victorian literature. His works provide insights into the social dynamics, values, and demanding situations of the time, making him a treasured discern in the literary panorama of the nineteenth century. "Basil and Annette" remains a testament to Farjeon's ability to capture the complexities of human relationships inside the context of the Victorian milieu.

CONTENTS

CHAPTER I
GRIF RELATES SOME OF HIS EXPERIENCES...................................7

CHAPTER II
HUSBAND AND WIFE..16

CHAPTER III
GRIF LOSES A FRIEND 27

CHAPTER IV
THE CONJUGAL NUTTALLS..37

CHAPTER V
THE MORAL MERCHANT ENTERTAINS
HIS FRIENDS AT DINNER 45

CHAPTER VI
FATHER AND DAUGHTER...54

CHAPTER VII
GRIF PROMISES TO BE HONEST 65

CHAPTER VIII
GRIF IS SET UP IN LIFE AS A MORAL SHOEBLACK..................84

CHAPTER IX
A BANQUET IS GIVEN TO THE MORAL MERCHANT.............96

CHAPTER X
ON THE ROAD TO EL DORADO.......................................106

CHAPTER XI
WELSH TOM 114

CHAPTER XII
THE NEW RUSH...122

CHAPTER XIII
OLD FLICK 127

CHAPTER XIV
LITTLE PETER IS PROVIDED FOR 133

CHAPTER XV
A HOT DAY IN MELBOURNE.........143

CHAPTER XVI
POOR MILLY.........158

CHAPTER XVII
BAD LUCK.........172

CHAPTER XVIII
HONEST STEVE.........181

CHAPTER XIX
THE WELSHMAN READS HIS LAST
CHAPTER IN THE OLD WELSH BIBLE.........184

CHAPTER XX
THE TENDER-HEARTED
OYSTERMAN TRAPS HIS GAME.........200

CHAPTER XXI
THE MORAL MERCHANT CALLS
A MEETING OF HIS CREDITORS.........207

CHAPTER XXII
ALICE AND GRIF MEET FRIENDS UPON THE ROAD.........215

CHAPTER XXIII
THE STORY OF SILVER-HEADED JACK.........224

CHAPTER XXIV
MRS. NICHOLAS NUTTALL TAKES POSSESSION.........238

CHAPTER XXV
MRS. NICHOLAS NUTTALL RECEIVES VISITORS.........244

CHAPTER XXVI
A NIGHT OF ADVENTURES.........251

CHAPTER XXVII
GRIF BEARS FALSE WITNESS.........265

CHAPTER I
GRIF RELATES SOME OF HIS EXPERIENCES

In one of the most thickly populated parts of Melbourne city, where poverty and vice struggle for breathing space, and where narrow lanes and filthy thoroughfares jostle each other savagely, there stood, surrounded by a hundred miserable hovels, a gloomy house, which might have been likened to a sullen tyrant, frowning down a crowd of abject, poverty-stricken slaves. From its appearance it might have been built a century ago; decay and rottenness were apparent from roof to base: but in reality it was barely a dozen years old. It had lived a wicked and depraved life, had this house, which might account for its premature decay. It looked like a hoary old sinner, and in every wrinkle of its weather-board casing was hidden a story which would make respectability shudder. There are, in every large city, dilapidated or decayed houses of this description, which we avoid or pass by quickly, as we do drunken men in the streets.

In one of the apartments of this house, on a dismally wet night, were two inmates, crouched before a fire as miserable as the night. A deal table, whose face and legs bore the marks of much rough usage; a tin candlestick containing a middle-aged tallow candle, the yellow light from which flickered sullenly, as if it were weary of its life and wanted to be done with it; a three-legged stool; and a wretched mattress, which was hiding itself in a corner, with a kind of shamefaced consciousness that it had no business to be where it was:--comprised all the furniture of the room. The gloominess of the apartment and the meanness of the furniture were in keeping with one another, and both were in keeping with the night, which sighed and moaned and wept without; while down the rickety chimney the wind whistled as if in mockery, and the rain-drops fell upon the embers, hissing damp misery into the eyes of the two human beings who sat before the fire, bearing their burden quietly, if not patiently.

They were a strange couple. The one, a fair young girl, with a face so mild and sweet, that the beholder, looking upon it when in repose, felt gladdened by the sight. A sweet, fair young face; a face to love. A look of sadness was in her dark brown eyes, and on the fringes, which half-veiled their beauty, were traces of tears. The other, a stunted, ragged boy, with pockmarked face, with bold and brazen eyes, with a vicious smile too often playing about his lips. His hand was supporting his cheek; hers was lying idly upon her knee. The fitful glare of the scanty fire threw light upon both: and to look upon the one, so small and white, with the blue veins so delicately traced; and upon the other, so rough and horny, with every sinew speaking of muscular strength, made one wonder by what mystery of life the two had come into companionship. Yet, strange as was the contrast, there they sat, she upon the stool, he upon the ground, as if they were accustomed to each other's society. Wrapt in her thoughts the girl sat, quiet and motionless, gazing into the fire. What shades of expression passed across her face were of a melancholy nature; the weavings of her fancy in the fitful glare brought nothing of pleasure to her mind. Not far into the past could she look, for she was barely nineteen years of age; but brief as must have been her experience of life's troubles, it was bitter enough to sadden her eyes with tears, and to cause her to quiver as if she were in pain. The boy's thoughts were not of himself; they were of her, as was proven by his peering up at her face anxiously every few moments in silence. That he met with no responsive look evidently troubled him; he threw unquiet glances at her furtively, and then he plucked her gently by the sleeve. Finding that this did not attract her attention, he shifted himself uneasily upon his seat, and in a hoarse voice, called,--

"Ally!"

"Yes," she replied vacantly, as if she were answering the voice of her fancy.

"What are you thinkin' of, Ally?"

"I am thinking of my life," she answered, dreamily and softly, without raising her eyes. "I am trying to see the end of it."

The boy's eyes followed the direction of her wistful gaze.

"Blest if I don't think she can see it in the fire!" he said, under his breath. "I can't see nothin'." And then he exclaimed aloud, "What's the use of botherin'? Thinkin' won't alter it."

"So it seems," she said, sadly; "my head aches with the whirl."

"You oughtn't to be unhappy, Ally; you're very good-looking and very young."

"Yes, I am very young," she sighed. "How old are you, Grif?"

"Blest if I know," Grif replied, with a grin. "I ain't agoin' to bother! I'm old enough, I am!"

"Do you remember your father, Grif?"

"Don't I! He was a rum 'un, he was. Usen't he to wallop us, neither!"

Lost in the recollection, Grif rubbed his back, sympathetically.

"And your mother?" asked the girl.

"Never seed her," he replied, shortly.

Thereafter they fell into silence for a while. But the boy's memory had been stirred by her questions, and he presently spoke again:

"You see, Ally, father is a ticket-of-leave man, and a orfle bad un he is! I don't know what he was sent out for, but it must have been somethin' very desperate, for I've heerd him say so. He was worse nor me--oh, ever so much; but then, of course," he added, apologetically, as if it were to his discredit that he was not so bad as his convict parent, "he was a sight older. And as for lush--my eye! he could lush, could father! Well, when he was pretty well screwed, he used to lay into us, Dick and me, and kick us out of the house. Dick was my brother. Then Dick and me used to fight, for Dick wanted to lay into me too, and I wasn't goin' to stand that. We got precious little to eat, Dick and me; when we couldn't get nothin' to eat at home, we went out and took it. And one day I was trotted up afore the beak, for takin' a pie out of a confetchoner's. They didn't get the pie, though; I eat that. The beak he give me a week for that pie, and wasn't I precious pleased at it! It was the first time I'd ever been in quod, and I was sorry when they turned me out, for all that week I got enough to eat and drink. I arksed the cove to let me stop in another week, so that I might be reformed, as the beak sed, but he only larfed at me, and turned me out. When I got home, father he ses, 'Where have you been, Grif?' And I tells him, I've been to quod. 'What for?' he arks. 'For takin' a pie,' I ses. Blest if I didn't get the worst wallopin' I ever had! 'You've been and disgraced your family,' he sed; 'git out of my sight, you warmint; *I* was never in quod for stealin' a pie!' And with that he shied a bottle at my 'ead. I caught it, but there was nothin' in it! I was very savage for that wallopin'! 'What's disgrace to one's family,' thought I, 'when a cove want's grub?' I was awful hungry, as well as savage; so I made for the confetchoner's and took another pie. I bolted the pie quick, for I knew they would be down on me; and I was trotted up afore the beak agin, and he give me a month. Wasn't I jolly glad! When I come out of quod, father had cut off to the gold-diggins; and as I wanted to get into quod agin, I went to the confetchoner's, and took another pie. The beak, wasn't he flabbergasted! 'What!' he ses, 'have you been and stole another pie!' and then he looks so puzzled that I couldn't help larfin'. 'What do you go and do it for?' ses he. 'Cos I'm hungry, your washup,' ses I. But the beak didn't seem to think nothin' of that; the missus of the shop, she ses, 'Pore boy!' and wanted him to let me off; but he wouldn't, and I wasn't sorry for it. I was five times in quod for takin' pies out of that confetchoner's shop. Next time I was nabbed, though. The old woman she knew I was jist come out, so she hides herself behind the door; and when I cuts in to git my pie, she comes out quick, and ketches 'old of me by the scruff. 'You little warmint,' she ses; 'you shan't wear my life out in this here way! Five times have I been before that blessed magerstrate, who ain't got no more heart than a pump! I wouldn't go,' she ses, keepin' hold of my collar, and looking me 'ard in the face--'I wouldn't go, but the ploesemen they make me. I ain't goin' agin, that I'm determined on. Here! Here's a pie for you!' and she 'olds out a big un. 'That's a rum start,' I thort, as I looked at the pie in her hand. 'It won't do, though. If I take her pie in a honest way, where's my blanket to come from?' But the old woman looked so worried, that I thort I'd make her a offer. 'If I take your pie, missus,' I ses, 'will you let me sleep under the counter?' 'What do you mean?' she ses. Then I tells her that it's no use her givin' me a pie, for I hadn't no place to sleep in; and that she'd better let me take one while she looked another way. 'When I've eat it,' I ses, 'I'll cough, very loud, and then you turn round as if you was surprised to see me, and give me in charge of a peeler.' 'What'll be the good of that?' she arks. 'Don't you see?' I ses. 'Then I shall have the pie, and I shall get my blanket at the lock-up as well!' She wasn't a bad un, by no manner of means. 'My pore boy,' she ses, 'here's the pie, and here's a shillin'. Don't steal no more pies, or you'll break my 'art. You shall have a shillin' a week if you'll promise not to worry me, and whenever you want a pie I'll give you one if you arks for it.' Well, you see, Ally, I thort that was a fair offer, so I ses, 'Done!' and I took my pie and my shillin'. I don't worry her more than I can help," said Grif; "when I'm very hungry I go to the shop. She's a good old sort, she is; and I gets my shillin' a week reglar."

"And have you not heard of your father since he went away?" asked the girl.

"No, 'cept once I was told permiskusly that he was cut tin' some rum capers up the country. They did say he was a bush-ranging, but I ain't agoin' to bother. I was brought up very queer, I was; not like other coves. Father he never give us no eddication; perhaps he didn't have none to give. But he might have give us grub when we wanted it."

"Yours is a hard life, Grif," the girl said, pityingly.

"Yes, it is 'ard, precious 'ard, specially when a cove can't get enough to eat. But I s'pose it's all right. What's the use of botherin'? I wonder," he continued, musingly, "where the rich coves gets all their money from? If I was a swell, and had lots of tin, I'd give a pore chap like me a bob now and then. But they're orfle stingy, Ally, is the swells; they don't give nothin' away for nothin'. When I was in quod, a preacher chap comes and preaches to me. He sets hisself down upon the bench, and reads somethin' out of a book--a Bible, you know--and after he'd preached for arf an hour, he ses, 'What do you think of that, 'nighted boy?' 'It's very good,' I ses, 'but I can't eat it.' 'Put your trust above,' he ses. 'But s'pose all the grub is down here?' ses I. 'I can't go up there and fetch it.' Then he groans, and tells me a story about a infant who was found in the bulrushes, after it had been deserted, and I ups and tells him that I've been deserted, and why don't somebody come and take *me* out of the bulrushes! Wasn't he puzzled, neither!" Grif chuckled, and then, encouraged by his companion's silence, resumed,--

"He come agin, did the preacher cove, afore I was let out, and he preaches a preach about charity. 'Don't steal no more,' he ses, 'or your sole 'll go to morchal perdition. Men is charitable and good; jist you try 'em, and give up your evil courses.' 'How can I help my evil courses?' I ses. 'I only wants my grub and a blanket, and I can't get 'em no other way.' 'You can, young sinner, you can,' he ses. 'Jist you try, and see if you can't.' He spoke so earnest-like, and the tears was a runnin' down his face so hard, that I promised him I'd try. So when I gets out of quod, I thort, I'll see now if the preacher cove is right. I waited till I was hungry, and couldn't get nothin' to eat, without stealin' it. I could have took a trotter, for the trotter-man was a-drinkin' at a public-house bar, and his barsket was on a bench; but I wouldn't. No; I goes straight to the swell streets, and there I sees the swells a-walkin' up and down, and liftin' their 'ats, and smilin' at the gals. They was a rare nice lot of gals, and looked as if butter wouldn't melt in their mouths; but there wasn't one in all the lot as nice as you are, Ally! I didn't have courage at first to speak to the swells, but when I did, send I may live! they started back as if I was a mad dawg. 'You be awf,' they ses, 'or you'll be guv in charge.' What could a pore beggar like me do, after that? I dodged about, very sorry I didn't take the trotter, when who should I see coming along but the preacher chap. 'Here's a slant!' ses I to myself. 'He's charitable and good, he is, and 'll give me somethin' in a minute. He had a lady on his arm, and they both looked very grand. But when I went up to him he starts back too, and ses, 'Begawn, young reperrerbate!' When I heerd that, I sed, 'Charity be blowed!' and I goes and finds out the trotter-man, and takes two trotters, and no one knows nothin' about it."

Before he had finished his story, the girl's thoughts had wandered again. A heavy step in the adjoining apartment roused her.

"Who is that?"

"That's Jim Pizey's foot," replied the boy; "they're up to some deep game, they are. They was at it last night."

"Did you hear them talking about it, Grif?" she asked, earnestly.

"A good part of the time I was arf asleep, and a good part of the time I made game that I was asleep. I heerd enough to know that they're up to somethin' precious deep and dangerous. But, I say, Ally, you won't peach, will you? I should get my neck broke if they was to know that I blabbed."

"Don't fear me, Grif," said the girl; "go on."

"Jim Pizey, of course, he was at the 'ead of it, and he did pretty nearly all the talkin'. The Tenderhearted Oysterman, he put in a word sometimes, but the others only said yes and no. Jim Pizey, he ses, 'We can make all our fortunes, mates, in three months, if we're game. It'll be a jolly life, and I know every track in the country. We can "stick-up"[1] the gold escort in the Black Forest, and we don't want to do nothin' more all our lives. Forty thousand ounces of gold, mates, not a pennyweight less?' Then the Tenderhearted Oysterman ses he didn't care if there was forty million ounces, he wouldn't have nothin' to do with it, if Jim wanted to hurt the poor coves. Didn't they larf at him for sayin' that!"

Footnote 1: "Sticking-up" is an Australian term for burglary and highway Robbery.

"Is he a kind man, Grif?"

"The Tenderhearted Oysterman, do you mean, Ally?" asked the boy, in return.

"Yes, is he really tenderhearted?"

"He's the wickedest, cruellest, of all the lot, Ally. They call him the Tenderhearted Oysterman out of fun. He's always sayin' how soft-hearted he is, but he would think as much of killin' you and me as he would of killin' a fly. After that I falls off in a doze, and presently I hears 'em talkin' agin, between-whiles, like, 'If the escort's too strong for us,' ses Jim Pizey, 'we can tackle the squatters' stations. Some of the squatters keeps heaps of money in their houses.' And then they called over the names of a lot of stations where the squatters was rich men."

"Did you hear them mention Highlay Station, Grif?" the girl asked, anxiously.

"Can't say I did, Ally."

The girl gave a sigh of relief.

"Who were there, Grif, while they were talking?"

"There was Jim Pizey, and Ned Rutt, and Black Sam, and the Tenderhearted Oysterman, and--" but here Grif stopped, suddenly.

"Who else, Grif?" laying her hand upon his arm.

"I was considering Ally," the boy replied, casting a furtive look at her white face, "if there *was* anybody else. I was 'arf asleep, you know."

The girl gazed at him with such distress depicted in her face that Grif turned his eyes from her, and looked uneasily upon the ground. For a few moments she seemed as if she feared to speak, and then she inquired in a voice of pain,--

"Was my husband there, Grif?"

Grif threw one quick, sharp glance upon her, and, as if satisfied with what he saw, turned away again, and did not reply.

"Was my husband there, Grif," the girl repeated.

Still the boy did not reply. He appeared to be possessed with some dogged determination not to answer her question.

"Grif," the girl said, in a voice of such tender pleading that the tears came into the boy's eyes, "Grif, be my friend!"

"Your friend, Ally!" he exclaimed, in amazement, and as he spoke a thrill of exquisite pleasure quivered through him. "Me! A pore beggar like me!"

"I have no one else to depend upon--no one else to trust to--no one else to tell me what I must, yet what I dread to hear. Was my husband there, Grif?"

"Yes, he was there," the boy returned, reluctantly; "more shame for him, and you a sittin' here all by yourself. I say, Ally, why don't you cut away from him? What do you stop here for?"

"Hush! Was he speaking with them about the plots you told me of?"

"No, he was very quiet. They was a tryin' to persuade him to join 'em; but he wouldn't agree. They tried all sorts of games on him. They spoke soft, and they spoke hard. They give him lots of lush, too, and you know, Ally, he *can*--" but Grif pulled himself up short, dismayed and remorseful, for his companion had broken into a passionate fit of weeping.

"I didn't mean to do it, Ally," he said sorrowfully. "Don't take on so. I'll never say it agin. I'm a ignorant beast, that's what I am!" he exclaimed, digging his knuckles into his eyes. "I'm always a puttin' my foot in it."

"Never mind, Grif," said the girl, sobbing. "Go on. Tell me all you heard. I *must* know. Oh, my heart! My heart!" and her tears fell thick and fast upon his hand.

He waited until she had somewhat recovered herself, and then proceeded very slowly.

"They was a-tryin' to persuade him to join 'em. They tried all sorts of dodges, but they was all no go. The Tenderhearted Oysterman, he comes the tender touch, and ses, 'I'm a soft-hearted cove, you know, mate, and I wouldn't kill a worm, if I thort I should 'urt him; if there was any violence a-goin' to be done, I wouldn't be the chap to have a 'and in it.' 'Then why do you have anythin' to do with it?' arks your--you know who I mean, Ally? 'Because I think it'll be a jolly good spree,' ses the Oysterman, 'and because I know we can make a 'cap of shiners without nobody bein' the worse for it.' But they couldn't get him to say Yes; and at last Jim Pizey he gets up in a awful scot, and he ses, 'Look here, mate, we've been and let you in this here scheme, and we ain't a-goin' to have it blown upon. You make up your mind very soon to join us, or it will be the worse for you.'"

"And my husband--"

"I didn't hear nothin' more. I fell right off asleep, and when I woke up they was gone."

"Grif", said the girl, "he must not join in this plot. I *must* keep him from crime. He has been unfortunate--led away by bad companions."

"Yes; we're a precious bad lot, we are."

"But his heart is good, Grif," she continued.

"What does he mean by treatin' you like this, then?" interrupted Grif, indignantly. "You've got no business here, you haven't. You ought to have a 'ouse of your own, you ought."

"I can't explain; you would not understand. Enough that he is my husband; it is sufficient that my lot is linked with his, and that through poverty and disgrace I must be by his side. I can never desert him while I have life. God grant that I may save him yet!"

The boy was hushed into silence by her solemn earnestness.

"He is weak, Grif, and we are poor. It was otherwise once. Those who should assist us will not do so, unless I break the holiest tie--and so we must suffer together."

"I don't see why you should suffer," said Grif, doggedly; "you don't deserve to suffer, you don't."

"Did you ever have a friend, my poor Grif," the girl said, "whom you loved, and for whose sake you would have sacrificed even the few sweets of life you have enjoyed?"

Grif pondered, but being unable to come to any immediate conclusion upon the point, did not reply.

"It is so with me," Alice continued. "I would sacrifice everything for him and for his happiness: for I love him! Ah! how I love him! When he is away from me he loses hope for my sake, not for his own, I know. If he is weak, I must be strong. It is my duty."

She loved him. Yes. No thought that he might be unworthy of the sacrifice she had already made for him tainted the purity of her love, or weakened her sense of duty.

"I've got a dawg, Ally," Grif said, musingly, after a pause. "He ain't much to look at, but he's very fond of me. Rough is his name. The games we have together, me and Rough! He's like a brother to me, is Rough. I often wonder what he can see in me, to be so fond of me--but then they say dawgs ain't got no sense, and that's a proof of it. But if he ain't got sense, he got somethin' as good. Pore old Rough! One day a cove was agoin' to make a rush at me--it was the Tenderhearted Oysterman (we always had a down on each other, him and me!) when Rough, he pounces in, and gives him a nip in the calf of his leg. Didn't the Oysterman squeal! He swore, that day, that he would kill the dawg; but he'd better not try! Kill Rough!" and, at the thought of it, the tears came into the boy's eyes; "and him never to rub his nose agin me any more, after all the games we've had! No, I shouldn't like to lose Rough, for he's a real friend to me, though he *is* only a dawg!"

The girl laid her hand upon Grif's head, and looked pityingly at him. As their eyes met, a tender expression stole into his face, and rested there.

"I'm very sorry for you, Ally. I wish I could do somethin' to make you happy. It doesn't much matter for a pore beggar like me. We was always a bad lot, was father, and Dick, and me. But *you!*--look here, Ally!" he exclaimed, energetically. "If ever you want me to do anythin'--never mind what it is long as I know I'm a-doin' of it for you--I'll do it, true and faithful, I will, so 'elp me--!" Her hand upon his lips checked the oath he was about to utter. He seized the hand, and placed it over his eyes, and leant his cheek against it, as if it brought balm and comfort to him; as indeed it did. "You believe me, Ally, don't you?" he continued, eagerly. "I don't want you to say nothin' more than if ever I can do somethin' for you, you'll let me do it."

"I will, Grif, and I do believe you," she replied. "God help me, my poor boy, you are my only friend."

"That's it!" he exclaimed, triumphantly. "That's what I am, till I die!"

CHAPTER II
HUSBAND AND WIFE

The rain pattered down, faster and faster, as the night wore on, and still the two strange companions sat, silent and undisturbed, before the fire. At intervals sounds of altercation from without were heard, and occasionally a woman's drunken shriek or a ruffian's muttered curse was borne upon the angry wind. A step upon the creaking stairs would cause the girl's face to assume an expression of watchfulness: for a moment only; the next, she would relapse into dreamy listlessness. Grif had thrown himself upon the floor at her feet. He was not asleep, but dozing; for at every movement that Alice made, he opened his eyes, and watched. The declaration of friendship he had made to her had something sacramental in it. When he said that he would be true and faithful to her, he meant it with his whole heart and soul. The better instincts of the boy had been brought into play by contact with the pure nature of a good woman. He had never met any one like Alice. The exquisite tenderness and unselfishness exhibited by her in every word and in every action, filled him with a kind of adoration, and he vowed fealty to her with the full strength of his uncultivated nature. His vow might be depended on. He was rough, and dirty, and ugly, and a thief; but he was faithful and true. Some glimpse of a better comprehension appeared to pass into his face as he lay and watched. And so the hours lagged on until midnight, when a change took place.

A sudden change--a change that transformed the hitherto quiet house into a den of riotous vice and drunkenness. It seemed as though the house had been forced into by a band of ruffianly bacchanals. They came up the stairs, laughing, and singing, and screaming. A motley throng--about a dozen in all--but strangely contrasted in appearance. Men upon whose faces rascality had set its seal; women in whose eyes there struggled the modesty of youth with the depravity of shame. Most of the men were middle-aged; the eldest of the women could scarcely have counted twenty winters from her birth: many of them, even in their childhood, had seen but little of life's summer. With the men, moleskin trousers, pea-jackets, billycock hats, and dirty pipes, predominated. But the women were expensively dressed, as if they sought to hide their shame by a costly harmony of colours. How strange are the groupings we see, yet do not marvel at, in the kaleidoscope of life!

The company were in the adjoining apartment, and, through the chinks in the wall, Alice could see them flitting about. She had started to her feet when she heard them enter the house, and her trembling frame bespoke her agitation. All her heart was in her ears as she listened for the voice she expected yet dreaded to hear.

"Get up, Grif," she whispered, touching the gently with her foot. On the instant, he was standing, watchful by her side. "Listen! Can you hear his voice?"

The boy listened attentively, and shook his head. At this moment, a ribald jest called forth screams of laughter, and caused Alice to cover her crimsoned face, and sink tremblingly into her seat. But after it short struggle with herself, she rose again, and listened anxiously.

"He must be there," she said, her hand twitching nervously at her dress. "Oh, what if I should not see him to-night! I should be powerless to save him. What if they have kept him away from me, fearing that I should turn him from them! Oh, Grif, Grif, what shall I do? what shall I do?"

"Hush!" Grif whispered. "You keep quiet. You pretend to be asleep, and don't let 'em 'ear you. If anybody comes in, you shut your eyes, and breathe 'ard. I'll go and see if he's there."

And he crept out of the room, closing the door softly behind him. Left alone, the girl sat down again by the fire, whispering to herself, "I must save him, I must save him;" as if the words were a charm. "Yes," she whispered, "I must save him from this disgrace, and then I will make one more appeal;" and then she started up again, and listened, and paced the room in an agony of expectation. Thus she passed the next half-hour. At the end of that time, Grif came in, almost noiselessly, and to her questioning look replied,

"He's there, all right."

"What is he doing?"

"He's a settin' in a corner, 'arf asleep, all by 'isself, and he hasn't sed a word to no one. Where are you goin'?" he inquired quickly, as Alice walked towards the door.

"I am going in to him."

"What for?" cried Grif hoarsely, gripping her arm. "Ally, are you mad?"

"I must go and bring him away," she replied, firmly.

"Look here, Ally," said Grif, in a voice of terror; "don't you try it. Pizey's got the devil in him to-night. I know it by his eye. It's jist as cool and wicked as anythin'! When he sets his mind upon a thing he'll do it, or be cut to pieces. If you go in, you can't do nothin', and somethin' bad 'll 'appen. Pizey 'll think you know what you oughtn't to know. Don't you go!"

"But I must save him, Grif," she said, in deep distress. "I must save him, if I die!"

"Yes," Grif said in a thick undertone, and still keeping firm hold of her arm; "that's right and proper, I dersay. But s'pose you die and don't save him? They won't do nothin' to-night. You can't do no good in there, Ally. The Oysterman 'll kill you, or beat you senseless, if you go; and then what could you do? I've seen him beat a woman before to-night. They're mad about somethin' or other, the whole lot of 'em. You'll do him more good by stoppin' away."

"Of what use can my husband be to them, Grif?" she cried, yet suppressing her voice, so that those in the next room should not hear. "What plot of their hatching can he serve them in?"

"I don't know," Grif replied; "he can talk and look like a swell, and that's what none of 'em can do. But you'll soon find out, if you keep quiet. 'Ark! they're a clearin' out the gals," and as he spoke were heard female voices and laughter, and the noise of the speakers who were trooping into the miserable night. "They won't be very long together. They won't be together at all!" he cried, as the door of the adjoining apartment opened, and heavy steps went down the stairs.

"But suppose my husband goes with them?" Alice cried, and tried to reach the door; but Grif restrained her.

"There's Jim Pizey's foot," he said, with a finger at his lips; "jist as if he was tramplin' some one down with every step. And there's Black Sam--I could tell him from a mob of people, for he walks as if he was goin' to tumble down every minute. And there's Ned Rutt--he's got the largest feet I ever sor. And there's the Tenderhearted Oysterman, he treads like a cat. I'll be even with him one day for sayin' he'd kill Rough! And there's--there's no more."

The street door was heavily slammed, and a strange stillness fell upon the house--a stillness which did not appear to belong to it, and which struck Alice with a sense of desolation, and made her shiver. A few moments afterwards Alice's husband entered the apartment. He was a handsome, indolent-looking man, with a reckless manner which did not become him. There were traces of dissipation upon his countenance, and his clothes were a singular mixture of rough coarseness and faded refinement. He did not notice Grif, who had stepped aside, but, gazing neither to the right nor to the left, walked to the seat which Alice had occupied, and sinking into it, plunged his fingers in his hair, and gazed vacantly at the ashes in the grate. He made no sign of recognition to Alice, who went up to him, and encircled his neck with her white arms. As she leant over him, with her face bending to his, caressingly, it appeared, although he did not repulse her, as if there were within him some wish to avoid her, and not be conscious of her presence.

"Richard," she whispered.

But he doggedly turned his head from her.

"Richard," she whispered again, softly and sweetly.

"I hear you," he said, pettishly.

"Do not speak to me harshly to-night, dear," she said; "this day six months we were married."

He winced as he heard this, as if the remembrance brought with it a sense of physical pain, and said:--

"It is right that you should reproach me, yet it is bitter enough for me without that."

"I do not say it to reproach you, dear,--indeed, indeed, I do not!"

"That makes it all the more bitter. This day six months we were married, you say! Better for you, better for me, that we had never seen each other."

"Yes," the girl said, sadly; "perhaps it would have been. But there is no misery to me in the remembrance. I can still bless the day when we first met. Oh, Richard, do not give me cause to curse it!"

"You have cause enough for that every day, every hour," he replied; "to curse the day, and to curse me. You had the promise of a happy future before you saw me, and I have blighted it. What had you done that I should force this misery upon you? What had you done that I should bring you into contact with this?" he looked loathingly upon the bare walls. "And I am even too small-hearted to render you the only reparation in my power--to die, and loose you from a tie which has embittered your existence!"

"Hush, Richard!" she said. "Hush! my dear! All may yet be well, if you have but the courage--"

"But I have not the courage," he interrupted. "I am beaten down, crushed, nerveless. I was brought up with no teaching that existence was a thing to struggle for, and I am too old or too idle to learn the lesson now.

What do such men as I in the world? Why, it has been thrown in my teeth this very night that I haven't even soul enough for revenge."

"Revenge, Richard!" she cried. "Not upon--"

"No, not that," he said; "nor anything that concerns you or yours. But it has been thrown in my teeth, nevertheless. And it is true. For I am a coward and a craven, if there ever lived one. It is you who have made me feel that I am so; it is you who have shown me to myself in my true colours, and who have torn from me the mask which I--fool that I am!--had almost learnt to believe was my real self, and not a sham! Had you reproached me, had you reviled me, I might have continued to be deceived. But as it is, I tremble before you; I tremble, when I look upon your pale face;" and turning to her suddenly, and meeting the look of patient uncomplaining love in her weary eyes, he cried, "Oh, Alice! Alice! what misery I have brought upon you!"

"Not more than I can bear, dear love," she said, "if you will be true to yourself and to me. Have patience--"

"Patience!" he exclaimed. "When I think of the past, I lash myself into a torment. Will patience feed us? Will it give us a roof or a bed? Look here!" and he turned out his pockets. "Not a shilling. Fill my pockets first. Give me the means to fight with my fellow-cormorants, and I will have patience. Till then, I must fret, and fret, and drink. Have you any brandy?"

"No," she said, with a bitter sigh.

"Perhaps it is better so," he said, slowly, for his passion had somewhat exhausted him; "for what I have to say might seem the result of courage that does not belong to me. I have refrained from drink to-night that my resolution might not be tampered with."

He paused to recover himself; Alice bending forward, with clasped hands, waited in anxious expectancy.

"Do you know how I have spent to-night and many previous nights?" he asked. "In what company, and for what purpose?"

She had been standing during all this time, and her strength was failing her. She would have fallen, had he not caught her in his arms, whence she sank upon the ground at his feet, and bowed her head in her lap.

"I have spent to-night, and many other nights," he continued, "in the company of men whose touch, not long since, I should have deemed contamination. I have spent them in the company of villains, who, for some purpose of their own, are striving to inveigle me in their plots. But they will fail. Yes, they will fail, if you will give me strength to keep my resolution.

Coward I am, I know, but I am not too great a coward to say that you and I must part."

"Part!" she echoed, drearily.

"Look around," he said; "this is a nice home I have provided for you; I have surrounded you with fit associates, have I not? How nobly I have performed my part of husband! How you should bless my name, respect, and love me, for the true manliness I have displayed towards you! But by your patience and your love you have shown me the depth of my degradation."

"Not degradation, Richard, not degradation for you!"

"Yes, degradation, and for me, in its coarsest aspect. Is not this degradation?" and he pointed to Grif, who was crouching, observant, in a corner. "Come here," he said to the lad, who slouched towards him, reluctantly. "What are you?"

"What am I?" replied Grif, with a puzzled look; "I'm a pore boy--Grif."

"You're a poor boy--Grif!" the man repeated. "How do you live!"

"By eatin' and drinkin'."

"How do you get your living?"

"I makes it as I can," answered Grif, gloomily.

"And when you can't make it?"

"Why, then I takes it."

"That is, you are a thief?"

"Yes, I s'pose so."

"And a vagabond?"

"Yes, I s'pose so."

"And you have been in prison?"

"Yes, I've been in quod, I have," said Grif, feeling, for the first time in his life, slightly ashamed of the circumstance.

"And you say," Richard said, bitterly, as the boy slunk back to his corner, "that this is not degradation!"

She turned her eyes to the ground, but did not reply.

"I was once a good arithmetician," he continued. "Let us see what figures there are in the sum of our acquaintance, and what they amount to."

"Of what use is it to recall the past, Richard?"

"It may show us how to act in the future. Besides, I have a strange feeling on me to-night, having met with an adventure which I will presently relate. Listen. When I first saw you I was a careless ne'er-do-well, with no thought of the morrow. You did not know this then, but you know it now. It is the curse of my life that I was brought up with expectations. How many possibly useful, if not good, men have been wrecked on that same rock of expectations! Upon the strength of 'expectations' I was reared into an idle incapable. And this I was when you first knew me. I had an income then small, it is true, but sufficient, or if it was not, I got into debt upon the strength of my expectations, which were soon to yield to me a life's resting-place. You know what happened. One day there came a letter, and I learned that, in a commercial crash at home, my income and my expectations had gone to limbo. The news did not hurt me much, Alice, for I had determined on a scheme which, if successful, would give me wealth and worldly prosperity. It is the truth--shamed as I am to speak it--that, knowing you to be an only child and an heiress, I deliberately proposed to myself to win your affections. I said, 'This girl will be rich, and her money will compensate for what I have lost. This girl has a wealthy father, not too well educated, not too well connected, who will be proud when he finds that his daughter has married a gentleman.' In the execution of my settled purpose, I sought your society, and strove to make myself attractive to you. But your pure nature won upon me. The thought that your father was wealthy, and that you would make a good match for me, was soon lost in the love I felt for you. For I learned to love you, honestly, devotedly--nay, keep your place, and do not look at me while I speak, for I am unworthy of the love I sought and gained. Yet, you may believe me when I say, that as I learned to know you, all mercenary thoughts died utterly away. Well, Alice, I won your love, and could not bear to part from you. I had to do something to live; and so that I might be near you, I accepted the post of tutor offered me by your father. I accepted this to be near you--it was happiness enough for the time, and I thought but little of the future. Happy, then, in the present, I had no thought of the passing time, until the day arrived when your father wished to force you into a marriage with a man, ignorant, brutal mean, and vulgar,--but rich. You came to me in your distress--Good God!" he exclaimed passionately; "shall I ever forget the night on which you came to me, and asked for help and for advice? The broad plains, bathed in silver light, stretched out for miles before us. The branches of the old gum-trees glistened with white smiles in the face of the moon--we were encompassed with a peaceful glory. You stood before me, sad and trembling, and the love that had brought sunshine to my heart rushed to my lips"--he stopped suddenly, looked round, and smiled bitterly. Then he continued--"The next day we fled, and at the first town we reached we were married. Then, and then only, you learned for the first time, that the man you had married was a beggar, and was unable to provide for his wife the common comforts of a home. We appealed to your father--you know how he met our appeals. The last time I went, at your request, to his house, he set his dogs upon me--"

"Richard! Richard!" she cried entreatingly. "Do not recall that time. Be silent for awhile, and calm yourself."

"I will go on to the end. We came to Melbourne. Brought up to no trade or profession, and naturally idle, I could get nothing to do. Some would have employed me, but they were afraid. I was not rough enough--I was too much of a gentleman. They wanted coarser material than I am composed of, and so, day by day, I have sunk lower and lower. People begin to look on me with suspicion. I am fit for nothing in this colony. I was born a gentleman, and I live the life of a dog; and I have dragged you, who never before knew want, down with me. With no friends, no influence to back me, we might starve and rot. What wonder that I took to drink! The disgust with which I used to contemplate the victims of that vice recoils now upon myself, and I despise and abhor myself for what I am! By what fatality I brought you here, I know not. I suppose it was because we were poor, and I could not afford to buy you better lodging. Now, attend to me--but stay, that boy is listening."

"He is a friend, Richard," said Alice.

"Yes," said Grif, "I am a friend that's what I am. Never you mind me I ain't a-goin' to peach. I'd do any thin' to 'elp her, I would--sooner than 'urt her, I'd be chopped up first. You talk better than the preacher cove!"

"Very well. Now attend. These men want me to join them in their devilish plots. I will not do so, if I can help it. But if I stop here much longer, they will drive me to it. And so I must go away from you and from them. I will go to the gold diggings, and try my luck there--"

"Leaving me here?"

"Leaving you here, but not in this house. You have two or three articles of jewellery left. I will sell them--the watch I gave you will fetch ten pounds--and you will be able to live in a more respectable house than this for a few weeks until you hear from me."

"How will you go?"

"I shall walk I cannot afford to ride. But I have not concluded yet. I have something to tell you, which may alter our plans, so far as you are concerned. I have a message for you, which I must deliver word for word."

"A message for me!"

He paced the room for a few moments in silence. Then, standing before Alice, he looked her in the face, and said:--

"I saw your father this evening."

"In town!" she exclaimed.

"In town. I do not know for what purpose he is here, nor do I care."

"Oh, Richard," cried the girl; "you did not quarrel with him?"

"No; I spoke to him respectfully. I told him you were in Melbourne, in want. I begged him to assist us. I said that I was willing to do anything--that I would take any situation, thankfully, in which I could earn bread for you. He turned away impatiently. I followed him, and continued to address him humbly, entreatingly. For your sake, Alice, I did this."

She took his hand and kissed it, and rested her cheek against it.

"Hearken to his reply," he said, disengaging his hand, and standing apart from her. "This was it. 'You married my daughter for my money. You are a worthless, idle scoundrel, and I will not help you. If you so much regret the condition to which you have brought my daughter, divorce yourself from her.'"

"No, no, Richard!"

"Those were his words. 'Divorce yourself from her, and I will take her back. When you come to me to consent to this, I will give you money. Till then, you may starve. I am a hard man, as you know, obstinate and self-willed; and rather than you should have one shilling of the money you traded for when you married my daughter, I would fling it all in the sea. Tell my daughter this. She knows me well enough to be sure I shall not alter when once I resolve.' Those were his words, word for word. That was the message he bade me give you. What is your answer?"

"What do you think it is?" she asked, sadly.

"I cannot tell," he said, doggedly, turning his face from her; "I know what mine would be."

"What would it be?"

"I should say this" (he did not look at her while he spoke)--"You, Richard Handfield, Scapegrace, Fortune-hunter, Vagabond (any of these surnames would be sufficiently truthful), came to me, a young simple girl, and played the lover to me, without the knowledge of my father, for the sake of my father's money. You knew that I, a young simple girl, bred upon the plains, and amidst rough men, would be certain to be well affected towards you--would almost be certain to fall in love with you, for the false gloss you parade to the world, and for the refinement of manner which those employed about my father's station did not possess. You played for my heart, and you won it. But you won it without the money you thought you would have gained, for you were disappointed in your calculations. And now that I know you for what you are, and now that I have been sufficiently punished for my folly, in the misery you have brought upon me, I shall go back to the home from which I fled, and endeavour to forget the shame with which you have surrounded me."

"Do you think that this would be my answer, Richard?"

He had not once looked at her while he spoke, and now as she addressed him, with an indescribable sadness in her voice, he did not reply. For full five minutes there was silence in the room. Then the grief which filled her heart could no longer be suppressed, and short broken gasps escaped her.

"Richard!" she exclaimed.

"Yes, Alice."

"Have you not more faith in me than this? As I would die to keep you good, so I should die without your love. What matters poverty? We are not the only ones in the world whose lot is hard to bear! Be true to me, Richard, so that I may be true to myself and to you. You do not believe that this would be my answer!"

There came no word from his lips.

"When I vowed to be faithful to you, Richard, I was but a girl--indeed, I am no better now, except in experience but I vowed with my whole heart. I had no knowledge then of life's hard trials, but since I have learned them, I seem also to have learned what is my duty, and what was the meaning of the faith I pledged. I never rightly understood it till now, darling! You do not believe that this would be my answer!"

Still he did not look at her. Although she waited in an anxious agony of expectation, he did not speak. The plain words he had chosen in which to make his confession, had brought to him, for the first time, a true sense of the unworthy part he had played.

"If in the time that has gone, my dear," she continued, "there is any circumstance, any remembrance, connected with me, that gives you pain, forget it for my sake. If you have believed that any thought that, you have done me wrong exists, or ever existed, in my mind, believe it no longer. Think of me as I am--see me as I am--your wife, who loves you now with a more perfect love than when she was a simple girl, inexperienced in the world's hard ways. Ah! see how I plead to you, and turn to me, my dear!"

She would have knelt to him, but he turned and clasped her in his arms, and pressed her pure heart to his. Her fervent love had triumphed; and as he kissed away her tears, he felt, indeed, that wifely purity is man's best shield from evil.

"You shall do what you have said, Richard; but not to-morrow. Wait but one day longer; and if I then say to you--'Go,' you shall go. I have a reason for this, but I must not tell you what it is. Do you consent?"

"Yes, love."

"Brighter days will dawn upon us. I am happier now than I have been for a long, long time! And oh, my dear!--bend your head closer, Richard--there may come a little child to need our care--"

The light had gone out and the room was in darkness. But mean and disreputable as it was, a good woman's unselfish love sanctified it and made it holy!

CHAPTER III
GRIF LOSES A FRIEND

"It's a rum go," Grif muttered to himself, as he wiped the tears from his eyes, and groped his way down the dark stairs; "a very rum go. If I was Ally, I should do as he told her. But she don't care for herself, she don't. She's too good for him by ever so many chalks, that's what she is!"

By this time Grif had reached the staircase which led to the cellar. Crouching upon the floor, he listened with his ear to the ground.

"I can hear him," he said, in a pleasant voice, "he's a beatin' his tail upon the ground, but he won't move till I call him. I don't believe there's another dawg in Melbourne to come up to him. Jist listen to him! He's a thinkin' to himself, How much longer will he be, I wonder, afore he calls me! And he knows I'm a-talkin' of him; he knows it as well as I do myself."

He listened again, and laughed quietly.

"If I was to mention that dawg's name," Grif said in a confidential tone, as if he were addressing a companion, "he'd be here in a minute. He would! It's wonderful how he knows! I've had him since he was a pup, and afore he could open his eyes. It would be nice sleepin' down in the cellar, but we can't do it, can we, old feller? We've got somebody else to look after, haven't we? You, and me, and him, ain't had a bit of supper, I'll bet. But we'll get somethin' to eat somehow, you see if we don't."

Here the lad whistled softly, and the next instant a singularly ugly dog was by his side, licking his face, and expressing satisfaction in a quiet but demonstrative manner.

"Ain't you jolly warm, Rough!" whispered Grif, taking the dog in his arms, and gathering warmth from it. "Good old Rough! Dear old Rough!"

The dog could only respond to its master's affection by action, but that was sufficiently expressive for Grif, who buried his face in Rough's neck, and patted its back, and showed in twenty little ways that he understood and appreciated the faithfulness of his dumb servant. After this interchange of affectionate sentiment, Grif and his dog crept out of the house. It was raining hard, but the lad took no further heed of the weather than was expressed by drooping his chin upon his breast, and putting his hands into the ragged pockets of his still more ragged trousers. Slouching along the walls as if he derived some comfort from the contact, Grif walked into a wider street of the city, and stopped at the entrance of a narrow passage, leading to a room used as a casino. The dog, which had been anxiously sniffing the gutters in quest of such stray morsels of food as had escaped the eyes and noses of other ravenous dogs, stopped also, and looked up humbly at its master.

"I'll stay here," said Grif, resting against the wall. "Milly's in there, I dare say, and she'll give me somethin' when she comes out, if she's got it."

Understanding by its master's action that no further movement was to be made for the present, Rough sat upon its haunches in perfect contentment, and contemplated the rain-drops falling on the ground. Grif was hungry, but he had a stronger motive than that for waiting; as he had said, he had some one besides himself to provide for, and the girl he expected to see had often given him money. Strains of music floated down the passage, and the effect of the sounds, combined with his tired condition sent him into a half doze. He started now and then, as persons passed and repassed him; but presently he slid to the earth, and, throwing his arm over the dog's neck, fell into a sound sleep. He slept for nearly an hour, when a hand upon his shoulder roused him.

"What are you sleeping in the rain for?" a girl's voice asked.

"Is that you, Milly?" asked Grif, starting to his feet, and shaking himself awake. "I was waitin' for you, and I was so tired that I fell off. Rough didn't bark at you, did he, when you touched me?"

"Not he! He's too sensible," replied Milly, stooping, and caressing the dog, who licked her hand. "He knows friends from enemies. A good job if all of us did!"

There was a certain bitterness in the girl's voice which jarred upon the ear, but Grif, probably too accustomed to hear it, did not notice it. She was very handsome, fair, with regular features, white teeth, and bright eyes; but her mouth was too small, and there was a want of firmness in her lips. Take from her face a careworn, reckless expression, which it was sorrowful to witness in a girl so young, and it would have been one which a painter would have been pleased to gaze upon.

"I have been looking for Jim," she said, "and I cannot find him."

"I sor him to-night," Grif said; "he was up at the house--him and Black Sam and Ned Rutt, and the Tenderhearted Oysterman."

"A nice gang!" observed the girl. "And Jim's the worst of the lot."

"No, he isn't," said Grif; and as he said it, Milly looked almost gratefully at him. "Rough knows who's the worst of that lot; don't you, Rough?"

The dog looked up into its master's face, as if it perfectly well understood the nature of the question.

"Is Black Sam the worst?" asked Grif.

The dog wagged its stump of a tail, but uttered no sound.

"Is Ned Rutt the worst?" asked Grif.

The dog repeated the performance.

"Is Jim Pizey the worst?" asked Grif.

Milly caught the lad's arm as he put the last question, and looked in the face of the dog as if it were a sibyl about to answer her heart's fear. But the dog wagged its tail, and was silent.

"Thank God!" Milly whispered to herself.

"Is the Tenderhearted Oysterman the worst?" asked Grif.

Whether Grif spoke that name in a different tone, or whether some magnetic touch of hate passed from the master's heart to that of the dog, no sooner did Rough hear it, than its short yellow hair bristled up, and it gave vent to a savage growl.

A stealthy step passed at the back of them at this moment.

"For God's sake!" cried Milly, putting her hand upon Grif's mouth, and then upon the dog's.

Grif looked at her, inquiringly.

"That was the Oysterman who passed us," said Milly, with a pale face. "I hope he didn't hear you."

"I don't care if he did. It can't make any difference between us. He hates me and Rough, and Rough and me hates him; don't we?"

Rough gave a sympathetic growl.

"And so you were up at the house, eh, Grif?" said Milly, as if anxious to change the subject. "What were you doing all the night?"

"I was sittin' with--"

But ignorant as Grif was, he hesitated here. He knew full well the difference between the two women who were kind to him. He knew that one was what he would have termed "respectable," and the other belonged to society's outcasts. And he hesitated to bring the two together, even in his speech.

"You were sitting with--?" Milly said.

"No one particler," Grif wound up, shortly.

"But I should like to know, and you *must* tell me, Grif."

"Well, if I must tell you, it was with Ally I was sittin'. You never seed her."

"No, I've never seen her," said Milly, scornfully. "I've heard of her, though. She's a lady, isn't she?"

"Yes, she is."

Milly turned away her head and was silent for a few moments; then she said,

"Yes, she's a lady, and I'm not good enough to be to about her. But she isn't prettier than me for all that; she isn't so pretty; I've been told so. She hasn't got finer eyes than me, and she hasn't got smaller hands than me;" and Milly held out hers, proudly--a beautiful little hand--"nor smaller feet, I know, though I've never seen them. And yet she's a lady!"

"Yes, she is."

"And I am not. Of course not. Well, I shall go. Good-night."

"Good-night, Milly," Grif said, in a conflict of agitation. For he knew that he had hurt Milly's feelings, and he was remorseful. He knew that he was right in saying that Alice was a lady, and in inferring that Milly was not; yet he could not have defined why he was right, and he was perplexed. Then he was hungry, and Milly had gone without giving him any money, and he knew that she was angry with him. And he was angry with himself for making her angry.

While he was enduring this conflict of miserable feeling, Milly came back to him. Grif was almost ashamed to look her in the face.

"She isn't prettier than me?" the girl said, as if she desired to be certain upon the point.

"I didn't say she was," Grif responded, swinging one foot upon the pavement.

"And she hasn't got smaller hands than me?"

"I didn't say she had, Milly."

"Nor smaller feet?"

"Nobody said so."

"Nor brighter eyes, nor a nicer figure? And yet," Milly said, with a kind of struggle in her voice, "and yet she's a lady, and I'm not."

"Don't be angry with me, Milly," Grif pleaded, as if with him rested the responsibility of the difference between the two women.

"Why should I be angry with you?" asked Milly, her voice hardening. "It's not your fault. I often wonder if it is mine! It's hard to tell; isn't it?"

Grif, not understanding the drift of the question, could not conscientiously answer; yet, feeling himself called upon to express some opinion, he nodded his head acquiescently.

"Never mind," said Milly; "it will be all the same in a hundred years! Have you had anything to eat to-night, Grif?"

Grif felt even more remorseful, for, after what had passed, Milly's question, kindly put, was like a dagger's thrust to him.

"Well, here's a shilling for you--it's the only one I've got, and you're welcome to it. Perhaps the lady would give you her last shilling! Any lady would, of course--that's the way of ladies! Why don't you take the shilling?"

"I don't want it," said Grif, gently, turning aside.

Milly placed her hand on the boy's head, and turned his face to hers. She could see the tears struggling to his eyes.

"Don't be a stupid boy," Milly said; "I have only been joking with you. I don't mean half I said; I never do. Though she's a lady, and I'm not, I'd do as much for you as she would, if I was able." And, forcing the shilling into his hand, the girl walked quickly away.

Grif looked after her until she was out of sight, and shaking his head, as if he had a problem in it which he could not solve, made straight for a coffee-stall where pies were sold, and invested his shilling. Carrying his investment carefully in his cap, which he closed like a bag, so that the rain should not get to the pies, Grif, with Rough at his heels, dived_into the poorer part of the city, and threaded his way among a very labyrinth of deformed streets. The rain poured steadily down upon him, and soaked him through and through, but his utter disregard of the discomfort of the situation showed how thoroughly he was used to it. Grif was wending his way to bed; and lest any misconception should arise upon this point, it may be as well to mention at once that the bed was a barrel, which lay in the rear of a shabby house. Not long since the barrel had been tenanted by a dog, whose master had lived in the shabby house. But, happily, master and dog had shifted quarters, and the barrel becoming tenantless, Grif took possession without inquiring for the landlord. Whereby he clearly laid himself open to an action for ejectment. And Grif was not the only tenant, for when he arrived at his sleeping-place, he stooped, and putting his head into the barrel, withdrew it again, and said, "Yes; there he is!" the utterance of which common-place remark appeared to afford him much satisfaction. Grif's action had disturbed the occupant of the barrel, who had evidently been sleeping, and he presently appeared, rubbing his eyes.

Such a strange little tenant! Such a white-faced, thin-faced, haggard-faced, little tenant! Such a large-eyed, wistful-eyed, little tenant! In truth, a small boy, a very baby-boy, who might have been an infant, or who might have been an old man whom hunger had pinched, whom misery had shaken hands and been most familiar with. He gazed at Grif with his large eyes and smiled sleepily, and then catching sight of Grif's cap with the pies in it, rubbed his little hands gladly, and was wide-awake in an instant.

"You haven't had nothin' to eat to-night, I'll bet," said Grif.

The little fellow's lips formed themselves into a half-whispered No.

Grif insinuated his body into the barrel, and stretched himself full length by the side of the baby-boy. Then he slightly raised himself, and, resting his chin upon his hand, took a pie from his cap, and gave it to his companion. The boy seized it eagerly, and bit into it, without uttering a word.

"You haven't got me to thank for it, Little Peter," Grif said. "It's Milly you have got to thank. Say, thank you, Milly."

"Thank you, Milly," said Little Peter obediently, devouring his pie.

There was another pie in the cap, but hungry as Grif was he did not touch it. He looked at Little Peter, munching, and then at his dog, who had crept to the mouth of the barrel, and who was eyeing the pie wistfully. Had the dog known that its master was hungry, it would not have looked at the pie as if it wanted it.

"*You've* had precious little to eat to-night, too," said Grif to Rough, who wagged its tail as its master spoke. "We'll have it between us." And he broke the pie in two pieces.

He was about to give one piece of it to Rough, when he heard a cat-like step within a few yards of him. "Who's there?" he cried, creeping partly out of the barrel. No answer came, but the dog gave a savage growl, and darted forwards. Grif listened, but heard nothing but a faint laugh.

"I know that laugh, that's the Tenderhearted Oysterman's laugh. What can he want here? Rough! Rough!" The dog came back at the call, with a piece of meat in its mouth, which it was swallowing ravenously. "Well, if this isn't a puzzler, I don't know what is," observed Grif. "Where did you got that from? You're in luck's way to-night, you are, Rough. All the better for Little Peter! Here, Little Peter, here's some more pie for you."

Little Peter took the dog's share of the pie without compunction, and expeditiously disposed of it. He then stretched himself on his face, and was soon fast asleep again. Grif, having eaten his half of the pie, coiled himself up, and prepared for sleep. No fear of rheumatism assailed him; it was no new thing for him to sleep in wet clothes. He was thankful enough for the shelter, poor as it was, and did not repine because he did not have a more comfortable bed. He was very tired, but the remembrance of the events of the day kept him dozing for a little while. Alice, and her husband, and Milly, presented themselves to his imagination in all sorts of confused ways. The story he had heard Alice's husband tell of how their marriage came about was also strong upon him, and he saw Alice and Richard standing in the soft moonlight on her father's station. "I wonder what sort of a cove her father is!" Grif thought, as he lay between sleeping and waking. "He must be a nice 'ard-'earted bloke, he must? I wish I was her father; I'd soon make her all right!" Then he heard Milly say, "She hasn't got smaller hands than me!" and Milly's hands and Alice's hands laid themselves before him, and he was looking to see which were the smaller. Gradually, however, these fancies became indistinct, and sleep fell upon him; but only to deepen them, to render them more powerful. They were no longer fancies, they were realities. He was crouching in a corner of the room, while Richard was speaking to Alice; he was groping down the stairs, and calling for Rough, and fondling him; he was standing at the entrance of the narrow passage, waiting for Milly, and he was sleeping, with his arm embracing his dog; he was talking to Milly, and asking Rough who was the worst of all Jim Pizey's lot? he was listening to the Tenderhearted Oysterman's retreating footsteps; and he was standing at the pie-stall, spending Milly's last shilling. But here a new feature introduced itself into the running commentary of his dreams. He fancied that, after he and Little Peter had eaten the pies, the Tenderhearted Oysterman came suddenly behind Rough, and, seizing the dog by the throat, thrust it into a small box, the lid of which he clapped down and fastened; that then the Oysterman forced the box into the barrel, and so fixed it upon Grif s chest that the lad could not move; and that, although he heard the dog moan and scratch, he could not release it. The weight upon Grif's chest grew heavier and heavier; it was forcing the breath out of his body. In his sleep he gasped, and fought release himself. And after a violent struggle, he awoke.

There *was* something lying upon his chest. It was Rough, who had crawled into the barrel, and was licking its master's face. It had been whining, but directly it felt Grif's hand, it grew quiet. The rain was falling heavily, and the drops were forcing themselves through the roof of the barrel. Grif shifted the dog gently on one side.

"There's 'ardly room enough for two, let alone three of us," Grif muttered. "Little Peter, are you awake?" The soft breathing of Peter was the only reply. "You've no right to come shovin' yourself in," continued Grif, addressing the dog, who gave utterance to a pleading moan; "but I ain't goin' to turn you out. What a night it is! And how wet the barrel is! It would be much nicer if it was dry. It's almost as bad as a gutter?" Here came a long-drawn sigh from Rough, and then a piteous moan, as if the dog were in pain. "Be quiet Rough! What's the use of botherin' about the rain!" exclaimed the boy. "There'll be a flood in Melbourne, if this goes on!" And drawing his limbs closer together, Grif disposed himself for sleep. He was almost on the boundary of the land of dreams, when a yelp of agony from Rough aroused him again, and caused him to start and knock his head against the roof of the barrel. "Blest if I don't think somethin's the matter with the dawg!" he exclaimed. "What are you yelpin' for, Rough?" The dog uttered another sharp cry of agony, and trembled, and stretched its limbs in convulsion. Thoroughly alarmed, Grif corkscrewed his way out of the barrel as quietly as he could for fear of waking little Peter, and called for Rough to follow him. Rough strove to obey its master's voice even in the midst of its pain, but it had not strength.

"Rough! Rough!" cried Grif, drawing the dog out of the barrel. "What's the matter, Rough? Are you hurt?" He felt all over its body, but could discover nothing to account for Rough's distress. He took his faithful servant in his arms, and looked at it by the dim light of the weeping stars. Rough opened its eyes and looked gratefully at Grif, who pressed the dog to his breast, and strove to control the violent shuddering of its limbs; but its agony was too powerful. It rolled out of Grif's arms on to the ground, where it lay motionless.

Cold and wet and shivering as he was, a deeper chill struck upon Grif's heart as he gazed at the quiet form at his feet. He called the dog by name, but it did not respond; he walked away a few steps and whistled, but it did not follow; he came back, and stooping, patted it upon its head, but it did not move; he whispered to it, "Rough! poor old Rough! dear old Rough! speak to me, Rough!" but the dog uttered no sound. Then Grif sitting down, took Rough in his arms, and began to cry. Quietly and softly at first.

"What did Ally arks me to-night?" he half thought and half spoke between his sobs. "Did I ever have a friend that I would sacrifice myself for? Yes! I would for Rough! There wasn't another dawg in Melbourne to come up to him! And now he's gone, and I ain't got no friend left but Ally." And he laid his face upon the dog's wet coat, and rained warm tears upon it.

"After all the games we've had together!" he continued. "After the times he's stood up for me! He'll never stand up for me agin--never agin!"

He knew that the dog was dead, and his anguish at the loss of his dumb, faithful friend was very keen. Had it been human, he could not have felt a deeper affliction.

"Everybody liked Rough! And he never had a growl for no one who spoke kind to him. Everybody liked him--everybody except the Tenderhearted Oysterman. The Tenderhearted Oysterman!" he cried, jumping to his feet as if an inspiration had fallen upon him. "Why, it was him as swore he would murder Rough! It was him as passed to-night when I was goin' to give Rough the pie! It was him as give Rough the piece of meat! The piece of meat! It was pizened! He swore he'd kill him, and he's done it! That's what I heerd him laughin' at."

Grif wiped the tears from his eyes with the cuff of his ragged jacket, and clenched his teeth.

"He's pizened Rough, has he?" he muttered, gloomily; and raising his hand to the dark sky, he said, "If ever I can be even with him for killin' my dawg, I will, so 'elp me--"

This time there was no one by to check the oath, and he uttered it savagely and emphatically. Then he put his head in the barrel, and shook Little Peter awake.

"Peter," he said, "Rough's dead. Ain't you sorry?"

"Yes," said Little Peter, without any show of feeling.

"He's been pizened. The Tenderhearted Oysterman's pizened him. Say Damn him!"

"Damn him!" Little Peter said, readily.

"I'm going to bury him," said Grif. "Git up and come along with me."

Very obediently, but very sleepily, Little Peter came out of bed. Grif looked about him, picked up a piece of rusty iron, and taking Rough in his arms, walked away, and Little Peter, rubbing his eyes, trudged sometimes behind and sometimes at Grif's side. Now and then the little fellow placed his hand half carelessly and half caressingly upon Rough's head, and now and then Grif stopped and kissed his dead servant. In this way, slouching through the miserable streets, the rain pouring heavily down, the funeral procession reached a large burial-ground. The gates were closed, but they got in over a low wall at the back. Everything about him was very solemn, very mournful, and very dreary. The night was so dark that they could scarcely see, and they stumbled over many a little mound of earth as they crept along.

"This'll do," said Grif, stopping at a spot where a tangle of grass leaves were soiling their crowns in the muddy earth.

With the piece of iron he soon scraped a hole large enough for the body. Some notion that he was performing a sacred duty which demanded sacred observances was upon him.

"Take off your cap," he said to Little Peter.

Little Peter pulled off his cap; Grif did so likewise; and the rain pattered down upon their bare heads. They stood so for a little while in silence.

"Ashes to ashes!" Grif said, placing the body in the hole, and piling the earth over it. He had followed many funerals to the churchyard, and had heard the ministers speak those words.

"Good-bye, Rough!" murmured Grif, with a sob of grief. "Dear old Rough! Poor old Rough!"

And then the two outcasts crept back again, through the dreary streets, to their bed in the barrel.

CHAPTER IV
THE CONJUGAL NUTTALLS

The March of Progress is sounding loudly in the ears of the people who throng the streets of Melbourne. It is not a lazy hum, a droning whisper, with an invitation to sleep in its every note; there is something martial in its tones, something that tells you to look alive and move along, if you do not wish to be pushed into a corner and lost sight of. It may be that the March of Progress is set to quicker time in the busy thoroughfares of Melbourne than in those of the cities of the older world. It makes itself more strongly felt; it asserts itself more independently; it sets the blood in more rapid circulation. It carries us along with it, past noble-looking stores filled with the triumphs of the workshops of the world which emigrants call Old; past great hotels whence men issue in the noonday light, wiping their months unblushingly, and through the swinging doors of which you catch glimpses of excited men, eating, drinking, talking, gesticulating, as rapidly and fiercely as if they thirsted to trip up the heels of Time, and take him prisoner by the forelock; past fine houses and squalid houses; through quarters where wealth smiles and poverty groans; to the very verge of the growing city, from which line the houses dot the landscape pleasantly, and do not crowd it uncomfortably--from which line are seen fair plains and fields, and shadows of primeval forests in the clouds. And here, the air which had been swelling louder and louder, until it grew into a clanging sound that banished all sense of rest, grows fainter and sweeter; here in the suburbs, as you walk in them by the side of the whispering river, over whose bosom the weeping willow hangs, the March of Progress subsides into a hymn, which travels on through the landscape to the primeval forests, and softly sings, that soon--where now grim members of the eucalypti rear their lofty heads; where now a blight is heavy on the bush, which before the burning sun had waged fierce war with it and sucked the juices from the earth, was bright and beautiful with tree and flower--the golden corn shall wave, and gladden the face of nature with rippling smiles.

The March of Progress sounds but faintly before a prettily-built weatherboard cottage in the suburbs, where dwell the family of the Nuttalls. It is a pleasant cottage, and so Mr. Nicholas Nuttall seems to think as he looks round the parlour with a smile, and then looks down again, and reads, for at least the sixth time, a letter which is lying open on the table.

"And Matthew is alive," he said, speaking to the letter as if it were sentient; "alive and prosperous! To think that it should be thirty years since I saw him; that I should come out here, scarcely hoping to find him alive, and that, after being here only a month, I should hear of him in such a wonderful manner. So amazingly rich, too! Upon my word," he continued, apostrophising a figure of Time, which, with a very long beard and a very long scythe, looked down upon him from the family mantel-shelf; "upon my word, old daddy, you're a wonder. You are," he continued, shaking his head at the figure; "there's no getting over *you!* You grow us up, you mow us down; you turn our hair black, you turn it white; you make us strong, you make us feeble; and we laugh at you and wheeze at you, until the day comes when we can laugh and wheeze no more. Dear! dear! dear! What a handsome fellow he was to be sure! I wonder if he is much altered. I wonder if he ever thinks of old times. I shall know him again, for certain, directly I clap eyes on him. He must have got grey by this time, though. Dear! dear! dear!"

And Mr. Nicholas Nuttall fell to musing over thirty years ago, fishing up from that deep well a hundred trifles which brought pleasant ripples to his face. They had been buried so long that it might have been excused them had they been rusted, but they were not so. They came up quite bright at his bidding, and smiled in his face. They twinkled in his eyes, those memories, and made him young again. In the glowing wood fire rose up the pictures of his past life; the intervening years melted away, and he saw once more his boyhood's home, and the friends and associates whom he loved. As at the touch of a magician's hand, the tide of youth came back, and brought with it tender episodes of his happy boyhood; he looked again upon faces, young as when he knew them, as if youth were eternal, and time had no power to wrinkle; eyes gazed into his lovingly, as of yore; and days passed before him containing such tender remembrances that his heart throbbed with pleasure at the very thought of them. He and his brother were walking hand-in-hand through a leafy forest; they came upon two girls (who were afterwards drowned but he did not think of that!) whom they greeted with hand-clasps, and then the four wandered on. He remembered nothing more of that woodland walk; but the tender pressure of the girl's hand lingered upon his even after so many years, and made the day into a sweet and loving remembrance. And thus he mused and mused, and all his young life passed before him, phantasmagorically. The flowers in the garden of youth were blooming once again in the life of Mr. Nicholas Nuttall.

But his reverie was soon disturbed. For the partner of his bosom, Mrs. Nicholas Nuttall, suddenly bouncing into the room, and seating herself, demonstratively, in her own particular arm-chair, on the other side of the fire, puffed away his dreams in a trice.

Mrs. Nicholas Nuttall was a small woman. Mr. Nicholas Nuttall was a large man. Mrs. Nichols Nuttall, divested of her crinolines and flounces and other feminine vanities, in which she indulged inordinately, was a very baby by the side of her spouse. In fact, the contrast, to an impartial observer, would have been ridiculous. Her condition, when feathered, was that of an extremely ruffled hen, strutting about in offended majesty, in defiance of the whole poultry race. Unfeather her, and figuratively speaking, Mr. Nicholas Nuttall could have put Mrs. Nicholas Nuttall into his pocket--like a doll.

Yet if there ever was a man hopelessly under petticoat government; if ever there was a man completely and entirely subjugated; if ever there was a man prone and vanquished beneath woman's merciless thumb; that man was the husband of Mrs. Nicholas Nuttall. It is a singular fact, but one which may be easily ascertained by any individual who takes an interest in studying the physiology of marriage life, that when a very small man espouses a very large woman, he is, by tacit consent, the king of the castle: it is an important, unexpressed portion of the marriage obligation; and that, when a very small woman espouses a very large man, she rules him with a rod of iron, tames him, subjugates him, so to speak, until at length he can scarcely call his soul his own.

This was the case with the conjugality of the Nuttalls, as was proven by the demeanour of the male portion of the bond. For no sooner had the feminine half (*plus*) seated herself opposite the masculine half (*minus*) than the face of Mr. Nicholas Nuttall assumed an expression of the most complete and perfect submission.

Mrs. Nuttall was not an agreeable-looking woman. As a girl she might have been pretty: but twenty-five years of nagging and scolding and complaining had given her a vinegarish expression. Her eyes had contracted, as if they had a habit of looking inward for consolation; her lips were thin, and her nose was sharp. This last feature would not have been an ugly one if it had not been so bony; but constant nagging had worn all the flesh away, and brought into conspicuous notice a knob in the centre of the arc, for it was a Roman. If such women only knew what a splendid interest amiability returned, how eager they would be to invest in it!

Mrs. Nuttall sat in her chair and glared at her husband. Mr. Nuttall sat in his chair and looked meekly at his wife. He knew what was coming--the manner, not the matter. He knew that something had annoyed the wife of his bosom, and that she presented herself before him only for the purpose of distressing him with reproaches. He waited patiently.

"Mr. Nuttall," presently said Mrs. Nuttall, "why don't you speak? Why do you sit glaring at me, as if I were a sphinx?"

To throw the *onus* of the interview upon Mr. Nuttall was manifestly unfair, and the thought may have kept him silent; or, perhaps, he had nothing to say.

"This place will be the death of me, I'm certain," Mrs. Nuttall remarked with an air of resignation.

Nicholas shrugged his shoulders with an almost imperceptible motion--shrugged them, as it were, beneath his shirt and coat, and in such a manner that no movement was imparted to those garments. Ever since they had been married, something or other was always going to be the death of Mrs. Nuttall; about six times a day, on an average, since the honeymoon, Mr. Nuttall had heard her utter the complaint, accompanied by an expression of regret that she had ever married. That regret she expressed upon the present occasion, and Mr. Nuttall received it with equanimity. The first time he heard it, it was a shock to him; but since then he had become resigned. So he merely put in an expostulatory "My dear"--being perfectly well aware that he would not be allowed to get any further.

"Don't my-dear me," interrupted Mrs. Nuttall, as he expected; he would have been puzzled what to say if she had not taken up the cue. "I'm tired of your my-dearing and my-loving. You ought never to have married, Nicholas. You don't know how to appreciate a proper and affectionate wife. Or if you were bent upon marrying--and bent you must have been, for you would not take No, for answer--you ought to have married Mary Plummer. I wish you had *her* for a wife! Then you would appreciate me better."

No wonder, that at so thoroughly illogical and bigamy-suggesting an aspiration, Mr. Nuttall looked puzzled. But Mrs. Nuttall paid no attention to his look, and proceeded,--

"I went to school with her, and I ought to know how she would turn out. The way she brings up her family is disgraceful; the girls are as untidy as can be. You should see the bed-rooms in the middle of the day! And yet her husband indulges her in everything. He is something like a husband should be. He didn't drag his wife away from her home, after she had slaved for him all her life, and bring her out to a place where everything is topsy-turvy, and ten times the price that it is anywhere else, and where people who are not fit for domestics are put over your heads. He didn't do that! Not he! He knows his duty as a husband and a father of a family better."

Mr. Nuttall sighed.

"The sufferings I endured on board that dreadful ship," continued Mrs. Nuttall, "ought to have melted a heart of stone. What with walking with one leg longer than the other for three months, I'm sure I shall never be able to walk straight again. I often wondered, when I woke up in a fright in the middle of the night, and found myself standing on my head in that horrible bunk, what I had done to meet with such treatment from you. From the moment you broached the subject of our coming to the colonies, my peace of mind was gone. The instant I stepped on board that dreadful ship, which you basely told me was a clipper, and into that black hole of a hen-coop, which you falsely described as a lovely saloon, I felt that I was an innocent convict, about to be torn from my native country. The entire voyage was nothing but a series of insults; the officers paid more attention to my own daughter than they did to me; and the sailors, when they were pulling the ropes--what good they did by it I never could find out!--used to sing a low song with a chorus about Maria, knowing that to be my name, simply for the purpose of wounding my feelings. And when I told you to interfere, you refused, and said it was only a coincidence! That is the kind of consideration I get from you."

Mr. Nuttall sighed again.

"There's Jane," observed Mrs. Nuttall, approaching one of her grievances; "the best servant I ever had. At home she was quite satisfied with ten pounds a year; and now, after our paying her passage out, she says she can't stop unless her wages are raised to thirty pounds. Thir-ty pounds," said Mrs. Nuttall, elongating the numeral. "And at home she was contented with twelve. Do you know how you are to meet these frightful expenses? I'm sure *I* don't. But mind, Nicholas, if we come to ruin, don't blame me for it. I told you all along what would be the result of your dragging us to the colonies. I pray that I may be mistaken; but I have never been mistaken yet, and you know it;" and Mrs. Nuttall spread out her skirts (she was always spreading out her skirts, as if she could not make enough of herself) complacently.

Still Mr. Nuttall made no remark, and sat as quiet as a mouse, gazing humbly upon the household prophet.

"Thirty pounds a year for a servant-of-all-work!" continued the lady. "Preposterous! The best thing we can do, if that's the way they're paid, is all of us to go out as servants-of-all-work, and lay by a provision for Marian."

A vision of himself, in feminine attire, floor-scrubbing on his knees, flitted across the disturbed mind of Mr. Nuttall.

"She must have the money, I suppose. I know who has put her up to it; it is either the baker's or the butcher's man. The two noodles are hankering after her, and she encourages them. I saw the pair of them at the back-gate last night, and she was flirting with them nicely. You must give information to the police, Nicholas, and have them locked up."

"Looked up!" exclaimed Mr. Nuttall.

"Certainly. Do you think the police would allow such goings on at home?"

"Perhaps not, my dear," said Mr. Nuttall, with a sly smile; "the police at home, I believe, are said to hold almost a monopoly in servant-girls."

"I don't understand your coarse allusions, Mr. Nuttall," said Mrs. Nuttall, loftily. "What I say is, you must give information to the police, and have these goings-on stopped."

"It is perfectly impossible, Maria. Do be reasonable!"

"Sir!" exclaimed Mrs. Nuttall, glaring at her husband.

"What I meant to say, Maria," said Mr. Nuttall, clearing his throat, as if something had gone down the wrong way, "is, that I don't believe it is a criminal offence for a servant-girl to talk to a baker, or even a butcher, over a gate; and I doubt if giving information to the police would lead to any satisfactory result."

"It will be a very satisfactory result--won't it?--if Jane runs away and gets married. Servant-girls don't think of that sort of thing at home. I shall be in a nice situation. It would be like losing my right hand. I tell you what this country is, Mr. Nuttall--it's demoralizing, that's what it is." And Mrs. Nuttall wept, through sheer vexation.

All this was sufficiently distressing to Mr. Nuttall, but he did not exhibit any outward show of annoyance. Time was when Mrs. Nuttall's tears impressed him with the conviction that he was a man of hard feeling, but he had got over that. And so Mrs. Nuttall wept, and Mr. Nuttall only experienced a feeling of weariness; but he brightened up as his eyes rested upon the letter which had occasioned him so much pleasure, and he said--

"Oh, Maria, I have an invitation for you. At short notice, too. For this evening. From Mr. and Mrs. Blemish. Great people, you know, Maria."

Mrs. Nuttall instantly became attentive.

"And whom do you think we shall meet? When I tell you, you will be as surprised as I was when I read it."

"Whom, Nicholas?" asked Mrs. Nuttall, impatiently. "Do *not* keep me in suspense."

"My brother Matthew!"

"Alive!" exclaimed Mrs. Nuttall.

"Of course. You would not wish to meet him in any other condition, would you?"

"That you should make such a remark," observed Mrs. Nuttall, "of a brother whom we all thought dead, is, to say the least of it, heartless, Nicholas. Of course, if the Blemishes are, as you say, great people, and he visits them, it is a comfort, as showing that his position is not a bad one. But, if we are to go, can you tell me what to wear? I don't know, in this outlandish colony, whether we are expected to dress ourselves like Christians or aboriginals."

"The last would certainly be inexpensive, but it would scarcely be decent, Maria," remarked Mr. Nuttall, slily.

"That may be very witty, Mr. Nuttall," responded his lady, loftily; "but it is hardly an observation a man should make to his own wife. Though for what you care about your wife's feelings I would not give that," and she snapped her fingers, disdainfully.

From long and sad experience, Mr. Nicholas Nuttall had learned the wisdom of saying as little as possible when his wife was in her present humour. Indeed, he would sometimes lose all consciousness of what was passing, or would find himself regarding it as an unquiet dream from which he would presently awake. But Mrs. Nuttall was always equal to the occasion; and now, as she observed him about to relapse into a dreamy state of inattention, she cried, sharply--

"Nicholas!"

"Yes, my dear," he responded, with a jump, as if half-a-dozen needles had been smartly thrust into a tender part.

"What am I to wear this evening?"

"Your usual good taste, Maria," he commenced--

"Oh, bother my good taste!" she interrupted. "You know that we are to meet your brother to-night, and I am only anxious to do you credit. Not that I shan't be a perfect fright, for I haven't a dress fit to put on my back. If I wasn't such a good contriver, we should look more like paupers than respectable people. My black silk has been turned three times already; and my pearl grey--you ought to know what a state that is in, for you spilt the port wine over it yourself. Is your brother very rich, Nicholas?"

"They say so, Maria; he owns cattle stations, and thousands of sheep and cattle. He is a squatter, you know."

"A what?" she screamed.

"A squatter."

"What a dreadful thing!" she exclaimed. "What a shocking calamity! Is he always squatting, Nicholas?"

"My dear;" said Nicholas, amazed.

"Not that it matters much," she continued, not heeding him; "he may squat as long as he likes, if he has plenty of money, and assists you as a brother should. Thank heaven! none of my relations ever squatted. Has he been squatting long, Nicholas?"

"For ever so many years," he replied.

"What a disagreeable position! Why, his legs must be quite round. You ought to thank your stars that you have a wife who doesn't squat--"

But observing a furtive smile play about her husband's lips, she rose majestically, and said,

"I shall not waste my conversation upon you any longer. I suppose the cab will be here at half-past nine o'clock; everybody else, of course, will go in their own carriages." (Here she took out her watch, and consulted it.) "Bless my soul! it is nearly seven o'clock now. I have barely three hours to dress."

And she whisked out of the room, leaving Mr. Nuttall, nothing loth, to resume his musings.

CHAPTER V
THE MORAL MERCHANT ENTERTAINS
HIS FRIENDS AT DINNER

On the same evening, and at about the same hour, of the occurrence of the foregoing matrimonial dialogue, Mr. Zachariah Blemish entertained his friends at dinner. Mr. Zachariah Blemish was a merchant and a philanthropist; he was also a gentleman of an imposing mien, and of a portly appearance. Some of his detractors (and what man lives who has them not?) said that the manly bosom which throbbed to the beats of his patriotic heart was filled with as earthly desires as other earthly flesh. If this assertion, which was generally made spitefully and vindictively, was the worst that could be said against him, Zachariah Blemish could look the world in the face without blushing. True or untrue, he did look, unmoved, in the world's face, and if either felt abashed in the presence of the other, it was the world, and not Blemish. There was a self-assertion in his manner when he appeared in public, which, if it could have been set down in so many words, would have thus expressed itself:--"Here am I, sent among you for your good; make much of me. You are frail, I am strong; you are mean, I am noble. But do not be abashed. Do not be afraid of your own unworthiness. I do not wish to hold myself above you. I will eat with you, and talk with you, and sleep with you, as if I were one of yourselves. It is not my fault that I am superior to you. Perhaps, if you look up to me, you may one day reach my level. It would be much to accomplish, but you have my best wishes. I am here to do you good, and I hope I may." As he walked along the streets, people fell aside and made way for him, deferentially. They looked after him, and pointed him out to strangers as the great Mr. Blemish; and it was told of one family that, when the children were put to bed at night, they were taught to say, "God bless papa and mamma, and Good Mr. Blemish." His snowy shirt-front, viewed from a distance, was a sight to look upon, and, upon a nearer acquaintance, dazzled one with its pure whiteness. At church he was the most devout of men, and the congregation wondered how so much greatness and so much meekness could be found in the breast of any one human being. There was not a crease in his face; it was fat, and smooth, and ruddy; it looked like the blessed face of a large cherubim; and it said as plainly as face could say, "Here dwell content, and peace, and prosperity, and benevolence." He was Chairman of the United Band of Temperance Aboriginals; President of the Moral Boot-blacking Boys' Reformatory; Perpetual Grand Master of the Society for the Total Suppression of Vice; the highest dignitary in the Association of Universal Philanthropists; and a leading member of the Fellowship of Murray Cods. He subscribed to all the charities; with a condescending humility he allowed his name to appear regularly upon all committees for religious and benevolent purposes, and would himself go round with lists to collect subscriptions. In this direction his power was enormous. Such a thing as a refusal was not thought of. People wrote their names upon his list, in the firm belief that twenty shillings invested in benevolence with Zachariah Blemish returned a much larger rate of interest than if invested with any other collector. Once, and once only, was he known to be unsuccessful. He asked a mechanic for a subscription to the funds of the United Band of Temperance Aboriginals, and the man refused him, in somewhat rough terms, saying that the United Band of Temperance Aboriginals was a Band of Humbugs. Blemish gazed mildly at the man, and turned away without a word. The following day he displayed an anonymous letter, in which the writer, signing himself "Repentant," enclosed one pound three shillings and sixpence as the contribution of a working man (being his last week's savings) towards the funds of the United Band of Temperance Aboriginals, and a fervent wish was expressed in the letter that the Band would meet with the success it deserved. There was no doubt that it was the mechanic who sent it, and that it was the magnetic goodness of the Moral Merchant that had softened his heart. At the next meeting of the United Band of Temperance Aboriginals (which was attended by a greasy Australian native clothed in a dirty blanket, and smelling strongly of rum) a resolution was passed, authorizing the purchase of a gilt frame for the mechanic's letter, to perpetuate the goodness of Blemish, and the moral power of his eye.

On the present evening he was seated at the head of his table, round which were ranged some dozen guests of undoubted respectability. He was supported on his right by a member of the Upper House of Parliament; he was supported on his left by a member of the Lower House of ditto. One of the leading members of the Government was talking oracularly to one of the leading merchants of the city. One of the leading lawyers was laying down the law to one of the leading physicians. And only three chairs off was Mr. David Dibbs, eating his dinner like a common mortal. Like a common mortal? Like the commonest of common mortals! He might have been a bricklayer for any difference observable between them. For he gobbled his food did Mr. David Dibbs, and he slobbered his soup did Mr. David Dibbs, and his chops were greasy, and his hands were not nice-looking, and, altogether, he did not present an agreeable appearance. But was he not the possessor of half-a-dozen cattle and sheep-stations, each with scores of miles of water frontage, and was not his income thirty thousand pounds a year? Oh, golden calf! nestle in my bosom, and throw your glittering veil over my ignorance, and meanness, and stupidity give me thirty thousand pounds a year, that people may fall down and worship me!

The other guests were not a whit less respectable. Each of them, in his own particular person, represented wealth or position. Could it for a single moment be imagined that the guests of Mr. Zachariah Blemish were selected for the purpose of throwing a halo of respectability round the person of their host, and that they were one and all administering to and serving his interest? If so, the guests were unconscious of it; but it might not have been less a fact that he made them all return, in one shape or another, good interest for the hospitality he so freely lavished upon them. This evening he was giving a dinner party to his male friends; and later in the night Mrs. Zachariah Blemish would receive *her* guests and entertain them.

The gentlemen are over their wine, and are conversing freely. Politics, scandal, the state of the colony, and many other subjects, are discussed with animation. Just now, politics is the theme. The member of the Lower House and the member of the Upper House are the principal speakers here. But, occasionally, others say a word or two, which utterings are regarded by the two members as unwarrantable interruptions. The member of the Government says very little on politics, and generally maintains a cautious reticence.

"I should like to have been in the House last night," said one of the conversational interlopers; "that was a smart thing Ritchie said."

"What was it?" asked another.

"Speaking of Beazley, who is awfully rich you know, and an incorrigible miser, he said, 'He congratulated himself upon not belonging to a party which had, for its principal supporter, a man whose office was his church, whose desk was his pulpit, whose ledger was his Bible, and whose money was his god.'"

"Very clever, but very savage," remarked one of the guests. "I do not believe in such unbridled licence of debate."

"I met Beazley the other day, and he complained that the times were dreadfully dull. He did not know what things were coming to. He had seventy thousand pounds lying idle, he said, and he could not get more than five per cent. for it. He shook his head and said, 'The golden days of the colony are gone!'"

"And so they are," said the member of the Lower House, whose proclivities were republican, "and they will not return until we have Separation and Confederation. That's what we want to set us going-- separation from the home country, and a confederation of the South Sea colonies. We don't want our most important matters settled for us in the red-tape office over the water. We don't want our Governors appointed for us; we want to select them ourselves from the men who have grown up with us, and whose careers render them worthy and prove them fit for the distinction. If we were in any serious trouble we should have to extricate ourselves as best we could, and if we *did* have help from the home country, shouldn't we have to pay the piper? That's the point--shouldn't we have to pay the piper?"

"Nay, nay," expostulated Mr. Zachariah Blemish. "Consider for a moment, I beg--we are all loyal subjects, I hope--"

"I maintain," said the member of the Lower House, excited by his theme, "that, notwithstanding our loyalty to the reigning Sovereign, the day must come when we shall not be dependent upon the caprices of a colonial office fourteen thousand miles distant, which very often does not understand the nature of the difficulty it has to legislate upon. I maintain that the day must come--"

"Gentlemen," called Mr. Zachariah Blemish, horrified at the utterance of such sentiments over his dinner table, "gentlemen, I give you The Queen! God bless her!"

"The Queen! God bless her!" responded all the guests, rising to their feet, and drinking the toast enthusiastically. And then the conversation took another turn. Presently, all ears were turned to the leading physician, who was relating a circumstance to the leading lawyer.

"It is a curious story," he said. "The man I speak of was always reported to be very wealthy. No one knows more of his early career than that, when the gold-diggings were first discovered, he was a Cheap-Jack, as they call them, trading at all the new gold-fields. He bought tents, picks, shovels, tubs, anything, from the diggers, who were madly running from one place to another. He bought them for a song, for the diggers could not carry those things about with them, and they were glad to get rid of them at any price. When he sold them he made enormous profits, and by these means he was supposed to have amassed a great fortune. Then he speculated largely in sheep and cattle, and grew to be looked upon as a sort of banker. Many men deposited their savings with him, and, as he did not pay any interest for the money, and traded with it, there is no doubt as to the profitable nature of his operations. The great peculiarity about him was that his face from beneath his eyes, was completely hidden in bushy, brown, curly hair, He had been heard to say that he had never shaved. Well, one night, at past eleven o'clock, he knocked up a storekeeper at the diggings, and bought a razor and strop, a pair of scissors, a pair of moleskin trousers, a pair of watertight boots, and a blue serge shirt. In the course of conversation with the storekeeper, and while he was selecting the articles, he said that they were for a man whom he had engaged as a shepherd, and who was to start at daybreak the following morning. That was the last indisputable occurrence that was known in connection with him; the next day he disappeared and was not heard of again. For a day or two, no notice was taken of his absence; but, after that, depositors and others grew uneasy, and rumour invented a hundred different stories about him. A detective who knew him intimately, said that he was standing at the pit entrance of the Theatre Royal in Bourke Street, when a man passed in, the glitter of whose eyes attracted the detective's attention strangely. He could not recall the man's face, which was clean shaven, and he thought no more about it at the time. The missing man was traced to Melbourne, but no further. Some three or four weeks after his disappearance, the body of a drowned person was found in a river in New South Wales, and, from certain marks about it, it was supposed to be that of our missing friend. The inquest was adjourned, to allow time for the production of evidence from Victoria, and twelve medical men, all of whom knew the missing party were subp��naed for the purpose of identifying him, or otherwise. The body was much decomposed, but some of the witnesses said that they would know if it was the missing man by the peculiar shape of one of his toes. The singularity of the affair lies in this. Six of the witnesses swore that it was the missing man, and six of them swore that it was not. Both sides were very positive. Some months after the inquest, a story was current that he had been seen at Texas, which story was shortly afterwards followed up by another, that he was shot in a tavern in South America. Then came other reports that he was living in great magnificence in all sorts of out-of-the-way places. But whether he is alive or not, no one in the colony knows, and to this day the mystery is not cleared up, and probably never will be."

"And the depositors' money?" asked the lawyer.

"Was never heard of. Vanished. If he was drowned, he did not like to part with it, and he took it into the other world with him."

Everybody at the table was much interested in the story, and commented upon it; after which there was a lull in the conversation.

"I have a great surprise in store for you to-night," said Mr. Blemish; addressing a gentleman of about sixty years of age, whose face was covered with iron-grey whiskers, beard, and moustache.

From some unexplained cause, the gentleman addressed looked suddenly and excitedly into the face of his host, and exclaimed, in a quick, nervous voice--

"A surprise!"

"Yes, and I hope a pleasant one."

"What surprise?" he asked, in the same agitated manner.

"Nay." returned Mr. Blemish, gently, "it will not be a surprise if I tell you beforehand."

The flush that had risen to that portion of the gentleman's face which the iron-grey whiskers, beard, and moustache allowed to be seen, slowly died away, and was replaced by a whitish-grey tint, which almost made him look like the ghost of an antique warrior. He debated within himself for a few moments, and then, taking out his pocket-book, wrote upon a leaf, "I shall take it as a particular favour if you will let me know what is the surprise you have in store for me; I have urgent reasons for asking;" and passed it, folded, to his host. Mr. Blemish read it, smiled, and wrote beneath, in reply, "Do you remember your brother?" and repassed the paper to his guest.

"Brother!" exclaimed that gentleman, in a voice betokening that, although he was considerably astonished, he was also considerably relieved.

"Yes," said Mr. Blemish, "your brother Nicholas."

"Good heavens!" exclaimed Mr. Matthew Nuttall; and the rest of the guests stared hard at him. Excepting Mr. David Dibbs, who was not disposed to be diverted from the serious occupation of eating and drinking. For Mr. David Dibbs lived to eat; he did not eat to live.

It *is* a shock to a man to be wrenched, without forewarning, from the groove in which his life has been gliding for twenty years. For fully that time Mr. Matthew Nuttall, engrossed in his own pursuits and his own cares, had never once thought of his brother; and now, at the very mention of his name, memories, long buried and forgotten, floated upon his mind like the sudden rising of a ghostly tide.

"Have you seen him?" he asked.

"No," said Mr. Zachariah Blemish, "I learned by accident that he has but lately arrived in the colony. Singularly enough, he had a letter of introduction to me from some of my people at home, and Mrs. Blemish, out of respect to you, invited him this evening to meet you."

"Mrs. Blemish is always kind. I shall be very glad to see Nicholas," said Mr. Matthew Nuttall, slowly and thoughtfully; and then the conversation became more general.

"Sheep are rising in the market, are they not, Mr. Dibbs?" asked the member of the Upper House.

"It's time they was," replied the great squatter, his mouth full of pine-apple.

"The people are complaining loudly of the price of beef," observed the democratic member of the Lower House.

"They're always a-growlin'," said Mr. David Dibbs, who, having swallowed his pine-apple, was enabled to speak with greater clearness. "They don't know what they want, don't the people. Beef ought to be double the price. My motto all'as has been, 'Live and let live.' They lay the blame on us squatters, but it's the butchers as sticks it on."

"It lies between the two of you, I suppose. Did you read in the papers that Mr. Froth said at the Eastern Market last night that the squatters were the ruin of the country?" asked the member of the Lower House, who, in virtue of his position, did all he could to make himself disagreeable.

"Mr. Froth wants his head punched," said Mr. Dibbs, elegantly, "and I wouldn't mind a-doin' of it for him. Why doesn't he stick to his business? He's a ignorant, lazy--a--a--" Here Mr. Dibbs wanted a word, and could not get it.

"Demagogue," suggested one of the guests.

"That's it. He's a ignorant, lazy demagogue, and is always trying to stir up the mob."

"The fact of it is, sir," said the member of the Upper House, seizing the opportunity to give a blow to democracy, "the people, as you call them, are a discontented set. Manhood suffrage has done it all. No man ought to have a vote who has not a property qualification."

"Quite right, sir," said Mr. Dibbs. "A glass of wine?"

"With pleasure. For, sir, what is the result?" (This oracularly, as if he were addressing the House.) "These men, sir, who have no property, but have a vote, exercise a pressure upon property detrimental to the interests of gentlemen who have property. What has property to do with them, or what have they to do with property? When they have property, let them speak; until then, let them be silent, and not interfere with what does not concern them."

"Them's my sentiments," nodded Mr. Dibbs, approvingly, helping himself to more wine and pine-apple.

"To what, sir, is this state of things to be attributed?" continued the orator. "The answer is plain. It is to be attributed to the unfortunate state of independence in which the working-man finds himself in these colonies. The working-classes all over the world, sir, are democratic, often dangerously democratic. But in such a country as England they are kept in their proper position by a sense of dependence. They cannot afford to quarrel with their bread-and-butter there. But, sir, when the working-man lands upon these shores, this spirit of dependence vanishes. Speaking vulgarly, sir, he says within himself, 'Jack's as good as his master;' and acting up to the spirit of that old adage (the author of it sir, ought to have been put into the pillory)--acting, I say again, sir, up to the spirit of that adage, he aims a blow at the interests of all of us who have property in the colony. He does not pay property the respect: to which it is entitled. He becomes democratic to a dangerous degree, and has no regard for conservative interests. This must be put a stop to, sir. It is incumbent upon us, who are loyal subjects, to put a stop to it--as loyal subjects, I say, sir, for we all know what is the meaning of democracy. It behoves all of us who have settled interests in the colony to look sharply about us. We must, if necessary, band together for the protection of our own interests; and, above all, sir, we must stick to the Constitution."

"Quite right again, sir," assented Mr. Dibbs, whose only idea of the Constitution was thirty thousand pounds a year for himself.

All the guests, with the exception of the member of the Lower House, agreed to the proposition that they must stick to the Constitution. The way that poor word was tossed about, and flung across the table and back again, was deplorable. It was settled that the Constitution was in danger, and, at all hazards, must be protected. No one could define precisely the nature of the danger. It appeared, as far as could be gathered, to resolve itself into this--that times were very dull, and that, therefore, the Constitution was imperilled. They all, with one exception, appeared to think that something was very wrong somewhere, and that the country was in a most distressing condition. Mr. Zachariah Blemish was the only person at the table who ventured to remark that "We are young, gentlemen, we are young, and have plenty of time before us for improvement. In all new colonies evils are sure to creep in. We have a fine estate in our hands, gentlemen; one of the finest estates in the world; and all it wants is proper management. Certainly the state of commercial morality is very bad--"

Ah, here was a theme! Commercial morality! The guests grew eloquent upon it. The member of the Upper House said it was deplorable; the member of the Lower House said it was disgraceful; the leading physician said it was frightful; the leading lawyer said it was unparalleled; Mr. Dibbs said it was beastly; and they raised their hands and their eyes, and shook their heads as much as to say, "Is it not dreadful that we, who are immaculate, who are undefiled, should live in the midst of such a state of things, without being able to remedy the evil?" But the most impressive of all was Mr. Zachariah Blemish; and, as a merchant of the highest standing, his words were listened to with deep attention.

Commercial morality (he said) was at its lowest ebb. The spirit of over-speculation among traders was something frightful to contemplate, and disastrous results were sure to follow. Indeed, indications of the approaching crisis were already observable in the records of the Insolvency Court. It was all occasioned by the easiness with which men got credit--men who commenced with nothing, who had nothing, with the exception of self-assurance, and who speculated recklessly, with the knowledge that when the crash came--and come it must, sooner or later, with such-like speculators--their creditors would only be too glad to take five shillings in the pound; would feel delighted at seven shillings and sixpence; would congratulate themselves at ten shillings; and then, after giving a full release, would actually do business again, upon terms, with the very man who had robbed them. Where was honesty? Where was morality? What would become of vested interests if that sort of thing were to continue? Steps must be taken--it behoved all of them to take steps. A check must be put to the spirit of reckless speculation, and he himself had some idea of initiating a movement in furtherance of the desired result. All that was required was that merchants should be true to themselves and to their own interests, and the country would soon recover from its present depressed condition.

And after the utterance of these platitudes, Mr. Zachariah Blemish stuck his thumbs in his waistcoat pockets, and looked round upon his guests, who, one and all, bowed down to the spirit of honour and integrity shining in the face of their merchant host!

CHAPTER VI
FATHER AND DAUGHTER

The house of Mr. Zachariah Blemish looked out upon the sea. It was a magnificent mansion, worthy of the greatness of its inmate, and was the resort of the most fashionable, as well as the most influential, residents of Melbourne and its charming suburbs. It had a balcony round three of its sides--a broad, spacious balcony, on which the guests could promenade, and talk politics, or love, or philosophy, as suited them. It was grand, on a quiet night, to sit thereon, and watch the moon rising from the sea; it was grand to watch the sea itself, cradled in the arms of night, while myriad cloud-shadows floated on its breast, and flashed into lines of snow-fringed light with the rising and the falling of the waves.

Lights were gleaming in the windows and round the balcony, and the house was pleasant with the buzz of conversation, and soft laughter, and sweet music. The party seemed altogether a very delightful one; for a smile was on every lip, and distilled honey dropped from every tongue, while the presiding genius of the establishment was benign and affable, and moved among his guests like Jove dispensing agreeability.

The brothers Nuttall had met in the ball-room. The only words they exchanged were "Matthew!" "Nicholas!" and then, after a long pressure of the hand, they adjourned to the balcony, where their conversation would be more private than in the house.

They felt somewhat awkward; the days they had passed together might have belonged to another life, so long gone by did that time seem. The bridge between their boyhood and their old age had crumbled down, and the fragments had been almost quite washed by the stream of Time. Still, some memory of the old affection was stirred into life by the meeting, and they both felt softened and saddened as their hands lay in each other's clasp.

They paced the balcony in silence at first. Then the elder, Matthew, asked some stray questions as to the old places he used to frequent, and smiled and pondered wonderingly as he heard of the changes that had taken place.

"And the yew, where the parrot used to swing, gone!" he said. "And the wood where we went nutting?"

"Almost a city, Mat. A tree here and there, that's all. I was thinking only to-night of that wood, and of one happy day we spent there--you know with whom?"

"I know--I know. Good God! I have not thought of it or them for twenty years. And now they come to me again. Do they live?"

"Drowned!"

"Poor girls! There, Nick, let us talk of something else. It is no wonder things have changed. We have changed more than they."

"Yes, we are old men now," responded his brother. "This is a strange meeting, Mat, and in a new world, too."

"What did you come out to the colonies for?" asked the elder brother.

"For the same reason, I suppose, that thousands of other people come out--to better myself. I don't know that I had any particular other reason, and I don't know that I exactly knew how I was going to better myself. But I thought it would come right somehow.

"Then there were the goldfields, eh, Nicholas?"

"Yes; then there were the goldfields. They did excite me certainly. I heard of people picking up nuggets--of course you laugh--and I thought it possible that such a thing might happen. I know now how foolish even the stray thought of such a thing was for me, an old man. But still the gold seemed to say to me, Come, and I came."

"You are not rich?"

"No," was the reply.

"Any fixed plans of what you are going to do?"

"No--a dozen things have occurred to me, but, to tell you the truth, I am puzzled. Everything here appears to be so--so go-ahead," he said, after hesitating for a term, "that I am bewildered somewhat. Then, there is Mrs. Nuttall!"

"Mrs. Nuttall!"

"Yes," replied Nicholas, smiling; "my wife. I will introduce you presently. She will be agreeably surprised at your appearance," and he chuckled to himself as he thought of his wife's notions of squatting. "Then there is the girl--"

"What girl?"

"My daughter."

"Daughter!" cried Matthew, almost convulsively. But he controlled himself the moment after, and said, "A spasm, Nicholas, nothing more. What is her age?"

"Sixteen," said Nicholas. "She is here to-night. I am very proud of her, and hope you will like her."

"Marian! That was our mother's name."

Then there was silence, and, as they stood on the balcony looking out upon the ocean, the snow-fringed waves might have been bringing back to them the time that seemed to belong to another life.

"Stay here a moment, Mat," said Nicholas; "I will bring Marian to you."

And going into the house, he returned with a beautiful girl, whose face was rosy with youth and health, and whose eyes beamed with pleasure. Her graceful person and her soft white dress made her a pretty figure in the scene.

"Marian, my dear, your uncle."

He turned and took her hand, and made a movement as if about to kiss her. But he restrained himself with a sudden impulse.

"This is her first ball, Mat," said Nicholas, with an affectionate look at his daughter. "Are you enjoying yourself?"

"Oh, so much, papa!"

As she spoke, her uncle dropped her hand, and faced the sea. She was moving away towards her partner, who was waiting for her, when her uncle wheeled round, and said, as if the words were forced out of him--

"Kiss me, child."

She raised her face to his, and he bent down and kissed her, then pushed her lightly towards her partner.

"She is a dear good girl, Mat," said Nicholas; "and the greatest blessing I have; that is," he added, not at all enthusiastically, "next to Mrs. Nuttall, of course. By the bye, Mat--how careless of me, to be sure, perhaps you have a family of your own. Are *you* married?"

"Nicholas," said his brother, not answering the question, "do you remember my character as a boy?"

"Quite well, Mat. Eager, pushing, brave, and determined."

"Very determined, Nicholas."

"Very determined. I often wish I had your determination of character. Old Mr. Gray, our schoolmaster--you remember him, Mat?--used to say your determination was so determined, that it was nothing less than obstinacy. I heard him say of you one day, 'When Mat Nuttall makes up his mind to do a thing, he'll do it, whether it be good or bad, and whatever may be the result.' He said it was not a good trait--but he was mistaken, Mat. There is nothing so manly as determination of character. I wish I possessed it."

"Don't wish it, Nicholas. It often proves a curse."

"It has not proved so to you, Mat, for it has brought you riches and prosperity."

"I am rich and prosperous, as the world goes; but let that pass. Whether it be good or bad, I am not a whit less determined now than I was when a boy. I cannot help it. It is my nature. Old Mr. Gray was right. I am not to be turned from a determined purpose, whether I think I am right or wrong. Now, I have made up my mind to do what is in my power, so far as prudence goes, to advance your fortunes. But when I say to you, you must not do such and such a thing, I expect you not to do it. You are attending to me?"

"Yes."

"I am glad to have seen you--I am glad to have seen your--your Marian. But there is one subject which must never be mentioned between us, and that is the question of my family. Say that I have none. Tell Mrs. Nuttall this, and spare me any questions from her. Tell her and your"--(and here the same indecision expressed itself when he spoke of his brother's daughter)--"your Marian, that I am wifeless and childless. I must not be questioned upon the point. I have made up my mind not to be. I will not allow it to be referred to, or hinted at."

He spoke with distinctness, and yet with a strange hurriedness, as if he wished to be done quickly with the subject.

"You see those two figures yonder," he said, pointing to where the shadows of two persons could be seen upon the seashore.

"Yes, Mat, I can see them, although my eyes are not so good as they were."

"Suppose those two should walk out upon the sea, and sink, and sink, and be lost to the world--you can suppose it?"

"I can suppose it, Mat," said his brother, wonderingly.

"Suppose they are walking out upon the sea, and that they are taking this subject with them, and that it sinks with them, and is heard no more. See" (and he waved his hand as the two figures disappeared), "they are gone, and the subject is gone, and they are lost to us for ever. And there is an end to them and to it. You understand me, Nicholas?"

"I understand you, Mat."

"Very well. We will go in now, and you shall introduce me to your wife."

Meanwhile, the two persons, whose shadows the brothers had noticed, were pacing the shore. The tide was running out, and each receding wave rippled in sympathy with the soft touches of melody which floated from the brilliantly-lighted mansion. The music brought no pleasure to the couple walking slowly upon the sands; they were too much engrossed in their melancholy condition. The boy had been crying at some tale he had told, and the girl's voice expressed much sympathy as she said--

"So poor Rough is dead!"

"Yes, he's dead," replied the boy. "I shall never see him agin. I hate the sight of dawgs now. I was very fond of 'em before. But didn't you say you wanted me to do somethin', Ally?"

"Wait a minute, Grif; I will tell you presently." Alice appeared to be struggling with some powerful agitation which threatened to master her, for she stopped, and placed her hand to her heart, as if to check its beatings. "You see that house," she then said.

"Yes," Grif said; "I peeped in there a little while ago. They're very jolly, all of 'em, Ally. There's lots of swells with their white chokers, and lots of gals lookin' very sweet and nice."

"They are happier than we are, Grif."

"I should think they was--they'd be precious fools if they wasn't! I got a squint at the kitchen--there's ducks, and geese, and turkeys, and jellies painted all sorts of colours, and sugar cakes--such a spread! I wish we had some of it here. They ought to be happy with such lots to eat. I tell you what, Ally; if I thought I was agoin' to be hung, I wouldn't mind it a bit if they'd put me down in that there kitchen jist as it is now, for about three hours. I'd like to have Little Peter with me, though--wouldn't we go it!" Grif's eyes glistened at the bare anticipation.

"I want you to take a letter for me to that house. You don't mind?"

"Not a bit of it. I'll jist do anythin' as you tells me, Ally."

"You can't read."

"I can spell large letters on the walls. I never bothered about nothin' else."

"Pay attention to what I say, and do exactly as I tell you," said Alice, placing her hand on the boy's shoulder. Grif's face assumed an expression of close attention. Alice took a letter from her pocket, and continued, "Go to the house, and ask if the gentleman to whom this letter is addressed is within. If they say he is, tell them that the letter is to be given to him at once--it is very important. Do not drop it, Grif, or lose it. It contains my hope, my happiness, perhaps my life. Be sure you give it to some one who will promise to deliver it without delay."

She spoke in short broken gasps, and stayed her speech to recover her breath.

"Don't cry, Ally," said Grif; "am I to arks to see the gentleman?"

"No. You can give the letter to any of the servants; then go away and keep out of sight. If you see a gentleman speaking with me, do not disturb us, but when he is gone, and I am alone, come to me, and we will go home."

Her voice was very desolate as she spoke the last word. Grif gave a nod of comprehension, and walked to the house, while the girl strained her eyes thitherward in eager watchfulness. The night was changing now; a low wail of wind came across the sea, striking a colder chill of desolation to her heart. She shivered, and wrapped her shawl more closely about her. But for this movement she might have been an image of Sadness, so drear and lonely did she appear as she stood upon the glistening sands.

Grif mused as he walked along; Alice's words had deeply impressed him. He weighed the letter in his hand, and thought, "It contains her happiness, perhaps her life; then the cove who gets it has got somethin' to do with Ally. I wonder who he is: I'll have a good look at him; I'll know him agin, I bet, after I've seen him once." Thus soliloquising, he reached the house, and, standing in the shade, watched the people flitting about. They were all so beautifully dressed that he felt ashamed of his rags; it was clearly, to his mind, an act of presumption to speak to such well-dressed people. With an instinctive exercise of good judgment, he resolved to ask one of the maids to deliver the letter. A man-servant might hustle him away; a girl would be more susceptible to pity. So, plucking up courage, he walked boldly to the back-door, and, seeing a girl with a pretty face, with a tray of custards in her hand, he approached her.

"Oh, dear!" exclaimed the girl, almost dropping the tray, as ragged Grif emerged from the shade into the light. "What do you want? Go away; I mustn't give you any."

Grif eyed the custards hungrily and longingly. Then he wrenched his attention from the tempting glasses, and said, falsely, "I don't want nothin', miss; only if you'll please to tell me if the gentleman's name writ on this letter is in this house."

The girl looked at it, and said he was, she thought.

"Will you please give him the letter? It's very partic'ler, it is."

The girl took the letter, and said she would deliver it. Grif ducked his head, and turned slowly away. But he cast a wistful glance over his shoulder at the food for which he was longing. The kind-hearted maid saw hunger in his face, and, catching up a half-devoured fowl, ran after him. She looked round hurriedly, to see that she was not observed, and saying, "Here, dirty boy!" thrust the food into his eager hands, and ran back to the house as fast as her legs would carry her. Grif, walking carefully in the shade, commenced at a wing; he was dreadfully hungry, but in the midst of his enjoyment he stopped, and thought of Rough, and wished the dog was there to eat the bones. The tears ran down the boy's face as he thought, and he strolled on, munching and crying. When he got to the front of the house, he saw the servant girl delivering the letter. The gentleman went in the light to read it, and Grif had an opportunity of seeing his face. "I shall know *you* agin," Grif thought. "You ain't much to look at, *you* ain't. He's goin' to Ally, and I'm not to bother 'em. All right; I'll watch for all that."

During the whole of this time Alice had not stirred. She stood where Grif had left her--her eyes turned towards the house. So fixed and rapt was her attention that her very breathing could scarcely be heard. As the form of the man came nearer and nearer to her, she shrank, and then stretched forth her arms, as if in supplication; but her feet seemed rooted to the spot. He came close to her, and said in a hard, stern voice--

"Is it you who wish to speak with me?"

"Father!" she cried.

"Alice!"

The sadden surprise robbed his voice of its sternness. He recoiled a step from her as she addressed him, and his face grew pale; but if the next moment the moon had shone upon it, no trace of emotion would have been there observable.

"So!" he said, coldly. "A trick! Another lesson you did not learn in my house."

She looked down and twisted her fingers nervously, but did not reply.

"Why did you address a note to me in a strange hand?"

"I thought you would not have come if you recognised my writing," she answered, sadly.

"What do you out at this time of night, and alone?"

"I am not alone, father," she said, glancing to where Grif was crouching.

"What! Is your husband here?" he exclaimed with suppressed passion, following her look.

"No, sir; it is but a poor lad. I was afraid to come out by myself."

"And your husband?"

"He does not know, sir, that I have come. If he had--"

"He would have kept you away; it would have been wise in him."

"Father, have you no pity?"

"What do you want of me?"

"Help and forgiveness."

"I will give you both. You can come to my home, and I will receive you as my daughter."

"And Richard--my husband--"

"I will have nought to do with him. I give you once again your choice. You are my daughter, or his wife. You cannot and shall not be both. As this is the first, so it shall be the last time I will see you upon the subject. You shall juggle me no more with false writing. The day you ran away from your home, from me who was hoarding and saving for you, I resolved to shut you from my heart as long as you were tied to that scheming scapegrace. You know how constant I can be when I resolve."

"Alas! I know."

"So I have resolved on this, and no power on earth can change me. Richard Handfield came to my house a guest, and he played the knave. He stopped in my house a servant, and he played the cheat. He took my money, he ate my bread, he displayed his fine gentleman's airs and accomplishments at my expense. And all this time he was stealing you from me, and laughing in his sleeve at the trick he was playing the wealthy squatter. He robbed me of the one object of my life. What! shall a father toil and scheme for a lifetime, and set his heart upon a thing, and be foiled in a day by a supercilious cheat! What does a child owe a father? Obedience. You owed me that--but a small return for all I had lavished upon you, but a small return for the fortune I was amassing for you. Did I ask you for anything else? What was this for a father to ask a daughter, that she should play the traitress to him?"

"Father, have pity!"

"You have thwarted the scheme of my life. But what was my strongest wish when it clashed with your girlish fancy? Listen. Do you know what

I have suffered in this colony? I have suffered privation, hunger, misery, raging thirst, over and over again. I have walked, with blistered feet, hundreds and hundreds of miles; I have laboured with my axe till I was faint with fatigue; I have hidden from Blacks in fear of my life; I have been left for dead upon the burning plains; I have been lost in the bush until my whole being was one great despair! Was this a pleasant life to lead, and did I deserve no recompense? Was life so sweet to me, with those burdens, that I should enjoy it in the then present? I had a child--a daughter. But for her I might have grown into a wild man of the bush, and growled at the world and at humanity. I had provocation enough, for I was poor. Men who knew me when I first came to the colony, and when I had money, knew me not when I lost it. I lost my wife, too; and I had but my daughter and my poverty left. Then, when men turned their backs to me, and I felt the bitterness of it--(I know now that they were right; poverty should be shunned)--I bent all my mind and soul to the one desire--to make money. A slice of good fortune fell to my share. I resolved to grow rich, and to make my daughter rich. I toiled, I slaved, I schemed for her. I had an object, and life was less bitter than before. I said, My daughter shall be the envy of those who knew me when I was poor; she shall marry riches, and grow into fashion and into power from the force of her father's and her husband's money. She shall be called the rich squatter's daughter, and her children shall be educated to rule the State. I knew well then, and know well now, the power of gold; it could do all this for me, and more. There is no aristocracy in this colony but the aristocracy of wealth; money is the god all worship here! It ennobles the mean, it dignifies the vulgar. It is all powerful. See what it does for me. What fascinations, what graces, what virtues, do I possess, that people should cringe to me and adulate me? And as they idolize me, a man of money, for my wealth, so I idolize my wealth for what it brings me."

As he spoke from the vile selfishness of his heart, did the wailing wind, sighing mournfully around him, suggest to his mind no more precious thing in the world than gold? Did the pale stars and the restless waves teach no lesson that such an egotist might learn, and be the better for the learning? Did they tell no story from which he might have learned a noble creed, had he but listened to their teaching? No! he felt not their influence. He lived only in himself. What was Nature to him? She gave him nothing that he should be grateful for; what he received, all others received. And so he beheld the swelling waves, and heard the wailing wind, and looked up to the glimmering stars with indifference. What was the glory of the heavens to him or to his life? A handful of gold and a sightful of stars! Was not the gold which bought him human worship, more precious to him than all?

"Oh, father!" murmured Alice: "money is not everything."

"Money is everything," he replied; "everything to me. Can you undo, with a word, the study of my life? It was but little I asked in return for the future I was working out for you. The man I selected for you had wealth, position. Even if you had failed (as you *have* failed, but in a different manner) in the duty you owed to me, I could not have forced the man upon you; even although you knew it was the only reward I coveted for my life's labour, and refused at the last moment to give it to me, you might still have been the daughter of my heart, as you are of my blood. But to fly from me to *him*--a penniless adventurer, a shallow, brainless coxcomb!" The thought seemed to cool his passion, and exclaiming, "Why do I waste my time here?" he made a movement towards the house.

"Stop, for pity's sake," Alice cried, stretching forth her arms; "stop and hear me."

"Speak on," he said, between his clenched teeth. There was no hope in his voice; it was hard and bitter.

"I came to-night, sir," Alice said, humbly bowing her head, and forcing back her tears, "to appeal to you for the last time. You may send me away, unhappy and broken-hearted--indeed, I am that already--but oh, sir! reflect before you do so, and let your better feelings guide you. Ah, sir! are all your thoughts about yourself and your money, and have you no thought of me? I do not know a parent's feelings, but soon"--and here her voice faltered--"soon I may become a mother--forgive me, sir, these tears--I try to conquer them, but they are too strong for me." She paused a few moments, and then continued: "What sympathy, sir, could you expect me, a simple girl, to have with your aspirations? I knew them not, and if you had confided them to me, I should not have understood them--"

"Have you come to tutor me, girl?" he asked, coldly.

"No, sir. If my distress and my misery have no weight with you, what can my poor words do? My husband--forgive me--I must speak of him."

"Go on."

"My husband, to whose fate and lot I am linked for ever--for ever," she repeated firmly, "is willing to work for me, is contented to keep me, poor and friendless as I am. But he needs help. Give it him; give it me, and I will trouble you no more. I will be content, so that you assist us to live."

"Your husband is a man; he can work like other men. Let him do so. He shall not live upon my bounty. No man need starve in this land of plenty. Let him work, if he be not too proud."

"He is not too proud, sir. He has tried to get work, but failed. Help him in his endeavor--you can do so. You have power, influence. And think, sir, that even if I would, I cannot undo the past."

"Would you, if you could?"

"For pity's sake, sir, do not ask me."

"Would you, if you could?" he repeated, relentlessly.

"Then, sir, as you insist," she returned, "I reply, as is my duty, No. He is my husband, and my future life is linked with his."

"Have you done?"

"I have but little more to say, sir. I feel from your voice that there is scant hope for me! But oh, sir, before you turn from me, think of what my future may be if you remain inexorable. You, who have undergone privations in your early life, know what a stern master is necessity. As yet, my husband is saved from crime--"

"Is this your last argument?" he interrupted. "It has no weight with me. You cannot more disgrace me than you have already done. Here let this end. I *am* inexorable."

His voice, stern and unforgiving, carried conviction with it.

"Heaven help me!" she exclaimed sadly. "Then we must trust to chance." And she turned from him, weeping.

There was a pause, and then he said, "I will not leave you entirely unsatisfied. It is money, I suppose, you want. Here are fifty pounds. It is the last you will ever receive from me while he and you are together. Good night."

She raised her arms imploringly, but he was making towards the house. He saw not the entreating action, nor did he hear the low wailing sobs which broke from her as he walked away. A sad contrast was her drooping figure upon the lonely sands to the glad life that moved in the merchant's house! A sad accompaniment were her sobs to the strains of music and the sounds of light laughter with which they mingled! The guests within were joyous, while she, who should have been his one joy, stood desolate on the shore. But despite her misery there was hope deep within her heart--hope of a happy future yet with the man with whose lot hers was linked. Her father had cast her off; but love remained--love strong and abiding. How great the contrast! A good woman's love and a hard man's greed of gold!

CHAPTER VII
GRIF PROMISES TO BE HONEST

Hunger has many phases; but in every phase except its physical one it is comparative. Thus, a person may be eagerly desirous, hungry, for something which his neighbour has, but which his neighbour, possessing, does not value and thinks of no regard. What is wanted is a moral, equable dispensation; yet if by any possibility such could be arranged, false weights would be sure to be introduced, and things would be unequal as before. And so the world goes on hungering, and one hungry class groans for that with which the belly of another hungry class is filled. Every step in the ladder of life is thronged with climbers ready to reach the next, and although some be twenty rounds above others, they are as restlessly unhappy in their high position, and as restlessly desirous of getting a foot higher, as those who are so far beneath them. It is the way of the world. The heaven is always above us, and we climb, and climb, and climb, and never reach our hopes.

And yet some of our desires are very small. Ambition is various; large-souled aspirations and the meanest of cravings come within its scope. Casually, we admire the aspirations of a noble mind which looks above and beyond the grovelling littleness of humanity, and strives to reach a goal where dwell the nobler virtues, studded with the jewels of their worth and goodness. Casually, we pass by, as scarcely worthy of contempt, certainly not worthy of notice, the paltry desires for common things which fill some creatures' souls. Nevertheless, the aspiration which stretches itself towards the nobler virtues may be no finer than the paltry desire which pines for common things. 'Tis ten to one that the latter is more human; and what is human must be good, notwithstanding what some preachers say about the corruption of flesh, and the vanity of desire.

Ask Grif. How paltry, how mean is his ambition! Ask him, in such language as he can understand, what it is he most desires, what it is he most craves for? He will answer, in his own way, Sufficient of the commonest food to eat in the day, and a shelter and blanket to cover him in the night. Is it his fault that he strives no higher? His hungry body cries out to him, and he responds to its prompting. He does not openly rebel against his fate. He knows that *it is*, and, without any concerted action of the mind to assist him to that conclusion, he feels that he cannot alter it. He does not repine;

he only wonders sometimes that things are so. Of course, when he is hungry he suffers; that he cannot help. But he suffers in silence, and thereby shows that he has within him the qualities that would make a hero. But still the fact remains that he aspires no higher; still the fact remains that he is dead to the conscious exercise of the nobler virtues. Spread them before him, if such were possible, and he would not even wonder. But his eyes would light up, and all his intellectual forces would be gratified, at the sight of a bone with a little meat upon it. Such is Grif, a human waif living in the midst of a grand and mighty civilisation.

Is it possible that this same civilisation, of which we comfortable ones prate and vaunt, depraves as well as ennobles? The thought is pertinent to the subject. For here is Grif (unquestionably depraved and debased in the eyes of that civilisation which does nothing for him, which absolutely turns its back upon him), a piece of raw material out of which much good might be wrought, suffering much unmerited suffering, and surrounded by an atmosphere of actively-conscious vice. The law looks unkindly upon him; policemen push him aside as if he were an interloper in the world; and well-dressed people shrink from contact with him as he slouches by. Civilisation presses upon him unkindly. He does not deserve it. There is a better nature within him than he is called upon to exercise in his intercourse with his enemy, the world. The chord of that better nature has been touched by Alice, so kindly, so commiseratingly, that every nerve in his frame quivers with a passionate longing to serve her. He can reckon on the fingers of one hand the objects for which he has any human affection. Alice he loves far beyond the others, for he feels that she is different to them. He has seen that she is unselfish and self-sacrificing; and he knows (though he could not express it in so many words) that she is good from principle, and that she is pure because it is her nature to be pure. He has heard her renounce ease and comfort, and choose poverty and suffering, so that she might play the good angel to the man whom she loves. And at the goodness of that renunciation, at the holiness of it, Grif fell down and worshipped her with all his soul. Then there was Milly: his love for her had no adoration in it, but was born of pity, tenderness, and gratitude. He would do much to serve Milly, for she had been very kind to him. Then came Little Peter. Grif loved that other little waif because he was so helpless, and because it was so sweet to have some one to cherish and take care of. His love for Little Peter had in it something of the love of a mother. He asked for no reward in the shape of gratitude. It was sufficient for him that Peter was dependent upon him--was his to protect. It is truly more blessed to give than to receive!

Counting, then, upon one hand the objects of his love, Grif could mention Alice, Milly, and Little Peter, and still leave a finger unprovided for. A short time since--only two days ago--the dog Rough would have closed the list; but Rough was dead, and the finger might be regarded as widowed. Yes, Rough was dead. Grif's faithful follower, his dumb companion, his honest servant, was gone--poisoned, murdered, meanly killed! Tears, born of rage and desolation, came into Grif's eyes as he thought of the death and the manner of it. But the murderer! Revengeful justice found strong expression when Grif swore and swore again that he would be even with the villain who had murdered his dog.

It was the second night after the burial, and Grif and Little Peter were sitting upon the ground near the grave. Grif was mourning for his lost friend; if Rough had been his brother he could not have mourned with more genuine grief. The night was chilly, and the wind whistled sharply about the rags in which the boys were clothed. But they were too much engrossed in special cares and griefs to pay more attention to the remorseless wind than was expressed by a cold shiver now and then, and an involuntary huddling together of their limbs. "I wouldn't care if Rough was alive," mused Grif. "If he'd only come when I whistle!" And the next moment he absolutely whistled the old familiar call, and looked down, almost expecting to feel Rough's cold nose rubbing against his hand. Disappointed in this, he looked to Little Peter for sympathy.

He got none. Little Peter's nature was not sympathetic, and Grif obtained no response from Little Peter's eyes or tongue as he placed his hand against the lad's cheek. How thin and pale was that poor little face of poor Little Peter's! What weariness of the trouble of living was expressed in the attitude of his body and in every line of his features! As he sat, drooping, trembling, hollow-cheeked, wistful-eyed, he looked like a shrunken old child-man with every drop of healthful life-blood squeezed clean out of him.

Gazing at the drooping figure, Grif forgot his own grief, and saying "Poor Little Peter!" in a tone of much pity, drew closer to the lad, and sat motionless for many minutes. Then he rose.

"Come along, Peter," he said, "it's time we was off."

But Little Peter did not move.

"Asleep, Peter?" asked Grif.

A slight quivering of Little Peter's body was the only reply.

"Wake up, Peter!" persisted Grif, shaking him gently by the shoulder.

Still Little Peter made no response, but sat quiet, with head drooping to his knees.

Grif knelt quickly upon the ground, and raised Peter's head. The large eyes opened slowly and gazed vacantly at Grif, and a strong trembling took possession of Peter. His limbs relaxed, and he would have fallen upon his face to the earth had not Grif caught him in his arms. Where he lay, trembling and shivering.

"He's took ill!" cried Grif, with a sudden apprehension. "They won't take him in at the horspital! What shall I do?"

Grif, aware of the necessity of immediate action, lifted Little Peter upon his shoulder. As he did so, and as Little Peter's head sank forward upon Grif s breast, a small stone heart, hanging from a piece of common string, fell from the little fellow's neck. Grif caught it in his hand and held it. Ever since he had known Peter this little stone heart had been round the boy's neck. He would have lost it long ago, had it been of any value; but its worthlessness was its security. So with the stone heart in his hand and Peter upon his shoulder, Grif walked slowly back to the city. Now and then a wayfarer stopped and looked after ragged Grif and his ragged burden. But Grif walked steadily on, taking no notice of curiosity mongers. Once he was stopped by a policeman, who questioned him.

"He's my brother," said Grif, telling the lie without the smallest compunction, "and he's took ill. I'm carryin' of him home."

Carrying of him home! The words caused Grif to reflect and ask himself where he *should* carry Little Peter. The barrel? Clearly, that was not a fit place for the sick lad. He knew what he would do. He would take Peter to Milly's house. Grif's instincts were nearly always right.

Soon he was in the city, and choosing the quietest streets, he made his way to the quarter where Milly lived. There was a light in her room. He walked slowly up the stairs, and knocked at the door. No answer came. He knocked again, and listened. A sound of soft singing reached his ears, and opening the door, he entered the room and stood still.

Milly was at the further end of the room, kneeling by the side of a bed on which lay a baby asleep. Her hands were clasped, and she was smiling, and singing softly to herself, and looking at the face of her baby, the while she gently swayed her body to and fro. He stood wondering. "I never knowed she had a baby," he muttered inly, under his breath.

Love and devotion were expressed in every curve of the girl's body. The outline of her face, her hair hanging loosely down, the graceful undulations of her figure, were beautiful to look at. She was singing some simple words which might have been sung to her when she was a sinless child, and the good influence of sweet remembrance was upon her, and robed her with tenderness.

"Milly!" whispered Grif.

She turned quickly at the sound, and seeing Grif, cautioned him by signs not to make a noise; and then, after placing her cheek caressingly against her baby's, came towards him.

"What do you want, Grif?" she asked. "Who have you got there?"

"It's Little Peter," said Grif, placing the boy on the ground; "he's took ill, and I don't know what to do."

Milly raised Peter's head to her lap, and bent over him.

"Poor Little Peter!" she said. "How white he is, and how thin! Perhaps he's hungry."

"No," said Grif. "I know what's the matter with him. He caught cold t'other night, when I took him with me to bury my dawg. It was rainin' hard, and we both got soppin' wet. It didn't matter for me, but he was always a pore little chap. I ought to have knowed better."

"To bury your dog!" repeated Milly. "Why, I saw him with you the night before last."

"Yes, Milly, that was when you gave me that shillin'. Rough was all right then. But he was pizened that night."

"Poisoned!"

"Yes," very mournfully.

"Who poisoned him?"

"The Tenderhearted Oysterman."

"The mean hound!"

"He heerd me say somethin' agin him when I was speakin' to you, Milly, so he took it out of me by pizenin' the dawg. But I'll be even with him!"

By this time Milly had undressed Little Peter, and placed him in the bed by the side of her baby.

"There!" she said. "He'll be all right to-morrow. I'll make him some gruel presently. He's got a bad cold, and wants keeping warm."

"You're a good sort, Milly," said Grif, gratefully. "I'd have carried him to the horspital, but I didn't think they'd take him in."

"No; they wouldn't take him there without a ticket, and where could you have got *that* from?"

"Blest if I know!" exclaimed Grif. "Nobody would give *me* a ticket, I shouldn't think!" This remark was made by Grif in a tone sufficiently indicative of his sense of his abasement.

"But I say, Milly," he continued, "I didn't know you had a baby. May I look at him?"

"It's a little girl," said Milly, smiling, leading Grif towards the bed, and turning down the coverlid so that he might get a peep of baby's face. "Isn't she a beauty?"

Grif bent over the bed, and timidly put his hand upon baby's. The little creature involuntarily grasped one of Grit's dirty fingers in her dimpled fist, and held it fast.

"It's like a bit of wax," said Grif, contemplating with much admiration the difference between baby's pretty hand and his own coarse fingers. "Will she always be as nice, Milly?"

"You were like that once, Grif," Milly remarked.

"Was I, though?" he replied, reflectively; "I shouldn't have thought it. How did I come like this I wonder?"

Here the baby opened her eyes--which had a very wide-awake look in them, as if she had been shamming sleep--and stared at Grif, seriously, as at some object really worth studying. To divert her attention from a study so unworthy, Grif smiled at the baby, who, thus encouraged, reflected back his smile with interest, and crowed into the bargain. Whereat Milly caught her in her arms, and pressing her to her breast, covered her face with kisses.

"How old is she, Milly?" asked Grif, regarding this proceeding with honest pleasure.

"Ten weeks the day after to-morrow," replied Milly, who, as is usual with young mothers, reckoned forward. "And now, Grif, if you will hold her, I will make some gruel for Little Peter. Be careful. No; you mustn't take her like that! Sit down, and I will put her in your lap."

So Grif squatted upon the ground, and Milly placed the child in his lap. He experienced a strange feeling of pleasure at his novel position. It was a new revelation to him, this child of Milly's. Milly herself was so different. He had never seen her in so good a light as now. Hitherto he had in his thoughts drawn a wide line between her and Alice; a gulf that seemed impassable had divided them. Now the gulf was bridged with human love and human tenderness. Alice was all good; but was Milly all bad?

He looked at her as she was making the gruel. Tender thoughts beautify; a mother's love refines. She was kneeling before the fire, pausing in her occupation now and then to bestow a smile upon her child. Once she rested her face in baby's neck, caressingly. Her hair hung upon Grif's hand, and he touched it and marvelled at the contrast between Milly of yesterday and Milly of to-day. Then he fell to wondering more about Milly than he had ever wondered before. Had she a father, like Alice, who was unkind to her? What was it that she saw in Jim Pizey that made her cling to him? Why was it that everything seemed to be wrong with those persons whom he loved? Rough had been poisoned, Little Peter was ill, Milly was attached to a bad man, and Alice--well, it was a puzzle, the whole of it! While he thus thought, Milly had been giving Little Peter the gruel.

"Milly," Grif said, when she returned from the bed, "have you got a mother and father?"

The girl turned a startled look upon him, and was about to make some passionate reply, but suddenly checked herself.

"Don't ask me, Grif," she said, in a hard voice. "How is your lady?"

Her old spirit was coming upon her. Grif knew that she meant Alice by "your lady," and he was hurt by the scornful ring of her voice. Seeing that he was grieved, Milly said:

"Don't mind me, Grif; now I'm soft, and now I'm hard. I've got the devil in me sometimes, and I can't keep him down. But I mustn't think--I mustn't think--I mustn't think. Of course, I've got a mother and father, and my mother and father's got a daughter they might be proud of. Everybody used to tell me so. I had a pretty face, pretty hands, pretty feet, pretty hair. I'm a pretty daughter altogether! Why wasn't I ugly? Then I might have been good!"

She took the baby from Grif s arms, and pressed it to her bosom.

"If I knew how to be good," she said, in a softened voice, "I think I would be. But I don't know how. If I was to go out of this house to-night, I shouldn't know which way to turn to be good. I'd be sure to turn wrong. I don't care!" And then she sang, recklessly, "I'm happy, I'm careless, I'm good-natured and free; and I don't care a single pin what the world thinks of me!"

"Don't, Milly! don't!" pleaded Grif, placing his hand upon hers, and looking earnestly at her.

She took his hand convulsively, and put it to her baby's lips.

"That won't do baby any harm," she said, after a pause. "I wonder if baby will grow up pretty, like me. Oh, I hope not, I hope not!"

"She's got eyes like your'n," said Grif, wishing to change her humour.

"Prettier than mine," Milly replied. "But if it wasn't that I should go mad if I was to lose her, I wish she would die! It would be better for her, but I think it would be worse for me. What's that in your hand?"

It was Little Peter's stone heart, which Grif had held all the while.

"It's Little Peter's heart," he said.

"Of course it is; I remember it now. It belonged to his mother."

"Where is she?" asked Grif, eagerly, for this was the first time he had heard of Little Peter's mother.

"She died two years ago in the hospital."

"Did you know her, Milly?"

"I went with a friend to see her when she was dying. She was a Welsh woman. She put the heart round Little Peter's neck when we took him to wish her good-bye, for the doctor said she would die before night."

"What did she die of, Milly?" The subject was full of interest to Grif.

"Broken heart. Somebody played her false, as usual. I shan't die of a broken heart--not I! Drink will be my death--the sooner the better! Hush! There's Jim. Who else? The Tenderhearted Oysterman."

Grif jumped to his feet, trembling with passion.

"He mustn't see you. He'll do you a mischief. Perhaps he won't stop long. Get under the bed-clothes, and pretend to be asleep. Quick! For God's sake!"

She thrust him hurriedly into the bed, and had barely time to conceal him and resume her position, before Jim and his companion entered.

Milly smiled at Jim, but neither he nor his companion took heed of her. They seated themselves near the fire, and Milly sat upon the bed, which was in the shadow of the room.

"We must have him," said the Tenderhearted Oysterman, apparently in continuance of a conversation. "The old bloke always keeps a heap of money in his safe at Highlay Station; and Dick Handfield knows every nook and cranny of the place. I've heard him say so. He knows all the secret drawers, too, I'll be bound, and where the keys are to be found, and where the hiding places are. We must have him, Jim."

At the mention of Highlay Station, Grif pricked up his ears. That was the Station which Alice had spoken of in their conversation a couple of nights ago. But when, the next instant, the Tenderhearted Oysterman uttered Richard Handfield's name, he started, and caught Milly's hand excitedly. Milly pressed him down with quiet, warning action, and, recalled to the necessity of being cautious, Grif lay still and listened. Milly paid but little attention to the conversation. She did not know anything of Highlay Station, nor that Alice was Richard Handfield's wife, and it was no novelty to her to hear schemes of robbery discussed by Jim and his associates.

"You talk," said Jim Pizey. "But I like to do."

"What do you mean by that?" asked the other.

"Not that you're not cool enough," continued Jim, "you're as good a pal as I ever want to have, if you'd only stop that damned cant of not hurting people." (The Tenderhearted Oysterman gave a quiet chuckle.) "I know well enough that you don't mean it."

"Now Jim," expostulated the Oysterman, and yet evidently regarding his comrade's words as a compliment. "It's a good job there's no one by to hear you take away my character."

"But others don't know you as well as I do, and there's plenty of them would think you were chicken-hearted."

"Do I look like it?" asked the Tenderhearted Oysterman in a tone of villanous humility.

"No, you don't. But you'd make believe that you was. If I didn't know you for one who would stick at nothing--nothing, not even short of--"

"Never mind what," interrupted the Oysterman, looking at Milly, who was employed nursing her baby, and did not appear to be taking heed of what was said.

"If I didn't know you for that, then, I'd have nothing to do with you, for your infernal cant sickens me."

There was a pause in the conversation. Grif still held Milly's hand hard. He felt there was something coming which would affect Alice, and every word that was being uttered stamped itself upon his mind.

"Dick Handfield we must have, and Dick Handfield we will have," resumed Jim. "If we can't have him one way, we will another. I've got a hook in him already, and if he hangs on and off as he's been doing, the white-livered skunk! the last two weeks, he'll get a dose that'll pretty well settle him."

"What sort of a dose, Jim?"

"I bought a watch of him this morning--here it is. I gave him five pounds for it. It's a pretty little thing. Just the thing for Milly! Milly."

"Yes, Jim," answered Milly, disengaging her hand from Grif's grasp, and walking towards Jim, for fear he should come to the bed, and discover Grif.

"Here's a watch I've bought for you. It belonged to a lady."

"Oh, what a beauty!" cried Milly, her eyes sparkling with eager delight as she looked at the pretty bauble.

"Well, it's yours now, my girl. I promised you should have one when the young 'un came."

"Thank you, Jim," said Milly, returning to the bed, with the present in her hand.

"He's just like me, Milly," said the Tenderhearted Oysterman; "he's as soft as a piece of putty. But I can't see how that watch is a dose, Jim."

"I gave Dick Handfield five pounds for that watch," said Jim, "and I paid him for it with a forged note."

At these words, Milly, who had been looking at the watch, and examining it with the pleasure of a child when it receives a new toy, dropped it upon the bed, with a heavy sigh.

"Then I took him to Old Flick's, and Old Flick gave him five sovereigns for the note. There was a man in the store when Dick Handfield changed the note, and Old Flick, who knew all about the lay, asked Dick Handfield all sorts of questions and regularly confused him. That's a pretty good dose for him, I think. I shall ask him to-morrow for the last time to join us. If he refuses, Old Flick shall give him in charge for passing a forged note, and the man who was in the store at the time will be the witness. Handfield will be glad enough to join us when he finds he's in the web. He'd sooner go up the country with us than go to quod--if it was only for the sake of that woman of his, that white-faced piece of virtue he calls his wife."

"Alice her name is," said the Tenderhearted Oysterman, sneeringly. "She's as much his wife as I am."

"It's a lie, Milly, a lie!" whispered Grif, in an agony of rage and despair at what he had heard. "She *is* his wife!" Oh, if he could get away from the room to tell Alice of the danger which surrounded her husband! He dug his nails in his hand, and his faithful heart beat furiously.

Milly placed her hand upon his lips.

"You're a liar, Oysterman!" she said, quietly. "The girl *is* his wife."

Grif took Milly's hand, and kissed it again and again for the vindication.

The Tenderhearted Oysterman turned sharply upon Milly, and was about to answer her when Jim Pizey said,--

"Milly's right. The girl is his wife. You don't know everything, Oysterman. But now I'll tell you that that girl is the daughter of Old Nuttall, the rich squatter of Highlay Station. Dick Handfield was living on the Station for a goodish time--that's how he came to know all about it. The girl fell in love with him, and they ran away and got married."

"And a pretty nice thing she made of it!" sneered the Oysterman. "I hate these milk-sop women!"

"I wonder what sort of a woman you'd ever be fond of, Oysterman!" said Milly, with bitter sarcasm. "I wonder if *you'd* ever get a woman to love you, and think you a model of anything but what's mean!"

"Serve you right, Oysterman," said Jim, laughing. "Never you speak against women when a woman is by."

The Tenderhearted Oysterman had turned white in the face when Milly spoke.

"You're a nice sort of woman, *you* are," he exclaimed, with a snarl. "I'd never want *you* to love me and think me a model."

"A good job for you," she exclaimed. "I pity the woman you'd take a fancy to, or the man either, for that matter. If I was Jim, I'd pitch you downstairs."

"Come, come, Milly," said Jim, "we've had enough of that."

"No, we haven't," cried Milly, who was thoroughly roused. "You're a man, you are. You're bad enough, God knows! but there *is* something of a man in you. But that cur!" She placed her baby on the bed, and advanced a step towards the men, and pointed to the Oysterman. "That cur!" she repeated in a tone of such contempt that the Oysterman's blood boiled with fury. "That kicker of women and poisoner of dogs! What do you think he did, the night before last, Jim? He crawled to where poor little Grif was sleeping, and gave a piece of poisoned meat to Grif's dog. He did, the mean hound! That was a nice manly thing to do, wasn't it!"

"Come along, Oysterman," said Jim Pizey, half angry and half amused, taking his comrade by the arm. "It's no use answering her. She talks to me sometimes like that. Come along, and have a drink."

And by sheer strength he forced the Oysterman out of the room.

"That's done me good," said Milly, when the men were gone, taking her baby to the fire.

Grif started to his feet.

"Thank you, Milly," he said. "I'll tell Ally how you stood up for her."

"Don't you do anything of the sort," said Milly, who, now her passion was over, was crying. "It isn't fit that my name should be mentioned to her. She's a good woman."

"And so are you, Milly," said Grif, inwardly struggling with his doubts.

"I'm not, nor ever shall be. That watch" (pointing to it) "was hers, I suppose."

"I s'pose so. I never sor it."

Milly took it in her hand and opened the case.

"Here's her name," she said. "Alice Handfield. And here's a motto: Hope, Faith, and Love. And she gave it back to her husband, because they were hard up, perhaps, and Jim bought it of him with a forged note. Oh, my God! What a web of wickedness and goodness!"

"I must go" cried Grif, "I must go and tell them--I must go and put Ally up to it."

"Up to what?" exclaimed Milly, a light breaking upon her. "Up to the forged note! You'll go and tell her that you heard Jim say he paid for the watch with a forged note? And her husband 'll have Jim took up, and you'll be witness against him!" She glided swiftly to the door, and turning the key, put it in her pocket.

"What do you do that for?" asked Grif. "I *must* go, Milly. I'll break open the door."

"No, you won't," said Milly, taking fast hold of him. "You shan't get Jim into trouble. He's been kind to me, though he is a bad man, and you shan't peach upon him."

"Let me go, Milly," cried Grif, gently struggling.

"You don't go till Jim comes in," she said, still retaining her hold of him, "and then--good God!" she cried, in a voice of despair and horror. "Then, he'll kill you!"

The conflict of thought was too much for her. She relaxed her hold, and Grif flew to the door, and broke the frail lock. Then he looked back. Milly had fallen to the floor, and was sobbing convulsively. Her baby was lying by her side.

Grif went to her and raised her.

"Milly," he said, "don't take on so. I won't hurt you or Jim. But I must be true to Ally. If I couldn't I'd go and drown myself. I couldn't live, and not be true to her. She said I was her only friend, and I swore that I'd be so till I die! And I will be, till I die--and I'd like to die for her, for she's a good woman, Milly!"

"She is--she is," groaned Milly; "and I'm a bad and wicked one."

"You're not, Milly, you're not," said Grif, emphatically. "You're good, but another sort of good! See what you've done for Little Peter to-night," and he kissed her hand; "see what you've done for me many and many a time; and see how you stood up for Ally jist now, although every word you said was agin yourself!" he kissed her hand again. "You can't be bad and wicked! And I won't hurt you, and I won't hurt Jim, because of you. I won't, you may believe me! I'll tell Ally that her husband must go away to-night. He was agoin' away--I heerd him say so--and perhaps he's gone already. I won't tell her about the forged note. I'll say that I heerd a plot, and I won't tell her what it is. She'll believe me, I know she will. And so I shall do her good, and I shan't do you any harm!"

Grif spoke earnestly, for as his words brought to his mind the remembrance of Milly' s unselfish kindness, the conviction that it would be wicked to harm her or wound her feelings, grew stronger and stronger.

"God bless you!" said Milly.

Truly, Grif was not entirely unhappy or forsaken. The blessing, even from Milly, fell upon his heart like dew upon a parched field.

"Ah, if you sor Ally!" Grif continued. "If you knew her! You wouldn't wonder at me then for sayin' I'd like to die for her! Why, do you know what I've heerd her do? I've heerd her refuse to go where she'd have everything she could set her heart upon. I've heerd her refuse it because it wouldn't be right, although lots of women would think it was, and because she means to keep good if she dies for it! She'd make you good, Milly!"

Milly looked at him and laughed hysterically.

"Make me good!" she exclaimed, half-defiantly. "She couldn't, she couldn't! It's too late for that?" Then, as Grif rose to go, she said, "You won't say anything about the forged note?"

"No, Milly. Take care of poor Little Peter. If ever I can do you a good turn, I'll do it--you mind if I don't!"

He went to the bed where little Peter was sleeping. The lad was lying on his side, hot and flushed, with his lips partly open, as if thought were struggling to find expression there. Grif placed his hand tenderly upon Peter's cheek, and then went out of the house.

When he arrived at Alice's lodging he crept up the stairs, and with a settled purpose, which gave intensity to his face, opened the door. Husband and wife were standing, looking into each other's eyes. Tender words had evidently been exchanged, for they stood hand in hand, he with the dawn of a good and strong purpose upon his face, she encouraging him with hopeful, loving speech. A blanket, rolled up, gold-digger fashion, was upon the ground. Grif walked swiftly towards them and asked abruptly--

"Are you goin' away to-night?"

There was so much earnestness in his manner, that, with startled looks, they asked for his meaning.

"I can't tell you," he said, in a rapid, sharp tone; "I'm under a promise not to tell. But you must go away to-night."

"We were thinking just now, Grif," said Alice, "whether it would not be better for him to go in the morning."

"Make up your mind at once," said Grif, looking round as if he were fearful of being overheard, "that it won't do to wait here any longer. I've overheerd somethin', Ally, and I'm bound down not to tell. If you stop till to-morrow, somethin' dreadful 'll happen."

"Richard, you must go," said Alice, with gathering alarm, for Grif's impressiveness was filling her with fearful forebodings. "You must go, and at once."

"But why?" asked Richard, fretfully, and regarding Grif as if he were anything but a friend. "Why must I go? Why can't he tell what he knows? What difference will a few hours make?"

"All the difference," said Grif; "in a few hours perhaps you won't be able to go at all, unless--"

"Unless--" repeated Alice, eagerly.

"Unless it's in company with Jim Pizey and the Tenderhearted Oysterman. They've set a trap for you that you won't be able to get out of, if you refuse to join 'em. Don't ask me again to tell you what I've overheerd, for I can't I mustn't I darn't! I've run all the way here to tell you that there's more and more danger every minute you stop. It'll be all the better for you to go away in the dark."

Weak natures like Richard Handfield's are easily impressed, and more easily impressed with fear, which springs from selfishness, than with any other feeling. Almost without knowing what he was doing, Richard proceeded to sling the blanket round his shoulders. Alice's eager fingers assisted him.

"Grif is right, dearest," she said; "I'm sure he is. His looks are against him, but he is a faithful friend." Grif nodded his head, and his eyes brightened. "After all, it is but a few hours more. They would soon be past. Bless you, darling I bless you, Richard!" She kissed him again and again, and clung to him, and broke away from him, choosing rather to endure the pain springing from repressed tenderness, than do aught, in word or deed, to weaken him in his purpose.

"Yes, I will go," he said, in a decided tone, and having made up his mind, he took Alice in his arms and held her to him. While thus they clung together, she whispered,--

"Be strong and firm, Richard dear!"

"I will, dearest and best," he said, as with a passionate love-clinging he held the good and faithful woman to his breast.

"If the thought that I am true to you, darling--that I am yours in life, and afterwards--that I would share a crust with you and be happy if you were so--if that thought will strengthen and comfort you, Richard, take it with you, keep it in your mind, for, oh! it is true, my darling, it is true!"

"I know it, Alice, I know it."

"I shall bless you and pray for you every day. Until we are together again, my eyes can never close without thinking of you. See, Richard, I am not crying." She put his hand to her eyes, which were hot but tearless. "I can send you away with gladness, for it is the beginning of a better time. Though I feel that it is hard to part with you, I can say cheerfully, Go, my dear, for I know that your going is for the good of both of us. Write to me often, and tell me how and where to write to you. Good bye, good bye-- Heaven bless and preserve you!"

And she broke from him, and then, meeting his eyes, a look of electric love brought them together again, and once more their arms were twined about each other's neck. Then she glided from his embrace, and sank upon the stool. Richard walked slowly out of the room, his heart filled with love and tenderness, his eyes seeking the ground. It was bitter to part. Even in the agony of separation he found time to murmur at the hardness of his lot which tore him away from the woman who was to him as a saint. As he walked down the stairs, his foot kicked against something. He stooped and picked it up. A stone heart! Indeed, Little Peter's stone heart which Grif had dropped without knowing it. Richard's nature was superstitious. The shape of the stone was comforting to him. A heart! It was a good omen. He put it carefully in his pocket, and was about to close the street door when an uncontrollable impulse urged him to look again upon Alice's face. He ran up the stairs into the room. Alice was still sitting upon the stool, her head and arms were resting upon the table; and she was convulsed with outward evidences of a grief she had no longer any motive to conceal.

He spake no word, but kneeling before her, bowed his head in her lap, as a child might have done. She looked at him through her tears, and placed her hands upon his head: in that action were blended the tenderness of a mother to her child and a wife to her husband. He raised his lips to hers; they kissed once more, solemnly, and he went out of the house with her tears upon his face. As he walked along the streets towards the country where was hidden the gold which had tempted thousands to break up happy homes and sever fond ties of affection, the picture of Alice mourning for him, and Grif quiet and sad in the background, was very vivid to his mind. No forewarning of the manner of their next meeting was upon him; if it had been, he would have taken Grif's hand, and kissed it humbly, penitently, instead of parting from him without a farewell nod.

Left alone with Alice, Grif, with a delicacy of feeling in keeping with his general character, was about to retire, when Alice, in a voice broken by emotion, said,--

"Do not go for a minute or two, Grif. I want to speak to you."

Grif gave a nod of acquiescence, and sat upon the floor, patiently.

Presently Alice dried her eyes and beckoned him to come closer to her.

"Grif," she said, in a sweet voice. "Why are you not honest?"

Now, Grif knew perfectly well the meaning of honesty--that is to say, he knew the meaning of the word literally. To be honest, one must not take what belongs to other people. Well, he was not honest; he had often taken what did not belong to him. But he was not a systematic thief; what he had stolen he had stolen from necessity. And he had never stolen anything but food, and then only when hunger sharply pressed him. The thought flew swiftly to his mind that if he had not taken food when he wanted it, he must have starved. Was that right? No, he was sure it was not. Little as he knew about it, he was sure he was not sent into the world to starve. But he must have starved if he had not taken what belonged to other people! Clearly, then, it was not wrong to steal. Grif's mind was essentially logical, as may be seen from the process of thought which occupied it directly after Alice asked him the question. And yet if he were right, Alice was wrong. Could she be wrong? Could the woman who was to him the perfection of women, the embodiment of all that was pure and noble--could she be wrong? Here came the doubt whether it would not have been the proper thing to have starved, and not stolen. "There'd have been an end of it, at all events," he muttered to himself, when his musings reached this point. After which he grew perplexed, and the logical sequence of his thoughts became entangled. He did not blame Alice for asking the question; but, for all that, he bit his lip and looked imploringly at her.

"You have been so good a friend to me and Richard," she said, "that it pains me to see you as you are. I would like to see you better, for your sake and for mine, Grif."

"I never know'd how to be honest, Ally," he said. Then he thought of Milly's words to him that night. "If I knew how to be good," she had said, "I think I would be. But I don't know how." That was just the case with him. He did not know how to be honest. And yet he had told Milly that Alice could make her good. Perhaps Alice could make him honest. Not that he cared particularly about being honest, but he would like to please Alice. "I don't want not to be honest," he said; "all I wants is my grub and a blanket."

"And those, Grif," she said, gently, yet firmly, "you can earn if you like."

"Can I? I'd like to know how, Ally?"

"You must work for them."

"Yes, that's all right. I'm willin' enough to work. I'd go out this minute to work, if I had it to do. But I couldn't get no work--a pore beggar like me! I don't know nothin', that's one thing. And then, if I get a 'orse to mind, the peelers take it from me and tell me to cut off. I tried to git papers to sell, and I did one day; but some of the other boys told the paper man I was a thief, and when I went for more papers the next mornin' he wouldn't give 'em to me. I've got a precious bad character, Ally, there's no mistake about that; and I've been to quod a good many times. I can't look a peeler in the face, upon my soul I can't!"

Grif did not make this last remark in a humorous manner; he made it reflectively. It really was a fact, and he stated it seriously.

But Alice was not convinced.

"You're willing to work," she said.

"Yes, I'm willin' enough."

"Every one can get work if he likes, and if he tries."

Grif looked dubious. His knowledge of the world was superior to hers. He had battled with it and fought with it since he was a baby. "She don't know what a bad lot we are," he thought. But he was sincerely desirous to please her.

"What do you want me to do, Ally?"

"I want you to give me a promise to be honest, Grif," she said, earnestly.

"I'll do it," he replied, without a moment's hesitation. And then he added seriously, for he felt he was undertaking a great responsibility, "I'll be honest, Ally, whatever comes of it."

"And if ever you want anything to eat and can't earn it, Grif, you will come to me."

"Yes, I'll come to you, Ally," he said, almost crying, for he knew how poor she was.

"Suppose now, to-morrow morning you go into all the shops and ask if they want an errand boy. That does not require any learning, Grif."

"No, I could do that all right; I can run fast, too. But you'll see, Ally; it'll be no go."

"You'll try, Grif, will you not?"

"I'll try, Ally."

"This is the last night I shall be here. I am going to other lodgings to-morrow, and shall remain there until my husband writes for me. Perhaps he will write for me to join him on the diggings; if he does, and you fail in getting work, you shall come with me, Grif."

He stood before her, mute and grateful. She wrote an address on a piece of paper. "This is where I am going to live," she said, giving it to him. He took it, and seeing that she was weary, bade her good night.

"Good night, Grif, my good boy. I am very grateful for the service you have done us this night."

"You've got no call to be grateful to me, Ally," said Grif. "Only let me be your friend, as you said I was, and I don't want no more."

Outside the door, Grif considered where he should sleep. He did not care to go to the barrel, for it would be so lonely there without Little Peter. It had been Grif's chronic condition, before he took possession of the barrel, never to know in the morning where he was going to sleep at night. It all depended upon where he found himself when he made up his mind to retire to rest. Knowing there was a cellar to the house, he groped his way down to it.

"I wish I had a match," he muttered, when he was at the bottom of the stairs. "There was a empty packin'-case somewhere about; I remember seein' it. Oh, here it is; it's hardly long enough, but I can double myself up;" thus soliloquising, he crept into it. "Now then," he said, as he lifted the cover of the packing-case on the top, popping his head down quickly to avoid a bump; "that's warm and comfortable, that is. It'd be warmer, though, if I had Rough here, or Little Peter. Wouldn't it be jolly! I'm honest now," he thought, recurring to his promise, as he closed his eyes. "I'm honest now, that's what I am. I ain't a-goin' to crib no more pies or trotters. It's a rum go, and no mistake!"

And Grif fell asleep, and dreamt that all the pies and trotters he had pilfered were transformed into little hobgoblins, and were holding a jubilee because he had turned honest!

CHAPTER VIII
GRIF IS SET UP IN LIFE AS A MORAL SHOEBLACK

Grif, although but a poor and humble member of the human family, was as gregariously inclined as the rest of his species, and loved, when opportunity offered, to associate with his fellows. The circumstance of birth had placed him upon the lowest rang of the social ladder, and, being grovelling by nature, he had no thought of striving upwards, and was always prowling about, like a hungry dog searching for a bone. Being gregariously inclined, he was to be depended upon as an item in a mob. The object of a gathering of people was not a thing to be considered--politics, religion, amusement, were all one to him. If he but chanced to come across a throng, he added one more to the number, from sheer force of habit. Thus he was a passive auditor of street preachers of every denomination, and being in the habit of standing quite still, with his mouth open and his hands in his pockets, or where his pockets ought to be, he grew to be looked upon as a godsend by the orators, who spoke at him, and scoffed at him, and humbled him, and hurled anathemas at his head, as representing a class entirely devoid of godliness. They twisted his moral nature, and picked at it, and pulled it to pieces, and grew eloquent upon it. They said--Look at his rags, look at his dirt, look at the ignorance written on his countenance. They told him to repent if he wished to be saved from damnation; and they prayed for him and wept for him so earnestly that sometimes he experienced a dull wonder that the earth did not open and swallow him, he felt so utterly and thoroughly bad. To the political orators who were in the habit of "stumping-it" in the Market-square he was not of so much importance. "The People" in the aggregate was what the stump politicians gnashed their teeth at and wept over; and it was remarkable to observe with what complacency the People listened to these bemoanings. At the period during which Grif played his insignificant part in the history of the gold-colony, working-men-politicians were in great force, and night after night the Market-square would be thronged with an auditory not unwilling to be amused by listening to the outpourings of half-crazy or wholly-knavish demagogues, who had either gone mad over "the people's wrongs," or were working to get into the parliament, where they could make "pickings" for themselves. Many a red-hot radical who could not get an audience in Great Britain, and who had emigrated to what he thought was to be the "people's paradise" here was listened to, and laughed at, and applauded, and--did no harm after all. Grif did not understand what it all meant. He heard a great deal about the ground-down people, the crushed people, the poor starving people, upon whose substance the oligarchs were fattening; but all he could make out was that things were wrong altogether, a conclusion which precisely tallied with his own experience. But he, for one, bore his lot uncomplainingly, and with an unconscious exercise of philosophy, walked in the gutters (not feeling himself good enough to indulge in the pavement) without a murmur. Grif did not object to gutters; he had formed their acquaintance in his earliest infancy, and time and association had almost endeared them to him. Everything in the world is comparative. Pleasure, pain, success, disappointment, act in different ways upon different people: the effect depends upon constitution and education. So, dirt and cleanliness are differently regarded by different classes of society. To a well-regulated mind the spectacle of Grif walking in a narrow street, and picking his steps carefully along the gutter, would have caused a sensation of wondering disgust; and a pair of well-polished Wellington boots might naturally have objected to come into contact with the dirty broken bluchers in which Grif's feet slip-slopped constantly. But, in the eyes of Grif, dirty boots were no disgrace; he felt not the shame of them. From the moment he came into possession of a second-hand pair (he had never known the respectable bliss of a new tight-fitting boot, pressing on corn or bunion), they were dragged down to his own level, and forfeited their position in society. They may have been occasionally scraped, but they were never polished; and so they lost their respectability, and became depraved and degraded, and their seams and soles were eaten into with mud and dirt, until they gave up the ghost in the boot world, and trod the earth no more.

It might be gathered from Grif's mutterings, as he walked along the streets the day after he had given Alice the promise to be honest, that his mind was disturbed. "She's right, o' course she is," he said, "I know that well enough; but what was I to do? I know it'll be no go my tryin'. He must be a precious green cove who'd have anythin' to do with me!" and he looked down upon his boots, not with disgust, but with distrust, and stepped out of the gutter on to the pavement. "I never wanted to steal; I only wanted my grub and a blanket. If any swell'd have given 'em to me, it'd have been all right. But they ain't a bit of use to any one, ain't the swells. I've got to try to got a billet as a errand boy. All right. It ain't a bit of good, I know. Every one on 'em knows what sort of a cove I am. But I'll try, at all events. I promised her I would, and I ain't agoin' to deceive her!"

And thus it fell out that Grif had issued from his last night's bed, the packing-case, with the intention, for the first time in his life, of endeavouring to obtain an honest livelihood.

But Grif did not seem destined to be successful. He walked into scores of shops and places of business with the timid yet half defiant inquiry, "Do you want a errand boy?" and was sometimes roughly, often ignominiously, turned out. Scarcely from one of the storekeepers did he obtain a kind word, and it was not in his favour that many of them knew him, and had been in the habit of seeing him prowl about the Melbourne streets. He was not a savoury-looking boy, and did not bear upon his outward appearance any recommendation to the situation he was soliciting. His boots were muddy, his clothes were ragged, his skin was dirty, his hair was matted. He did not add another word to the query, "Do you want a errand boy?" and he did not at all take it in bad part that he was treated with contumely. Indeed, if such a state of mind can be conceived, he was in a sort of measure exultant at each rebuff. "I told her so," he muttered to himself, triumphantly; "who'd have anything to do with a beggar like me? But I promised her I'd try, and I ain't agoin' to deceive her." Two or three times he was surlily spoken to by the policemen, and on each occasion he slunk off without a murmur, not without a dim consciousness that he was absolutely compromising his character by attempting to obtain an honest livelihood. Readers who are not acquainted with colonial life, must not suppose that the police, or that other "institutions," differ in any essential in the colonies from those of the older countries. The colonies are certainly new, but they do not commence their career at the year One, but at the year Eighteen Hundred and Odd. There is just about the same comparative amount of vice and virtue, goodness and wickedness, ruffianism and kind-heartedness, as is to be met with in any other part of the world. Those who say otherwise, and cause others to think otherwise, are in the wrong. There are in the colonies, just as much average unkindness and uncharitableness, just as much charity and benevolence, just as much ignorance, just as noble-mindedness, as can be found amongst of human creatures anywhere. It is true that men get into false positions oftener than in older countries, but that is scarcely to be wondered at in new colonies where people of all classes are thrown indiscriminately together, and have not had time to settle into their proper positions. Those readers will therefore please not to wonder that Grif should be looked upon in precisely the some light as he would be looked upon if he were prowling about London streets. To the Melbourne constable, he was just what a ragged pilfering boy would be to London constable. It did not much affect him. He was accustomed to be buffeted, and cuffed, and maltreated. The world had given him nothing but hard knocks since his birth, and he took them without murmuring. He looked upon it quite as a matter of course when the conservators of public peace spoke harshly to him. But he had a promise to perform; and he resolved to perform it conscientiously. So it happened that he stood at the door of the great place of business of Mr. Zachariah Blemish, with the intention of asking for the situation of an errand boy. The green baize folding doors somewhat daunted him; but hesitating for one moment only, he pushed them open and entered. It chanced that, exactly upon his entrance, Zachariah Blemish came out of his own particular private room for the purpose of putting a question to one of his clerks, and that the great Blemish and the small Grif stood face to face. It was a marvellous contrast! The great Blemish, sleek and shining; the small Grif, rough and muddy: the great Blemish clean and polished, smooth-shaved and glossy; the small Grif, dirty and ragged, with the incipient stubble of manhood upon his chin and cheeks. For nature is impartial in her supply of beard and whiskers. Money will not buy them, nor will grease produce them, though it be puffed and perfumed.

The rich, great Blemish, then, looked down upon the poor little Grif. For a moment, the great man's breath was taken away at the sight. In his counting-house, sanctified by the visits of Members of Parliament, of Ministers, and of merchants of the highest standing--in sight of his books, wherein were daily entered records of transactions amounting to thousands of pounds--the appearance of a ragged boy, and such a ragged boy, was, to speak of it in the mildest terms, an anomaly.

"What do you want here?" asked Blemish.

"Do you want a errand boy?" asked Grif, in return.

"A what?" inquired Blemish, sharply.

"A errand boy," replied Grif, calmly.

At this juncture, a policeman, who had watched Grif enter the office, and who was sycophantishly disposed to protect the interests of wealth and position, popped his head in at the door, and touching his hat, begged Mr. Blemish's pardon, but the boy was a thief, and he thought he was up to no good.

"Umph!" said Mr. Blemish. "He looks like it. But thank you, policeman," this with a stately affability, "I do not think you will be wanted."

Whereupon the policeman touched his hat again, and vanished, determining, however, to keep an eye upon Grif, and find out what he was up to.

"Come this way," said Mr. Blemish to Grif, who, considerably astonished that he had not been given into custody, followed the great man into his private room. There he found himself in the presence of two other gentlemen, Mr. Matthew Nuttall, and Mr. David Dibbs. Mr. Nuttall was sitting at a table, writing, and his face was hidden from Grif. "Now, then," said Mr. Blemish, when Grif had disposed himself before the great merchant like a criminal; "what do you mean by coming into my place of business?"

"I wants a sitiwation as a errand boy," immediately replied Grif.

"The policeman says you are a thief," interrogated Mr. Blemish; "what do you say to that?"

"Nothin'," replied Grif, shortly.

"You *are* a thief, then?"

"No, I ain't," said Grif: "I'm honest, now," and he blushed with shame as he made the confession.

"Oh, you are honest now," Mr. Blemish observed, with a slight dash of sarcasm. "Since when has that occurred?"

"Since this mornin'; this is my first day at it."

Grif's candid statement appeared to perplex the great merchant. He paused a little before he said,--

"You *were* a thief, then?"

"When I couldn't get nothin' to eat for nothin', I took it," returned Grif, uncompromisingly; "I wasn't a-goin' to starve."

"Starve!" exclaimed Mr. Blemish, lifting up his hands in pious wonderment. "Starve! In this land of plenty!"

"It ain't a land of plenty to me; I wish it was."

"Really," observed Mr. Blemish, to surrounding space, "the unblushing manner in which such ragamuffins as this give the lie to political economists is positively frightful. Do you believe in statistics, boy?"

"Not as I knows on," said Grif.

"Did you expect a situation here?" inquired Mr. Blemish, looking down upon the lad, as if wondering what business he had in the world.

"No."

"Why did you come, then?"

"I promised her to try, though I told her it wasn't a bit o' good."

"Who is 'her'?" inquired Mr. Matthew Nuttall, turning suddenly round, and facing Grif.

Grif gave a great start, and threw a sudden sharp look at the questioner's face. He knew him at once. The likeness was unmistakeable. Even in his deep voice there was a ring of Alice's sweeter tones. If anything could have shaken Grif, it was the sight of that stern face, and the knowledge that the man before him could make Alice happy if he chose. Eager words rushed to Grif's lips, but he dared not give them utterance. What good could a ragamuffin like him do? He had best hold his tongue, or he would make matters worse.

"Who is 'her'?" repeated the gentleman.

"She's a lady, that's what she is," replied Grif, recovering his composure.

"A lady!" and Mr. Nuttall laughed.

"Ah, if you knew!" thought Grif, but he contented himself with saying, "Yes, she is, and so you'd say if you sor her."

"Upon my word," remarked Mr. Blemish, blandly, "I did not know that vagabonds like you associated with ladies. This boy is evidently an original."

"Don't you call no names," said Grif. "If you don't want a errand boy, say so, and send me away."

"Better and better," observed Mr. Blemish, composedly. "Now, this is something in my way, although I am not aware that I have met with such a character before to-day. Why did you start when this gentleman spoke to you?"

"I thort I knew his voice," returned Grif.

"And do you know it? Have you had the pleasure of this gentleman's acquaintance?" this said so pleasantly that both the gentlemen smiled.

"Never seed the gentleman afore, as I knows on," said Grif, to whom a lie was of the very smallest consequence.

"What do you do for a living?" asked Mr. Blemish.

"Nothin' partikeler."

"And you find it very hard work, I have no doubt," observed Mr. Blemish.

"Yes, I do; very hard," replied Grif, literally; and then, with sudden exasperation, he exclaimed, "What's the use of badgerin' me? You ain't agoin' to do nothin' for me. Why don't you let me go?"

"Come," said Mr. David Dibbs, who up to this time had taken no part in the dialogue, "I tell you what it is, young feller! You keep a civil tongue in your head, or I'll commit you on the spot. I'm a magistrate, that's what I am, and I'll give you a month, as sure as eggs is eggs, if you don't mind what you're up to!"

"I don't care," responded Grif. "I ain't a-goin' to be badgered."

"You don't care!" exclaimed Mr. David Dibbs, turning as red as a turkey-cock. "Send for the policeman, Blemish. I'll have him put in jail, and flogged. Is a magistrate to be sauced at in this here way?"

The small puffed-up soul of Mr. David Dibbs swelled with indignation. Things were come to a pretty pass, indeed, when the possessor of thirty thousand pounds a year, and a magistrate into the bargain, was thus openly defied by a ragged boy, probably without sixpence in his pockets! They glared at each other, did Grif and Mr. David Dibbs, and Mr. Dibbs did not have much the best of the situation.

"Nay, nay, Mr. Dibbs," said Mr. Blemish, soothingly; "you have every right to be angry, but let me deal with the boy, I beg.--Now, suppose," he said, addressing Grif, impressively, "suppose I were to take it into my head (I haven't any such idea, mind you) to give you a situation as errand boy, what remuneration would you require in return?"

"What what?"

"What remuneration--what salary--how much a week would you expect?"

"I don't expect nothin' a week," answered Grif; "I only wants my grub and a blanket. But if you ain't got no such idea, what's the good of keeping me here?"

"Of course you know nothing of religion?"

"I've been preached to," responded Grif, "till I'm sick of it."

"This boy interests me," remarked Mr. Blemish, speaking to society in general; "I should like to make an experiment with him. Who knows but that we might save his soul?"

"You can't do that," said Grif, moodily.

"Can't save your soul!"

"No; the preacher chap sed it'd go to morchel perdition; and I s'pose he knows."

Mr. Blemish raised his eyes to the ceiling, and an expression of sublime pity stole over his countenance. Grif edged closer to the door, as if anxious to be dismissed.

Mr. Blemish folded his hands with a sort of pious horror, and exclaimed- -"I am amazed!"

"What are you amazed at?" inquired Mr. David Dibbs. "I've seen hundreds of boys like this here one--he ain't no different to the rest. They're a bad, vicious lot."

Grif assented to the last remark by a nod.

"But our duty is clear," said Mr. Blemish, as if in answer to a voice within him, perhaps the voice of morality. "Listen to me"--this to Grif, with a forefinger warningly held up; "I am about to give you a chance of reforming."

"All right; I'm agreeable," said Grif, in a tone that betokened utter indifference of the matter.

"In my capacity as President of the Moral Boot Blacking Boys' Reformatory, I will provide you with a boot-stand, a set of brushes, and a pot of the best blacking. You can polish boots?"

"I've only got to rub at 'em, I s'pose," said Grif, wishing his own feet, with their dirty bluchers, would fly off his legs.

Mr. Blemish waived the question as one of detail, which it was evidently beneath him to enter upon.

"You can take up your stand at once. What do you say? Are you willing to be honest?"

"Didn't I tell you that this is my first day at it," replied Grif. "I'm willin' enough; I only wants my grub and a blanket. It don't matter to me how I gets 'em, so long as I do get 'em."

"Very well," and Mr. Blemish touched the bell, which on the instant brought a clerk, to whom he gave instructions. "Go with this young man, and he will provide you with everything that is necessary, and come to-night to the meeting of the Moral Boot Blacking Boys' Reformatory. Do you know why it is called the Moral Boot Blacking Boys' Reformatory?"

"No."

"Because all the boys are moral. If they are not moral when they are admitted, they are made moral. So mind that you're moral. The more moral you are, the better you will get on."

"I'll be very moral, I will," promised Grif, without the slightest idea of the meaning of his promise.

"Now you can go; I shall keep my eye on you, and watch how you conduct yourself;" and Mr. Blemish straightened himself, and swelled and puffed, as who should say, "I have done a noble and a moral action, and now I can transact my business with an easy conscience."

Grif, finding himself set up in life as a moral shoeblack, felt uncomfortably strange as he stood behind his stand in one of the Melbourne streets. He had been provided with a boot-stand, a set of brushes, and a pot of the best blacking; and as he surveyed his stock in trade, he was not quite certain whether he ought to be gratified or disgusted. He was so awkward altogether; and he did not know what to do with his hands. He placed them behind him--that was not business-like; he let them hang before him, and he became so painfully conscious of them, that he absolutely began to hate them. Never until now had he experienced what a dreadful responsibility it was to have two hands and not know what to do with them.

For an hour no customer came. Thinking that the state of his own boots was not a recommendation to business, he set to work brushing and polishing them up. It is amazing what a difference a well-polished pair of boots makes in one's appearance. As he surveyed his shining leathers, Grif felt that an important change had taken place in his prospects. He was already a respectable member of society. But still no customer came. He was a shrewd lad, and, thinking to tempt the passers-by, he took off his boots, and placing them upon his stand, courted custom with bare feet. In vain. Most of those who passed took no heed of him; a few looked at him and smiled--some in pity, some in derision. It was like standing in the pillory. He turned hot and cold, and flushed and paled, by turns. In truth, it was no enviable task for Grif, who had been a Bedouin of the byeways all his life, to stand stock-still, as if proclaiming that he was ashamed of his past life, and begged to be admitted into the ranks of honest respectability. Besides, he was hungry, and gnawing sensations within made him restless and unhappy. But Grif behaved bravely. He did not flinch from his post. For hours he stood, patiently waiting. And then an incident occurred. Two men, Jim Pizey and the Tenderhearted Oysterman, stopped before him. The sight of the Oysterman so inflamed Grif, that he felt inclined to do one of two things--to catch up his boots and fly away, or to spring upon the Oysterman and choke him for murdering Rough. But he did neither.

"Here's the young imp," I said Jim Pizey; "he's turned respectable," Grif's first impulse was to indignantly deny the imputation, but no time for utterance was given him. "Have you seen Dick Handfield to-day?" asked Pizey.

"No," answered Grif, shortly.

"Where have they gone to, him and his wife?" asked Jim. "Tell me any lies, and I'll break your neck for you. Here, clean my boots." Jim bade him do this, for he was fearful of attracting attention.

Grif would have liked to refuse; but he felt that to do so would be a clear infraction of his promise to Alice.

"How should I know where they are?" exclaimed Grif, brushing at Jim's boots.

"You were there last night, and they were there last night. You and the girl have been together lot a of times, and you know well enough where they're gone to. You're a pet of hers, I'm told."

"She's been very good to me, Ally has," said Grif, gently. "And because o' that, you don't think I'd let on where they are, do you? You don't think I'd let on, if I know, do you? No, I'd have my tongue cut out first."

"I'll tear it out and pitch it down your throat, if you talk to us like that," said the Oysterman, fiercely.

"Will you?" said Grif, standing up. "Or you'll pizen me, the same as you pizened my dawg! You'd like to, wouldn't you? And because o' that, if I didn't have no other reason, I wouldn't tell you where Dick Handfield is, if I knew where you could put your hands on him this minute. There!"

"You won't tell us?" asked Jim.

"No," answered Grif, bravely.

Jim looked darkly at him, and giving the stand a kick, sent the blacking-bottle, the brushes, and Grif's boots, rolling in the gutter; and, while Grif was busy picking them up, he took his companion's arm, and walked away.

This was not an encouraging beginning to Grif's honest career, and dark doubts entered his mind as to whether he really had made a change for the better.

"What's the use of bein' moral," he grumbled, as he rearranged his stand, "if this is the way I'm to be served? They've soon found out that Dick Handfield's gone; and ain't they mad at it, neither! It's a good job he went away to-day. Old Flick will be mad, too, at buyin' the bad note. It's a reg'lar game, that's what it is. I'm precious hungry. I wish I was near the confectioner's. I'd go and arks for a pie. But I'll see it out. I promised Ally I would, and I will. Hallo! what do *you* want?"

This was addressed to a boy, if possible dirtier and more ragged than Grif himself. Indeed, dirt and this boy had become so inseparable that he was known by the simple but expressive name of Dirty Bob. Now, Dirty Bob had seen Grif take up his stand, and had disdainfully watched him wait for customers. In Dirty Bob's eyes Grif was a renegade, a sneak, for setting up as a shoeblack. And he determined to show his disdain in his own particular way. He possessed only one sixpence in the world, and he resolved to spend it luxuriously.

"Oh, it's you, Dirty Bob, is it?" said Grif.

"Yes, it's me," responded Dirty Bob, loftily.

"What do you want?" asked Grif.

"What do I want?" echoed Dirty Bob. "Why, you're a bootblack, ain't you?"

"Yes," replied Grif, with dignity. "I'm a moral shoeblack now."

"Ho! crikey!" exclaimed Dirty Bob. "What do you call yourself?"

"I'm a moral shoeblack," repeated Grif, with an inclination to punch Dirty Bob's head.

"'Ere's a go!" cried Dirty Bob. "A moral shoeblack, are you? Well, then, clean my boots, and mind you clean 'em morally;" and he flopped upon the stand a foot encased in a boot in the very last stage of decay.

In Grif's eyes this was a humiliation, and he almost quite made up his mind to pitch into Dirty Bob; but the thought that by so doing he might injure his character as a moral shoeblack, restrained him.

"Now, then," exclaimed Dirty Bob, "what are you waiting for? Clean my boots, d'ye hear! What are you block in' up the street for if you won't clean a genelman's boots when you're told?"

"Where's your tanner?" asked Grif, gloomily.

"'Ere it is," replied Dirty Bob, producing it. "It's a good un. It's the only one I've got, but I'm goin' to spend it 'spectably and genteelly. Brush away."

After a little uncomfortable communing, Grif spat upon his brush, and commenced to rub, submitting silently to the scornful observations of Dirty Bob.

"I say, sir," observed Dirty Bob (and be it remarked that the "sir" was a nettle which stung Grif sharply); "I say, sir, do you want a 'prentice?"

"I don't want none of your cheek," said Grif, rubbing so smartly that he almost rubbed off the upper leather; "that's what I don't want. So you'd better hold your jaw."

"I beg your pardon, sir," said Dirty Bob, meekly; "I forgot that I was speakin' to one of the Hupper Class. And ho! sir!" he exclaimed, in a tone of anguish, "don't tell the perlice, or they'd put me in quod for cheekin' a moral shoeblack."

"There; your boots are done!" ejaculated the disgusted Grif. "Where's the tanner?"

"Don't you think, sir," said Dirty Bob, surveying his boots critically, "that one on 'em is a little more polished than t'other? Would you please make 'em even, and give this cove another rub?"

Grif commenced again rubbing viciously.

"Ho! don't rub so 'ard, sir," exclaimed Dirty Bob.

"I was brought up very tender, I was, and I've got a wopping corn on my big toe. Thankey, sir! 'Ere's the tanner; and when you're Lord Mayor, don't forget Dirty Bob!"

And he walked off, whistling. It was late in the day now, so Grif prepared to close business. His heart was not very light, for the first sixpence he had honestly earned in his life had been earned with a sense of bitter humiliation.

CHAPTER IX
A BANQUET IS GIVEN TO THE
MORAL MERCHANT

The world is full of shams. As civilization advances, shams increase and multiply; indeed, they multiply so fast that human nature in the nineteenth century might be likened to a pie, with very little room inside for the fruit, so thick is the crust of shams with which it is overlaid. And as a chief lieutenant of shams--as a sham which takes precedence of a host of other shams, from its very shamelessness, may be ranked the toast of Our Guest, or Our Host, proposed at public dinners and entertainments. The unblushing fibs told in the speeches are dreadful to contemplate. Surely, some day a fearful retribution will fall upon that man who is in the habit of rising when the dessert is on the table, and endowing Messrs. Smith, Brown, Jones, and Robinson with every virtue under the sun, and who unctuously dilates upon their sublimities, their virtues, and their goodnesses. Beware! thou weak and false platitudinarian! Think not to escape thy fate, because the word which describes thee is not to be found in the dictionary. Beware! and reform thy evil courses ere it be too late!

It is not to be supposed that any such thoughts as these entered the mind of Mr. Zachariah Blemish, as he sat on the right hand of the chairman at a grand public dinner given in his (Blemish's) honour. For public enthusiasm with regard to this great and good man had risen to a very high pitch--to such a pitch indeed, that it was resolved to give Mr. Zachariah Blemish a banquet; and, all the preliminaries being arranged, more than two hundred gentlemen, representing wealth and position, sat down, and ate and guzzled to do him honour. The guest himself ate sparingly, but Mr. David Dibbs made up for him. Mr. Dibbs had but few articles of faith, and to eat as much as he could was one of them. If it had not been that his gold threw a glare of sanctity around him, Mr. Dibbs would have been looked upon as a glutton. As it was, what would have been a vice in a poorer man, was in him nothing but an amiable eccentricity. The company was composed of very influential atoms: politics, religion, and L.S.D. were largely represented, the latter especially. The Honourable Mr. Peter Puff was in the Chair; another Honourable undertook the Vice; and a Bishop said grace before meat. It was curious to note the conduct of the guest in whose honour the entertainment was given. He appeared to be quite oblivious of the occasion, and but for a shade of self-consciousness which now and then passed across his face, he might have been regarded as a perfectly disinterested observer. The committee would have been justified in regarding this conduct as somewhat ungrateful, for they had been indefatigable in their exertions. Fish of river and sea, game of forest, fruit of hothouse, were cunningly served up in every possible variety in honour of Blemish. For long weeks, celebrated cooks had ransacked their brains to invent new dishes, and every one admitted, when the dessert was laid, and the wine was passing, that the result produced was glorious and worthy of the occasion.

Thump--thump--thump! Rattle--rattle--rattle! Gentlemen, Her Most Gracious Majesty the Queen! Proposed with patriotic enthusiasm. The Queen! Each gentleman, standing, drains his glass, and sits down again with becoming solemnity. Buzz of conversation. Thump--thump--thump! Rattle--rattle--rattle! Gentlemen, His Royal Highness the Prince of Wales, and the rest of the Royal Family; and may he and they, etc., etc., etc. Enthusiasm and general geniality. Thump--thump--thump! Rattle!--rattle--rattle! Gentlemen, His Excellency the Governor! With appropriate flunkeyism. As Her Most Gracious Majesty's Representative--most important and flourishing portion of Her Most Gracious Majesty's dominions upon which the sun never sets--and so on, and so on; with The Army and Navy, The Clergy, etc., until the important moment arrives when the toast of the evening is to be proposed.

"Gentlemen, are your glasses charged?"

"All charged in the East," responds an indiscreet Freemason, and then there is a shifting and shuffling, until the Honourable Mr. Peter Puff rises. He looks round upon the guests, blows his nose, lifts his glass, puts it down again, coughs, and proceeds to speak.

"Gentlemen, it is now my proud task to perform a duty, which is no less a duty than it is a pleasure. (Hear, hear.) I wish that it had fallen to the lot of some more eloquent speaker than myself--(No, no!)--to propose the toast or the evening; but being asked to preside on this memorable occasion, I felt that I should have been wanting in respect to myself, and in respect to the gentleman who sits upon my right hand, if I had not at once joyfully and gratefully accepted the honourable position. Gentlemen, some men are born great, some achieve greatness, and some have greatness thrust upon them. (Considerable doubt here intrudes itself the minds of fifty per cent, of the guests, whether this is an original observation or a quotation.) Gentlemen, I have, in this instance, had greatness thrust upon me; for no one can doubt that the devolvement upon me to propose the toast I am about to propose, reflects honour and greatness upon--upon the proposer. We have amongst us this evening, a gentleman--(here every one looks at Mr. Zachariah Blemish, who looks up to the ceiling, as if he considers it likely that the gentleman about to be referred to may be discovered somewhere in that locality)--a gentleman whose undeviating rectitude, whose integrity, whose moral character, whose wealth, whose position, are not only creditable and honourable to himself, but creditable and honourable to the city which he has made his dwelling-place. (Hear, hear.) We might say, with Hamlet, that in this gentleman (in a moral sense) may be seen a combination and a form indeed, where every god doth seem to set his seal to give the world assurance of a man. (Great rattling of glasses and thumping of knives; Mr. Zachariah Blemish looks curiously and unconsciously interested, as if still wondering who is the individual indicated; and the Honourable Mr. Peter Puff gives a sigh of relief, having delivered himself correctly of a quotation which he had taken great pains the day before to learn by heart.) Need I say, gentlemen, that I refer to our guest, Mr. Zachariah Blemish? (Prolonged applause; the thumping and rattling are terrific. Mr. Blemish appears much astonished to learn that he is the individual referred to, and perceiving that all eyes are turned towards him, wrinkles his brows, as much as to say, 'Really! can this be? I *am* surprised?' and afterwards assumes an air of exceeding humility.) Gentlemen, we all know him (Cries of 'We do!') and we are all proud to know him. (Cries of 'We are!') Say that we know him only as Chairman of the United Band of Temperance Aboriginals, and he is entitled to our approval; say that we know him only as President of the Moral Bootblacking Boys' Reformatory, and he is entitled to our respect; say that we know him only as the Perpetual Grand Master of the Society for the Total Suppression of Vice, and he is entitled to our esteem; say that we know him only as the head of the Association of Universal Philanthropists, and he is entitled to our admiration; say that we know him only as a leading member of the Fellowship of Murray Cods, and he is entitled to our veneration. But say that we know him as all of these combined, and as a merchant of integrity, and as a gentleman of honour, and words fail us in speaking of him. Gentlemen, words fail *me* when I speak of him. Far better for me to stay my speech, and leave what is unsaid to your discrimination and your intelligence. Suffice it for me to say that I am proud to know him, and that I am proud of this opportunity of expressing my sentiments. With these few remarks--inadequate as they are to the occasion--I conclude, and propose the health of our guest, Mr. Zachariah Blemish--in bumpers!"

Hurrah! In bumpers! Our guest, Mr. Zachariah Blemish. No heeltaps! Three cheers for Mr. Zachariah Blemish! with a hip, hip, hip, hurrah! hurrah! hurrah! Three cheers for Mrs. Zachariah Blemish! Three cheers for the little Blemishes (which fell flat, for the little Blemishes were not, and had never been). For he's a jolly good fellow--for he's a jolly good fellow--which nobody can deny--with a hip, hip, hip, hurrah! hurrah! hurrah! And a little one in--hurrah!

All which being enthusiastically performed, the guests, somewhat exhausted with their exertions, sat down with the consciousness of having nobly done their duty.

Mr. Zachariah Blemish, in voice which trembled with emotion, rose to thank the gentlemen who had so enthusiastically responded to the toast of his health.

"Mr. Chairman, Vice-Chairman, and Gentlemen," he said, "this is the happiest moment of my life, and I am naturally much affected. (Pocket-handkerchief.) When I look around and see the leading members of every profession and every important interest in the Colony, and when I consider that they are assembled here to render a tribute of respect to so unworthy an object as myself (cries of 'No, no!')--yes, I repeat, so unworthy an object as myself, I am lost in wonder as to what I have done to entitle me to such an honour. I am conscious, gentlemen, of having only performed my duty. It is no very hard task, and yet it is not always done. As a merchant, as a citizen, and as a public man, this has been my endeavour. In the performance of my duty I may have done some little good. (Cries of 'A great deal.') You are kind enough to say so. The good I have done reflects but small credit upon myself; for it has been, as I may say, evoked by my position as a not inconsiderable merchant in this city. Gentlemen, I *am* proud of my position as a merchant; and never in my hands shall commerce be degraded--never in my hands shall the spirit of fair and honest dealing which characterises the British nation be abused. (Thumps and rattles.) I am extremely affected by this demonstration. (Pocket-handkerchief.) You will excuse me if my emotion overcomes me, and you will pardon the little incoherences you may detect in my speech. (Pocket-handkerchief.) It is usual on such occasions as this to give a brief *r❖❖sum❖❖* of the movements and acts of the individual upon whom is conferred an honour like the present; and I, with your permission, will touch upon one or two little matters in which I have taken a slight interest. Our worthy chairman, my friend, the Honourable Mr. Peter Puff (a beaming smile from that individual)--has mentioned the names of a few societies and associations with which I am connected. You all know, gentlemen, the difficulties with which the formation of the United Band of Temperance Aboriginals was attended. When the white man first set his foot upon these shores he found the native savage wallowing in ignorance and immorality. They ran about naked; civilisation was a dead letter to them; they knew nothing of Christianity; and although attempts have been made to throw a doubt upon their practice of cannibalism, we are all perfectly well aware that the Australian aboriginals were in the habit of eating and enjoying one another. Then, again, they were given to intemperance, and would sacrifice anything for a pint of rum. What was the duty of a Christian when these things became known? To reform the savage. For this purpose the United Band of Temperance Aboriginals was formed, blankets were distributed, moralising influences were brought to bear, and I am proud to be able to state my opinion, founded upon, statistics, that in the course of fifty years from the present time, not a single intoxicated aboriginal will be found in the length and breadth of the colony. (Loud applause.) As for the Society for the Total Suppression of Vice, we do our best. Vice is not yet totally suppressed; but we look forward to the time when we shall view, perhaps in the spirit, the successful accomplishment of the work we have initiated in the flesh. The operations of the Moral Bootblacking Boys' Reformatory, of which I am President, are well known. The institution of boot-stands in the streets of Melbourne has been attended with inconceivable blessings. A large number of boys, who did not even know the meaning of morality, having been made moral through the influence of boot-stands. It is but a few days ago that I was made the humble instrument of redeeming a vagrant--a boy in years--who unblushingly admitted that he was a thief; he had never before worked at any honest employment, and when I incidentally introduced the subject of salvation, he actually told me that his soul would go to immortal perdition, and could not be saved. The saving of this lad's soul--who bears the extraordinary name of Grif--dates from the moment when he received from the Reformatory a set of blacking-brushes and a boot-stand; and he may now be seen, daily, in the streets, waiting for customers. (Cheers.) What shall I say, gentlemen, of the Murray Cods? You are acquainted with the gigantic difficulties with which we had to contend, and which we have successfully overcome. Here was a fish, vast in its proportions, delicious in its flavour--(Hear, hear, from Mr. David Dibbs),--which could only be caught in the River Murray. Why should it not be transplanted, if I may use the word, to other waters? That was a question, gentlemen, which naturally suggested itself to the Murray Coddians. A society was formed, subscriptions were raised, and the monopoly the River Murray enjoyed in its Cod was destroyed. This is a single but significant proof of the determination of the colonists. In our hearts, gentlemen, we are all Murray Coddians. The energy which the Murray Coddians threw into their task reflects credit upon the Colony-- (here the Honourable Mr. Peter Puff whispers to the speaker)--and I am informed by our honourable Chairman, that on this very dinner-table was placed a Murray Cod which was not caught in the River Murray, (Frantic applause.) I look upon the Cod placed upon the dinner-table this evening as a mark of respect paid to me for my efforts in its cause; and looking upon it in that light, I cannot restrain a natural feeling of emotion. (Pocket-handkerchief.) Gentlemen, here I pause. The remembrance of this happy evening will always be with me. You have imposed upon me a debt of gratitude, which is the only debt, gentlemen, which I doubt of ever being able to pay."

In the next morning's papers appeared glowing accounts of the dinner, and verbatim reports of Mr. Blemish's speech. But if the reporters, while they were transcribing their shorthand notes, could have seen the object of the night's adulation, they might have been puzzled to account for the singular change that had come over his appearance. For, say it was two o'clock in the morning when they sent away the printer's devil with the last slip, at that very hour Mr. Zachariah Blemish was locked in the private room of his mansion near the sea, his table strewn with papers and documents, and his head resting wearily on his hands. Surely that was not the face of Mr. Zachariah Blemish! Its freshness and roundness had departed from it; it looked positively thin and haggard. Did the great Blemish possess a skeleton, and was it even now staring at him in the face in his own sanctum? It looked uncommonly like it. Or, perhaps the triumph of the evening had been too much for him, and he was thinking of his own unworthiness. Under any circumstances, it was well for the credit (moral and commercial) of Mr. Zachariah Blemish that he kept such expressions as his face then wore for his own private use, and that he did not exhibit them in public.

It was about two o'clock in the morning, also, that Mr. Nicholas Nuttall was wending his way, somewhat; unsteadily, homeward. He had been at the Blemish banquet, and had lingered until the very last moment. Then he had been cajoled into joining half a dozen gay fellows in "just another glass," which just another glass having been submitted to a multiplication process, rendered him a decidedly unfit companion for a lady with such a strong sense of the proprieties as Mrs. Nicholas Nuttall. Some notion of this sort floated across his mind, and produced therein considerable disturbance, inasmuch as he stopped suddenly in the midst of the chorus--"We won't go home till morning," which was being trolled out by himself and a couple of young gentlemen, who had volunteered to see him home, and shook his head gravely and reproachfully.

"Ni--hic!--cholas Nuttall!" he observed, leaning his back against a lamp-post, "Ni--hic!--cholas Nuttall, you are an immoral cha--hic!--character."

The two young gentlemen, who had been induced to see Mr. Nuttall home solely because he had a pretty daughter, endeavoured to persuade him to walk on, and said, coaxingly, "Come along, old fellow. Come home."

"Home!" scornfully exclaimed Mr. Nicholas Nuttall, and regarding them with an expression of deep disdain. "Home!--hic!--do you know what home is--hic!--Home is a--hic!--place where you are badgered--hic!--and nagged--hic!--and worried. I wish you were married to Mrs. Nuttall!"

Here Mr. Nuttall began to cry, and called himself a villain, and a destroyer of domestic hearths. He allowed himself, however, to be prevailed upon to resume his homeward course, and in a very miserable condition he arrived at his street-door.

"Gentlemen!" he then said, "my wife--hic!--does not--not allow me a latch--hic!--key. Pull the bell. When you are married--hic!--have a latch key put down--hic!--in the settlements. This--hic!--is the advice of a miserable wretch."

The sound of steps along the passage drove Mr. Nuttall into a condition of abject despair. "Don't go--hic!"--he exclaimed, affectionately clinging to his companions. "Don't go--hic!--come in and have a glass--toddy."

The person who was unfastening the door had evidently heard strange voices, for it was suddenly thrown open, and a glimpse of a white nightgown flying hastily up the stairs, flitted across the vision of the three inebriates.

"Come in," said Mr. Nuttall, with a mingled feeling of exultation and dismay, for he knew that the figure in white was the figure of the wife of his bosom. "Hic!--come in, and we'll make a night of it."

But when they got in, they were doomed to disappointment. The cupboards were locked, and not a bottle or glass could be found. The young gentlemen were therefore compelled to beat a retreat. Left to himself, Mr. Nicholas Nuttall sank into a chair. He was in the enemy's camp, and he felt that there was no hope for him. With his head sunk upon his bosom, he waited doggedly for the blow.

Mrs. Nicholas Nuttall, in her nightgown, looked ridiculously diminutive; but her moral power was tremendous. Mr. Nuttall felt its effects the instant she made her appearance; and he shivered. When she seated herself opposite to him, he had not the courage to raise his head. He thought that she would speak first, but he was mistaken. He waited for a long time, and the silence grow so awfully oppressive that he was compelled to break it.

"Why did you lock up all the de--hic!--canters?" he asked.

"Because I knew the state you would come home in," returned his spouse; "and I have some regard for your health, little as you deserve it."

"You've no right, Mrs. Nuttall, to make me look--hic!--ridiculous in the eyes of my friends."

"Ridiculous!" said Mrs. Nuttall, with lofty sarcasm "As if you don't make yourself look ridiculous enough without my help! You may outrage my feelings as much as you like, sir, but you shall not turn the parlour into a tap-room, although it *may* be the custom in this country!"

"The two gentlemen who came home with me are very respect--hic!--table."

"Don't tell me, Mr. Nuttall!" said Mrs. Nuttall. "Gentlemen, indeed! A couple of tipsy brutes!"

"Why didn't you--hic!--go to bed? You must be very cold, sitting up with scarcely anything on."

"I *am* very cold. But what do you care for that?"

"Not a bit," murmured Nicholas, recklessly.

"And this man I married!" exclaimed Mrs. Nuttall, in a horror-struck voice, appealing to the chairs and tables. "This is the man I sacrificed myself for. This is the man I sit up for night after night, while he is dissipating and destroying the happiness of his family!"

"Don't be stupid--hic!--Maria!" said Mr. Nuttall, rising, and staggering to the door. "I am going to bed. Where's the door-handle? You haven't locked that up, have you?"

Mrs. Nuttall made no reply, but walked after him, statelily, with the chamber-candlestick in her hand.

"A nice example you are to your children!" she said, when she got between the sheets. "A nice example!"

"Children, Maria!" exclaimed Mr. Nuttall, before she could proceed any further. "Children! You--hic!--forget yourself, my dear. We've only got one."

"A pretty thing to reproach me with, upon my word!" exclaimed Mrs. Nuttall, indignantly. "A nice example you are, then, to our only child! I wonder you don't want to come to bed with your boots on! Oh, if I had known this before I was married--"

"It's too late now, Maria," observed Mr. Nuttall, maliciously, tugging at his boots.

"That's right," sobbed the lady, the frills of her nightcap fluttering in sympathy with her agitation. "Taunt me with my folly! But I deserve it. I brought it all on myself. Mamma warned me of the consequences, when

I told her that I had accepted you; but I wouldn't listen to her, and now I am justly punished. Oh! turn your head the other way. How you smell of tobacco! 'Take my word for it,' mamma said, 'if you marry that ninny, you will repent it all your life.'" Here Mrs. Nuttall jumped up suddenly in the bed, and said, "Mr. Nuttall, there is some one walking about in the parlour."

"I don't care," murmured Nicholas, digging his head into his pillow. "He won't find much to eat and drink; that's one comfort."

"Get up and see if there is any one there, or I shan't be able to sleep a wink all the night."

"Get up yourself, and see," suggested Nicholas, drowsily.

"Is it possible," indignantly continued Mrs. Nuttall, "that any man can be so unmanly? Nicholas! Do you hear me?"

"Don't bother! Let me go to sleep!"

"Perhaps it's the new servant I took this morning. I shouldn't wonder if Australian servants walked in their sleep."

"If I thought so," murmured Nicholas, "I would go and admonish her. She's a very pretty girl."

Wifely indignation kept Mrs. Nuttall silent for awhile, but she soon commenced the nagging system again, and so worried her husband that, in an agony of desperation, he sprang up like a Jack-in-a-box, and after driving his fist fiercely into his pillow half-a-dozen times, fell back exhausted.

"Very pretty!" exclaimed Mrs. Nuttall, sarcastically. "Very pretty, indeed! I wonder you don't beat me!"

"The man who raises his hand against a woman," said Mr. Nuttall, slumberously, "except in the way of kindness, is--is--I don't exactly remember what he is. There's a thing, Maria, I have thought of often, and have never spoken of to you. It isn't right--there should not be any secrets between man and wife."

"My very words, Nicholas, my dear! What is it you are going to say?"

"In the course of our confidential conversations--as we are having now, Maria"--(in her eagerness not to lose a word, Mrs. Nuttall placed her close to her husband's lips, for he spoke very drowsily, and appeared to be addressing his pillow)--"you have frequently mentioned your respected mamma. Did she know a lady of the name of Mrs. Caudle?"

"I am not aware that she knew any person with such a vulgar name."

"You never heard her speak of Mrs. Caudle?"

"Never!"

"Strange!" murmured Mr. Nuttall. "There is a deep mystery here. For you have the Mrs. Caudle spirit so very strongly developed, Maria, that I am certain a family connection exists between you."

Not knowing whether this were meant for a compliment or a reproach, Mrs. Nuttall deemed it wise to make no comment upon it. So she proceeded to ask him about the dinner at which he had been present.

"It was a very nice dinner," said Mr. Nuttall.

"And how many people were there, Nicholas?"

"A room full."

"How do I know what sized room it was--it might hold twenty, or it might hold a thousand--how many sat down to dinner?"

"A hundred--a hundred and fifty--two hundred--two hundred and fifty," said Mr. Nuttall, vaguely.

"Was your brother there, Nicholas?"

"No."

"Did Mr. Blemish make a speech?"

"What did he say?"

"All sorts of things."

"Nicholas, you are enough to vex a saint. Tell me instantly, what did Mr. Blemish say?"

Instead of replying, Mr. Nuttall groaned, and screwed himself up tight in the bed-clothes.

"That's right," said Mrs. Nuttall, tugging at the sheets. "I'd take up the whole bed, if I were you!" Mr. Nuttall partially unscrewed himself. "I'm much obliged, I'm sure! And now, Nicholas, answer me one question. Are we going to spend Christmas at your brother's Station?"

"Yes. I have told you so a dozen times."

"I wanted to make certain," she said, sweetly. "Good night, Nicholas."

"Oh, good night," he said, somewhat savagely, muttering between his clenched teeth, "I wish the man who invented Caudle lectures had been at the bottom of the Red Sea first!"

And sleep then descended upon the Conjugal Nuttalls.

CHAPTER X
ON THE ROAD TO EL DORADO

Far and wide, through the length and breadth of Victoria, over its borders into New South Wales, and over the seas to neighbouring Colonies, floated marvellous stories of the New Rush. Ears burned, eyes glistened, and fingers tingled at the news. Men, separated from the spot by hundreds of miles of land, by thousands of miles of ocean, made frantic arrangements to fly thither incontinently. The hearts of those in Great Britain who contemplated emigration beat faster at the news brought by the overland mail; and the tongues of the Celestials who meant to move from China to the Land of Gold chattered and wagged at a fearful rate when rumours of the big nugget reached them. Merchants grew exultant as they thought of shipments on the road, and reckoned up the profits beforehand. Servants threw up their situations; family men broke up their homes; and tradesmen wound up their businesses at any sacrifice. Cherished ambitions, life-dreams approaching to fruition, calm, peaceful ways of living, were all forgotten and forsaken in the fever of gold-greed, which spread itself through many lands.

Over the waters came regiments of adventurers, each man burning to give Nature a bruise or a blow. What brought them? Gold! It beckoned them with its golden finger, it flung a yellow shade before them, it filled their minds with desire in the day, it hopped about their brains in the night. It wooed them, and kissed them, and embraced them, and nestled in their hearts, and smiled in their eyes, and made their fingers tingle. Down to the ports of distant countries hurried cohorts of warriors, with beds upon their backs, and picks upon their shoulders. The Gold God that had awakened into life threw its irradiations thousands of miles around it, dyed the steeps of far-off mountains and illumined far-off plains. From those plains and mountains shoals of men hurried down to the ports. Ships were laid on, labourers shouted and bellowed, chains creaked and squeaked, anchors groaned and moaned, ropes strained every fibre, and bales and cases piled themselves above another, jealous not of elbow-room. Blow winds, and fill the sails! The sun is setting, and the shimmer of the Gold God is in the west, and lights the waters with a golden radiance; the sun is rising, and the shimmer of the Gold God is in the east, and is reflected on the rosy clouds;

the ship is rushing onward, and the sails puff out their grey cheeks towards the promised land; the men are sleeping in their bunks, and a little image of Queen Mab, cast in pure gold, is sitting on a throne in the centre of each brain. If thought were not immaterial and colourless, the fashion of that epoch would have been bright yellow.

The Colony itself was in a ferment, and night and day the roads to the locality of the New Rush were thronged with eager pedestrians. Scraps of news, picked up Heaven only knew how, about wonderful "finds" of gold, about great nuggets and bucketfuls of the precious metal, flew from mouth to mouth. The stories lost nothing in the transmission; for pennyweights were magnified to ounces, ounces to pounds, pounds to hundredweights. Troops of sturdy diggers, their heavy "swags" upon their backs, and their tin pots and pannikins buckled to their waists, marched on bravely and cheerfully, and felt not fatigue. Truly have such men been called the bone and sinew of the gold colonies. For thorough manliness, for sturdy courage, for indomitable perseverance, they are scarcely to be paralleled in the world's history. Strings of shambling Chinamen, with pigtails and sallow faces, dressed in half-modern costume, and bearing on their shoulders poles, upon which were slung their boots, picks, shovels, and "cradles,"[2] were also there, toiling patiently along to the El Dorado, and receiving with good humour the badinage of the Saxon and the Celt. They did not travel as swiftly as the Europeans; but, like the tortoise, they were slow and sure, and were not unlikely to win the race. Drays creaked and sighed in woeful tribulation beneath the weight of bags of flour and cases of spirits, sent off to the New Rush by watchful speculators. Many were the perils the goods encountered in gullies and creeks; and many were the accidents, most of them, however serious, having some ludicrous features. Here might be seen a waggon piled up with diggers' swags, chiefly Chinamen's, the owners being perched on the top, while the remainder trudged patiently along in the dust. There, a troupe of Nigger serenaders, with bones and banjos, their faces already blackened for the amusement of the wandering hordes. Here, a couple of drays, in which were packed cases of type and printing-press for the printing of a newspaper in the bush! There, a travelling theatre, consisting of a huge tent with all the paraphernalia of scenery and dresses: the leading tragedian (descended to dull earth) played the part of driver for the nonce, entertaining his cattle with morsels of morality from Hamlet or Macbeth; while the low-comedy man, his face woefully begrimed with dust, tramped sturdily along, bearing upon his shoulders the infant prodigy of the company. Day after day the roads were thronged with workers from all parts of the colony, and when night came, trees were cut down and fired, horses and oxen were turned loose, water was fetched from adjacent creeks, tea was prepared, and pipes were lighted, and tents and "mi-mis"[3] hastily thrown up, beneath which the nomades rested their weary limbs, hopefully and cheerfully. It was a pretty sight to see the fires glancing out along the miles of dusky bush, and it was pleasant to feel the sense of rest which had fallen upon the busy plains. The tinkling bells attached to the necks of hobbled horses led musically on the air, and from silver-toned flutinas, in the hands of rough-bearded men, sounded "Home, Sweet Home," and many other airs as touching, the strains of which lingered lovingly about the trees, whose dark forms were glanced with light from a clear and brilliant moon.

Footnote 2: Machines in which diggers wash the gold from the auriferous soil.

Footnote 3: A shelter for the night, made with the boughs and branches of the trees. Pronounced "mī-mīs."

Amongst those who were attracted to the promised land by the news of the wonderful discoveries was Richard Handfield. He had picked up as a mate an old digger, whose Herculean frame appeared fit to bear any amount of fatigue--a man known as Tom the Welshman, and commonly called Welsh Tom for brevity's sake. He was a simple, kind-hearted creature, always ready to do a good turn, and not always able to avoid being imposed upon. He was fond of nursing children, and drawing water, and chopping wood, to lighten the labours of the women who were fortunate enough to be living in his neighbourhood. He was a lucky digger, and he scattered his gold about freely. He had been in the Colonies since his youth, and for a great portion of his time he had been a bullock-driver. One might have thought that this would have been sufficient to make him cruel and hard-hearted; but the contrary was the case. He swore at his bullocks like other bullock-drivers, but he did not lash them. Even when he swore at them, the poor oxen seemed to know that he was not unkindly; and if such a feeling as gratitude be inherent in bullock nature, it must surely have been strong in the Welshman's oxen, for he regarded with pity a sore shoulder or a wound, and would apply such simple remedies as he was acquainted with to ease the pain. And yet, gentle as he was by nature, loved as he was by all his acquaintances, there was a stain upon him which would never, in this world, be wiped out. He had been convicted of some offence in the home country, and had been sentenced to life transportation. He did not often refer to this portion of his career, although, when the subject arose, he solemnly and consistently protested his innocence. He never travelled without his concertina, from which he extracted the most exquisite music. But his greatest treasure was an old Welsh Bible; which had been his mother's, and no night passed without his reading a chapter from it. He was fond of his glass, was the Welshman, and sometimes he took more than was good for him. On such occasions he would retire to some secluded spot, and, bareheaded, preach to the hills in red-hot Welsh. It was a thing to remember, was the sight of this gaunt, strong man, flinging his arms wildly about in his enthusiasm, while the impassioned gutturals rolled fast and furious from his throat. Those who knew him never interfered with him when he was in such ecstasies; he was perfectly harmless, and on the succeeding morning was always up with the sun, ready for work.

Richard Handfield was fortunate in picking up Welsh Tom for a mate; for Richard was an idle fellow, while the Welshman buckled to his work with overwilling zeal. When their day's walking was done, and a suitable place had been found to camp in, it was the Welshman who felled the tree, and the Welshman who fetched the water from the creek, and the Welshman whose ready hands extemporised a sleeping-place; while all that Richard did was to gather a few branches and to make the tea. Even this he did unwillingly and grumblingly, repining at what he thought his hard lot. He had never been used to work, and, although he and his mate had walked but twenty-five miles that day, his feet were blistered, and he was sore and weary. The Welshman, whose limbs were hardened by constant exposure and years of toil, felt as fresh as when he started in the morning, and could have walked another twenty-five miles with ease. But, anxious as he was to arrive quickly at the new diggings, he did not grumble at the short day's journey, and, when tea was over, he sat down, pipe in mouth, with perfect contentedness.

Of course, the talk between them was of the new gold discovery, which had been made upon an immense plain.

"Discovered by Chinamen, eh, Tom?" queried Richard.

"Yes, Dick," answered the Welshman. (It is soon Tom and Dick with new acquaintances upon gold-fields. The conventional "Mr." is but seldom used, and never among diggers.) "John Chinaman got the first bite."

"Just like their luck," grumbled Richard; "why couldn't a white man have found it?"

Tom did not reply, for in common with most of the European gold diggers, he entertained a very low estimate of the Mongolian race, and looked upon them in the light of interlopers.

"I always thought gold would be found in that quarter," he said, presently; "I passed over the flat six years ago, and I almost fancied I could see the gold at the bottom."

"I should have tried it," said Richard.

"I was taking a load of wool down to Melbourne at the time, and I was single-handed. Besides, it's a thousand chances to one if I had hit upon gold. A rich gold-field gets scratched over a hundred times before it's found out. No gold-field ever is any good, or ever proves itself very rich, until a big rush sets into it."

The conversation not being continued, Welsh Tom took his concertina from its case, and played some simple melodies. Attracted by the sounds, a party of diggers, camping not many yards away, strolled towards the spot, and stood about the musician in easy attitudes, listening to his music. At the conclusion of a little piece of delicious extemporising, one of the party asked the Welshman to play "Shades of Evening," which he did very sweetly; and then the same man said, "Play 'Alice Gray,' mate." It was an especially favourite air with the Welshman, and he played it with much feeling. As the last note died softly away, the diggers strolled back to their camping-place.

Perhaps the only one who heard the melodies, and who was not thoroughly softened by them, was Richard Handfield. In the hearts of the rough diggers there was a stir of deep emotion as the sounds travelled into space; the music of sweet remembrance dimmed many an eye, and took their thoughts from the strange present into the realms of long ago. But not so with Richard. His was a nature that needed constant control. With Alice by his side to strengthen him, he could be strong; left to his own resources, his weak nature asserted itself in repinings. He pined for a result, but had not sufficient strength of purpose to work for its accomplishment. Thus, fortified as he was, brave as he felt himself to be, when he parted from Alice, no sooner was he torn from the influence of her presence, than he became again a murmurer at hardships of his lot. The picture of this man's nature is a true one, and is not overdrawn.

He sat, on this evening, moody and discontented, looking with a dash of contempt at the Welshman, who, reclining upon the earth, with his back against a tree, was playing softly the old familiar airs. He could not help thinking that this man was beneath him, this man who could be contented with so little, and who had no disturbing memories to render him miserable. At the same time he was envious of him, as was evidenced by the remark he made.

"I wish I was like you, Welshman."

"Like me!" the Welshman exclaimed, in a tone of simple surprise.

"Yes; you haven't a care. No wife, no children, no ambition. Give you your pipe and your concertina, and you are happy and contented."

Welsh Tom sighed, and said, "And you?"

"I am the most miserable dog in the world. I wish I had never been born."

"There's no use in wishing that, mate. The best way is, to make the best of it."

"That's all very well for you. You have led a rough life, and are used to it. I wish I had been brought up like you. It would have been all the better for me."

Welsh Tom sighed again, but did not reply.

"I was brought up as a gentleman," continued Richard, following the current of his own selfish thoughts, "and just at my age, when I ought to be enjoying life, I have to sweat for my living. You would not think of it so lightly if you were married--"

"I think it would make life all the sweeter," said the Welshman, simply.

"*You* think!" exclaimed Richard, so disdainfully, that any man but the Welshman would have fired up. "What do you know of marriage and its responsibilities?"

"Nothing."

"What do you know of the weight it is upon a man, what a clog it is upon him when he is in misfortune; how it frets him and worries him, and drives him almost mad? Why, I doubt if you have ever been in love!"

"I don't think I have."

"Well, then," said Richard, impatiently, "what's the use of talking about it?"

"Not much; yet I've sometimes wished that my life had been different. I've sometimes wished that I had a woman to love me, and children to bring up. I've often thought, What use am I, rough and strong as I am, in the world? I have been sinful enough at times to envy my mates who had wives and children; and, as I've laid myself down upon my bed, have wished that I could hear the prattle of children about my pillow. Foolish of me, no doubt!"

"Better to be without them. You have no cares and no one but yourself to look after. Why, look here! I have a wife whom I married for love--her father is a wealthy hunks, but he discarded her for marrying me. What is the result? Misfortune pursued me, and we are both miserable. Would it not have been better that we had never met? Of course it would. So you may thank your stars that you haven't a wife to drag your thoughts down to desperation point, as my wife does mine."

"Isn't she a good wife?"

"Fifty thousand times too good for me."

The Welshman refilled his pipe, and, after puffing for a few moments, said--

"What one man sighs for, another man groans at. Of course it's absurd tor such a rough-and-ready chap as me to say that if I had a wife fifty thousand times too good for me, I should look upon her as a blessing. I've never had much experience of women. The only woman I ever loved was my old mother; but although I dare say I am ignorant enough with regard to womankind, I often think that the world is like a garden, and that the women and children are the flowers in it."

"Is the world like a garden to you! I've heard that you've had pretty hard lines in it, too."

"So I have. But, you see, it is not my fault. I might make things worse for myself, but I don't know how I could make them better."

"Very fine philosophy that, I dare say," Richard continued to grumble; "but all men are not made the same, and all men don't think the same. What is one man's meat is another man's poison. You like this sort of life; you don't feel it any hardship to walk thirty or forty miles a day. You were never brought up to expect anything better. I was. And I can't sit still, and be grateful for misfortune."

Far away, through the miles of tall gaunt trees that stood in dark relief, like sentinels of the night, the watch-fires were glimmering! men bodily weary, but into whose hearts had stolen the peacefulness of nature, were lying contentedly about, enjoying the sweet incense of repose. Heaven's eyes were looking down upon them; God's handiwork surrounded and encompassed them. The solemn trees, the bright stars; the evanescent flash that marked the lizard's track; the hushed air that glided through the forests of the New World, the faintest tracery of whose minutest leaf is more marvellous than man's greatest work; and all the myriad visible and invisible wonders of the wondrous earth: contributed to the holiness of the night. The Welshman looked round and beyond, where the glimmering watch-fires lost themselves in dark depths. Then he looked at Richard, and said, as if wishful to woo him to a softer mood,--

"If she were here--"

"My wife?" queried Richard.

"Your wife. If she were here, she would think this very beautiful."

"If she were here," said Richard, less fretfully; and then more softly still, he repeated, "If she were here--ah! I know what I would wish."

"What?"

"I should wish but first (I don't mind telling you, Welshman, for you are a good fellow, I think), I should like to lie with my head in her lap, and see her soft eyes looking into mine--I should wish that we might fall asleep upon this peaceful night, and never wake up again! What a grand and awful thing to think of! All of us, as far as we can see, to fall asleep for ever, and for it to be always quiet and peaceful as it is now. Yet quiet as it is, I do not feel inclined for sleep."

"I will tell you my story, if you like," said Welsh Tom. "It isn't very long, and I don't suppose it is very interesting. But I feel as if I should like to tell it to-night."

"All right," said Richard, with some slight show of curiosity. "I'm listening."

CHAPTER XI
WELSH TOM

"I was born in North Wales," commenced the Welshman, "near the Valley of Clwyd, in Denbighshire, and I passed my days at home in idleness. My father died when I was very young, and I cannot remember him. My mother was a little dark-skinned woman. I can see her now in her widow's weeds; she never left them off from the time of my father's death. I got some little education from an old clergyman, but not much, for I was too fond of roaming over the hills and valleys to pay attention to study. You can tell by my accent that I am Welsh born. My dear mother was very proud of her descent, and like many old Welsh families, hers had a pedigree which she could trace back many centuries, and which connected us with a royal line. My father left some property which brought in about forty pounds a year. Upon this we lived, and we were looked upon as quite rich people. There were three of us at home--my mother, my sister, and myself. We were the family. When I say I passed my days in idleness, I mean that I was brought up to no trade, and did not work for money. But I found the days quite short enough. I fished, and hunted, and made excursions to the neighbouring mountains. One day, when I was returning from Moel-Fammau, I fell in with a gentleman, who told me he was making a pedestrian tour for pleasure. We got into conversation together, and he walked with me until we came to my mother's house. I was pleased him, and I invited him to our evening meal. He made himself very agreeable, and we offered him a bed for the night. The chance acquaintance ripened into intimacy, and he stayed with us some time. Lake and woodland round about the Valley of Clwyd are magnificent. He was delighted with the scenery, and, being an artist, was desirous of taking away with him some sketches of what he called a paradise upon earth. So, he with his sketch-book, and I with my gun and rod, would go in search of pretty bits of scenery, and he would sketch while I shot or fished. We were away from home sometimes for two or three days. We climbed Snowdon together, and caught otters on the banks of shy streams, which seemed to be trying to hide themselves from our sight. Many weeks passed in this manner, and we became much attached to one another--that is, I became much attached to him. The life of seclusion I had led made me like him better than I should have done, perhaps, had I been a worldly man, or had I been, as I am now, better acquainted with the world. He was to my life as bright clouds are to the sky. We were all fond of him: I, because I had never had a friend; my mother, because he would indulge her in her pet pride of royal descent (he would talk with her for hours about ancient Wales and its noble kings); and my sister--half a minute, mate, my pipe's out."

He paused to relight it, and continued:

"My sister liked him too well, although I did not suspect it at the time. We took no notice of their being often together, for you see he was our guest, and no suspicion of wrong entered our minds. Even when the time drew near that he must depart, I did not think it strange that my sister should look grieved at his going from us. We all felt sorry--he had so enlivened our quiet home with his gay manners and conversation, that it was impossible he could have been easily forgotten. I accompanied him many miles on his road, and with expressions of friendship we parted. For some days after his departure, the sunshine of our home seemed to have disappeared; but little by little it came back, and our quiet life was resumed. But not for long--for one day my sister was missing, and all our anxious searchings and inquiries brought us no tidings of her. My mother was distracted, and I thought at the time it would be her death. A few weeks after my sister's disappearance, a letter came from her, asking our forgiveness for her flight, and saying that she hoped soon to visit us, a happy wife. She made no allusion to any person in the letter, but a mother's loving perception detected the sad strain in which it was written; and many were the bitter tears she wept over the letter. I looked at the postmark on the envelope, 'Wenlock,' and resolved to go to Shropshire to try and find my sister. Dishonour had never fallen on our family, and although no word of the fear which haunted us passed between my mother and myself, I saw and knew the dread which possessed her. I went to Wenlock. I did not think, as I left my home, with a look at my gun and my fishing-tackle, that I should never see them again, and that the Valley of Clwyd would receive me no more. The day after my arrival at Wenlock, I met the man whose name was Hardy who had made our home so bright while he stopped with us. Then, when I saw him, the suspicion that had entered my mind that he was connected with my sister's flight, flashed into conviction. I questioned him, but he denied all knowledge of her. It needed not the unquiet look or the hesitating speech to convince me that he lied. He did lie, as I knew. It was not long before I found my sister, and learned from her lips the shame that had fallen upon our family. I can see her now, crouching before me, as she sobbed out her confession; indeed, it was little she said, but it was enough. I can see her face--it might be looking upon me in the light of this beautiful moon!--as she raised it, tear-covered, to me, and implored my forgiveness. Poor child! I could not reproach her; she was punished enough already for her sin. But I determined to seek my false friend, and to force him to make reparation. He received me civilly enough, but almost laughed in my face when I asked him to marry my sister. I spoke of the honour of our family, and begged him not to tarnish it; I recalled to his mind the welcome and the hospitality he, a stranger, had received at our hands; I spoke of my mother, and of the blow it would be to her;--but he only sneered at me, and with his specious tongue tried to put me off. I was hot, and he was cool, and when he left me, I was goaded almost into madness. It appeared to me incredible that hospitality should be so violated. That night, after I had once more visited my sister, I determined to see this man again, and to appeal more strongly, if I could, to his sense of honour. And if he does not marry her, I thought, I will kill him! For what reason I do not know, for I was strong enough for anything, I put a pistol into my pocket. It was late in the night when I went to his residence. The doors were closed, but at the back of the house I saw a light shining in a window, and a shadow I could swear was his upon the blind. I soon climbed over the low wall which enclosed the garden, and then I scrambled up to the window, and dashed into the room. He was half undressed, and his face turned very white when he saw me. My words were few: I told him I was determined not to submit to dishonour. He would have called out, but I presented my pistol, and swore I would shoot him if he raised his voice. He knew that I would keep my word, and he promised me that he would marry my sister on the morrow. I held out my hand to him, and he shook it. We spent a few minutes in friendly talk, and then, with a light heart, I prepared to leave the house the way I had entered it. But no sooner had I got my leg over the window-sill than he rushed to the door, and throwing it open, called loudly for assistance. I was bewildered. The pistol I had brought with me dropped to the ground. He picked it up quickly and pulled the trigger, then let it fall again to the ground. As he did so I jumped back into the room, which in an instant was filled with people, and the next moment I was seized and dragged off to prison on a charge of burglary and attempted murder. The case was quite clear: my presence in the room, the smashed window-panes, the pistol, which was proved to be mine, the bullet in the wall, made up a chain of evidence too strong, of course, to admit of doubt. There was only my bare word that the story was false; they shrugged their shoulders when they heard it, and the judge himself said that it was nothing but a shallow fabrication. They did not hesitate over the verdict; they found me guilty, and I was sentenced to transportation for life."

The Welshman paused for a few moments, and puffed away at his pipe before he resumed.

"While I was lying in prison, my sister fled. I wanted sadly to see her, but it was denied me. She was nowhere to be found. Three days before the ship sailed which was to convey me from my country, my mother came to see me. Poor thing! she had almost lost her reason. She wept over me, and gave me this little Welsh Bible, which I have never parted with, and which shall be buried with me when I am dead. Then she was taken away, and I never saw or heard of her again. I was chained by the leg to a fellow-convict, and put on board ship. We were eight months getting to Botany Bay. The ship was a leaky old tub. The Government in those days picked out the rottenest vessels it could get to convey the convicts from their native shores. The filth and dirt of the ship were horrible. The water was poisonous; the food was disgusting. A plan was mooted among the convicts to murder the officers, and seize the ship; but it was discovered, and half-a-dozen men were shot and thrown overboard. After that we were kept nearly the whole of the time under close hatches. How that old tub creaked and strained! Many a time I thought we were going down, and I prayed that the vessel might be dashed to pieces, and make an end of us. For during a great part of the voyage, I was angry and despairing, and almost doubted the goodness of God. But this" (and here he touched the Bible) "has taught me better! We arrived at our destination safely enough, and were set to work. Some of the convicts in our ship did well. The man I was chained to during the voyage is now a millionaire. He bought some land in Sydney with his savings, and sold it at twenty thousand pounds an acre. I was never very fortunate. I got my ticket-of-leave, and worked for myself, chiefly at bullock-driving. I could tell you some queer anecdotes of colonial life in those days. Bushranging was all the go, and it wasn't safe to travel a hundred miles with anything valuable about you. I remember once, as I was coming into Sydney with my dray, seeing a buggy, without a horse, standing on the road. When I drove up to it there was a man inside, stark naked. He had been stuck up by bushrangers, and they had stripped him of every bit of clothing, down to his socks. They had torn from the buggy everything that he might have converted into a covering: otherwise, they did not ill-treat him. I have been a shepherd, too, and have lived by myself for months and months, without seeing the face of a single human creature. It is a trying life. I have known men grow into a state of incurable idiocy after a few months' solitariness. It is not disagreeable at first; one takes a pride in the sheep, and enjoys the sense of independence which is the great feature in a shepherd's life; but, after a time, it is awful. To sit, night after night, with no soul to speak to, with nothing to read, with nothing to do but to smoke and think-- it is no wonder that men go mad! The wonder is, that so many escape with reason. I remember a narrow brush I had with the natives. I remember it with pleasure, for even the sight of a savage, although he was eager to kill me, was a relief. I had missed some sheep, at odd times, within two or three weeks. I was actually pleased when I first made the discovery, for it gave me something new to think of. One night I determined to watch; and, sure enough, I came upon the natives, carrying off half-a-dozen or so of the fattest sheep. I did not see them sooner than they saw me, and I had to run for it. I had provided for such a contingency, and when I arrived, almost breathless, at the hut, I made all fast in a twinkling, and prepared to receive them. They came up pretty fast at my heels, but I saluted them with three barrels from my six-shooter, and all but two retreated, yelling, faster than they came. The hut was rather queerly built, just in a nook of some overhanging rocks, and there was only the front of it exposed. This was an advantage to me, for the savages could not get at me at the back. I watched their dusky forms in the distance with absolute pleasure. It must have been quite four months since I had seen anything in the shape of a man, and though I saw him now in the shape of a deadly foe, it was better than living any longer the devil's life of solitude. Besides, I did not care much for them. If they had fought fair, I could have kept them off as long as my powder lasted. But they don't fight fair. The 'noble' savage will take any mean advantage he can of an enemy. They are a skulking, idle, dirty lot of thieves. They came to the attack three times, and each time I received them with my six-shooter, and sent them scampering back. Then they made preparations for doing what I expected, and what I was prepared for. They collected all the dead timber and dry brushwood they could lay their hands on, and threw it before my hut, topping it with a lot of green branches. They were going to smoke me out. But I was ready for them. My hut, built in the cleft of a mass of rock, concealed a great fissure at the rear. In fact, the fissure served as a sort of tunnel. I had worked at it for a long while, and had dug along the natural tunnel until I came to an outlet. This outlet I had filled up carelessly, with loose pieces of rock, so that no one unacquainted with the secret would have suspected that it was a place of concealment. When the savages in front of the hut set fire to the pile of wood, which they did by throwing lighted branches into it from a distance, I crawled through the tunnel. A feeling did come over me, that if the savages knew of this retreat they would be sure to guard it, and it would be all up with me; and when I reached the outlet, I was a bit curious to know if I should see any black skins knocking about. Luckily for me, there were none, and I crept away. I did not have much time to lose, for I knew they would rush the hut before it was half burnt, and would discover the tunnel; so I only crept slowly along until I thought I was out of sight of them, and then I scudded off. I ran a good many miles that night, and I thought I was pretty clear of them. But the next day, when I was within eight or ten miles of the station I was making for, I saw three of the black devils racing after me, with their skinny legs. They haven't much superfluous flesh about them, haven't the blacks. They are all skin, bone, and muscle. They had tracked me the whole way, nearly thirty miles, and when they caught sight of me, they set up a hullaballoo of delight. I was pretty tired at the time, but the sight of them put fresh life into me, and I ran my fastest. But they were too much for me. I saw one of them disappear round a clump of timber for the purpose of cutting me off, while the other two followed straight after me. I soon came to where there was a bend in the track, and just as I turned it, the first one sprang out of the timber. He was within two hundred yards of me, and when he saw me he raised his 'boomerang,' and sent it whizzing into the air. Quick as lightning, for I knew how true those savages could aim, I turned, and ran towards the other two. Seeing this, and knowing that I had turned upon them to escape the 'boomerang,' they stopped short, suddenly, and threw their spears at me. I felt that there was nothing for it but fight. I had my revolver in my hand, loaded in its six barrels. One of their spears grazed my cheek as I flew along; and when I got close enough, I sent a bullet into the nearest one, which dropped him. Then, with a sudden rush, I closed with his companion. I had not climbed the Welsh hills in my young days for nothing. The hardy life I had spent served me now; and, as I flung my arms round the dirty savage, I knew that I could master him in the end. But, in the meantime, the one who had thrown the 'boomerang' was after me with raised spear. He did not dare to throw it, for fear of hitting his comrade; for we were by this time upon the ground, locked in each other's arms, and rolling over one another, enveloped in a thick cloud of dust. Throughout the struggle, I kept my revolver in my hand, but had no opportunity of using it. My finger was on the trigger, and, in the scuffle, I must unconsciously have pressed upon it; for, to my surprise, it suddenly went off. For a moment I thought I was hit; but presently the clasp of the savage with whom I was struggling relaxed, and he rolled back dead. The one who had thrown the 'boomerang,' took to his heels upon hearing the report. When I rose, and got away from the dust, I could see him scampering off. I did not care to follow him. I made my way as quickly as I could to the station: and so ended my shepherd's life. After that, I turned bullock-driver. That is a dreary life enough, but it's better than being a shepherd: it's more humanising. You get a chance, now and again, of giving a lift to a poor fellow, and that does a man good, you know. I remember, one morning, missing two of my bullocks. I did not find them till pretty late in the day. I was glad enough when I heard the tinkle of their bells, I can tell you; and as I was following the sound, I came upon a man lying in the bush. At, first, I thought he was dead; but I felt his heart beat--

very faintly, though. I carried him to the dray, and after a good deal of trouble, I brought him to. He had lost his way in the bush, and had wandered about without food for three days, until, what with hunger and despair, he had almost lost his senses. I remember he told me a curious impression he had, while he lay waiting, as he thought for death. He had quite resigned himself to die, and as he was waiting, waiting, his thoughts of course wandered back to the time when he was a boy at home. And he came to a day when he was lying, quite a little lad, on the grass, listening to the bells of his village church. His thoughts, just then, did not wander farther back, for the death-forest he was imprisoned in changed to the field of waving grass; he saw the leaves bending over him and about him. And the death-silence which had shrouded him was suddenly invaded by musical bells: they were the bells of his village-church, playing the old familiar peals, and they actually brought to his mind a long-forgotten rhyme, which he murmured with parched lips to the ringing of the bells. He heard them sure enough, but they were not the bells of his village church; they were the bells on the necks of my lost cattle. If my bullocks hadn't strayed, it would have been all over with him, for he couldn't have lasted another day. So what I looked upon at first as precious hard, turned out to be a piece of real good fortune. When the goldfields were discovered, I turned to gold-digging; and between that and bullock-driving I have spent all my time. It isn't a very attractive story, mine--is it, mate? I don't think I ever had an ambition, and my life was over when I was transported. I have often thought that if I were to meet the false friend who wrecked my life, and who destroyed the happiness of my family, I should kill him. But there is no chance of our ever meeting, and I do not yearn for it. But I *do* yearn, and have for many a year yearned, to know what became of my sister. Once I thought--it was in Melbourne three years ago, when I was loading flour for up-country--that I saw a face like hers, but it passed like a flash, and I did not see it again. It was but fancy, I know, yet it has often haunted me since. I am not the only innocent convict in the Colonies. I know some who were transported for life, for less crimes than mine--perfectly innocent men, who are living victims of what is called justice. If I had happened to stroll a different way the day I met that false friend, my life might have been very different. I might have married, and had children, and been a happy man. I wonder if, by and by, those who suffer unjustly are recompensed in any way!"

"You are a queer fellow, Welshman," said Richard Handfield. "If I were you, and had been treated as you have been treated, I should have turned desperate, I think. By what right are men oppressed and hunted down? Say I owe a duty to society; does not society owe a duty to me? Just think for one moment of what I have suffered--"

"Of course," said the Welshman; "I do not mean to say I have as much to complain of as you. You were educated and brought up in luxury--"

"That's where it is. If I had been brought up as roughly as yourself, I might take the same view of misfortune."

"Certainly," said Welsh Tom, but in a voice which struck somewhat strangely upon his companion's ears. "There's no comparison between the hardship of our lives. But it is time to turn in. We must be up with the sun. Good night!"

And then they prepared for their night's rest. Before falling asleep, Richard glanced at the Welshman, and saw him, with an earnest expression on his face, reading, by the light of the moon, a chapter from his mother's old Welsh Bible.

CHAPTER XII
THE NEW RUSH

Early in the morning the plains were busy with moving life. Refreshed by their rest, the hardy gold-diggers, full of health and vigour, rose from their primitive beds, and raced to distant creeks to lave their faces, and draw the water for the morning meal. Little do the constant residents in a crowded city know of the vigorous healthful life that stirs in the veins of these sturdy pioneers in the New World. "Take up thy bed and walk," was literally illustrated by thousands of eager men. Quickly were their rough toilets completed; quickly were the hobbles taken from the horses' feet and the bells from their necks, and quickly were they harnessed and ready to play their parts in the moving panorama; quickly were the heavy-jawed, wisdom-faced oxen yoked to the drays and waggons, patiently waiting for the flick of the whip which bade them move along, which they did at a snail's pace, as if they were weary of their day's work before it was begun; and soon were log fires blazing, chops and steaks frizzling, and boiling tea impatiently bubbling in the queerest of utensils. Scant time was given to breakfast; scantier time was employed in rolling up blankets; less time still was occupied in arranging them over broad backs and shoulders, and starting on the march to the promised land. But one operation all performed, and all took time in performing. When everything else was adjusted, a black stump of a pipe was carefully produced, carefully loaded, and carefully lighted by the aid of a burning branch. Then, refreshed by their first pipe, the adventurers whistled away dull care, and "stumped it" at the rate of four miles an hour. It was a lovely summer morning. The sun was rising over a snow-capped range, which reared its head in the distance, a picture of beauty. As the warm rays fell upon the moss-clad giant, rills of sparkling snowdrops gemmed its face with myriad silver tears. It was a marvellous picture. But few stayed to pay it tribute. Among the few, a ragged German, upon whose shoulders were placed all his worldly treasure--a calico tent, a couple of blankets, and a flat-faced, stolid-looking little boy, who, as his father pointed to the range, crowed and clapped his hands at the glorious sight.

When evening came, and they were within twenty miles of the New Rush, Richard Handfield and the Welshman halted at a wayside inn, which had been built but a few days, and in which the proprietors were making their fortunes rapidly. It belonged to two young Scotchmen, upon whom fortune had descended unexpectedly. They had taken to woodsplitting, and were happy at that, and contented even with the little they earned, as is the proverbial way of Scotchmen. But they had the national characteristic, an eye to the main chance: and they had the still more national characteristic, the wit to take advantage of the chance. So, directly the gold fever broke out, and they saw the signs of it floating past their little six-feet-by-nine tent of drill, they built themselves a building of gum-tree slabs. In less than two days it was finished; the same evening they bargained for a dray-load of bottled beer and spirits, the first on the road to the new gold-fields; and the next morning, as impromptu hotel keepers, they commenced to make their fortunes to the tune of two hundred pounds a day. Their building was the only one for miles around, and as it stood in the midst of an amphitheatre of hills, they dignified it by the title of the Amphitheatre Hotel. Night and day it was crowded with men who recklessly squandered their money at the bar in a state of the wildest excitement.

At ten o'clock at night, Richard and his mate were standing by the door of the Amphitheatre Hotel. The riotous noise within the hotel precluded all idea of sleep, and they stood there, looking at the moon, whose brightness was hardly dimmed by a screen of light floating clouds, and talking over the chances of their being able to get a good piece of ground at the New Rush. What is that in the distance? A white object! Moving? Yes, and moving fast. Running, racing, like one demented. White trousers, white guernsey shirt, bare arms, and bare head--running like mad, under the white face of the moon. Who can he be? Where has he come from? Is he mad? All the inmates of the calico hotel came out to the door, waiting for the racer. And here he is, panting, his strong chest heaving, his brawny arms waving, his blue eye glaring! "Well, mate, what's the row! What's up?" Without returning any answer to these questions, the racing individual points in the direction of the New Rush, whence he has come, and gasps out, "There--got a claim--heaps of gold--saw a bucketful dug up just before I left--off to fetch my mates!" And off he is, without--wonder of wonders!--stopping to drink. There he goes, racing off to fetch his mates: a large white speck dotting the plain beyond--a small white speck--a smaller white speck--an infinitesimal white speck--no speck at all! Meanwhile, the conversation has become very animated. They all thought so--that was the real El Dorado--they had been waiting for it for a long while, and here it was at last! Anecdotes are related as authentic, of fortunes made in a week, in a day, in an hour. Goodness knows how the information has been obtained, but suddenly these men are relating to each other wonderful accounts of thousands of ounces obtained by single individuals at the New Rush, although, before the arrival of the racing individual, they did not appear to know very much about the new field. Gradually the conversation dies out, and the diggers retire to their rest. Nothing disturbs the stillness of the night. The scene is so lovely that it might serve for the Kingdom of Dreamland. On the top of yon lofty mountain stands an old castle, wrapped about, grim shadow as it is, by the soft moonlight. Near it, each rugged rock and stone assumes a living shape. Why creep they away so stealthily? Are they rock or human? Psha! They are but two diggers, who, excited by the news, have given up all thoughts of sleep, and are stealing away to the New Rush, so that they may not be too late for the chance of digging up a bucketful of gold!

At noon on the following day, Richard and the Welshman arrived on the ground. There were thousands of diggers there, and a long street of calico stores was already erected to supply their wants. As the new arrivals poured in, they had to traverse this street, which commenced at the mouth of the main road, so that it presented a very animated appearance, and was always thronged. Flags of all nations and flags of no nations, were waving over the stores, many of which rejoiced in high-sounding titles. There were the Great Wonder, the Little Wonder, the Wonder of the World, and a great quantity of other Wonders. There were the Monster Emporium (which, properly, would represent an Emporium for Monsters); the Blue Store, and the Red Store (which were impositions, for they were built of unbleached calico); and the Bee Hive, which looked like one, for it was crowded with customers. There was the Right Man in the Right Place, which was the sign of a stationer's store, where old newspapers were being sold at exorbitant prices, and where you had to pay half-a-crown for two sheets of notepaper, two envelopes, and a pen. This store was also a kind of post-office, where you might deposit letters on payment of one shilling each, and receive them, if there were any to receive, at the same price. There were half-a-dozen auctioneers, going, going, going, with all their might. There were scores of draymen unloading their drays, and blocking up the road with cases of goods. There was a horse sale-yard, where horses were being galloped madly up and down, to the infinite risk of life and limb; and wherein the salesman talked the most outrageous nonsense, and told the most outrageous fibs, as to the wonderful qualities of the cattle he was anxious to dispose of. There were scores of hotels and restaurants for the accommodation of the natives of almost every nation under the sun. There were the Hibernian, the Spanish, the French, the American, and a host of others. Those who could not find their native clime indicated on the broad strips of calico in front of the stores, might console themselves at the All

Nations; while philanthropists might rest their weary limbs at the Live and Let Live.

Forcing their way through the bustling crowd, Richard Handfield and the Welshman soon reached the end of the straggling street of stores, and came upon the gold diggings. These were situated upon a great plain, which was dotted with strong sunburnt men, straining at windlasses. Round some of the shafts small knots of diggers were congregated, waiting eagerly for the "prospect." One shaft had just come upon the gold, and great excitement was produced by the statement that the first bucketful of earth had yielded twelve pennyweights of the precious metal. There was no chance of getting ground near this spot, for every inch for a mile around was monopolised; so the new-comers had to walk on till they came to a less busy part of the plain. A claim was there soon measured and marked out with pegs, and the orthodox custom of sticking the pick[4] in the centre was duly performed. Then Richard and his mate went in search of a spot to put up their tent, and before evening their house was built, and Richard was sitting at the door smoking his pipe, while Welsh Tom commenced to build a new chimney. Welsh Tom was in his glory. He worked and sang, and looked every inch a man of might; even Richard could not help admiring him. His shirt sleeves of blue twill were tucked up to his shoulders, and the hard muscles of his arms stood out so grandly that Tubal-Cain himself might have been proud of them. Every now and then he fell back and contemplated his mud chimney, which grew like magic beneath his hands. Sad as was the story of this man's life, he was happy and contented. Work--God's heritage to man--sweetened his days for him!

Footnote 4: This sticking the pick in the ground is an honoured gold-digging custom. It is the title-deed to the property. The first thing gold-diggers do when they arrive upon a newly-discovered gold-field is to look about them for a piece of ground which is most likely to be auriferous. Having made their selection, they measure as much of it as the gold-mining regulations of the colony allow them to occupy (perhaps forty feet by sixty), stick a boundary wooden peg at each corner, and then drive their pick into the centre of their ground, which is called "claim." Then they reconnoitre, and set about putting up their tent, and building a chimney. After-comers seeing the pick in the ground, consider it a good title-deed, and pass on to fresh spots.

Night was a busy time in the township. The bars of the calico restaurants and hotels were crowded, and money was lavishly squandered in the dancing-saloons and concert-rooms, with which the township abounded. The men danced with each other; a barmaid was a *rara avis* indeed, and could, with impunity, give herself as many airs as the most fashionable drawing-room belle. The fever excitement of a New Rush is most intense: men grow frantic from mere contagion. There was one free-and-easy concert-room, filled with diggers, who shouted out the choruses to the songs, and smoked and drank amidst a very Babel of riot and noise. In this room, one night, a little excitable Frenchman drunk himself into a state of madness, and, calling for a dozen of Champagne, knocked the necks off half the bottles, and poured the wine upon the ground; and three minutes afterwards, in a wild delirium, he lit his pipe with a five-pound note.

So days and weeks passed, and every day and every week the gold-field grew and grew until it extended over many miles. With magical celerity a city was built, and before the birth of a new moon the thousand and one institutions of a civilised life were growing in the light of enterprise and industry. Streets were laid out, roads were made, newspapers and banks were established, a theatre was erected; and while the busy life of the city was in full glow, homely men were building modest snuggeries in the suburbs, and the welcome faces of women and children began to be seen.

CHAPTER XIII
OLD FLICK

Old Flick's dwelling-place was in a narrow thoroughfare--so narrow, that Old Flick might have shaken hands with his neighbour on the opposite side of the way without moving from his own side of the pavement. Not that he ever tried the experiment; Old Flick was not given to the shaking of hands and was as secret and close as the grave. The thoroughfare was a misnomer; for if you walked about twenty yards beyond Old Flick's dwelling-place, you came, to your great discomfiture, plump upon the dead wall of a building which checked all further progress. Many deluded pedestrians, who had strolled into the place, curious to know whither it led, had been compelled to retire in dudgeon. A clever speculator had purchased the land round about Old Flick's dwelling, and had mapped it out and built upon it with so much ingenuity, that when he came to Old Flick's Thoroughfare, which was the last built upon, he, to his exceeding surprise, found himself blocked in; and rushing to his plans, discovered that he had given himself a few feet of land more upon paper than he actually possessed upon earth. But he derived consolation from the thought that he had accomplished his object, which was, to build as many tenements as he could crowd upon his freehold, and to allow as little walking and breathing space as possible to his tenantry. This result being successfully attained, he took a first-class passage home, and retired to Bermondsey, where he lives to the present day upon the results of his ingenuity, and talks continually, in grandiloquent strains, of his Estates in Victoria.

Old Flick's Thoroughfare, as it had grown to be called, boasted of about two feet of pavement and six feet of road, and contained sixteen tenements--eight on each side. In the owner's plan of the estate, which decorated the walls of his parlour in Bermondsey, it was represented as a magnificent street, lined on each side with handsome edifices, four storeys high, and crowded with carriages and pedestrians of the most fashionable character; whereas, in truth, the tenements were each composed of but one storey, and there was scarcely room in the road to wheel a barrow. Over the portico of Old Flick's dwelling was the inscription:--

OLD FLICK'S
ALL-SORTS STORE.
WHOLESALE, RETAIL, AND FOR EXPORTATION.

For be it here remarked, it is the fashion of all small traders in the colonies to sell everything down to oranges and gingerbread, "wholesale, retail, and for exportation." It is an idiosyncrasy peculiar to the class. In the windows of Old Flick's All-sorts Store was heaped the most worthless collection of worthless articles that could possibly be compressed within so small a space. Blunt saws, dirty pannikins, broken crockery, worn-out dog collars, two-bladed penknives, empty ink bottles, rust-eaten picks and shovels, a few torn books, the broken works of two or three clocks and watches, with a multitude of other utterly incongruous things, were tumbled indiscriminately upon each other. In one pane there was an advertisement to the effect that "Doctor Flick prescribed for and cured every disorder incidental to the human frame, at the lowest possible rates;" and in another pane appeared the announcement that Old Flick was a land and estate agent, and collected rents and debts, and acted as the confidential adviser of all persons in trouble and difficulty, and that secrecy and despatch might be relied upon. To show that he was ready for consultation or active business, Old Flick, with his palsied frame and blear eyes, might be seen, half the day, standing in ragged slippers, at his door, on the watch for customers. He might not inaptly have been likened to an ugly spider on the look-out for flies.

The origin of Old Flick was wrapped in mystery. Nothing further was known of him than that he had sprung up suddenly in Canvas Town, in the early days of the gold-diggings, and that, when that motley delectability was swept away, he had migrated to the blind alley to which he gave his name, and which had just then been formed by the operations of the Bermondsey speculator. Canvas Town, when Old Flick first made his appearance there, was indeed a delectable locality. Take a few acres of level ground, where in the winter people sank over their ankles in thick mud, and where in the summer they were blinded with the fine dust which an Australian hot wind drove mercilessly in their faces; divide the ground into the narrowest and most irregular of streets and lanes; erect (if it may be so called) upon it a few hundreds of canvas tents, of all sizes and shapes, which in a civilised city would not be thought fit for pigs or poultry; smoke-dry the entire space until the canvas of the tents becomes black and rotten, and hangs in shreds from weak battens and crazy poles; let the wretched habitations be tenanted by gaol-refuse, by unscrupulous traders, by dismayed and distressed immigrants who have journeyed over stormy seas in search of gold, by brute faces and kind faces, by flaunting women and ladies of tender rearing; let the spaces be choked up with packing-cases, and immigrants' trunks, and crying children, and perplexed wanderers from distant lands; above all, let no vice be hidden, let no shame be shame-faced: and a reasonably correct picture of Canvas Town, Melbourne, in the early days of the gold-diggings, will be portrayed. But even in Canvas Town, where probably was assembled the most incongruous mass of human beings ever congregated together; where thief and gentleman slept with but the division of a strip of calico between them, and where ladies cooked their family meals, and washed their family clothes, in the open thoroughfares--even there, Old Flick was a mystery. He was a tall, thin, stooping man, with an unwholesome-looking face, always stubbled and dirty. He was a dealer in everything, whether honestly come by or not, and professed himself a doctor; and as a proof of his skill he was in the habit of exhibiting a musty, yellow, old cash-book, in which were inscribed more than fifty testimonials from grateful patients who had been cured of lumbago, tooth-ache, and other plagues which human flesh is heir to. He was sixty years of age, or thereabouts, and he was so shaky that he could scarcely hold a glass to his lips without spilling half its contents. He said it was ague; others said it was rum. At the time of his introduction to the reader, he was standing at his door, as usual, in his ragged slippers, with his blear eyes looking frequently over his shoulder to the room at the back of his store. While thus engaged, he was accosted by Milly, whose manner and appearance betokened that she had been drinking.

"Hallo! Old Flick! Who is inside?"

"No one, Milly," he answered.

"What a liar you are, Flick!" said Milly. "Jim's inside, and you know it."

"Jim isn't inside," he returned. "You're drunk."

"I say, Old Flick," said Milly, "I never saw you blush. Tell the truth for once, and set your face on fire."

Old Flick looked venomously at the girl, but she only laughed at him in return.

"Go in, and tell Jim I want to speak to him," she said.

"I have told you he isn't there."

"All right. Then I'll sit here and wait for him;" and she sat down on the pavement in front of the store. Old Flick was in despair. He glared at her, and swore at her.

"Get up, you she-devil!" he quavered, in a voice shaking with passion.

"I shan't. If you call me names, I'll pull your whiskers out."

"Go away, Milly," said Old Flick, coaxingly; "go away, there's a dear! You'll have the peelers on you, and if Jim hears you--"

"Oh, he *is* in there, is he!" exclaimed Milly, rising to her feet.

"Yes, but it's more than my life's worth to disturb him. Go away, quietly, there's a dear!"

"All right; just you tell him, when you go in, to come home soon. I didn't want to see him, you old fool. I only wanted to know where he was. Oh, what a liar you are, Flick!"

And giving him a playful pinch on his withered cheek, she walked away, singing.

In the back room of Old Flick's dwelling was assembled a quartette, each member of which bore upon his face a certificate for the gallows. It was composed of Jim Pizey, Black Sam, Ned Rutt, and the Tenderhearted Oysterman. Spirits and glasses were on the table, and the room was filled with smoke.

"That's arranged, then," said Jim Pizey; "we meet at Gisborne this day fortnight?"

His companions nodded.

"Until then," he continued, "try quietly to find out where Dick Handfield has got to."

"If I knew where that milk-faced woman of his was," said Ned Rutt, with a dark look, "I'd soon work it out of her."

"Strike me blind!" exclaimed the Tenderhearted Oysterman. "You don't mean to say you'd hurt a woman!"

"Wouldn't I?" sneered Ned Rutt. "You wouldn't hurt a woman, of course, Oysterman?"

"Strike me dizzy!" exclaimed the Oysterman. "I wouldn't hurt a fly."

"There's that young devil, Grif," says Pizey; "he knows where Dick Handfield is. If you could get hold of him and frighten him, Oysterman, he might tell."

"I'd frighten him if I got hold of him," muttered the Oysterman, with a villanous scowl.

"Come here, Old Flick," shouted Jim Pizey, striking the table violently, and putting an end to the discussion. "Come here, you bag of rattling old bones, and let's settle up with you."

Which settling-up caused a great deal of whining on the part of Old Flick, and a great deal of cursing on the part of the quartette.

"Milly's been here, Jim," said Old Flick, when the settling was arranged, and Ned Rutt and Black Sam had departed. "She kicked up a nice row! I had as much as I could do to prevent her coming in."

"She'll be whimpering nicely when she knows I'm going away," said Pizey, with a touch of softness in his voice, for bad as he was, he had a sincere affection for the girl. "I haven't told her, and don't intend to. I shall leave that job to you, Flick. And now just listen to what I say, and don't miss a word."

With their heads close together, Jim Pizey and the Tenderhearted Oysterman laid bare their scheme. It was complete in its villanousness. Highway robbery, burglary, murder--they would stop short at nothing.

"Never mind about Dick Handfield giving us the slip," said Jim. "He's gone up the country, that's certain; we shall hear something of him, and when we do, he shan't escape us a second time."

"I'll lay a trap for him when I come across him," said the Oysterman with a lowering look, "that he'll be clever to get out of. A better trap than the forged five-pound note."

"What do you think of our plan, Flick?" asked Pizey.

"It sounds very well, Jim," said Old Flick. "But I've heard such lots of these schemes, and they've all ended in smoke."

"And why?" asked Jim Pizey, with passion. "Why have they all ended in smoke? Because, when everything has been cut and dried, some white-livered thief grew squeamish, and backed out of it; or because the infernal cowards have turned dainty at the sight of a drop of blood, and didn't have heart enough among the lot of 'em to kill a man! But this shan't end so--if any man turns tail when I am leading, I'll give him six barrels, one after another; he shall never turn tail again! We've got the right lot this time; there are four of us down here, and I can reckon upon four up the country. Grif's father's one of 'em. When we've got them all together, perhaps we'll 'stick up' the gold escort. I'll take care we won't bungle over it. We'll kill every damned trooper among 'em."

"But we won't hurt 'em, Flick," said the Tenderhearted Oysterman. "If I thought we should hurt the poor coves, I wouldn't have anything to do with it."

"There shan't be many left to blab about it," said Jim. "How would you like to have your hands in the gold-boxes, Flick, and run the dust through your fingers, eh?" Old Flick's eyes glistened, and his fingers twitched, as if they were already playing with the precious dust. "How would you like to buy it at so much a measureful,--eh, Flick? That's the way lots of it was sold after the 'Nelson' was stuck up in Hobson's Bay."

"Ah," said Old Flick, pensively, "that was a smart trick, that was! But them men had pluck in them."

"It's all very well to say that," grumbled Jim; "I could find men with lots of pluck, but there are no opportunities, worse luck!"

"Only think," said Old Flick, gloating upon the subject; "the dark night; the ship ready for sea, and going to sail the next day; the gold on board; the captain and officers on shore. I can see it all. The ship lies snugly at anchor; a boat with muffled oars, comes quietly to the side; half a dozen plucky men glide up like snakes on to the deck. Down goes the watch, gagged and bound in no time! The iron boxes, filled with gold--thousands and thousands of ounces--are lowered into the boat, and in a few minutes the brave fellows are pulling back to shore, made for life." And old Flick's villanous face brightened, and his eyes glistened.

"Made for life!" sneered Jim. "Not they! They were robbed right and left by such villains as yourself. I could lay my hands on a man in this town who would only put down a hundred sovereigns for every tin measure of gold-dust he bought. A fairish-sized measure, too!"

"That's the way they do us poor hard-working coves," grumbled the Oysterman. "Why, every one of them measures was worth a thousand pounds! He ought to be had up for embezzlement."

And thus conversing, they sat together until late in the night, hatching their villanous schemes; and when they departed, Old Flick chuckled, and rubbed his hands, and with one leg, and nearly the whole of the other in the grave, indulged in anticipations of a glowing future, as he drank his rum-and-water.

CHAPTER XIV
LITTLE PETER IS PROVIDED FOR

Sailing down the stream of life in his new moral boat, of which he, the Moral Shoeblack, was the Skipper, Grif was often at a loss what to do with his leisure time. Having relinquished his profession of vagrancy, he no longer felt himself at liberty to wander through the streets without an object. He had an instinctive foreboding that the Eye of the public was upon him, and was watching that he did not misconduct himself. Every time he met that Eye (and he met it as often as he dared to look into the human face) it appeared to be holding up a warning finger, if such a metaphor may be allowed. It appeared to say, Take care, now; be careful; no slouching about and trying to deceive ME; I am watching you! He was so acutely sensitive of this that it soon became his custom of an evening, when his day's work was done, to wander into the suburbs, that he might escape from the Eye which distressed him in the city's crowded streets. His day's work often proved, in its result, a delusion and a snare; and on many and many an evening did he gather together the implements of his trade, and walk away without a sixpence in his pocket. He had no place where he could safely deposit his bootstand and brushes, so wherever he wandered he carried them with him.

Behold him now, with these badges of his office slung round his shoulders, sauntering down a shady lane, with Little Peter by his side. For Little Peter was better. Milly had nursed him through his illness, and by her care had restored him to health. Was he grateful? It is hard to say. Little Peter's mind was almost a blank. He suffered without repining; he enjoyed without rejoicing. He took things as they came, and never dreamt that any effort on his part could alter them. After a scanty meal came hunger, and he waited patiently for the next poor crumbs which charity bestowed him, and which he received without gratitude. Then he hungered again and so on. It was all one to him. Whether it were night or day was a matter of indifference.

Walking along listlessly by the side of his best friend, he paid no heed to the beauty of nature, nor to the balmy air of evening. With Grif it was different. He was keenly alive to the joys and sorrows of life, and to all its surroundings. Even now, although he was hungry, and heart-sore, and weary, he looked from side to side with eager wonder and delight. The soft breeze was sweet to him, and he breathed it in so gratefully that the shadow of a spiritual beauty stole into his common face. He felt and rejoiced with nature that summer was coming. The clouds smiled at its approach, and as Zephyr whispered the glad tidings to field and forest, pretty blossoms peeped shyly out from the bosom of the earth, wondering if winter had really taken its departure. Grif was far from insensible to these influences, and the delicious air of spring was in some measure a recompense to him for the sufferings of his lot. So he sat him down under a hawthorn edge, hungry yet grateful, and Little Peter sat beside him, looking at the blood of the dying sun staining the western sky.

Not far from where he sat was the house of Nicholas Nuttall. The female head of that house was in a high state of glorification, for Matthew, their rich brother, had dined with them that day, and had behaved so graciously that visions of future greatness grew in her imagination. Matthew was a single man; of that fact she had made herself sure by a process of cross-examination to which she had subjected her lord and master the previous night. Certainly, her task had not been an easy one, for Nicholas was singularly reticent and hesitating in his replies to her eager queries; but goaded, pushed thereto by his wife's perseverance, he had at length given her to understand that his brother had no family.

"And why you should have endeavoured to keep the fact from me," Mrs. Nicholas had said, before composing herself to sleep, "is beyond my comprehension. I am not a murderess, and I don't wish to poison your brother--I may say *our* brother--to-morrow at dinner. But you always *were* aggravating, Nicholas. I wonder I've a bit of flesh left on my bones!"

"You haven't much," thought Nicholas as, shifting himself in bed, he came in contact with some of her bony protuberances; "you have worn it nearly all away by nagging."

But Mrs. Nicholas Nuttall was satisfied. She had ascertained that Matthew had no family, and that was sufficient for her. Whether he were a widower or a bachelor was immaterial. He had no ties, and Nicholas was his only brother. Nicholas was, therefore, the natural heir to the property, and the one remaining duty her newly-found brother-in-law owed to his family was not to remain too long upon earth. Such a proceeding would be manifestly indecent.

Dinner was over, and Matthew and Nicholas were sitting in the verandah, smoking their cigars. Had Matthew wished to smoke in the drawing-room he might have done so; indeed, Mrs. Nuttall had hinted as much, had even tried to prevail upon him to do so. She was so fond of smoke! nothing was so agreeable as a good cigar! the fragrance, and all that, was so delicious! (It was lucky for Nicholas that the wife of his bosom did not see the sly smile which played about his lips while she was uttering these rhapsodies.) But Matthew Nuttall would not be persuaded. He was too shrewd a man not to see through the small soul of Mrs. Nicholas, and he valued her excess of politeness at exactly its proper worth.

Thus it was that, notwithstanding the importunities of Mrs. Nuttall, Matthew and his brother were sitting in the verandah smoking their cigars. When he had consented to dine with them he made it a special provision that no guests were to be invited to meet them; it was to be a quiet family dinner. And Mrs. Nuttall, although inwardly disquieted--for she had laid out plans for a grand entertainment in honour of the rich squatter, an entertainment which would humiliate her neighbours (there is even that sort of pride in the Australian colonies)--wisely deferred to his wish. They had spent a pleasant afternoon. Mrs. Nuttall was amiability personified, although her graciousness was a trifle too obtrusive; and both Matthew and Nicholas, without any thought of pounds, shillings, and pence, were genuinely glad to renew brotherly relations. They sat together in silence, each engrossed in his own special thoughts. Nicholas was speculating upon his brother's previous life. From what Matthew had said to him on the occasion of their first meeting, he knew that there was present unhappiness connected with it--some domestic misery which even now, in spite of all his obstinate attempts at concealment, was preying upon his heart. Nothing could more surely denote this than his behaviour to his niece, Marian. Now, he would be all tenderness to her, would speak to her affectionately, caressingly; and now, as if some sudden remembrance had risen, which chilled the tender feeling, he would turn cold and stern, and would strive to steel himself against her girlish graces and fascinations. It was happiness and torture to be in her society, for she reminded him of his daughter. When she was present he juggled with his senses, and, shutting his eyes, believed that it was Alice who was in the room. Ha could feel her presence about him, and while the impression was strong upon him, the love he bore to her came back to his heart, bringing with it a painful sense of desolation. For he did love her, in spite of all; he did love her, although he would never look upon her face again. To that he was pledged. He had told her he would never see her again unless she renounced her husband; at the time he had told her, and ever since, he knew that she would be faithful to her marriage vows--he knew that she would be faithful till death to the man she had chosen. The words he had spoken to her on the night she made her last appeal to him were constantly recurring to him: "The day you ran away from your home I resolved to shut you from my heart as long as you were tied to that scheming scapegrace." Ah! but could he shut her from his heart? No, he felt that he could not do that. Her sweet pale face was for ever pleading to him. It was indelibly stamped upon his mind, and he could not efface it. Not long ago, when he was in his grand house at Highlay Station, he rose from his bed one night, and went to the room she used to occupy. There he sat down, and conjured her before him. Then he went outside the house, and looked around. All was his as far as he could see, and miles beyond and on every side of him. He was lord of range and gully, and all that was thereon. Forests of iron-bark and gum, tens of thousands of sheep, vast herds of oxen, droves of horses, the growing wealth of mountain and plain, were his. He was lord of all. Yet, as he stood there gazing on his greatness, he would gladly have bartered it for his daughter's love. Thus much he confessed to himself. He knew his own weakness, but the world should not know it. He owed it to himself that he should be consistent in this. Often and often he thought to himself that Alice might be in want, might be suffering. Well, if she suffered, did he not suffer also? The worst of suffering was his. The suffering of a lonely life, unblessed by a single caress. No, not one--not one loving smile, not one bright look, of the tender light of which he could say, "This is for me, from the heart; it is not bought." Worshipper as he was of the power of money, these thoughts came home to him, and brought desolation with them.

The soft sycophancy of Mrs. Nuttall disgusted him; he knew well enough what evoked it. And he marvelled how it was that his brother, who was unselfish and tender-hearted, could have married such a cross-grained woman. "But I suppose Nicholas did not know her nature until it was too late," he thought; "all women are false--all women are two-faced, deceitful, or mean, or selfish, or something worse." All? He knew he was lying to himself. All women were not so. The remembrance of his married life rose before him, for it had been a happy one. His wife had been to him an angel of devotion and goodness. All women were not bad; but he took a stern delight in striving to make himself believe so.

Nicholas had been watching the shadows of sad remembrance pass over his brother's face; he was getting to be an old man, but his heart was very tender to his brother, and he yearned to administer consolation.

"Mat," he said, "you are not happy."

"No, I am not." The reply was drawn from him almost involuntarily.

"Can I do anything?"

"Nothing, Nic." He paused for a short while, and then, laying his hand upon his brother's arm, he said, "When we first met I hinted that I did not wish my domestic life touched upon. I may one day speak of it to you; until then let it remain a sealed book between us." Nicholas bent his head. "I think it is your pretty little blossom, Marian, that has opened my wounds this afternoon, for I--I once had a daughter myself." He passed his hand across his eyes, and rose. "I see Marian in the garden," he said; "I will take a stroll with her."

He pressed his brother's hand, and joined Marian. Nicholas looked after him, and sighed. "So rich," he said, "and so unhappy! I am happier than he, notwithstanding--yes, notwithstanding that I am blessed with Mrs. Nuttall." The appearance of that lady upon the verandah just at the moment he uttered this qualification, made him feel very guilty, and he mutely thanked Heaven that she had not heard him.

"Where is brother Matthew, my dear?" she inquired, in her most sugary tones.

"He is taking a stroll with Marian," replied her spouse, pointing to the two figures in the distance. "They are just turning into the lane."

Mrs. Nicholas Nuttall looked, and seated herself with a satisfied air. Things were going on famously. Matthew would make his niece his heiress. Should they stop in the colony, or return to England when that event occurred? It might occur any day. People went off so suddenly in these hot climates. As she pondered, the servant came on to the verandah with coffee, of which Nicholas took a cup thankfully. It was not every day that such attention was paid him. Mrs. Nicholas Nuttall declined coffee. Her soul was too highly attuned for such common beverage.

"She is a dear good girl!" she mused.

"That she is, Maria," assented Nicholas, sipping his coffee, "and her wages are not at all high, as wages go. So neat and tidy, too!"

"Of whom are you speaking, Mr. Nuttall?" asked Mrs. Nuttall, with a lofty stare of surprise at her husband.

"Of Jane, my dear, the new servant, of course."

"I referred to our child," said Mrs. Nuttall, in her grandest tones, which always conveyed a frozen sensation to Mr. Nuttall's marrow; "to our child, Marian. You do not suppose that I should speak in that manner of a menial."

"Oh, I beg your pardon, I am sure," apologised Nicholas, very crest-fallen. The next moment he almost choked himself in an attempt to hide his shame by swallowing his coffee too hastily.

Mrs. Nuttall regarded with complacency his efforts to recover his breath. His punishment was just.

"A dear good girl," repeated the lady, with emphasis, when Nicholas's struggles had subsided. "And I shouldn't wonder if she mightn't look as high as a lord, or even a marquis."

"I shouldn't wonder either, Maria," said Nicholas, profoundly stupified by his wife's words. "I have often looked as high myself."

"The coffee has surely got into your head, Mr. Nuttall," observed Mrs. Nuttall, with a look of supreme contempt.

"I must have coughed it up, I suppose, my dear," said Nicholas, jocularly; he was fond of his joke, and enjoyed it even when Mrs. Nuttall's freezing influence was upon him. "Don't be alarmed, Maria. It will settle down eventually."

"Your coarse wit is beneath contempt," exclaimed Mrs. Nuttall, severely, "and is cruelly out of place when the happiness of our only child is concerned."

"Upon my soul, I haven't the slightest idea what you mean, Maria."

"Then I shall not explain, sir," said Mrs. Nuttall, rising with dignity, and walking away.

Nicholas, perfectly satisfied at being deprived of her company, disposed himself for a nap. Clearly, Mr. Nicholas Nuttall was not a model for husbands.

In the meantime, Grif and Little Peter had not moved from where they had at first seated themselves, under the shadow of the hawthorn hedge. Their conversation had not been very animated. Once, Grif had asked Little Peter if he was hungry, and Little Peter had answered, Yes. And then Grif had unconsciously constituted himself a committee of ways and means, and found that he was totally unable to vote the supplies. Time was when, Little Peter being hungry, Grif would issue forth and prowl about and beg, or steal perhaps; at all events, he would seldom return to Little Peter without food, obtained somehow or other. He could not do that now; he had taken the pledge of honesty; he had renounced vagrancy, and he was helpless. Glancing at Little Peter every now and then, he began to be perplexed with an entirely new consideration. It was this. Little Peter was hungry. Grif had only one means open of obtaining food. Supposing he was unfortunate the next day, and was unable to supply Little Peter's stomach, what was to be done? Here was a great difficulty; and looking it steadily in the face, it dawned grimly upon Grif's mind that Little Peter was a serious responsibility.

Engaged in the contemplation of this subject, Grif became suddenly aware of the approach of two long shadows, and looking up, saw Matthew Nuttall and Marian. Although the day was waning fast, he recognised Alice's father on the instant. Their eyes met, and Matthew stopped. Marian, whose hand was resting lightly on her uncle's arm, looked at the two lads with compassion.

"You are the boy who came to Mr. Blemish's office for a situation one day when I was there," said Matthew Nuttall in a tone of inquiry.

Grif looked an affirmative. He did not dare to trust himself to speak just yet.

"And Mr. Blemish kindly gave you one," said Matthew.

Grif looked another affirmative.

"Are you doing well?"

"No, sir," Grif found voice to reply.

"He looks very miserable, uncle," said Marian, in a half whisper; "and see that other little boy there. Is he asleep?"

"No, miss; he is hungry," Grif had to check a rising sob as he said this. "Look up, Little Peter."

Little Peter looked up with his large pleading eyes, and then turned his face to the ground again.

"He seems ill, uncle," whispered Marian. "Shall I run to the house, and bring him something to eat?"

"Hush! my dear," said Matthew Nuttall, taking the girl's hand in his. The little bit of womanly sympathy reminded him of his daughter, who never allowed a poor man to go hungry from Highlay Station. "Wait a moment. Is he your brother?" This to Grif.

"No, sir."

"Any relation?"

"Not as I knows on."

"Why are you two together?"

"I takes care on him," said Grif; "but I don't know what to do now. I ain't got nothin' to give him to eat."

"Oh, uncle!" cried Marian.

But he did not release her hand.

"Where is his mother and father?"

"Got none."

"And yours?"

"Got none." Grif told the lie readily enough. He was ashamed of his father, and did not want to be questioned about him.

"What have you earned to-day?"

"Nothin'."

"And have you had nothing to eat?"

"Not since this mornin'."

"How am I to know that you are telling the truth?"

The tears came to Grif's eyes. He would have given a saucy independent answer, but the thought of Little Peter restrained him. He did the best thing he could. He was silent.

"And you have no money?"

Grif turned out his pockets. Every one of them was full of holes. He had answered Matthew Nuttall's questions quietly and sadly, not in that reckless defiant manner which Matthew remembered he had used in Mr. Blemish's office. This itself pleaded for him. The stern man of the world knew genuine suffering when he saw it before him. The very hopelessness which spoke out of Grif's voice was in the lad's favour. He felt a desire to befriend Grif. But there were more questions to ask before he determined.

"When you applied to Mr. Blemish for a situation, you said you had given a promise to a lady. What was your promise?"

"I promised to be honest," answered Grif, wondering whether Matthew Nuttall had any suspicion who the lady was.

"And you have kept your promise?"

"Yes."

"Why do you not go to the lady now you are hungry, and ask her for assistance?"

"I don't like to," said Grif. "Somethin' pulls me back. She's hardly got enough for herself, I think. She'd give it me out of her own mouth, she would. She's poor--but she's good, mind! I never knowed any one so good as her! And I'd lay down my life for her this minute if she wanted me to!" He burned to tell who she was; he forgot his own cause when he spoke of her. Ah! if he could make her happy! But some feeling restrained him--some fear that he might make matters worse for Alice if her father knew that she was a friend and companion to him, who was no better than a thief.

"He speaks the truth, uncle, I am sure," said Marian.

"And so am I, my dear." He considered how he could best assist them. "You lead a hard life," he presently said.

"I don't care for myself," Grif said; "only for Little Peter."

"Well, I will send you and Little Peter on to one of my Stations, if you like, where you can learn to make yourself useful, and where at all events you will have enough to eat and drink. Anything else will depend upon yourself. What do you say?"

Grif's mind was made up in an instant. For Little Peter--yes. For himself--no. He could not leave Alice. He would starve sooner.

"Will you take Little Peter, sir, and not me?" he asked, in a trembling voice. "I can't leave this, sir. I've made a promise, and daren't break it. The lady who's been kind to me might want me, and I mustn't be away. I shan't like to part with Little Peter, sir, but it'll be for his good. He's often hungry when I've got nothin' to give him to eat. I ain't give him anythin' to-day, and p'rhaps shan't be able to to-morrow. Don't say no, sir! Take Little Peter, and not me, and I'll do anythin'--anythin' but go away from where she is." And Grif burst into a passion of tears, and stood imploringly before Alice's father.

He turned to his niece, and she caught his hand and pressed it to her lips. He needed no stronger appeal in his then softening mood.

"It shall be as you ask," he said. "Little Peter, as you call him, shall go with us now."

Grif lifted Little Peter to his feet. "This gentleman's going to take care of you, Peter," he said. "You'll never be hungry no more." Little Peter opened his eyes very wide. "You're to go with the gentleman," Grif continued, "and he'll give you plenty to eat and drink. You are not sorry to part with me, are you?"

"No," replied Little Peter, with perfect sincerity.

A keen pang of disappointment caused Grif to press his nails into his hands; he threw a troubled look at Little Peter, but he soon recovered himself, and taking the child's wasted hand, he said tenderly, "Good bye, Little Peter."

"Good bye," said Little Peter, without the slightest show of feeling.

A big lump rose in Grif's throat as he stooped to kiss the lad. He touched his ragged cap when Matthew Nuttall gave him a piece of silver.

"Thank you, sir," he said. "You'll take care on him?"

Matthew Nuttall nodded, and the three walked away. So Grif and Little Peter parted. Grif gazed after the lad, but Little Peter did not turn his head to give his more than brother one parting look of affection. "Never mind," Grif thought, with a heavy sigh; "he'll never be hungry no more." He sat upon the ground, and watched them till they were out of sight. He was alone now. Rough was dead, and Little Peter was gone, for ever. How lonely everything seemed! But there was comfort in the thought that Little Peter was provided for, and would always have his grub and a blanket. And with that reflection to console him, Grif laid him down beneath the hawthorn hedge, and went to sleep with the stars shining upon him.

CHAPTER XV
A HOT DAY IN MELBOURNE

A hot, scorching day. The winds having travelled, over hundreds of miles of arid plain and smoking bush, floated into Melbourne, laden with blazing heat. The sky glared down whitely, and the blinding sun scorched up moisture and vegetation with its eye of fire. The very clouds where white with heat, and to look up at them made one dizzy. In the city, mankind panted with thirst and fatigue, and, regardless of consequences, revelled, inordinately and greedily, in ices and cool drinks. Womankind retreated to cellars and shady nooks, and, divested of superfluous attire, indulged, gratefully, in water-melons; and mankind, coming home wearied and parched, joined womankind in her retreat, and lay at her feet, tamely. Dogkind panted, and lolled out its tongue, distressfully; but though it wandered in despair through the streets, it found no relieving moisture in kennel or gutter; and being, by its constitution and laws, debarred from the luxury of ices and cool drinks, it endured agonies of silent suffering. Clerks fell asleep over their ledgers, and storekeepers grew dozy behind their desks. At the sea-side the very waves were too wearied to roll, and lay, supine, beneath the dreadful glare of the sun. The beaches were deserted: not even a crab was to be seen. In the country, the bush smoked and blazed, and wretched oxen strained at their chains, and did their half-a-mile an hour in dire distress. With suffering noses almost touching the ground, they smelt in vain along the earth for liquid life. The drivers with their cabbage-tree hats slouched over their eyes, were too lazy to crack their whips, and too fatigued to swear loudly at their cattle; but, determined not to be cheated of their privilege, they growled and cursed in voices almost inaudible. The leafless trees smoked beneath the glare of the sun, and stretched their bare branches to the sky as if for pity, but got none. On the goldfields, diggers stripped to their shirts, and were glad to hide themselves at the bottom of deep pits, with bottles of lager beer or cold tea by their side; those who could find no such shelter threw themselves upon their rough beds, and longed eagerly for the night. Everywhere, business, except where bare-armed men or muslin-clad barmaids served long drinks to thirsty souls, was at a standstill. Merchants were too lazy to haggle. Percentages were forgotten, and invoices disregarded. Even Zachariah Blemish, dressed in white linen from the top of his head to the sole of his foot, and looking, with his rubicund face, like a white and pink saint, ready and fit to fly heavenward, lolled idly in his sanctum, and refreshed himself with hock and seltzer water. The conjugal Nuttalls were in the deepest misery. The head of the family, Nicholas Nuttall, was in his dressing-room, pouring jugfuls of cold water over his head, as if he were afraid of its taking fire: and, directing his eyes to the bed, beheld thereupon the partner of his bosom, whose face was puffed up with mosquito bites, and who, glaring reproachfully at her husband, said as plainly as eloquent looks could speak, Fiend! behold your handiwork! Walls and pavement were smoking; and all nature, excepting the flies and the fishes, was in a state of misery. The blazing wind was comparable to nothing but the blast from a fiercely-heated furnace, and high and low succumbed to its power.

High and low! Ay, even down to Old Flick, who, in the back-room of his All-Sorts Store, in Old Flick's Thoroughfare, gasped, and growled, and cursed, as he drank his rum-and-water. Old Flick was attired in shirt, trousers, and slippers. Nothing more. His shirt was open at the bosom, thereby displaying a sinewy chest, covered with dirty gray hair; and was tucked up to the shoulders, showing his lean and bony arms. He was not a pleasant object to look upon, with his straggling hair, and his blotched face, and his bloodshot bleary eyes. One might have wondered while looking upon him, Was this man ever a child, and was he ever blessed with a mother's love? One might have so wondered, and, doubting, might have been pardoned for the doubt. For indeed he looked terribly sinful and depraved: a very blot upon humanity. Sitting and drinking and growling, he became conscious of a shadow before him, and looking up and seeing the girl Milly, who had just entered the room, he made a motion as if he would like to spring upon her. She, too, was not pleasant to look upon; for she also had been drinking, and her eyes were bloodshot. Her hair was hanging loosely about her face, and she had a reckless and defiant manner which almost unwomanised her.

"What do you want?" growled Old Flick.

She did not answer him for many moments. She had come there for a purpose, and she knew she was not fit for it, and that she was no match for the crafty man who sat before her. Milly's condition was very pitiable. She depended upon Jim Pizey for support, and she had not received a line from him since his departure from Melbourne. He had left her without wishing her good-bye, but he had sent her a message that Old Flick would give her money when she required it. Depending upon this, when she wanted funds she had applied to the old man, but getting a few shillings from him was like squeezing life's blood from his heart. The process was such a sickening one to Milly, that she had lately but seldom attempted it. He had so wearied her with his whining protestations, that she had not applied to him for assistance for a long time; but now necessity was driving her hard. There was another reason besides the want of money, which induced Milly to visit Old Flick at the present time. He had, she knew, received a letter from Jim, and she wanted to read it. You see, Jim was the only rock the poor girl had to cling to.

As for Old Flick, the sight of Milly was torture to him. He thought he had got rid of her for good, and here she was to torment him again. He knew what she wanted well enough--money, money, always money! But he would not give her a doit--not a doit! He did not think that part of Milly's purpose was to get Jim's letter; he was not aware that she know he had received one. His tribulation would have been sore indeed had he suspected that; for there was something in the letter about Milly which would be enough to drive her mad. "I wish she would die!" he muttered, inly. "What's the use of her? Why don't she die?" If he could, he would have killed her with a look.

"What do you want?" he growled again.

She seized the bottle from the table, and placed it to her lips. Old Flick did not attempt to restrain her. Indeed, he was frightened of her.

"I want money!" Milly exclaimed, with a kind of drunken scream.

"The old cry!" he screamed, in return.

"Yes, the old cry. You thought you weren't going to hear it again, eh! I want money!"

"I haven't any."

"Lies! You're rolling in it. You've enough to fill your grave. I want money."

"You're a pretty article to want money," said Old Flick, with a sneer. "Go and earn it."

"Don't say that again, Flick," said the girl, with a threatening flash in her eyes, "or I'll tear your liver out! Oh, I don't care for your looks! What do you think I've got in me to-day?"

"I don't know, and I don't care," he replied.

"I've got the devil in me!" she cried. "Mind how you let it loose. I feel it here--here!" and she drew her hand, with a nervous twitching of the fingers, across her forehead. "I try to deaden it to sleep with drink, but it won't rest. It dances in my brain, and laughs at me through my eyes! Oh! you're frightened at my talk, are you? What wonder! I'm frightened at it myself."

"You want rest, Milly," the old man said, with a sort of lame compassion in his voice.

"Rest!" she echoed, bitterly. "What rest can I expect or do I deserve? What did I come here for?" she asked herself, in a confused, wandering manner. "I came here to ask you for something, Flick. Not money alone; no, no! something else. I have it!" she steadied herself in an instant. "The letter!"

"The letter!" he repeated, his face turning ashen white.

"The letter!" she reiterated. "The one you received from Jim Pizey yesterday. You have a lie ready! I see it trembling on your lips. Send it back, and mind it don't choke you! Where's the letter?"

"I haven't it."

"Where's the letter?"

"I've burnt it."

"You are a liar!" she said, quietly, looking steadily at him.

"You're drunk!" he cried, in a voice thick with passion, "If you don't go away I'll set the police on you."

"Do!" she replied, laughing scornfully, "and I'll tell them who you are in league with. Who do you think they will believe? You or me? You'll set the peelers on me, will you? You worn-out parcel of bones, it's more than your soul's worth--though that's not worth much. I'll tell them that you are in league with two of the biggest scoundrels in the colony. And I'll prove it too. You shall go out of here into quod, and out of quod into hell, Old Flick! You'll set the peelers on me, will you? Shall I call 'em in?" and she moved towards the door.

He threw one of his evil looks upon her, and, in his shaking voice, told her to stay where she was.

"Give me some drink," exclaimed Milly, taking the bottle as she spoke, and drinking from it again. "Do you know what I am going to do, Flick?" she asked, her mood suddenly changing. "I'm going to kill myself with drink."

"All the better," he growled.

"Right you are!" she returned, recklessly. "I'm tired of my life. It's time I was dead! Look here, Flick; if you don't tell me where Jim is, I'll set the place about your ears."

"I don't know," he whined; "how should I know? What's the use of asking me where he is? I know nothing about him. He wrote me a letter, but you don't think he put his address in it, do you? You ought to know him better than that, Milly!"

"You miserable gray-head, ain't you afraid that your lies will choke you? Ain't you afraid of dying? What an old sinner you are! Do you ever think of the worms creeping over your ugly carcase, and gloating over you when you are in your grave? Do you ever think of the cold slimy earth falling on your face through the coffin, and sucking all the hope out of you, even after you are dead? Ain't you afraid when you think of it? I am! I am!" she exclaimed, with a shuddering shriek; "or I should have killed myself long ago!"

The drunken old man's face twitched with terror as she spoke these dreadful words, and he whined piteously, "Don't, Milly, there's a good girl. Talk of something pleasant."

"I haven't the courage to do it," she continued, in a musing tone, not heeding his remonstrance. "I have thought of it often--have dreamt of it often. I have woke up in the night and seen it looking at me, from the foot of the bed--my thought that seemed to be all eyes, and no shape. It speaks to me, and I can never hear it; it clings about me, and I can never feel it. It takes me through the dark streets to the water side, and I look down and see the stars bidding me come--I see the shadows of the trees moving about at the bottom--and then and then," she said, shudderingly, "I see myself lying in the mud, and things crawling over me--and I run away, I run away!"

Old Flick moved nearer to the wall, and regarded her with cowardly fear.

"If I wasn't afraid of that," she continued, "I should have been out of the world long before now. I bought some poison one day, and was very near taking it. But I got such a fit of shaking all at once, that I threw it on the floor, and stamped on it, and ran away, mad with fright. Did you ever try to take poison, Flick? Pour it in a glass, and look at it for a moment, and you see a lot of devils glaring at you and clutching at you, and you feel a lot of creeping things dancing in your brain, and stirring in your hair, and tingling at your fingers' ends!"

Old Flick shook with fear now, and not with ague. "Don't talk like that, Milly," he cried again, looking fearsomely about him; "do talk of something pleasant."

"Something pleasant!" Milly exclaimed. "What have I got pleasant to talk about? I wish the sun would burst through the ceiling, and strike me dead, and so put an end to it!" and she threw her hair from her face, and looked up wildly. "Do you know, Flick, I think something is going to happen to me! My head is whirling about strangely. I've an old father and mother at home, and I've been thinking of them at odd times, all the day. Father is an old man--a basket-maker--and I can see him as plainly as I see you, sitting down in our little room, weaving the canes, and thinking of me. Yes, I can see him thinking of me. He used to stroke my hair and my face, and call me his pretty Milly. Pretty Milly! That's what they called me at home. I *was* pretty--I had the prettiest hands!"--she put them close to her eyes, with a caressing motion, and hid her face in them. "I can see father with my eyes shut. He weaves the canes in the back room, sitting by the window. There is the little garden outside, and the two pots of mignonette on the window-sill. And there's the speckled hen that used to eat out of my hand. There is the picture of me on the wall, over the mantel-shelf, with my hair all in curls. Father is smiling at it. And now--now it is raining, and what do you think he is doing? He is looking at me, and crying, and I am lying dead in a basket cradle, with flowers all about me!" (She stood silent for a little while, with her face still buried in her hands, as if she could see the picture she had described.) "He was too fond of me, father was; he was so fond of me that he didn't look after me properly; he used to let me do as I liked."

"Why don't you go home to him?" asked Old Flick, in a voice which he strove to make gentle.

"Home!" she exclaimed. "Home! As I am! What would they say of me, I wonder? No; thank God, they think me dead. But there! I don't want to think of them, and they still keep coming up;" and she passed her hands over her face, confusedly.

"What's the matter, Milly?" Old Flick said, soothingly. "What's made you like this?"

"Drink!" she cried. "Drink and thought. And the more I think, the more my head is filled with awful fancies. Why did Jim go away from me? What right had he to leave me alone by myself?" and here she began to cry. But, seeing that Flick was about to speak, she said, "Stop a minute. I haven't done yet. I must work myself out first, and then I shall be all right. How long is it since you were a boy, Flick?"

"I don't remember," he muttered.

"What happiness! Not to be able to remember! But if you could remember, you would have to go a long way back, Flick; you're old enough to be my grandfather. It isn't so long ago since I was a little girl, and I can't help remembering. Oh, if I could forget! if I could forget!" And throwing herself upon the ground, she sighed, and trembled, and sobbed; and then, as if angry with herself, she bit her white lips, and tried to suppress her passion.

"Now, then, you are more quiet," said Old Flick, after a little while. "Get up, Milly, like a good girl, and go home."

"I'm not a good girl--I'm a bad woman; and," she said, folding her arms resolutely, "I'm not going to stir until you give me what I want, and tell me what I want to know."

"I haven't any money, Milly," whined Old Flick, "and I can't tell you anything you don't know."

"Didn't Jim say, before he left, that you were to give me money when I wanted it?"

"Yes, but he hasn't sent me any, and I have no more to give. I'm a poor man, Milly."

"What was in that letter Jim sent you?"

"That letter?" exclaimed Old Flick, almost instinctively putting his hand to the pocket in which it was hidden.

"Yes, that letter," repeated Milly, her quick eyes noting the old man's action.

"There was nothing in it, Milly, upon my--my honour, and I burnt it."

"All right," Milly said, quietly, rising. "I suppose there was nothing in it, as you say, for you never tell a lie; and I suppose you burnt it, for you never tell a lie; and I suppose you haven't got any money, for you never tell a lie. That's right, ain't it?"

"Yes, that's right," he exclaimed, sullenly.

"And you can tell me what's to become of Jim's baby--for it is Jim's, you know. How am I to keep it?"

"How do I know what's to become of it?"

"I'll kill it," Milly said, composedly.

"Milly!" cried Old Flick, catching her arm.

"Let me go! You don't think I meant it, do you? I haven't come to that yet. No, I won't kill it. I'll do something better," and without another word, Milly walked away.

"A good job she's gone," muttered Old Flick. "I must tell Jim about her. She's getting mischievous. If she had known I had that letter about me, she would have torn it from me, I believe. The cat! Does she know there is anything in the letter about her? No, she can't; she only suspects. I must read it once more, and destroy it. It implicates the whole gang; I must burn it--burn it. What a turn she gave me when she talked about killing the baby! I am glad she's gone;" and, in self-gratulation, Old Flick drank some more rum-and-water, and, raising his eyes, exclaimed--"The devil take the cat! Here she is again!"

And there she was again, sure enough, with her baby in her arms.

"Now then, Old Flick," she said, "I've got rid of all my fancies. When Jim went away, he told me you would give me money as I wanted it, so long as I didn't ask for too much. I haven't asked for too much, have I? You precious old flint, you've taken good care of that. You've screwed me down so tight that I've been obliged to pawn every blessed thing I could lay hands on; and I haven't a shilling left, and haven't anything more to pawn."

"You've plenty of money to get drunk with, anyhow."

"The drink was treated to me. People will give me lush, but they won't give me bread. Can you tell me how I am to keep Jim's baby?"

"How do I know? I suppose you can get your own living."

She gave him another of her threatening looks, and then she asked--

"Are you going to give me some money?"

"I haven't any."

"Very well. I love my baby; let alone that it's mine, it is a pretty little thing. Of course you can't understand how it is a bad girl like me can love an innocent pet like this; but then you never loved anything in your life, and can't be supposed to understand my feeling. I love it dearly, but as I can't keep Jim's baby, and as you are in partnership with Jim, you'd better keep it yourself;" and she laid the baby on the table, where it sprawled contentedly amongst the bottles and glasses.

"What do you mean?" demanded Old Flick, it considerable alarm.

"What do I mean? Just this--I'm going to leave the baby here. You'll have to feed it and wash it. It will be a nice companion for you, and you can bring it up your own way. What a blessed father you'll make!"

"Are you mad?" cried Old Flick, with a rueful look at the baby.

"Not a bit of it. I've often thought what a pity it is you haven't got a lot of young Flicks of your own. Never mind. Here's one you can try your hand upon."

"Take the brat away!"

"Will you give me some money?"

"No!" he snarled.

"Then here's your baby!" Milly said; and taking the child from the table, she placed it dexterously in Old Flick's arms, and moved towards the door.

"Come back, you jade!" roared Old Flick, looking disgustedly at his burden. "Come back, and I'll give you what you want."

"How much now?" asked Milly, with a laugh, standing by the half-open door.

Old Flick fumbled in his pockets, and, with much difficulty, produced three half-crowns.

"Seven-and-six," he said.

"Baby will cost you more than that the first week," said Milly. "Then, how am I to live? 'Tain't half enough.

"I haven't another shilling in the world!" cried Old Flick, tearing at his gray locks in a delirium of drunken despair. "You'll ruin me, you jade!"

"Say two pounds," suggested Milly, regardless of his appeal; "and out with it quick, or I'm off. Now, then, before I count three. One--"

"Milly, dear, say a pound," implored Old Flick.

"Two--"

"Thirty bob!" screamed Old Flick, in anguish.

"Three. I'm off."

"Stop, stop!" roared Old Flick; "here's the money, and I wish you'd kill yourself with it."

"And what did Jim say about me in the letter?" asked Milly, coming back.

"Not a word," said Flick, pretending to consider, as he counted out a pound's worth of silver. "Oh, yes, he did; he sent his love to you. You'll find that right, Milly."

"All right," said Milly, pocketing the money carelessly. "You know, Flick, if you'd like to keep the baby--"

"Take it away--take it away!" cried Old Flick; "and curse you, the pair of you," he added, in an undertone.

"You fool!" exclaimed Milly, scornfully, as she took the baby in her arms, and kissed her. "You gray-headed, cold-hearted, old fool! Did you think for a moment that I would leave this angel from heaven here, for you to contaminate with your filthy breath! Did you think it, old sinner? You might have saved your money, if you weren't a coward as well as a thief. And so you've burnt the letter, eh, Flick!"

"Yes, yes," said Old Flick, as Milly walked away with the child, "it is burnt, sure enough. Phew! what with her, and what with the heat, I'm melting away. How cantankerous she was about the letter! She'd have gone mad if she'd seen it. I must burn it; it isn't safe to keep; but I must copy the address first."

His shaking hand sought his pocket, and drew therefrom the letter. He opened it, and read it again by fits and starts, muttering the while. But when he tried to copy the address, his fingers trembled so that he could not trace the letters.

"I'll wait till the evening, when if s cool," he said, returning the letter to his pocket, "when it's cool. The devil take the sun! It's enough to scorch one to a cinder!"

As a counteractive, Old Flick applied himself industriously to his rum-and-water, which he swallowed with a running accompaniment of oaths and curses. Now, as too much rum-and-water will make a man drunk, and as Old Flick had drunk a great deal too much rum-and-water, and still continued drinking it, he soon got very drunk indeed--so drunk, that he began to cry, and to beat his breast, and to tear his hair, and to shake so, that the table trembled when he leant upon it.

"To scorch one to a cinder," he mumbled, pursuing his previous remark. "Supposing it should come, and scorch me to a cinder!"

He held up his hands, as if to ward off a blow, and as he looked about him, his fevered fancy conjured a thousand crawling things upon the ceiling and the walls. With sight-terror fixed he gazed at them as they crept nearer and nearer to him. As fast as he brushed them away, they came again. In desperation he drank more rum, and strove to rid himself of the terrible fancies.

"Go away--go away," he cried, menacing them with impotent fingers; "I know what it is. I've been drinking too much. I must leave it off, or I shall have the deliriums." To strengthen his good resolution he applied himself again to the bottle. "I'm better now. What a cat that Milly is! Beast--beast--beast! Why don't she die? What good is she in the world? She wished to frighten me by asking me if I had ever tried to take poison. What did she mean by 'the devils in the glass?' Ugh! I can see them glaring at me!"--and Old Flick staggered to his feet in dire terror, and then dropped down in a drunken swoon.

It was late in the afternoon now, and people began to breathe more freely. A slight but refreshing breeze set in from the sea, and the cooler air, floating through the streets, brought a sweet relief to exhausted nature. To no person did the grateful change bring more satisfaction than to Grif, whose sufferings during the day had caused him to fret exceedingly. The whole of that day, as he stood blistering in the sun, he had been propounding questions to himself--questions to which he could find only one answer, dictated by hunger and misery. Why was he so unfortunate? All other boys were not so. He was trying hard to be good, and something would not let him. He felt that his requirements were modest, that he did not ask for too much. The constant pressure of misery had caused him to look about him and compare his condition with that of other boys. There were plenty of them walking the streets--well-fed, well-dressed boys; not sons of gentlemen, but working boys--boys occupying the social sphere to which he aspired. What had he done that his lot should not be as comfortable as theirs appeared to be? He was sure he was trying hard enough to deserve it. "I've been bad, I know," he reflected, "but I can't make out as it was all my fault. I couldn't help it. There's father, he was bad, and in course I was bad too; I didn't know nothin' else. Then Ally come, and she made me good--leastways, she tried to. But what's the good of bein' good? I usen't to be 'arf so hungry when I was bad!" This was the argument which clenched the matter. When he was bad, his stomach was better supplied, as a rule, than now that he was good.

Not only was Grif's mind argumentative, but his nature was sensitive. How this came about was strange, for his father's nature was brutal enough; he did not remember his mother, and had never given her a thought. His sensitiveness was a positive misfortune; it intensified his sufferings just now. What with the awful heat, which made his heart faint and sick, the hunger which gnawed at his vitals, and the sorrow he felt at being parted for ever from Little Peter, his condition was an utterly miserable one. He could not battle against such influences; they were too powerful for him. He felt an irresistible conviction that he should never see Little Peter again. "I wonder if he ever thinks of me?" Grif mused; and in his then despondent mood he groaned at the thought that all remembrance of him was wiped out of Little Peter's mind. "No matter, it was all for his good. He's a precious sight better off where he is, I'll be bound. I suppose he's got good clothes and good boots, and plenty of grub. That's jolly for him, poor Little Peter! If he was here to-day, it'd pretty well settle him, I think." There was some small consolation in this reflection, and Grif tried to make the most of it.

From this it will be perceived how unfortunate Grif had been in his new vocation. Honesty and morality had not taken to him kindly. As a moral shoeblack, his career had been the very reverse of prosperous, notwithstanding that he had striven to deserve better. He had attended some meetings of the Moral Bootblacking Boys' Reformatory, and had heard a great deal about morality; and, albeit he would have been considerably perplexed if he had been asked to define the meaning of the word, it could not but be presumed that he had been much edified by the moral essays and exhortations to which he had listened. And yet his mental condition, when he came away from those meetings, was one of perplexity. He could not see the connection between morality and a bellyful of food. "It's all very well," he would mutter, "for them coves who's got lots to eat and drink to talk about morality; but what good does it do me?" Exhortations, moral lessons, pious sermons, would often be given by well-meaning men at the meetings of the Moral Bootblacking Boys' Reformatory. At one of these meetings, the speaker had fixed Grif with his eye during the whole of his discourse, which occupied nearly an hour. The burden of his exhortation was an oppressive beseeching to Grif to "look up." By day and by night, awake or asleep, standing still or walking, always through his life, Grif was entreated to "look up." Never mind how persistent misfortune might be in persecuting him, never mind what calamities might overtake him, everything would come right if he would continue to "look up." "But how *can* I do that," Grif asked of himself, "when I'm forced to be always lookin' down?" whereby he meant, literally, looking down at the boots of the passers-by to see if they wanted polishing. Which coarse perversion of the pious speaker's exhortation was another proof of the baseness of Grif's nature.

Many such sermons did Grif hear; they sounded well, all of them. But they shrank into very nothingness when he applied them to his own case. To him they were nothing; they did him no good. Grif wanted practical arguments. Theory was valueless to him. As for good advice he had enough of that, goodness knows. He received it by the bushel; it was literally heaped upon him. But he did not get an ounce of meat out of it for all its virtue. He was an especial object of attention to Mr. Zachariah Blemish. That great man and princely merchant had at various times condescended to be gracious to Grif by word of mouth. Mr. Blemish would inquire of Grif how he was getting along, and Grif did not have courage to answer that he was getting along badly, or rather that he was not getting along at all. It would have sounded like an impeachment of the conduct of the great man in providing him with the implements of his occupation. "That is right--that is right," Mr. Blemish would remark. "You are moral, are you not?" "Very moral, Sir," Grif would answer, humbly. "Very good; mind you keep moral," Mr. Blemish would exhort. And Grif invariably ducked his head and promised that he would keep very moral. But when the great merchant was gone, Grif would shrug his shoulders, and ponder and puzzle over the good advice given him without arriving at any satisfactory conclusion.

Occasionally he visited Alice, and argued matters with her. Alice truly was his good angel. Many and many a time had they two sat together, he listening to her gentle voice, she striving to impress upon him truths which would have seemed to him the bitterest of lies if he had judged them by the light of his hard experience. But Grif did not interpret her words by that light. If he did not understand, he believed; his nature did not rebel against her sweet words and gentle voice as it did against the sermons preached at the Moral Reformatory. What Alice said to him was good, was true, and he was satisfied. It was happiness to hear her, to sit near her, to look up into her face now and then: it was more than happiness, it was heaven. With such an influence upon him, Grif could not be otherwise than good. She kept him from crime. Bad promptings had no chance with him when he thought of her. Ill as she could afford it, poor girl, she fed him often, although every day her means grew less and less, and although Hunger, with its white eyes and despairing face, crept nearer and nearer at every turn of the hour-glass. All she could do was to wait for it, and shudder at its near approach. The first few weeks after her husband left her, she had heard regularly from him, and had received long letters filled with love, and tenderness, and hope. And she would read them again and again, and cry for joy over them, and press them to her lips, to her heart, and place them under her pillow at night. Many a happy dream did they bring her, and she would rise in the morning with a light heart, hopeful and smiling. But lately his letters had become shorter and shorter, and the intervals between them longer. And now three weeks had passed, and she had received no letter. Three or four times every day she went to the post-office, until her face became so familiar to the clerk that, directly he saw it looking almost beseechingly through the little window, he would shake his head without waiting for her to speak. How hurriedly she would throw on her bonnet and shawl, and hasten to the little window, and how sadly and slowly she would walk back to her poor lodgings, heartsore and disappointed! That little window! It might have been likened unto heaven's gate, or the gate of despair. Sometimes, when she reached it, panting, she lingered before she asked, as if fearful to have her hope destroyed. That would be mostly when there were no other applicants; but when there was a crowd round it, drawn thither by the arrival of an important mail, she would take her stand among them, and burn with impatience until her turn came. Then she would think it cruel that others had letters and she had none. Many of them had three, four, a dozen, and she not one! The pleased expressions upon the faces of women who opened their letters and read as they walked, made her feel as she ought not to have felt; and to drive away envious thoughts she would lower her veil, and soon could see nothing through her blinding tears. The last letter she had received from Richard was written in a very despondent mood, and that made her more anxious to hear from him. There are some men who cannot fight with the world--who cannot battle with misfortune. The first blow floors them, and they lie helpless, and make no effort to rise. There are others who, at every knock-down blow, jump up again, hurt but not killed, and who, to speak metaphorically, square up at misfortune with courage and vigour. Richard Handfield was one of the former, and because he did not find a rich patch of gold at the bottom of the first hole he sank, he whimpered at Fate, and did not care to try again. All that Alice could glean from his last letter was, that misfortune pursued him and mocked at his efforts. That was the way he expressed it; he chose to believe that the world had a special spite against him, and that he, of all the hundreds of thousands of soldiers who are fighting life's battles, was singled out for the victim. The fault, which was in himself, he laid upon fate; he was partial to the common platitude, "fate was against him." He was naturally indolent, and if he had known how to work he would scarcely have cared to do so. There are thousands of men of this type in the world.

Alice often fed Grif. But Grif was shrewd enough to perceive that Alice was daily more unable to spare him the food she pressed upon and forced him to eat. One evening, when he was in the midst of eating a thick slice of bread and butter which Alice had given him, he stopped suddenly, and, looking at her, was overcome with remorse at the thought that he was eating her meal. He could not eat any more; he placed the bread upon the table, and said, with his eyes filled with tears, that he was satisfied. From that day, he never tasted food in her room. Often when he was hungry, often, when he had stood about all the day patiently, without earning sixpence, he refrained from going to her, and crept, supperless, to sleep. At other times he waited until he knew Alice had finished her poor meal, and then, in answer to her inquiry as to whether he had had his tea, would say that he had had a jolly good tuck-out, and would make his mouth water by particularising what he had eaten.

On this afternoon Grif was particularly miserable. He had suffered much during the day from heat, and although he had plenty of cold water to drink, it must be admitted that that was but poor satisfaction to a hungry boy. He would have gone to his pie-shop, but the old woman had been gathered to her foremothers, and the pie-shop had passed into other hands. Grif had stood behind his boot-stand all the day broiling in the sun. No passer-by had been mad enough to stay blistering for a quarter of an hour in the heat, while his boots were being blackened. And, when evening came, it found Grif faint, and weary, and unhappy. The tears actually welled into his eyes as the sense of his forlorn condition came upon him. He could not stand it any longer! He looked round, with such a sense of desolation expressed in his face, that if any humane person had noticed it, it must have touched his heart with pity. He thought of the exhortations he had listened to, and of the good advice which had been heaped upon him. He thought of the promise he had given Mr. Blemish that he would continue to be moral. To break that promise would not pain Grif much; but there was the pledge he had given to Alice. He was about to be false to her. But he could not starve; she wouldn't ask him to do that, he knew. "No, she wouldn't arks me to do that," he muttered. "I'd die for her yes, this minute. If I went to her now, she would give me somethin' to eat--in course she would! But I *won't* go to her; I'll starve first! She stinted herself the other night, and didn't have enough to eat, because I was there. I know what I'll do. I'll go to Old Flick's, and sell my stand and brushes. He'll give me a bob for 'em, I dessay. Ally won't like it when she hears it, but I can't help it; I'm hungry."

Then the thought came upon him that, although he might have some right not to be moral if he pleased, he had no right to sell the stand and brushes. They were the property of the Reformatory. But he was stung to desperation, and he drove the thought from his mind.

"I don't care," he said recklessly. "I've been moral long enough. It ain't a bit of good! I ain't agoin' to starve any more. If they find it out, they can put me in quod agin, that's all. They'll give me my grab and a blanket there, at all events, and that's what I can't get here. I s'pose I am a bad lot, and I shall never be no good. How can I be good when I haven't got nothin' to eat?"

Asking this question of himself with much sternness, Grif put his stand and brushes under his arm, and wended his way towards Old Flick's Thoroughfare.

CHAPTER XVI
POOR MILLY

When Milly walked out of Old Flick's store, she walked out with the full determination of returning and possessing herself of the letter he had received from Jim Pizey, and which she was certain the old man had not destroyed. She had two reasons for her determination. One was a woman's reason--she had made up her mind to have it, and have it she would. A woman's logic is not always logical. The other reason was, that she was convinced there was something in the letter concerning herself. She did not stop to consider whether it would be good for her to read it; it was a letter from Jim; and read it she would. She felt hurt that he had sent her no word since his departure. There was nothing strange in her affection for him. She had no one else to love except her baby, and he was its father. He had deserted her, and still she clung to him. There is no human being in the world who is so complete an isolation as not to have a love for something; and the unfortunate class to which Milly belonged is no exception to this rule, for it is capable of strong, if misguided, affection.

To fortify herself for her task, Milly, after she had lolled her baby to sleep, adjourned to the bar of a public house, where she told how she had "done" Old Flick, and where she spent the greater portion of the two pounds in treating her associates to drink. Having soon made herself most thoroughly and desperately drunk, she set off staggering, but very earnest, towards Old Flick's All-sorts Store. Her mind was in a dangerous state of tension. She was almost blind from the fumes of the spirits she had taken, and everything swam before her; but she swung onwards, trolling out snatches of songs, and laughing and talking to herself incoherently. She did not attract much attention. A woman drunk was no novelty in that neighbourhood--indeed, her state was chronic to the locality; and she was allowed to proceed unmolested--some few people turning to look after her, but most avoiding her. She had not far to go, and when she arrived at her destination, she staggered in at the door, and sinking into a seat, gazed confusedly about her. Brushing her hair from her face, she looked round in vain for Old Flick.

"Now then, Flick," she said, almost inarticulately, "it's no use hiding away. Lord! how my head swims! Come out and give me the letter!"

She waited for an answer, but received none, for Old Flick was deep in his drunken swoon upon the floor.

"Are you coming out, old sinner?" she asked, looking vaguely about her. "I will have the letter--I will! I will! I will! You haven't burnt it. You're not half cunning enough; I saw your hand go to your pocket when you told me you'd burnt it. I'll tear your hair out of your head if you don't give it to me!"

She felt dizzy and confused, and seeing a bucket filled with water in the corner, she staggered instinctively towards it, and, tumbling down by its side, plunged her face into it. It was deliriously cool; she kept her face in it, until she almost lost her breath, and then raising the bucket, she poured the water over her head. It refreshed, if it did not sober her. A moment afterwards, as she seized her hair to wring the water from it, she shivered, and turned cold as ice; and then flashed into a burning heat. Wiping her face with her dress, Milly, for the first time, observed Old Flick lying upon the floor. Her eagerness to obtain possession of the letter appeared to desert her for a time. But presently she crept towards the prostrate man, and feeling in his pockets, found the letter. The old man murmured some almost incoherent words, among which she heard her own name. She laughed as she heard it, and said, "Oh, you old fox! Milly's done you, this time. Here's Jim's letter. What does he say in it?" She wiped her face again with her wet dress, and commenced to read the letter slowly. She read to herself until she came to the last page, when she cried, "What's this? 'After what you have told me about Milly, I never want to look at her face again. I didn't think she would turn informer against Jim Pizey. If ever I come across her, I'll mark her, by G--!'" She read these lines twice over, and then, letting her hands fall idly in her lap, looked before her, bewildered. "He never thought I would turn informer against him!" she exclaimed, a cold shuddering taking possession of her. "Oh, Lord! What's this feeling coming over me? Somebody's been telling lies to him about me. Who is it? Me split upon Jim! Who said so? She quite forgot the letter which she held tightly clutched in her hand. She threw the damp hair back from her forehead, and looked shudderingly round the room. Her skin was blazing, and there was an awful brilliancy in her eyes. She was burning hot, and she placed her hand upon her throbbing forehead, trying to press out the pain; in a little while her condition changed, and she sat still, shivering, and burst into a strange, wild laugh.

"What's the matter with me?" she murmured. "I never felt like this before. Get up, Old Flick!" she said, softly, to herself, and with no idea of addressing the old man. "Get up, Old Flick!"

She repeated the words almost in a whisper, twenty times at least, in a wondering kind of voice, and sang them over and over again, in a vacant manner.

"Oh, my head! my head!" she moaned, and then she commenced again singing softly to herself, her voice breaking occasionally into a kind of wail. She continued in this state for some time, and made no sign of recognition of Old Flick when, after a series of growls, he sat up on the floor. He gazed at her with stupified amazement, and he growled as he looked down at the pool of water in which he had been lying. As he raised his eyes, she caught his look, and introduced his name into the meaningless words she was singing.

"Milly!" he cried, half frightened; but she showed no consciousness of him. "She's going mad, I believe," he muttered. "Get up, Milly, there's a dear, and go home."

But she was deaf to all his entreaties, and presently she began to scream.

"There, Old Flick?" she cried. "Do you see the spiders creeping up the wall? There they go, creeping, creeping, creeping, and now they're on the ceiling, looking down upon us. Keep away--keep away!" she screamed, clutching at the old man, who, almost scared out of his senses, followed her gaze with fear. "They'll drop down upon us! That's right Jim. Crush 'm--smash 'em! Ugh! You can't kill 'em half quick enough. Do you see that big one leering down? That's Old Flick. Smash him, Jim. Ugh! keep off! They're dropping from the ceiling upon me!" and she writhed upon the floor, and plucked at her dress with her hands, and shuddered and moaned distressfully.

At this moment, Grif, with his boot-stand on his shoulder, and his brushes under his arm, entered the store. Receiving no answer to his taps upon the counter, he peeped into the back room, and saw Milly tearing madly at her dress, and Old Flick looking on helplessly, in an agony of terror.

"What's up?" inquired Grif.

Old Flick rose instantly, and he clung to Grif as though the lad were an anchor of hope.

"Don't grip so hard, Flick," cried Grif, who, being faint with hunger, scarcely had strength to shake the old man off.

"Milly's mad, I think," said Old Flick. "Take her home, Grif--take her home."

"How am I to take her home?" asked Grif, looking at Milly. She had covered her face with her hands, and was in a terrible fit of trembling. He went to her, and tried to remove her hands from her face, but he could not succeed. Then, glancing about him, he caught sight of a loaf of bread in the cupboard, the door of which was half open. There it was--the bread for which he was craving! His heart beat painfully as he saw it. Not even pity for the girl could overcome his natural sensations of hunger. The gnawing within was more powerful than pity. "What'll you give me if I take her away?" he inquired, eyeing the loaf yearningly.

"Anything--anything--that is, anything in reason," quavered Old Flick, qualifying his answer. "And if she ever darkens my door again," he muttered, "I'll have her dragged to the lock-up, as sure as my name's Flick."

Man is a bargaining animal. Despite his hunger, Grif pretended to consider for a few moments. He knew that if he exhibited too much eagerness, he would have less chance of obtaining the food.

"I'll take her away," he said slowly, "if you'll give me that loaf of bread"--and he moved wistfully towards the cupboard,--"and this tin of sardines--"

"Yes--yes," assented Old Flick, eagerly, taking the food from the cupboard.

"And five bob for this stand and set of brushes," concluded Grif, boldly.

"They're not yours," said the old man, all his cunning intellect on the alert directly the question of barter arose.

"Never you mind that," said Grif; "it's not the first time you bought what didn't belong to parties you bought 'em of. I won't take her away for less. I'm hungry now, and I shall be hungry to-morrow. I must have some tin."

"Take two and six, then, Grif," said Flick. "I'll give you two and six."

Grif shook his head.

"Say four bob," he said, "and it's a bargain."

Old Flick hastily produced four shillings, and gave them to Grif, who deposited on the table his vouchers to respectability, feeling, as he did so, that he had lost his character as a moral shoeblack, and was once more a vagrant and a thief. The next thing Grif did was to tear a piece out of the loaf and wolfishly devour it. Theoretical philanthropists might have learned a useful lesson if they had witnessed the ravenous eagerness with which Grif swallowed the stale dry bread. Old Flick was neither a theoretical nor a practical philanthropist, and he viewed the proceeding with a feeling of impatience, urging Grif to take Milly away quickly. It was not a difficult task--indeed, it was so easily accomplished, that Flick was filled with considerable remorse at the price he had paid for it. Milly's fit was over for a while, and she rose almost passively as Grif took her hand. She looked at Old Flick without recognising him; but she instinctively shrank from him.

"You've been frightenin' of her," Grif said to the old man. "I've a good mind to pitch into you."

Grif was stronger now, and having relapsed into vagrancy, felt himself at liberty to indulge his organ of combativeness. But Old Flick, in a quavering voice, protested that he had not been saying anything to Milly to frighten her.

"She looks as if she had been scared out of her life," Grif remarked.

"She's been drinking herself mad, Grif," Old Flick said, "that's what she's been doing. She'll be all right when she's had a good sleep."

Grif nodded his head, and led Milly away. She trembled violently as they walked to her poor lodgings; and when she got to her room, she threw herself upon the bed, and moaned and cried deliriously. She had placed the letter she stole from Old Flick in the bosom of her dress, and she kept her hand over it as if to guard it.

"She's orfle bad," mused Grif, seating himself on a stool at the foot of the bed, and employing himself with the bread and sardines. "I wonder if she knows me. Milly!"

The girl made no reply, and tossed about on the bed, sobbing piteously. Grif tried the experiment of placing her baby near her; but although he put the child into her arms, she did not notice it. She was so restless that he took the baby on his lap, and offered her a crust of bread, which, much to Grif's astonishment, she grasped with her little fists and sucked at vigorously, staring contentedly at Grif the while. But Milly's distress drew his attention from the study of baby.

"Milly!" he cried again, shaking her, and attempting to raise her. "Send I may live! if she ain't like a ball of fire! And she's all wet, too. What did you say, Milly? Say that agin."

"And they've got hold of Dick Handfield," she murmured. "Oh! what a wicked plot! If Grif knew--but I won't tell, no; though you do suspect me."

"If I knew!" exclaimed Grif. "If I knew what? She said somethin' about Dick Handfield! What does it all mean?"

He listened eagerly for her next words, which might give him a clue to her meaning, but Milly's fancies had changed.

"Go home!" she said. "Why don't I go home, he asked? What would they think of me? Don't come near me, father! Keep away; I'm not your Milly--she's dead, long ago--dead! dead! dead! Do you see that sheet of water?" and she half rose from the bed, and clutched Grif by the shoulder. "Father's standing on the other side. What an awful way off he is! He looks like a ghost. Does the water stretch into the next world, I wonder! There it is--miles, and miles, and miles of it. And look! just over the hill, where it flows out of the world, there's father and mother, and they're looking at me, and crying, and I am sinking down, down! I'm choking--take me out! take me out! Now I'm in my coffin. They are nailing the cover on me! Don't shut out the light; everything is black: now it's red. I can't breathe!" and she struggled madly with Grif, who was holding her down. It was as much as his strength could accomplish, and presently she grew calmer.

"I can't leave her like this," said Grif. "She's very ill, and she'll do herself a mischief, if she ain't took care on. She's quiet now. I'll run and fetch a doctor."

Acting on the impulse, Grif, first taking the baby from the bed, and placing it upon the floor in a corner of the room, ran quickly to an apothecary's shop hard-by. It happened fortunately that a doctor was in the shop at the time, giving some directions for a prescription. He listened to Grif's story, and, without a moment's hesitation, accompanied Grif to Milly's lodgings. He looked very grave as lie placed his hands upon Milly's burning forehead, and felt her pulse.

"How long has she been in this condition?" he asked.

Grif told him.

"Is she married? Umph! What a question! Of course she's not. Poor creature! So young, too, and pretty. Sad case! Sad case!"

He took his pocket book from his pocket and made a memorandum, and then observed, "If the poor girl has any friends, they should be here. She wants care and nursing, although even they will not save her, I fear. A female friend should be with her all the night. Come with me, boy, and I will give you medicine."

In silence, Grif followed the doctor to the apothecary's shop, and in silence he received the medicine which the doctor himself made up.

"You can read?" said the doctor.

"I know some of the letters," replied Grif, "when they're stuck upon the wall very large."

"Ah!" mused the doctor, looking attentively at Grif. "Give her a wineglassful of this medicine every hour; but don't wake her to give it, if she is sleeping quietly. I will call again in the morning to see how she is getting on."

"Is she very bad?" inquired Grif.

"Very," laconically replied the doctor

"Will she die?"

The doctor placed his hands upon Grif's shoulders, and noticed the boy's eyes luminous with tears. "Would you be sorry?" he asked.

"Yes, sir; very sorry."

"What are you--brother, cousin, any relation?" was the next question, carelessly asked.

"No, sir, not as I knows on; but she's been very kind to me."

"Don't stand chattering here!" the doctor exclaimed, abruptly. "Go and give the girl her medicine."

Grif was on the point of quitting the shop, when the thought occurred to him that the doctor ought to be paid. Taking from his pocket the four shillings for which he had sold his boot-stand and brushes, he placed them on the counter, immediately beneath the doctor's nose.

"What is this for, my lad?" asked the doctor.

Struck with a sense of the insufficiency of the remuneration, Grif said, apologetically, "I ain't got another mag about me, sir. I'll bring you some more when I gets it."

"Confound you, you young scamp!" exclaimed the doctor, in a fiery manner. "Do you think I have no humanity? Take your four shillings away, and here are ten more to add to them. Run off, and give the girl her medicine, and mind she has some one with her during the night;" and he pushed the boy hastily out of the shop.

When Grif returned to Milly, he found her still lying on the bed. He spoke to her, but she did not reply to him. He was the more alarmed at this because Milly was not asleep; her eyes were staring round the room, and her cheeks were burning with an unnatural fire. He moistened her parched lips with water, and tried to make her take the medicine, but she pushed him away, fretfully, and turned from him.

"What's to be done?" asked Grif of himself, in serious perplexity. "The doctor chap says she ought to have some one with her. He's a good sort, he is! I can't get her to take her physic." Then, struck with a sudden idea, he said, "I'll go and arks Ally."

Without another thought he hurried to Alice's lodgings. There was no need to entreat her help. Her bonnet and shawl were on before he had concluded his story.

"But she ain't a good girl, Ally," said Grif; "mind that!"

"God help her!" said Alice. "She is in the more need of assistance. And the poor baby, too! Come, Grif."

And very soon our Alice was in the sick girl's room, attending on her, and nursing her with a good woman's loving zeal. No thought of the difference in their social positions interfered with the performance of what Alice deemed to be a duty. She undressed Milly, and placed her in the bed; and, raising the poor girl's head on her bosom, she gave her the medicine, which Milly swallowed without resistance. Then Alice tidied up the room, and hushed the baby to sleep by the mother's side. She almost forgot her own grief in the sad spectacle before her, and the tears came to her eyes out of very pity, as she sat beside the sick girl's bed.

"Will you stop here all night, Ally?" asked Grif, who had retired from the room, and who now entered at a signal from Alice.

"Yes, until the doctor comes in the morning."

"She's a angel, that what she is," soliloquised Grif, retreating to a corner, and squatting himself upon the floor, "and I'm her friend. She said so herself. There never was anybody 'arf so good as her!"

When Alice was undressing Milly, she observed the letter which lay concealed in the bosom of Milly's dress; but, unconscious of all else, the sick girl clutched the paper tightly in her hand, and, seeing her desire to retain it, Alice made no effort to take it from her. Many hours passed, and still Alice sat patiently by Milly's side. During this time Milly was delirious, and raved and spoke words which caused Alice to shudder. But pity for the poor girl's condition overcame every repugnant feeling, and she nursed Milly tenderly and gently, as if she were, indeed, a good and virtuous, instead of an erring, sister. Shortly after midnight, the moon being nearly at its full, Milly turned her eyes to Alice's face, and asked in a weak wondering voice,--

"Who are you?"

"I am your friend, Milly," replied Alice. "Do you feel better?"

"Yes, I feel better." The words came from her lips slowly, and with an effort. "Give me your hand."

Alice placed her hand in Milly's, and the sick girl raised it to her lips, and to her forehead.

"Who sent you here?"

"No one. Grif told me you were ill, and I came to nurse you."

"I never saw you before. Good God!" Milly exclaimed, feeling Alice's wedding ring. "You are married!"

"Yes."

"And you come to nurse me! Do you know what I am?" and she raised herself in the bed, and her eyes dilated with horror as she looked round the walls of the room.

"Hush, my dear! Lie down."

"What is this?" Milly cried, seizing Alice by the arm, and trembling violently. "Everything is fading from my sight. Don't let me go! Hold me-- hold me! My heart is fainting--dying!" And a wild shriek issuing from her lips, as she fell back powerless on the bed, roused Grif from his slumber, and caused him to start to his feet.

A great change had come over Milly. Her face had grown pinched and white, her hands were clammy, and a wild despairing look in her eyes made them awful to look upon. Alice needed all her courage to keep herself from swooning.

"Has she any friends, Grif?" she asked.

"None as I knows on," replied Grif. "Don't you know who she is?"

He was about to answer his own question, and tell Alice of Jim Pizey, but just then Milly murmured the man's name.

"Why did you go away, Jim Pizey," she said, "and leave me to starve and drink myself to death? And then to write, you never want to see my face again. It is cruel--it is cruel! Look at me--I am dying, and you have killed me. I don't want to die! Lord help me, I'm not fit to die!"

"Grif," whispered Alice, "was not Jim Pizey the man who tempted my husband to crime?"

"Yes," answered Grif, "and before I came for you she was speaking of him."

"Of my husband, Richard?"

"Yes, but I couldn't make out what she meant."

Milly's wandering speech prevented the continuance of the subject.

"There's mother and father again," she said; "they're always haunting me. I am glad they have come to wish me good-bye, though. I have been a bad daughter to them--a bad daughter--a bad daughter. I'm punished for it now. Forgive me, daddy! I think he does forgive me, his face is so kind; but it was always kind when he looked at me. I can smell the mignonette on the window-sill. And see! there's my little sister; she died yesterday. How sad she looks in her shroud! She was prettier than me. I slept with her the night before she died, and she told me to be always good. I say, Jim, don't you think little Cis is prettier than me?--she's better than me! I should like father to make me a basket coffin. Where's baby?"

Alice placed the child in her arms, and as Milly pressed it to her breast, the haggard look in her face quite passed away. She was very young-- scarcely nineteen years of age: but it was better for her to die, young as she was, than live her life of shame.

"Do you know where there's a clergyman, Grif," asked Alice.

"No; what for?"

"I don't want a clergyman," gasped Milly. "Yes, my dear, I am quite sensible now. I don't want a clergyman. Your good face is better than all. Will you kiss me?"

Alice bent down and kissed her.

"Don't cry for me. I wonder why you should be here; for you know I am a bad girl, and you are a respectable woman. Give me a little drink--my throat is so dry! Oh, what a wicked life I have led! Will God forgive me, do you think?"

"Yes, dear Milly," said Alice, weeping. "God will forgive you if you ask Him."

"I do ask Him," said Milly, earnestly, but very slowly, for her voice was failing her. "Fold my hands, dear. I do ask Him, humbly. Forgive me, God!"

There was solemn silence in the room. Alice, kneeling by the bed, checked her sobs, and watched every movement in the face of the dying girl. Grif, bare-headed, stood by, in awe; his eyes were not crying, but his heart was. For Grif was very troubled. He had never prayed to God, and here in the quiet night, in the dread presence of death, the thought of his own utter wickedness and unworthiness filled him with gloom. He crept down on his knees, and lifting his hands, as if to a visible Presence, he said--"Forgive me, God!" and trembled, and cried softly to himself.

"Mine has been a wicked life," said Milly; "but I did not know what I was doing--indeed, indeed I did not! I never stopped to think. You believe me, don't you, dear?"

"I do believe you, my poor, poor Milly!"

"You break my heart, my dear, when you speak like that," said Milly, the tears stealing down her face. Alice stooped and kissed her again. "Thank you! it is more than I deserve. You are like a good angel standing by my bed. What could I do? I was persuaded to run away from my home by a young man, three years ago. We came out here, and he left me. What could I do? Is all the sin mine? I was led away. It was not all my fault. Oh, my dear! You are a married woman, and respectable; you don't know the sufferings we poor girls endure!"

Ah! poor Alice! she thought of herself and of her own sad lot, and laid her cheek close by the side of Milly's.

"How good you are!" said Milly, as thus they lay. "What is your name, dear?"

"Alice."

A look of horror crept into Milly's eyes, and a change so ghastly came over her countenance, that Alice caught at her as though she would arrest the life she thought was passing away.

"Alice?" whispered Milly, slowly and painfully, for her strength was leaving her. "Alice? Grif's friend?"

"Yes, dear," replied Alice, holding Molly's hand fast.

"And Richard Handfield is your husband?"

"Yes."

"If you knew--bend your head, for my breath is going--if you knew that the man who is the father of my child had striven to do you a great wrong, to blast your life--had schemed to sting your husband to crime--your husband whom you love, do you not--?"

"Whom I love," repeated Alice, softly.

"--For whom, as I have heard Grif say, you would give your life--"

"For whom, if needed, I would give my life."

"--If you knew that Jim Pizey, my baby's father, was his bitterest enemy, you would leave me to die alone--alone!"

"No, Milly, dear, I would not. I know that Jim Pizey tempted my husband; but he escaped, thank God!"

"You think so--come closer--take this letter--and by-and-by, not now"--she could not control her shudders as she said these words, and gave Alice the letter she had stolen from Old Flick--"by-and-by, read it. It is from Jim Pizey--he is a bad, wicked man, but I was living with him. If ever you see him, let him know that I am dead, and that with my last breath I asked you to forgive him."

"I will, Milly."

"Alice--may I call you Alice?--thank you--Alice, my dear, say you forgive me, for any unconscious wrong I may have done you."

"I forgive you, Milly."

"God bless you! Ask him to give baby to some respectable people to keep, and never to come near it--do you hear me?--never to come near it. He is baby's father, but he must never come near it, or she will be bad like me. Promise me this. I have no one else to ask."

"I promise, Milly."

"God be kind to you!" She lay quiet for a little while, and then she whispered, "How dark it is! Is the moon shining, Alice?"

"Yes, Milly; it is at its full."

"Open the window, dear, and let it shine upon me. Thank you. What a dreadful day this has been, and how quiet the night is! I can see the moon--there is a ladder of light to it from my bed. There are figures moving about in the light--I see your shadow in it, Alice, with your dear eyes. Oh, God bless you! my dear, for being by my side. Kiss me again. Good-bye! Place my baby's hand to my lips. God bless you, baby, and make you good! Is that Grif? Good-bye, Grif!"

"Good-bye, Milly," said Grif, in a choking voice.

"And now, my dear, fold my hands once more. Forgive me, God!"

A rippling smile passed over Milly's face, and in that smile she died. The light from the silver moon might have kissed away her life, she yielded, it up so peacefully.

For half an hour no sound disturbed the silence. Then Alice, after covering the face of the dead girl, opened the letter. She read, and as she read, her eyes dilated, and with a shudder she sank into Grif's arms. But she recovered herself by a strong effort, and reading a few more lines, cried, in a voice of such anguish, that Grif's knees trembled and his face turned ashen white.

"Oh, Grif! Grif! my heart is broken!"

"What is it, Ally? Are you ill?"

"Listen to me, Grif," said Alice, rapidly, and in a voice of strong emotion. "The crisis of my life has come. You said once that you would help me if you could--"

"And so I will!" cried the boy. "With my life! So help me G--!"

"This is a letter from Jim Pizey, that poor girl's associate. In it he details his devilish schemes. He discloses how he and his vile associates are going to rob Highlay Station--"

"Go on, Ally, go on," said Grif, eagerly, as Alice paused to recover her breath.

"That is my father's Station, Grif. My father is displeased with me, and that is the reason I am poor. He is rich--he always keeps large sums of money in the house; and these men are going to rob him--perhaps murder him."

"Jim Pizey don't stick at nothin'," put in Grif, rapidly. "I've heerd him talk of Highlay, but I didn't know it was your father's. Let's go and tell the peelers."

"I cannot! I dare not!" cried Alice. "For, oh, Grif! Grif! they have entrapped my husband, who knows where my father keeps his gold. They have entrapped him in the gang, and they, with my husband in their company, are on the road to rob and murder my father. If I tell the police, my husband is lost--lost!"

"What can we do?"

"We must get up there somehow. We must walk, if we cannot ride. We must beg upon the road, Grif. They intend to wait--thank God! we may be in time. They intend to wait, the letter says, until my father has in his house a very large sum, with which he is about to purchase a new Station. It is the whim of the seller that he should be paid in gold. We may be in time. Oh! thou beneficent Lord!" exclaimed the girl, as, falling upon her knees, she raised her streaming eyes to the bright heavens, which shone upon her through the open window. "Grant my prayer! Save my husband from this dread crime, and then let me die!"

A silence, as of death, was in the chamber. The glory of the moon shone full upon the upturned face of Alice, quivering with a strong agony, and upon the death-couch of poor Milly, whose life of shame was ended.

"You will come with me, Grif?" said Alice, presently.

"I am ready, Ally," Grif replied. He had been quietly packing up the remains of his bread and sardines in a pocket-handkerchief.

She turned to leave the room, but her eyes fell upon Milly's baby, who was lying asleep, with her hand on her dead mother's breast. She wrote hastily upon a piece of paper, "To the kind doctor who gave medicine to the poor girl who is dead: Take care of the baby, for the love of God!" and pinned it upon the child's frock. Then, with one last look--a look of blended pity and despair--at the form of the dead girl, Alice took Grif s hand, and went out with him into the open.

CHAPTER XVII
BAD LUCK

"It is of no use, Tom; luck is dead against us."

"It almost looks like it, Dick; but never mind, old boy. Faint heart you know."

Although Welsh Tom said this in a tone of cheerfulness, there was a serious expression on his face. The difference between Welsh Tom and Richard Handfield was, that one was always trying to make the best of things, and the other the worst. Just now they were standing by the side of a muddy creek; along the banks of the creek were two or three score of gold-diggers, puddling the auriferous soil in wooden tubs, or washing it in tin dishes, or rocking it in "cradles," as tenderly as if those strangely-named implements for the extraction of gold contained their own precious flesh and blood. Black-bearded and brown-bearded men, these! A gold-digger's occupation is favourable to the growth of hair. Here were men with beards hanging upon their breasts, godlike; here were men whose great curling mustachios gave to their faces a leonine appearance; here were men whose strong whiskers kissed their shoulders, and gave to their wearers a noble grace, albeit they were not perfumed or bandolined. The open-air life, the freedom of action, the absence of that mental contraction which seems to grow upon one in crowded cities, causing the mind to brood upon subjects confined in narrow circles, tend to make the gold-digger handsome, and brave, and strong. Yet his aim and the aim of the city man are the same; both work for gold. But in the search for it, on new gold-fields, there is more generosity and less meanness than in the cities.

Our two mates, Richard Handfield and Welsh Tom, had come upon the gold strata in the hole they had been sinking for the past three weeks. The gold-diggers on both sides of them were getting at the rate of an ounce of gold a-day per man, and they had every reason to justify them in the hope that they also were in possession of a golden claim. But when they reached the strata of earth in which the gold, from all surrounding indications, ought to have been imbedded, they were dismayed at finding only the merest speck of the metal here and there. And this morning they had washed a tubful of the soil which should have been auriferous, and were rewarded by not quite two grains of fine gold. It was at these two disappointing grains they were looking, very despondently, when they made the above remarks.

Throwing the tin dish containing the "prospect" to the ground in disgust, Richard asked, petulantly, "What is to be done now?"

"Look out for some fresh ground," answered the Welshman, applying himself to the gold-digger's consolation, a pipe.

"And work for three weeks more, and get nothing at the end of it!"

"Perhaps; and perhaps not." Welsh Tom said this laconically. He was more accustomed than Richard to such-like rebuffs, and was ready to go to work again with a very perfect faith.

"You take it coolly enough," Richard said, digging at the earth viciously with the heel of his boot.

"It's of no use growling," replied the Welshman, with a quiet shrug. "If it was, I'd growl."

Richard looked enviously at the party next to them, who had washed more than half-an-ounce of gold from a tin dishful of earth.

"Just see that," he said, jerking his head spitefully in the direction of the lucky gold digger.

Welsh Tom nodded. He saw nothing to envy in the other man's good fortune.

"Half-an-ounce to a tin dish," grumbled Richard, "and we got two grains to a tub!"

"Come, come, Dick," said the Welshman, "it can't be helped. Let us go back to the claim. We may find a bit of gold in it yet."

They returned to their ground, and Richard worked at the windlass, while his mate burrowed at the bottom of the hole. But though Tom drove in his pick here, and drove it in there, and although he worked until the perspiration soaked his shirt through and through, Dame Fortune did not smile upon his efforts.

"We will abandon the claim, Dick," he said in the evening, as he stood, hot and tired, at his mate's side, by the windlass. "I don't think we should get a pennyweight of gold out of it if we worked for a month. We will start in the morning for Deadman's Flat. They are getting plenty of gold there, and we may hit upon a good piece of ground. It is only five miles off."

Richard gave a sullen assent, and commenced to dig np the slabs which supported their windlass. Early the next morning they started off for the new locality.

At the very commencement of the gold-rush a hole had been sunk in Deadman's Flat, and soon afterwards deserted. Most of the adventurers who came on to the field saw this deserted hole, and inferring that the ground had been tested for gold-digging purposes and found worthless, passed on to other spots. But one day, two mates who had been everywhere unfortunate, descended this hole in search of gold, and found the body of a dead man. In the side of the hole was a rusted pick, and as they pulled the pick out of the earth, which was composed of blue clay and cement, they pulled out also some pieces of the conglomerate, which to their infinite delight they discovered to be richly studded with gold. Examining the pick they found upon its point human hair and stains of blood, and they knew that a murder had been committed. A. struggle had evidently taken place at the bottom of the hole, and the man had been murdered with the pick. Then the pick had been driven into the side of the hole, and the murderer had climbed to earth's surface and fled. All this was inference, but it was clear as truth, which spoke at the bottom of the pit, where lay the murdered man. The two hitherto unfortunate mates were made rich by a murder! they dug their wealth out of a grave, for the hole had an amazing quantity of gold in it, which was theirs by right of conquest. The murderer was never discovered, and in honour to his victim the gold-miners christened the place Deadman's Flat.

Richard and his mate chanced to light upon a vacant piece of ground, of which they entertained great anticipations. All around them the diggers were getting gold--not a mere hand-to-mouth living, but gold to spend, to squander. They had to sink nearly forty feet to get to the gold strata, and part of the sinking was through a toughish kind of rock. The day following that on which they commenced to work, the men in the claim next but one to theirs found a nugget of gold weighing ninety ounces, and hey, presto! no sooner was a nugget found in one claim than nuggets began to be found in many of the others. Not large ones certainly, but nice pieces of gold to handle and look at. The miners on Deadman's Flat were jubilant, not to say uproarious. In the very next claim to theirs the men one day obtained more than a hundred ounces of gold. "All right, this time, Dick!" said the Welshman with a knowing wink; and Dick at once began to reckon up how many thousands of pounds they would make out of the claim. It was jolly working the sinking of that hole, and they indulged in fond anticipations of the nuggets of gold waiting for them at the bottom. They ate their meals with a relish. Better than all, the heavy gold seemed to be trending in their direction. "We shall find some big bits in the wash-dirt," said Tom. "The gold gets heavier and heavier as it comes down to us; it is more water-worn too. What if we should drop down upon a big nugget!" Ah, what indeed! A big nugget! The dream of a gold-digger's life. When the Welshman indulged in the speculation, he half smiled. Yet why should it not occur to them? It had occurred to scores of other men.

Then Richard began to build all his hopes upon the finding of a nugget larger than any that had been found before, and asked sly questions of his mate as to the biggest nuggets he had ever seen or heard of. He led up to the engrossing subject as if he were putting questions out of a book of catechisms. As thus:--

"Where was gold first discovered, Tom?"

"In New South Wales." (It will be observed that they both ignored ancient history, and that to them the story of Solomon's Temple was a fable.)

"When Tom?"

"In 1851."

"Where was it found next?"

"In Victoria."

"When Tom?"

"In 1852."

(Please to understand that these questions were not asked straight off, but at intervals, and artfully, as if the questioner did not wish to be suspected of having any interest in the subject.)

"Were there any large nuggets found in New South Wales, Tom?"

"Yes, lots of 'em. But none came up to the first specimen, which was got near the surface at Bathurst, and which was sold for heaps of money."

"Who found it?"

"An aboriginal shepherd."

"How much did it weigh?"

"Over a hundred pounds--nearly a hundred-weight, I think I heard. There are all sorts of stories told about the first piece of gold, Dick. They say that the shepherd, an Australian Native, you know, had been sitting on it or lying on it for years, while he was watching his sheep, until at last he had worn the earth away from the stone which peeped up at him, all yellow and brown. Being an uncivilized savage, he did not know anything about gold, and did not imagine there was anything strange in the appearance of the stone. But one day he happened to mention to his master that he was in the habit of resting upon a large yellow stone. That led to the discovery; the master took the gold-stone and sold it, and gave the Native ten pounds, who spent it in rum and tobacco, I dare say. I don't know whether this is the true account, Dick: I have heard the story told all sorts of ways."

Richard listened somewhat impatiently, for he was burning to hear of the largest nugget, so that he might estimate the size of the one waiting for them at the bottom of their claim.

"That was only a hundredweight," he said.

"Yes, only a hundredweight," said Welsh Tom, drily.

"There have been plenty of heavier ones, haven't there, Tom?" Richard asked, anxiously.

"There was the Sarah Sands nugget," replied the Welshman, plunging into the subject to please his mate; "found at Ballarat; weighed more than a hundred and thirty pounds."

Richard calculated rapidly; one hundred and thirty pounds, troy, fifteen hundred and sixty ounces, at four pounds an ounce, six thousand two hundred and forty pounds. That was better.

"Then there was the Blanche Barkly nugget, dug up at Kingower," proceeded Welsh Tom, "weighed a hundred and forty-five pounds, that did."

Better and better. Richard was immediately engrossed in his process of mental calculation, and achieved a result of six thousand nine hundred and sixty pounds. What a fine sight it would be, all in sovereigns! But it was a pity it was not an even seven thousand pounds, he thought.

"Then there was the Welcome nugget--the biggest lump of gold found yet--found at Ballarat, nearly two hundred feet down. Weighed a hundred and eighty-four pounds."

A hundred and eighty-four pounds! Something like a nugget that! Richard quickly multiplied it by twelve; two thousand two hundred and eight ounces, at four pounds an ounce, eight thousand eight hundred and thirty-two pounds.

He said this aloud, "Eight thousand eight hundred and thirty-two pounds."

"They sold the nugget for ten thousand pounds," said the Welshman.

"Did they? That was glorious. And that was the largest nugget?"

"The largest nugget ever found."

He had obtained the information at last. The largest nugget! Ten thousand sovereigns for one piece of gold, discovered merely by a blow from a pick. The largest nugget ever found! Why they might find a larger! Three hundredweight, four hundredweight, a quarter of a ton, perhaps!

"Do you think that bigger nuggets will be discovered than those you speak of, Tom?"

"To be sure. There are some places where gold will be found in great lumps."

This was once a favourite fancy with gold-miners, and some theorists to this day persist that by-and-by men will be cutting solid gold out of the rock with a cold chisel. When that time comes we must have our sovereigns made of iron.

"If we find a big nugget in the claim," said Richard, "and make our fortunes, I shall bid good-bye to the colony, Tom."

"Where will you go?"

"Home!"

It is a simple word and was spoken without much feeling, but the strong Welshman's heart beat more swiftly than usual at the sound of it, and there was a momentary dimness in his eyes.

"I have suffered enough in this colony," Richard continued, "and shall be glad to turn my back upon it. So will Alice. Perhaps you will come with us, Tom. We'll all go home together in the same ship."

"You forget I am a ticket-of-leave-man," said Tom. "My ticket-of-leave only extends to Victoria. If I cross the boundary, the police will soon be on my track."

He spoke a little bitterly. Home! Yes: he would like to see the Welsh mountains once more. But it was not to be.

"I beg your pardon, Welshman," Richard said, carelessly. "It was forgetfulness on my part."

They worked cheerfully, day after day, digging out the bowels of their gold-pit. The miners in the locality would cluster round the hole, which they prophesied would be the richest on Deadman's Flat. One day, a smooth-faced man with a scar beneath his eye, as if it had been burnt, came and looked down the shaft. Richard was working at the windlass, and as the stranger came up a chill crept over him.

"When do you expect to come on the 'gutter,' mate?" the stranger asked.

"In two or three days," replied Richard, his uneasy feeling increasing. But the man was a perfect stranger to him. He had never seen him before.

"Do you want to sell a share in the claim?" the new-comer asked, presently.

"No."

"I will give you twenty ounces for a third share."

"Don't want to sell, mate."

Richard spoke very shortly, and showed so evident a disinclination to talk with the stranger that the man walked away. That night Richard dreamt that they found a tremendous lump of gold, and that the man with the burnt scar under his eye stole it.

The following day the stranger came again. This time the Welshman was at the windlass, and the stranger found him more sociable than Richard. He lingered for half-an-hour or so, chatting with Welsh Tom.

"He wants to buy into the claim very bad," said the Welshman to Richard, afterwards. "But we won't sell a share in our big nugget, Dick." (He spoke this in a sly tone, for he did not share his mate's dreams of the lump of gold waiting for them at the bottom of the hole.) "His name is Honest Steve, he says."

As they approached nearer and nearer to the gutter of gold, Richard became more and more excited. His brain was busy with schemes for laying out his money to advantage. He had delayed writing to Alice until he could write to her the good news of their wonderful fortune. So unfortunate had he been in his gold-digging career, that he had been unable to send Alice a shilling since he bade her good-bye; and the last letter he had written to her was full of complaining and repining. But the next should not be. No; he would be able to tell her that all their sufferings were ended at last. His heart felt so glad that he spoke to the Welshman about her; and his mate encouraged him, and drew him on to talk of Alice. Welsh Tom, in his simple way, was a true friend to Richard's wife.

At length the indications in their shaft told them that they were very near the golden gutter. Richard examined every bucketful of earth as he pulled it np. Then he received the signal that his mate wished to ascend, and the next time he pulled up the bucket, it had Welsh Tom in it instead of dull clay.

"Now, Dick," said Tom, with a pale face, "we are on the gutter. All the stuff that comes out of the hole must be put aside by itself. Before we commence, let us go and have a nobbler."[5]

Footnote 5: Nobbler--the Australian term for a glass of wine or spirits.

They went to a shanty where grog was sold on the sly--that is to say, where grog was sold without a licence--and spent their last two shillings in two nobblers of whisky, which they drank with the usual salutation of "Here's luck, mate!" They drank it hurriedly, for they were dreadfully anxious to get back to their shaft. It had got wind that Welsh Tom and his mate were on the gutter, and a little knot of diggers was assembled to see the gold out of the first tubful of stuff. Half-a-dozen buckets of earth, taken from the gutter, were soon on the surface, and Welsh Tom ascended the shaft, looking very much disturbed. The earth was carried to a neighbouring creek, and put into a tub, and then the process of gold-washing commenced. Richard poured water into the tub with a ladle, and Tom puddled the stuff with a short-handled shovel, and let the overflow of muddied water run into the creek. All heavy metal, of course, sank to the bottom of the tub, and only the refuse earth which contained no gold, or out of which the gold had been puddled, floated to the top, and was allowed to escape. Soon, the contents of the tub were reduced by one-half, and then the stuff was manipulated more carefully. Every now and then the Welshman lifted a shovelful of the muddy mixture from the bottom of the tub, and poured clear water over it, and examined it. Richard noticed with uneasiness that every time he did this, his face grew paler.

After about an hour's tub-work, the stuff was passed through a riddled dish, and the large stones thrown aside. By this time, the tub was only one-fifth full. When the riddling process was completed, what remained was put into a "cradle," and submitted to a gentle rocking, Richard continuing to pour water over it. There then remained not quite a tin-dishful of stuff. Taking the dish in his two hands, the Welshman bent over the creek, and scooped up a little water with the dish, which he rotated deftly and delicately. Either the stooping or some inward excitement brought the blood to his head, but when he stood upright to rest, his face grew quite white.

The diggers pressed anxiously round as the Welshman continued to work, and as they followed with watchful eyes the progress of the operation, a grave expression stole into their countenances. The stuff grew less and less. The tin dish was only half-full now. Another five minutes, and half of this was gone; a few minutes more, and nine-tenths of the contents of the dish had floated off. The on-lookers shook their heads, and crept slowly away, one by one.

Biting his lips, Richard watched the earth melt in the water, and grudged every speck of it that floated out of the dish. Now came the trying moment. The stuff was reduced to about sufficient to fill a large tablespoon. This lay at the side of the dish, and beneath it all the gold which the tubful of auriferous soil had contained must of necessity have been collected. Taking some clear water in the dish, the Welshman rotated it gently, delicately. Little by little, the pasty remnant melted off; then, with one skilful swing, the promised treasures of their golden claim were laid bare, and Richard saw--

Two minute specks of gold mocking him from the bottom of the dish!

The claim was worthless.

CHAPTER XVIII
HONEST STEVE

Richard Handfield groaned, and looked with a kind of dismay at the gold.

There lay the fulfilment of his extravagant hopes--there lay the promise of his precious nugget, which he would not sell for ten thousand pounds--there lay his dreams of the future, the happiness of his life, the compensation for past suffering--two miserable specks of gold, not worth twopence! He clutched at his hair, and sitting upon the inverted tub, rested his chin in his palms, and despaired.

What was the use of working? He was marked out by misfortune, and it was labour thrown away to struggle against it. It pursued him, and mocked him with false hopes. Of what use was it for him to continue to struggle?

A pretty thing! That he should so lower himself for such a result he,--a gentleman! That he should slave, walk till his feet were blistered, work till his hands were like the hands of a common man, sweat in the sun till the skin peeled off his face, mix with common men, herd with common natures, be "hail, fellow" with creatures so far beneath him--and all for this! The two little specks of gold lay in the bright tin dish, and seemed to mock him with their yellow light. He wished he could have hurt them as they hurt him. He would have liked to dash them to the ground and tread them into the rock with his iron heel, till he made them groan as they made him groan!

Welsh Tom took the matter much more philosophically. If it had not been that he saw Richard's distress, and sympathised with him, he would have been inclined to smile at the two-pennyworth of gold which lay in the dish. Your true heroes are those who accept the inevitable, and who, knowing they are defeated, still retain their courage. It is easy to be brave when fortune is with you--then, the virtue of bravery is of the milk-and-water kind. But to be brave when fortune is against you is god-like. Welsh Tom did not blame mankind and all the world because he was unfortunate. It was a fair fight he was fighting with nature for her treasures. Well, he was unsuccessful that was all. He would try again.

All the gold-diggers but one had strolled away when they saw the result of the washing. The one who remained was Honest Steve, the man who had offered to give twenty ounces of gold for a third share in the claim. Looking up, Richard Handfield saw him.

"Would you give twenty ounces for a third share now?" Richard asked, in a bitter tone.

"Not likely," was the reply.

What was the sudden fear that came upon him as the stranger spoke? Richard tried to shake it off, not quite successfully. Psha! What was there in the man to be afraid of?

"Not likely," the stranger repeated. "It was a good job for me you didn't take my twenty ounces, mate. I laid it out to better advantage, I think."

Honest Steve spoke this in a tone which invited further inquiry. But as neither Richard nor the Welshman said anything just then, he volunteered a piece of gratuitous information.

"I bought a claim on the gutter," he said.

Now, this was interesting; and the Welshman asked, "Are you on the gold?"

"Not yet. I'm in a bit of a fix. I haven't a mate. I am looking out for one now."

"Ah," Richard said, querulously, thinking of their last two shillings which they had spent that morning in whisky. "I suppose you want some one to give you twenty ounces for a share."

"No," Honest Steve said, carelessly. "I would like a mate or even two mates, and go fair shares, and stand all the risk myself, for the claim is sure to turn out well."

"That's magnanimous," Richard said, contemptuously. He hated ostentatious generosity. The insolence of his tone might have fired any man with resentment, but it did not appear to make any impression upon Honest Steve.

"I tell you what it is," he said, quietly and respectfully, addressing himself especially to Richard, "I like the way you two work together, and I should be glad if you would let me go mates with you."

Both matter and manner were mollifying to Richard. They were eminently respectful, as if Honest Steve knew and admitted Richard's superiority. He took the Welshman aside, and said,

"Well, Tom, what do you think?"

"I don't like him," Tom said.

It is a singular proof of the contrariety of human nature, that no sooner did the Welshman say he did not like Honest Steve than Richard's dislike began to melt away.

"I did not know you were prejudiced, Tom," he said.

"I'm not prejudiced, but there is something about him that tells me not to mate with him."

"What is it?"

"I can't say. It is beyond me. The people round about where I was born and bred are a little superstitious."

"That's it! Superstition is always unreasonable. Look here, Tom. The claim we hold is a duffer, isn't it?"

"I think so."

"His claim may be a golden one. Why should we throw a chance away? If he did not believe it to be good, he wouldn't have given twenty ounces for it."

The Welshman saw that Richard was in favour of the stranger's proposition; he was in the habit of practising unselfishness--it was his nature to do so. It *would* be a pity, perhaps, to throw away the chance. Yet Honest Steve's generosity puzzled him. Never mind, he would do as his mate wished.

"All right, Dick!" he said. "We will join him."

They returned to where Honest Stove was standing. He had been watching them furtively as they held their conference.

"Well, Steve," said Welsh Tom, "we will go mates with you.'"

"Good!" said Honest Steve. "Let us shake hands upon it."

They shook hands; a cold shiver chilled the Welshman's marrow as Honest Steve's hand rested in his.

"Dick," he whispered, as they proceeded towards their new claim, "I feel as if some one was walking over my grave!"

CHAPTER XIX
THE WELSHMAN READS HIS LAST CHAPTER IN THE OLD WELSH BIBLE

In a small blind gully, rejoicing in the name of Breakneck, to which there had once been a slight rush, but which was now almost deserted, there still remained a solitary tent. It attracted no particular attention. It was not unusual for diggers to put up their tents in out-of-the-way places, some distance from the claims they were working; and no comment was caused by the circumstance that but very lately this tent had been sold for a trifle to new-comers. Breakneck Gully had been so named because, to get to it, one had to descend a range of precipitous hills, with here and there dense clumps of bush and timber, leading into treacherous hollows. From its peculiar situation, Breakneck Gully always wore a dismal appearance; it almost seemed as if the surrounding ranges were striving to hide it from the sun. In the day-time, when little streaks of light peeped timidly into its depths, but never lingered there, it was cheerless enough: in the night its gloom was terrible. The gully was about four miles from the main rush; and those who had to walk past it in the night were glad when they left it and its gloomy shades behind them. When it was first discovered, great hopes were entertained that some rich patches of gold would be found there; but, although the ground had been pretty well turned over, none of the claims yielded more than sufficient to purchase flour and meat, and it was soon deserted for more auriferous localities.

One evening, a few weeks after Welsh Tom and Richard Handfield had admitted Honest Steve into partnership, four men were busy within this solitary tent. They might have been ordinary diggers, preparing for supper and their night's rest. They were dressed in the regular digger's costume; and tub, cradle, and tin dishes, huddled into a corner, would have been considered sufficiently indicative of the nature of their pursuits. Yet there was about them a manner which did not favour the hypothesis of their being honest workers of the soil. They had an evil look upon their faces; they moved about the tent stealthily and suspiciously; and there was somewhat too ostentatious a display of firearms. Indeed, they were none other than Jim Pizey and his gang.

"Keep a good look-out, Ralph," said Jim Pizey to one who was stationed as a sentinel near the door. "Let us know if you hear anyone coming."

"All right," was the reply.

"How much longer are we going to hang about here?" asked Ned Rutt. "I'm tired of waiting. It's my opinion we're only wasting our time."

"I don't know," said Jim Pizey. "It will be the first time the Oysterman ever failed, if he fails now. He seems pretty confident. But I wish he would finish his job. We shall have to be away from here, anyhow, in a couple of days."

"Isn't Nuttall to have the money in his place by Christmas?"

"Yes; we shall have lots of time to get to the Station. We have to hang on there a bit, you know. We've had cursed bad luck as yet; but we'll make up for it. I'd like to have Dick Handfield with us. He'd save us a lot of trouble, and it would prevent his peaching afterwards."

"He knew about the plant in Melbourne, didn't he?" asked the sentinel.

"Yes, but he escaped us somehow. I wish we had cut the skunk's damned throat for him. Directly the affair is blown, he'll know who did it, and he'll split upon us to a certainty."

A dark look came into Jim Pizey's face as he said this.

"I'd think no more of squeezing the life out of him who'd split than I would of--" he finished the sentence by knocking the ashes out of his pipe in a significant manner. "Out of *him* especially," he continued, taking a letter from his pocket, and reading part of it; "I've a score of my own to settle with him. I couldn't make out at first what made Milly, turn informer against us; but I know now how it was. Dick Handfield's white-faced wife got hold of and frightened her. I didn't think Milly would do it, though, for I liked the girl, and I thought she liked me. There's the baby, too. It's a pity for *that!* If the Oysterman succeeds in what he is trying, I'll write to Old Flick telling him how we're getting along."

At this moment, the man at the door, who had been addressed as Ralph, turned his head, and said, "Hush! some one coming."

Not a word was spoken in reply, but each man grasped his weapon, and assumed an attitude of watchfulness.

"All right," presently said the sentinel. "It's the Tenderhearted Oysterman."

And in walked, whistling, Honest Steve!

He nodded to his comrades, and, seating himself upon a stretcher, took out his pipe. Having slowly filled it, and lighted it, he said,

"Well, Jim, how is it getting on?"

"How do I know?" returned Jim Pizey. "We're waiting for you to tell us that. Here we are, hanging about for you, and, for all I know, wasting our time to no purpose."

"Strike me cruel!" exclaimed the Oysterman. "Did you ever know the Oysterman bungle a job?"

"No: but you're a precious long time over this one. I'd strangle the pair of them before I'd be done by them."

"And so will I, before I'm done by them. I don't want you to tell me how to do my work."

"How much longer are we to wait here?"

"Mates and gentlemen," said the Oysterman, speaking very slowly, "it is my pleasing duty to inform you, as we say in Parliament, and notwithstanding the insinuations thrown out by my honourable friend and mate, Jim Pizey, Esquire, that I think we may look upon the job as pretty well done."

"Stop your palaver and tell us all about it," observed Jim Pizey.

"Well, then, mates and gentlemen," said the Oysterman--

"We've had enough of that infernal nonsense," interrupted Jim Pizey, angrily. "Can't you speak straightforward?"

"Strike me patient!" exclaimed the Oysterman, "Let a cove speak according to his education, can't you! I'll tell the story my own way, or I won't tell it at all."

"Go on, then," growled Pizey.

"Well, then, to commence all over again: Mates and gentlemen, you know that I'm now an honest, hardworking digger, and mates with Dick Handfield and an infernal fool of a Welshman. When I happened promiscuously to drop across the pair of them, says I to myself, Tenderhearted Oysterman, here's a little bit of work for you to do, and you've got to go in and do it well. There's that plant of Nuttall's at Highlay Station, says I to myself. What if the old cove should have some place to put his money in that we don't know of? Here's Dick Handfield knows every foot of the house and Station. If we can get him to join us, we can make sure of the tin. We can settle him afterwards, if we like; but have him we must, if we can get hold of him. But, says I to myself, Dick Handfield is an honest young thief. He gave us the slip once before. And, says I to myself, Dick Handfield'll get a good claim, perhaps, and I can't get no hold of him if he does, unless I come it very artful. So, mates and gentlemen, I laid a plot, invented it every bit myself, and when I tell you all about it, as I'm going to do now, I think you'll say I did come it artful, and no mistake."

The Oysterman settled himself upon his seat, in an evident state of enjoyment, and resumed:

"The first thing I thought of, mates and gentlemen, when I came across the pair of them, was that Dick Handfield mustn't suspect that he knew me. You know, mates and gentlemen, that I hadn't shaved for ten years, but I sacrificed everything for my artful plot. I shaved my chin as smooth as a bagatelle ball, and took care to keep myself pretty clean. It was such a long time since I saw my own face, that I assure you, mates and gentlemen, I hardly knew it again. But to prevent any chance of discovery, I bought some acid, and burned this black mark under my eye. That was rather artful, wasn't it? And, mates and gentlemen, as it spoils my good looks, I hope you'll take it into consideration when we square up, and make me an allowance for it. Then, says I to myself, what name shall we take, Oysterman? And I hit upon Honest Steve, as one that would exactly suit me. Then I began to look about me; it didn't take me long to strike up an acquaintance with the Welshman. He's a simple kind of fool, and will believe anything. It was different with Dick Handfield. I do believe he had some kind of suspicion at first; he looked at me as if he had a sort of an idea that he knew me, and in his damned proud way wouldn't condescend to be civil to me. But I didn't rile up at that; it wasn't my game. I was a bit frightened that my trap wouldn't click, for they had got a claim which every one of us believed was going to turn out pounds weight of gold. But it was a duffer." (Here the Tenderhearted Oysterman chuckled.) "A regular duffer--two grains to the tub--not enough to keep 'em in salt. I was there when they washed out the first tub, and wasn't Dick Handfield down on his luck! Before they came on the gutter I had offered 'em twenty ounces for a third share, but they wouldn't take it. And when Dick Handfield looked up and saw me, he turned awfully savage. But I had nothing but soft words for him, mates and gentlemen. I put up with all his airs, for I knew my day would come, and it has come, mates and gentlemen, as you will say, presently."

He paused to indulge in the pleasing anticipation of his coming day, and then resumed--

"I had a claim marked out upon the line of the gutter--of course I did not know whether it would turn out good or bad--and I offered to take them in as mates. They jumped at the offer, like a couple of mice jumping into a trap;

and after that I got more artful than ever. The long fool of a Welshman, he's a soft sort of cove, and he reads his Bible every night before he goes to bed. Says I to myself, I must turn religious, I must. So I buys a Testament, and I makes it dirty and ragged, as if I had used it a good deal, and I writes my name inside the cover. One day, I leaves this Testament lying on the table- -quite by accident, mates and gentlemen--and the Welshman, he comes in, and I twigs him take it up and look at my name on the cover. 'Is this yours, Steve?' he says. 'Yes,' I answers; 'how stupid of me to leave it out; I've had it for twenty years, and I wouldn't take anything for it.' 'I like you for that, Honest Steve,' he says, the tears almost coming into his eyes--a nice soft fool *he* is!--and he gave me a regular hand-gripe. 'You're a better sort of fellow than I thought you was.' He had never shook hands with me before, and I knew that I had got *him* all right. I was awful pious with him, I can tell you! Then I set on to Dick Handfield. Whenever I spoke to him I called him 'Sir,' and was very respectful. I got him to talk of his being a gentleman, and what a shame it was that such a swell as him should have to work like a common digger. 'The Welshman,' says I, 'he's used to it, and don't mind it; but you ought to be different. It isn't a very gentlemanly thing,' I says to him, 'for you to have to go mates with an old lag'--for the Welshman, you know, mates and gentlemen, is a lag--a lifer, too. Then I got him to drink, and set him and the Welshman quarrelling; and after that, mates and gentlemen, my artful job was pretty well done."

"What are you going to make of all this?" asked Jim Pizey. "I don't see how this will get Dick Handfield to join us. And we must have him, Oysterman, or we shall all swing for it. He's the only one, besides Old Flick, who knows what we're up to."

"Wait till I've done," said the Oysterman, "and you'll see quick enough. I've been mates with the Welshman and Dick Handfield now for four weeks, and the claim's washed up. It has turned out pretty well but not so well as the diggers round about think it has, which makes it all the better for us. They think we've been keeping them in the dark as to what we've got out of the claim. We haven't divided the gold yet; the Welshman's got charge of that. We're going to divide to-morrow. All the diggers know that we're going to divide to-morrow"--and the Tenderhearted Oysterman laughed and rubbed his knees. "I've took care that they should all know it. That's coming it artful, ain't it?"

"How?" asked Jim Pizey.

"How!" repeated the Oysterman, scornfully, but dropping his voice. "Can't you see through it? The Welshman and Dick Handfield, they've been quarrelling for the last two weeks, as if they'd like to cut each other's throats. I've took care of that. I told Dick Handfield that the Welshman said he was a proud, lazy fool; and I told the Welshman that I heard Dick Handfield swear, if he could get hold of the Welsh Bible, he'd pitch it into the fire. Dick Handfield, he's been drinking like mad; and this afternoon, mates and gentlemen, this afternoon, they had a regular flare-up; if they hadn't been parted, they'd have had a stand-up fight. Dick Handfield, he goes away swearing that he'll be even with the Welshman yet. And that's the end of my story, mates and gentlemen."

"But what's to come of all this?"

"Can't you see through it yet? What would you say if, before to-morrow morning, I was to bring you the gold the Welshman's taking care of? There's nearly a hundred ounces of it. What do you think I've been working for all this time? You be on the watch to-night, and I'll bring you the gold safe enough. See here, mates and gentlemen"--and he looked about him cautiously, and pulled out a knife--"this is Dick Handfield's knife, this is; I prigged it from him this morning. What if the poor Welshman was to be found to-morrow morning dead in his bed? What if Dick Handfield's knife should be found on the ground, under the bed, with blood on it? The quarrel between Welsh Tom and Dick Handfield remembered--the gold that was going to be divided to morrow gone--the Welshman stabbed with Dick Handfield's knife: eh, mates and gentlemen? Do you see now how artful I've been coming it? When Dick Handfield knows that they're after him for murdering his mate when he knows that his knife is found, covered with blood he'll be too glad to come with us, so as to get out of the way? Oh, you let the Oysterman alone for doing a job properly! In a dozen hours from now we'll be on the road to Highlay Station, and Dick Handfield will be with us."

"And all this will be done to-night?"

"As sure as thunder!"

"By God! Oysterman," exclaimed Jim Pizey, "you've got a heart of iron!"

"Strike me merciful!" said the Tenderhearted Oysterman. "Me a heart of iron! I've got a heart as soft as a woman's! If I thought I should hurt the poor cove to-night, I'd go and give myself in charge beforehand. There's Ralph, there, if you call hard-hearted, you wouldn't be far out. But me!" No words can express his villanous enjoyment of this appeal.

"What do you mean?" growled Ralph.

"Mean, you flinty-hearted parent!" said the Tenderhearted Oysterman. "What's the use of your being a father? We've never heard you ask once after your offspring, Grif!"

"How's the young rip getting on?" asked Ralph, surlily. "He's always a disgracing of me!"

"He's getting on very bad," replied the Oysterman; "very bad, isn't he, Jim? He's turned honest, and blacks boots in the streets for a tanner a pair. We gave him a turn, Jim and me, but we didn't pay him; I wasn't going to encourage him. He'll come to no good, won't Grif; he's a downright sneak."

"There, that's enough of him," growled Ralph; "talk of something else, can't you?"

"Here's an unnatural father for you!" exclaimed the Oysterman, looking round. "Objects to speak about his own offspring! It makes my tender heart bleed to think of his unnaturalness. Give us something to drink; I'm dry with talking. I'll stop for a couple of hours before I go back. Everything'll be quiet then."

Brandy was produced, and the gang of ruffians sat together for some time in the dark, talking in whispers over their vile projects.

The Welshman was alone in his tent. He was lying upon his bed, thinking over his quarrel with Richard Handfield; thinking how sorry he was that there should have been any quarrel at all, and how he would like to make it up. He could not help reflecting how strange it was that he had never quarrelled with Richard until Honest Steve had joined them. He had not been quite imposed upon by Honest Steve; he had all along entertained a doubt of that worthy's genuineness, and all his simple predilections were in favour of Richard Handfield. But he had been taken in by Honest Steve's story of the Bible. There were two common beds in the tent, one belonging to Handfield, the other to himself. Honest Steve had a little tent of his own, close by. The Welshman cast many glances at the unoccupied bed, wishing that Handfield would come, so that the difference between them might be healed. The more he thought over the matter, the more he was convinced that an explanation would set it all right. There were many good points about Handfield, which had won upon the simple Welshman; and he did think that his mate's lot was a hard one. He had seen the picture of Alice, too, which Richard kept about him, and he thought that no man could be bad who was loved by such a woman; her sweet face seemed to elevate his mate in his eyes. And so, as he lay upon his bed thinking over these things, the Welshman yearned for Richard's return, that a reconciliation might be effected between them.

Richard Handfield was far from a bad man; but he was a weak man and a coward. He was vacillating, and was easily led for good or evil. Above all, he could not face misfortune. The change in his circumstances before he married Alice, his bitter disappointment at the conduct her father had pursued towards them, and their subsequent misfortunes and poverty, had completely prostrated him. He really looked upon himself as most harshly treated: in his heart he did not believe that any other man in the world had as much to bear as himself; and he writhed and fretted at his hard lot. The weak points in his character would scarcely have made their appearance in prosperity; but under the lash of misfortune they thrust themselves out, pricking him sorely, and causing him to appear in a very unamiable light. He was intensely weak, intensely vacillating, intensely selfish; and his utter want of moral courage was bringing him to the brink of a terrible precipice.

It was past nine o'clock in the evening when Richard, who had been drinking at some of the sly grog-shanties, came to the tent. It would have been better for him had he not come home that night. It is awful to think upon what slight threads of chance a man's destiny hangs! He had not intended to sleep that night in the Welshman's tent, but a stray remark had changed his resolution. The quarrel between the two mates had been incidentally mentioned in conversation at the shanty where Richard was drinking, and a digger jokingly observed that he supposed Richard would be afraid to sleep that night in the Welshman's tent. That remark decided him. He was not going to have the charge of cowardice brought against him. It also prevented his drinking to excess, for he determined to go home early.

When he entered, the Welshman sprang from his bed, and Richard started back, expecting a blow. He was much astonished when the Welshman, holding out his hand, said,--

"Dick, let's shake hands. If you are sorry for the quarrel we have had, so am I. Why should we two fall out?"

Richard made no response.

"I have been thinking over things, Dick," the Welshman said, "and the more I think the more certain I am that it is all a mistake. Come--we have seen bad luck and good luck together. Let us shake hands."

Richard put out his hand, but not so readily as the Welshman, nor with a similar heartiness.

"I'll shake hands with you, Tom," he said; "and I'm sorry that we quarrelled. But you had no right to say of me that I was a proud, lazy fool."

"I said nothing of the sort," said the Welshman. "Whatever I've said, I've said to your face. I'm not mean enough to speak against a man when his back's turned. Who told you I said so?"

"Honest Steve."

It flashed across the Welshman's mind, that they had both been deceived by Honest Steve.

"You remember my telling you my story, Dick, when we camped out?" he asked.

"Yes."

"You remember that part about my mother?"

"Yes"

"And the Bible she gave me?"

"Yes."

"All the gold in Victoria could not buy that Bible Dick."

"I don't think it could, Tom."

"And yet I was told that you swore to burn my Bible, when you could lay hands on it."

"Whoever told you so told a lie. I'm not very sober, but you can believe me."

"I do. We're both been put upon by Steve. He told me you swore this, and you may guess my blood was up."

"I should think so. But why didn't you tell me this before?"

"Because Steve made me promise not to say anything about it. I suppose he made you promise the same."

Richard nodded, and said, half musingly, "What could be his motive?"

"Never mind his motive. To-morrow morning we share the gold, and when we have squared up, we'll break with Steve, and you and I will stick together as mates, if you like. I'll tell him my opinion of him, too. Shake hands again, Dick."

They shook hands once more, and the two were friends again. Softened by the reconciliation, they fell into confidential conversation.

"I can't fathom his motive, Tom," said Richard, harping upon the theme. "Steve has done this for a purpose. Did you ever meet with him before?"

"No."

"You remember how he came and offered to mate with us? There didn't seem anything strange in it then, but now it seems to bear a different light. He has been playing upon both of us. He played upon me, knowing my cursed pride"--the Welshman patted Richard's knee--"he told me it was a degradation to me to mate with a--a--"

"Say it, Dick," said the Welshman, gently. "It was a degradation to you to go mates with a ticket-of-leave man."

"Yes, he said that. And I--although I know that you are innocent, Tom, old fellow,--"

"Thank you, Dick,"

--"And, although I know that you are the best-hearted fellow in the world--I listened to him, and believed him."

The Welshman sighed, and said, "It was natural, Dick; it was natural."

"It was nothing of the sort; I ought to have known better. But I didn't think, Tom, that's the truth." Richard spoke in a tone of self-reproach; he was ashamed of his selfishness, and of the unjust thoughts he had harboured towards his mate.

"There's enough of him," said the Welshman, heartily. "We'll talk no more about him, and to-morrow we will wash our hands of him. And now, Dick,"--he hesitated before he proceeded, for he was about to speak of a subject which needed delicate handling--"And now, Dick, I want to speak to you about your wife."

"Well, Tom," said Richard; in his then mood, when all harsh feeling was banished from his mind, the thought of his wife harmonised with his gentler humour. But even at that moment a sharp pang quivered through him, as the image of Alice, alone in Melbourne, without a friend, rose before him. Then there was the additional sting of his own misconduct. If Alice knew how he had been drinking lately, after all his promises and good resolutions! Little thrills of shame tingled through every nerve of his body.

"When men and women marry," said the Welshman, made bold by Richard's subdued voice and manner, "they owe a duty to each other, which I think it is sinful to forget. You have forgotten your duty, Dick. If your wife is anything like the picture you have of her, she wouldn't forget hers, I'll stake my life on it."

"She is the best and dearest woman in the world," said Richard; "and the most unfortunate, for she met me, and--and loved me, who am no more worthy of her than I am of heaven." (It is often in this way that weak selfish men atone for their bad conduct. As if gentle self-accusation can heal cruel acts!) "If she had never seen me, it would have been better for her."

"But she did see you, and she married you, Dick, so it's not very wise to speak like that now. How long is it since you have written to her?"

"It must be five or six weeks." The Welshman looked grave. "There is no excuse for me, I know. But I had not courage."

"There is no excuse for you. I wish I had the good fortune to possess such a wife."

"You deserve one better than I do, Tom," said Richard, remorsefully.

"That's a good hearing--not for me, but for you. It sounds as if you were more grateful. Think of her without a friend in Melbourne, waiting, waiting, waiting! Poor thing! who has she to lean upon but you? Write to her to-morrow. I tell you what we'll do, Dick? When we've divided the gold--there are more than ninety ounces--we'll put our two shares together, and well take your wife in mates with us. We'll divide our shares into three, and you shall send her her share with your letter."

Richard pressed his mate's hand.

"You are a good fellow, Welshman," he said. "We'll talk over it in the morning."

"No; we'll settle it now. I've no one depending upon me. I haven't much use for my share. For the matter of that, you might have the lot. Why not go to Melbourne, and bring her here? While you're away, I can be putting up a tent for you and her. I will line it with green baize, and make it quite a snuggery. I'll get a good claim, too, before you return; you see if I don't."

"She will never be able to rough it, up here."

"Dick," said the Welshman, "what do you think she is doing now, in Melbourne? She must be dreadfully unhappy, away from you, although you do not deserve her. Come, now, make up your mind. This may be a turning-point for you. We may find a big nugget yet, you know, and then you'd be all right again."

"You put new life into me, Welshman. I think I will go to Melbourne, and ask her if she'll come."

"Bravo, Dick! You shall start the day after to-morrow. She'll come, depend upon it. I'll be your friend, Dick, yours and hers. You will see what sort of a tent I'll have ready for you by the time you come back. Now then, write her a letter."

"What is the use, if I am going to Melbourne to-morrow?"

"The post will travel faster than you. Write just two or three lines, and give her a glimpse of sunshine. Her face will be all the brighter for it when she sees you."

Welsh Tom placed writing materials on the table, and Richard sat down to write. Before he commenced, he took from his pocket a small pocket-book, containing the letters Alice had sent him, her picture, and Little Peter's stone heart, which he had picked up on the stairs when he parted from his wife. He opened Alice's last letter, and read it; his heart grew very tender to her as he read. The letter was full of hope, full of encouraging counsel; it bade him not to be cast down, not to despair, not to let any thought of her disturb his mind. She yearned to be with him, but she could wait without repining if he would persevere in his good resolutions. "As I know you will, dear," she wrote, "for my sake, to whom you are all the world. I am not dull, for I think of you always, and of the brighter days to come. Never mind if you are not fortunate at first; fortune will smile upon you--I know, I feel it will. God will never desert us, if we are true to ourselves and to each other. And oh, Richard darling! since you have gone I have witnessed such suffering in others--such misery, endured with patience by poor unfortunate persons--that I feel our lot to be a happy one in comparison with theirs. I think the experience was sent to me as a lesson." Richard read to the end with moistened eyes.

"God bless her!" he said, and he took her portrait from his pocket-book, and kissed it.

Then he wrote a short letter--a few lines merely--telling Alice that he would be with her almost directly, and mentioning incidentally that he had got rid of a bad man, who was his mate, and that he would bring some gold to Melbourne. He had a postage-stamp in his pocket-book, and to get it he turned out the contents of the book upon the table. As he did so, Little Peter's stone heart rolled away, and would have fallen if the Welshman had not caught it. Richard sealed his letter, affixed the postage-stamp, and looking towards his mate, started to his feet in surprise.

Welsh Tom was all of a tremble, and his eyes were fixed with a terrified expression upon the stone heart, which lay in his hand.

"Tom!" Richard cried, in alarm.

The Welshman grasped Richard's wrist, and asked, in a husky voice--

"Where did you get this from?"

"That heart! I picked it up on the stairs when I bade Alice good-bye in Melbourne. I thought it was a good omen. What makes you look upon it so?"

As the Welshman gazed upon that little piece of stone, he saw the woodland, lake, and mountain, which lay around his old Welsh home, where love and peace had reigned until the false friend came to wreck their happiness. The heart-shocks, the stern resolves born of desolation, the flight of his sister, the agony of his mother, his pursuit of the villain who had so ruthlessly violated the sacred ties of friendship and hospitality, the promise of reparation, the false charge, the trial, the condemnation: all this he saw in that little stone heart.

"It is like a sign from the grave." he said. "And you don't know to whom it belongs?"

"No."

"It was my sister's--my poor, lost sister's. I gave it to her in Wales, when she was good. I told you I fancied once I saw her in Melbourne. If she should be alive, Dick--if she should be there! Oh, Dick! Dick!"

"When I get to Melbourne, Tom," Richard said, "I will try and find out all about it. Perhaps Alice knows." And then he thought pityingly of the bad character of the house in which he had found the heart. "Take courage, Tom, we will find her if she be alive."

"Yes, we will find her," Welsh Tom said, as if speaking to himself; "her and hers, perhaps. It is my duty. If anything happens to me, Dick, promise me that you will take care of her, and be a brother to her."

"What should happen to you, Tom?"

"I cannot tell. I have a foreboding of evil upon me. Promise."

"I do promise."

"Thank you. We will talk to-morrow morning about this"--he placed the stone heart to his lips, and taking from his pocket a chamois-leather bag, nearly filled with gold, he dropped the heart in it, and placed the bag beneath his pillow. "I shall turn in now. I am tired, and I want to go to bed and think."

"All right, Tom, I shall turn in too. I heard to-day of a good bit of ground, and I shall be up early in the morning to have a look at it before I go to Melbourne. Good-night, old fellow."

"Good-night, Dick."

Richard was soon asleep, but the Welshman lay awake for a longer time than usual, reading his mother's Bible. He had a strange sort of feeling about him. His mind was thronged with old associations. Impelled by some heaven-directed influence, he crept out of bed, and knelt down and prayed. Then he got into bed again, and thought of his sister, and of their once happy home in the old Welsh mountains. He kissed the Bible before he fell asleep; and, as consciousness was fading from him, the last thing he saw, with his inner sense of sight, was the face of his old mother, as he remembered it in his boyish days.

Everything in and around the tent was wrapped in deepest shade. The moon had not yet risen. The stars glimmered dimly in the heavens, and the wind floated by with soft sighs. Scarce the barking of a dog disturbed the stillness. Nothing but the deep breathing of strong men was heard. A solemn hush was over all. Yet there was wakeful life within the tent--wakeful life in the person of the Tenderhearted Oysterman, who, with but little trouble, had succeeded in unfastening the calico door from without. When he was inside, he softly closed the door, and crouched upon the ground, listening to the regular breathing of the sleepers. Satisfied that his entrance had not disturbed them, he took a piece of phosphorus from his pocket, and rubbed it on the sleeve of his serge shirt. As he held his arm up to his face, a dim, ghastly glare was reflected in his cruel eyes, and upon his cruel lips. He then took out Richard's clasp-knife, and opened it slowly, so as to avoid the click of the spring. His plans were well matured. In the event of any struggle, and of Richard's awaking, he would call out for assistance, and accuse Richard of the murder. He could easily account for his appearance in the tent, and, for the rest, Richard's knife, and the quarrel between the mates, would be sufficient evidence. He thought over all this as he crouched upon the ground, with the open knife in his hand. He slowly drew the bright blade across the phosphoric glare on his sleeve, and then suddenly rose, and bent over the sleeping form of the Welshman. The doomed man was lying upon his back; and his arm, carelessly thrown over his pillow, rested upon the old Welsh Bible. The coverings on the bed were disarranged, and the Welshman's strong, muscular chest was partially bared. If, at that awful moment, he had awakened, it would not have saved him: for the hand of the murderer was raised, and, with one strong, cruel flash the knife was buried to the hilt in the heart of the sleeping man! A sudden start an agonised quiver of every nerve--a choking, gasping sigh and moan--and the murdered man lay still in death. Not more still was his form than was the form of his murderer. Motionless as a statue, the Tenderhearted Oysterman stood, as if petrified. For a brief space only he so stood; for presently his muscles relaxed, and he groped under the dead man's pillow for the gold. He uttered a stifled scream as his hand came in contact with the dead man's face; but directly afterwards, he cursed himself in silence for his folly. When he had found the gold, he turned his phosphorus-lighted sleeve towards the murdered man. He felt sick and faint as the ghastly blue glare fell upon the Welshman's bleeding breast, and with a shudder which he could not repress, the Tenderhearted Oysterman crept stealthily from the tent.

Pale and trembling, he halted for a few moments outside, as if for rest. He could hear nothing but the beating of his heart against his ribs; he could see nothing but the phosphorescent glare upon his arm. As though he had looked into some weirdly-illuminated mirror, in which he saw a fadeless picture of his crime, he hurriedly turned up the sleeve, and so shut out the glare. Then he walked towards Breakneck Gully. The loneliness was awful to him. As he crept slowly along--for he had to thread his way for the first mile between deserted claims, and over white hillocks of pipeclay soil--he listened eagerly for the barking of a dog, for any sound that would break the dreadful silence, and divert his thoughts from the deed he had committed. But no sound fell upon his ears; for him the air was full of silent horrors. Strive as he would, he could not rid himself of the fancy that the shadow of the murdered man was gliding after him as he walked alone. He dared not look behind him. He almost tumbled into a hole as he quickened his steps, the sooner to reach his comrades' tent; but, recovering himself, he started back with an oath upon his coward lips, for he saw the Welshman's face rise suddenly from the claim. It disappeared as suddenly at his fancy had conjured it up, and he went on his way. As he came to the end of the diggings, a faint light was spreading over the verge of the horizon. The moon was rising. He was thankful for this; the thought that he should have to walk, surrounded by black night, through the wooded range which led to Breakneck Gully, somewhat daunted him; but he would have the moon now to light him through the bush. He cursed his weakness; he cursed his folly in not having provided himself with brandy to keep up his courage. He needed it; for he could not shake off the idea of the appalling shadow gliding after him. His thoughts travelled back to the tent, and fascinated by the horror of the last hour, he lived it over again. Once more he enters the tent, vividly recalling each minute circumstance; once more he crouches upon the ground, intent and watchful! He takes the piece of phosphorus from his pocket, and rubs it upon his sleeve--there is a blue glare across his eyes as he thinks this part of the tragedy over again--he opens the knife softly, cautiously--he bends over the sleeping man, raises his arm, and strikes! Horror! what is this? Standing directly in his path is a tall, dark form, with gaunt arms stretched towards him. He can see its hair stir, he can hear a sobbing wail issue from its mouth. His craven heart leaps with terror; then a sickly smile of relief passes over his face, for he sees that he has been startled by a tree, its branches trembling in a gust of wind which has just swept by. All nature seemed to cry against him for the coward deed he had committed. The moon rose slowly behind a veil of mournful clouds; the stars paled; the wind gasped and sobbed; and every leaf and branch quivered as he crept along. Once he closed his eyes as if shut out the terror which encompassed him; but more thickly thronged his ghastly fancies, making themselves visible. And when he looked before him once more, a shadow seemed to glide swiftly by him, and to hide itself behind a clump of timber at his right. So strong was this fancy upon him, that he took a knife from his pocket, and held it ready to strike. A sigh of relief escaped him when he had left the clump of timber at his back; but still he dared not look behind, for the awful shadow was following on his steps. Louder grew the moaning of the wind; more strongly trembled every leaf and branch; and a flash of pale lightning glancing suddenly upon his sight, almost blinded him. But not so suddenly that he did not see within it a picture of the Welshman lying upon his stretcher, with a stream of blood flowing from his breast. Then the clouds began to weep; thick clots of rain fell, like clots of blood, in his path; and he trod in them, shuddering. He was near the end of his journey now. Within fifty yards of his comrades' tent stood a solitary tree. As he passed it the heavens opened, and he saw again the vision of the Welshman's bleeding heart, while the now fast-pouring rain seemed to coil a host of bloody symbols round about his feet.

CHAPTER XX
THE TENDER-HEARTED OYSTERMAN
TRAPS HIS GAME

Before the rising of the son, Richard Handfield was on his way to inspect the new ground, of which he had spoken to his mate on the previous night. When he rose, he did not strike a light, and he trod softly out of the tent, so as not to wake the Welshman. A tender feeling of regard for his mate had sprung up within him; and as he hastened along, with pick and shovel slung over his shoulder, a new happiness took possession of his heart. The reward of right doing is very sweet, and Richard was tasting this, in anticipation, for the first time in his life. To-morrow he would start for Melbourne to join his wife. He knew that no persuasion would be required to induce her to live with him on the gold-fields. He felt very remorseful at his neglect of her: never, since he had known her, had he so truly appreciated her goodness. He thought of her patience, of her sufferings; and the memory of her sad, sweet face came upon him as he walked along. "She's a dear, good girl," he said to himself. "The Welshman is right; I don't deserve her. Never mind, I'll make it up to her, now; she shall not suffer for me any more." And, with heart and step rivalling each other in lightness, he wended his way to the new ground.

The sun was up when he retraced his steps. He had marked off a claim, and intended returning with his mate, after the gold was divided, and they had broken with Honest Steve. When within a quarter of a mile of his tent, just as he was revolving in his mind what could have been Honest Steve's intention in setting him and the Welshman against each other, he heard the word "Murder," spoken by one of two diggers who were coming out of a tent, a few yards before him. Murder! His heart almost ceased to beat, and a sense of impending evil fell upon him. At the rear of the tent, there was a little straggling bush, through which Richard was walking when he heard the word. It arrested him for a moment or two. "Murdered in his bed," the man said; "the knife sticking in him, too! Let's run and see." And they ran off at full speed in the direction of the Welshman's tent. A feeling of dread came upon Richard, and he was preparing to hasten after the two diggers, when a hand was laid upon his shoulder, and a warning voice cried, "Hist!" in his ear. Turning, he saw the face of Honest Steve.

"Turn back," said Steve: "all's discovered."

"What's discovered?" asked Richard, looking round, bewildered.

"If they catch you," continued Steve, not heeding the question, "they'll lynch you; I heard them swear they'd do it, and I came away, fearful they might set on to me."

"What are you talking about?" asked Richard, a vague terror stealing over him.

"They have read the letter in which you said you had got rid of a bad mate, and was going to Melbourne with the gold. What a mistake it was for you to leave that letter about! I thought you were more fly than that, Dick."

"I don't understand," muttered Richard, putting his hand to his head, confusedly.

"But it wasn't so much that," pursued Honest Steve, "as it was the knife. It was the knife that settled it. It wouldn't have looked so bad, if the knife hadn't been found sticking in him. What made you leave that behind you?"

Instinctively, Richard felt in his pockets; his knife was gone!

"Then they know you've been quarrelling together--"

"Good God!" cried Richard, the full horror of his situation breaking upon him. "The Welshman--"

"Murdered, as you know."

"Murdered!"

"It was an infernal cowardly thing for you to do," said Honest Steve, with simulated indignation.

"Do you believe?--" Richard gasped out.

"Look here! What's the use of asking me if I believe? Who wouldn't believe, I should like to know? Here he is, found murdered in the tent this morning, your knife sticking in him, the gold gone, your letter upon the table, and you cut away--"

"But I'm going back," cried Richard, in despair.

"Say your prayers first, then. They'll hang you on the nearest tree-- they've got the rope already slung. I heard one of them say that he told you last night you was afraid to go home, and that you started off in a rage directly afterwards. The men were speaking of it just now. When you quarrelled with him yesterday afternoon, you know you said you'd be even with him."

"But we made friends last night."

"Who knows it?"

Richard staggered and almost fell. The question struck him like a blow. Who knew it? No one. None but the Welshman and himself knew of the reconciliation that had taken place between them. In the eyes of the world they were still enemies. Of what use would be his simple word? He felt that the chain of evidence was too strong for him to attempt to struggle against. What a change had come over his prospects within the last hour! The new life of happiness that had dawned upon him had faded away, and now his future was full of horror. "Fate is against me," he groaned; "what is the use of my struggling?"

But in the midst of his great peril came the thought of the disgrace that would attach to his name. Alice, too; it would be her death. Weak, vacillating, he was, but she must not think him infamous. He was unworthy of her, but he would not bring that disgrace upon her. "I must save her from this misery," he thought; "I must save myself from this shame, if only for her sake. This is some foul plot against me. I may unravel it, if I have time. Where can I hide?" And then with that marvellous rapidity of thought which conquers time, he reviewed, in a few brief moments, the whole of the circumstances. He felt that there was no chance of escape if he gave himself up--the net of circumstantial evidence was too strong for him, unaided, to break through. In this most dread extremity, strong points in his character came out, and he determined, if possible, to clear himself from the imputation of the infamous crime. But to accomplish that, he must be free. Where could he hide? As if in answer to his thought, Honest Steve said--

"See here, Dick. We're mates together, and I ain't going to desert you. You may have killed the Welshman, or you may not, I'm not going to be squeamish about that. One thing's certain--it couldn't look blacker against you. But then it looks a little black against me, too; because you know I'm not a prime favourite. If you like to come with me, I'll show you where you can hide away for a time."

"If you believe I did this deed, why do you wish to save me?"

"I'm coming to that. I don't do it out of love for you, don't deceive yourself. You will find out soon enough. I've got a purpose to serve. I fell in with some old mates yesterday, and I'm going to join 'em again. You can make one, if you like."

"Explain yourself."

"Let's get away from here, first. The diggers'll about directly."

Even as they spoke they saw strangers, talking excitedly, coming towards them. They crouched down in the bush, and hid themselves from the men.

"The damned villain!" Richard heard one say. "The mean, cowardly villain, to kill poor old Tom! And he put himself up for a gentleman, too, and didn't think us good enough for him!" Honest Steve nudged his companion as if to direct his attention to the speaker. But Richard needed no reminding; he heard the words, and they burnt into him and made him writhe. "If we catch him, we'll lynch him, by God!" exclaimed another. Richard caught sight of their faces, and felt that there would be no mercy for him at their hands. Guiltless as he was, he breathed more freely when they had passed out of hearing.

"Come now," said Honest Steve, "we can't afford to lose time. It is too precious."

In silence, Richard rose and followed him.

They set off stealthily, looking warily about them, and walked for nearly an hour, Honest Steve leading the way. So well did he know the locality, that they did not encounter a single person. When they came to Breakneck Gully, and were within sight of Jim Pizey's tent--

"Do you know whose tent that is?" he asked.

"No."

"That's Jim Pizey's tent."

A light broke upon Richard, but he checked the expression of the thoughts which rushed upon his mind.

"Is Jim Pizey there?" he asked, almost calmly.

"Yes, he's there, waiting for us."

"Waiting for us!"

"Yes. That's lucky, isn't it?"

"Your voice suddenly sounds familiar to me," said Richard, turning his eyes upon Steve's face. "Who are you?" Honest Steve passed his hand over his face, and on the instant, Richard, looking at him, recognised him. "Great Heavens!" he exclaimed. "You are the Tenderhearted Oysterman."

The Oysterman nodded and smiled.

"You have shaved the hair off your face to deceive me," Richard cried. "You made that black mark under your eye for the same purpose. And you came to us, and lied to us, and played your pious part--"

The Oysterman with a self-satisfied leer, took his Bible from his pocket, and, tearing out a leaf, lit it from the light of a match, and applied it to his pipe.

"That's the use I make of it now, Dick," he said. "Pity to waste it!"

"You villain! We found out last night, Tom and I"--at the mention of his mate's name, Richard trembled so that he could scarcely stand; he had to steady himself before he could proceed--"we found out last night that you had been lying to both of us, and raising ill blood between us. We found it out last night, and we shook hands and made friends. Thank God, at least, for that!"

"That's a consolation for you at all events," said the Tenderhearted Oysterman, in a mocking voice.

"You devil!" Richard cried. "*You* killed poor Tom, and with my knife!"

He struck wildly at the Oysterman, but the Oysterman caught his hand and forced him to the ground. He had not tasted food that morning, and hunger and excitement made him very weak.

"Listen to me," the Oysterman said, "or I will tie your arms behind you, and give you up to the diggers. That would set me clear with them if nothing else would. With you, they would make short work. Everybody loved Welsh Tom"--(Richard groaned)--"he was so good, and kind, and considerate. Why, I was fond of him in my way--ay, I was," he repeated, chuckling, as Richard looked at him with a kind of wondering horror. It was one of the most revolting features in this man's character that he was continually vaunting himself as being full of tender feeling. "You know what we wanted you to do in Melbourne: we laid all our plans open to you, and thought you were going to join us. But, somehow or other, you gave us the slip. We thought we had you all right, too, but you was too clever for us that time. Now, you will find we are too clever for you. Do you remember the five-pound note Flick changed into gold--the five-pound which Pizey gave you for your wife's watch? Well, that note was a forged one. So it is a good job you are not going back to Melbourne, for the detectives are after you there, my lad. I was pretty mad when I found you had cut away; but I determined to have you. And when the Tenderhearted Oysterman makes up his mind, blood can't stop him."

He spoke vindictively, almost savagely, and Richard shuddered as he listened.

"I hated you in Melbourne for your infernal airs of superiority. You were too good for the likes of us. Are you too good now? I hated you then, and you were mixed up with some I hated worse than you. There was Grif--that friend and lickspittle of your wife's--if ever I set eyes on him again, I'll strangle him, by God! I hated you and all your lot. I made up my mind to snare you, and I have. I came to these diggings because I heard you were here; I laid my plans well, you will confess, I won you over by playing upon the meanness in you which makes you think yourself superior to everybody else. I humbled myself enough to you, I hope. Though I did think, at first, that you suspected me."

"I did suspect you."

"I thought so; but I was too clever for you. Well, now my part is played out. What are you going to do? Give yourself up?"

"No."

"What then?"

"What do you want me to do?"

"To join us. There is only one of two things for you to do. Choose."

"What are your plans?"

"We are going to rob Old Nuttall's station. That's what we want you for. You know the lay of the house, and where the old man would be likely to hide his gold. You owe the old fellow a grudge; you can pay it off. He has treated you badly enough. As he would not give you any of his gold, you can help yourself to some of it. Now for your decision. I have spoken pretty plainly, haven't I?"

"Yes. Give me two minutes to reflect. Nay; you can put up your pistol. I shall not run away, with that charge of murder hanging over my head."

He turned his back to the Oysterman, and thought. He saw it all now; the whole plot was bare before him. He remembered the anxiety of Jim Pizey, when they were in Melbourne, that he should join the gang, for the purpose of sticking up Highlay Station; he remembered the threats they used in their attempt to coerce him. The story of the forged five-pound note he heard now for the first time. Well, that was a portion of their scheme. The part of "Honest Steve" had been played to trap him. The Oysterman had sown dissension between him and the Welshman, had committed the murder, and had stolen his knife for the purpose of implicating him. If he made his escape from the gang, and was taken, he could not establish his innocence: the chain of evidence against him was complete. But if he consented to join the gang, he might gain information which would clear him from the charge. He had been the dupe; now he would play the fox. He would blind them; he would go with them to his father-in-law's station; in the next few days he would be able to get evidence of the Oysterman's guilt, and then-- But he could not think out the rest. Chance might aid him. If the worst befell, when they got to the station, and he had no means of establishing his innocence, he would save Alice's father; that would be one good thing done. It might be the means of reconciling father and daughter; that would be sweet, though he himself were lost. It would be sweet to be able to do some little good for Alice, even though she would not know he had done it. He knew the desperate character of the men he had to deal with, and that it behoved him to be wary. All this was thought out in less than the two minutes he had asked for.

"I will join you," he said to the Oysterman; "not because it is my inclination to do so, but because I must, as you say. It is better than being strung up by the diggers; I'll keep my life as long as I can."

"That's well said," returned the Oysterman; "but look here, mate. You go in heart and soul with us. No treachery, mind. We know who we've got to deal with. You'll be looked after, I can tell you."

"I suppose I shall," said Richard; "but I must take my chance. It's bad enough being compelled to turn thief and bushranger, but it would be worse if I was caught. I speak as plainly as you, don't I?"

"Bravo, Dick," said the Tenderhearted Oysterman, clapping him on the shoulder; "you're more sensible than I took you for. We shall make a good haul with this job, and when it's done you can get off to America, and turn honest again, if you like. There's Jim Pizey at the door. Let's join him. We'll start directly."

CHAPTER XXI
THE MORAL MERCHANT CALLS A MEETING OF HIS CREDITORS

The office of Mr. Zachariah Blemish was situated in one of the busiest and most respectable portions of the City. There was an air of business about it which unmistakeably stamped its character; its polished mahogany panels seemed absolutely to twinkle with riches. The spirit of pounds, shillings, and pence peeped out of its every corner, and appeared to be cunningly busy over the sum of multiplication--a sum which may be said to comprise the whole duty of mercantile man. The swing-door of the office had a hard time of it--from morn till night it creaked upon its hinges, complainingly. If ever door had occasion to growl that door had. If ever door bemoaned its hard fate, or protested against being worked to death, that door did. Sometimes it sent forth a piteous wail; sometimes a long-sustained groan; sometimes an agonised little squeak, as much as to say, "Now it is all over with me!" But it wailed, and groaned, and squeaked in vain. There was no rest for it. For weeks, and months, and years, it had been flung open with ferocity, and slammed to with vindictiveness; for weeks, and months, and years, it had been pushed and banged with venomous cruelty. But a day came when it rested from its labours, and when its wails, and groans, and squeaks, ceased to be heard.

It is surprising what consternation the simple closing of a door can produce. If the swing-door of the office of Mr. Zachariah Blemish had been aware of the dreadful tremor that thrilled through commercial circles on the day that it hung quiescent on its hinges, it would have squeaked of its own accord with fiendish satisfaction. If it could have seen the dismal faces of those ruthless men who had for years so cruelly pushed, and slammed, and banged it, it would have laughed in its baized sleeve, vindictively. But it had no means of satisfying its vindictive feelings, for it was shut out from the busy world, and a gloomy shade encompassed it.

There was great dismay in the City. The office of Mr. Blemish shut up! What could it mean? Was it a temporary suspension, or a total smash? Why, everybody thought he was rolling in wealth. Everybody asked questions of everybody else. Quite a crowd was congregated outside the office during the whole day; and the outer door was stared at with feelings somewhat akin to awe, as if, like the Sphinx, it contained within its breast the knowledge of an awful mystery. Among the crowd were many members of the Moral Boys' Bootblacking Reformatory, who stood and stared with the rest, wondering what heroic deed their Moral President had performed. In the midst of the general wonderment came whispers of disastrous speculations; losses in sugar, losses in flour, losses in saltpetre, losses in quicksilver, losses by underwriting, and losses by guarantying. Ships had been wrecked, cattle stations had fallen in value, large firms in India had failed, debtors had absconded. But still, these were trifles to a man of such immense wealth as Blemish was reputed to be. And such a moral man, too.

Later in the day, it was reported that a meeting of creditors had been called, and a dark rumour was circulated that the estate would not pay a shilling in the pound. What were his liabilities? Some said fifty thousand pounds, some said a hundred thousand, some said half a million. The smaller sums were soon indignantly rejected, and the liabilities were fixed, to the satisfaction of everybody, at half a million. No--not to the satisfaction of everybody; not at all to the satisfaction of his creditors, who were furious. They were a numerous class, but they were small in number compared to those who were not his creditors. With the public, Mr. Zachariah Blemish had never been so popular as he was now. If he had made his appearance in the streets, he would have been stared at and adulated more than ever. For had he not failed for half a million of money? What a rich, unctuous sound the words had, as they were pronounced! They rolled deliciously round the tongue. Half-a-million of money!

Certainly, he was a public benefactor. If he had poisoned his wife, and murdered every one of his ancient clerks--if he had enticed a dozen inoffensive (and of course lovely) females into his office, and killed them then and there with a deadly vapour--if he had been for years quietly strangling unsuspicious strangers, and hiding their remains in his cellar until it was so full that it could not hold another limb--if he had been the author of any or all of these highly-spiced sensations, he could not have been more popular than he was in the present circumstances of his position. He had provided the public with something to talk about, something that it could take home to its wife, and moralise over, and dilate upon virtuously. It was not every day that a man failed for half-a-million of money, and especially so good a man as Mr. Blemish.

Great was the marvel how he had managed to keep his state unknown and unsuspected for so long a time. For the rumoured losses had not come upon him at once. People had heard him speak, upon various occasions, of losses upon shipments here, of losses upon consignments there, of debtors absconding heavily in his debt, &c., &c.; but he had spoken upon those subjects so pleasantly, that it rather enhanced his credit than otherwise. The impression conveyed was, that those losses had been sustained, but that, large as they were, they were too trifling to a affect the position of such a merchant as Blemish. How had he managed to sustain his credit through all those losses, which now, it was seen, must have been enormous? Why at the time the great banquet was given to him, he must have been hopelessly insolvent! He was certainly a marvellously clever man. He was undoubtedly a very great genius; for he had failed for half-a-million of money!

And Mr. Blemish himself--how did he bear the publication of his downfall? Was he pale, anxious, nervous, humbled, crestfallen? Was he crying and fretting inwardly at his displacement from the pedestal upon which public opinion had seated him? Not at all. He was comfortably located in one of the cosiest rooms of his mansion, in handsome dressing-gown and slippers. He was smoking a fragrant Havanah cigar, and drinking iced claret, which he poured from a costly jug, a portion of one of the numerous testimonials presented to him in the course of his moral career. From where he was sitting, he commanded a view of his garden, wherein were blossoming the choicest exotics. His face was as ruddy and as fat as ever--he looked like a man at peace with himself and with all the world. And yet to-morrow he was to meet a host of furious creditors, men whom he had deceived, robbed, swindled, perhaps ruined. He had given instructions that he was at home to nobody except a legal friend, and he was passing the afternoon luxuriously, and enjoying his leisure as such a moral man as himself deserved to enjoy it.

In the evening he had a long consultation with his lawyer, the most eminent man in the profession. Long statements of accounts were examined and discussed; as to what might be said of this item, and of that. The conversation sometimes assumed an anxious turn, but leisure was found for a little pleasantry. "Do you think it is all right?" asked the honest merchant, the slightest dash of nervousness in his voice. "Quite right," replied the honest lawyer, cheerfully. Then a few documents were burnt, Mr. Blemish devoting an unusual amount of care to so trivial an operation. After which the honest merchant and the honest lawyer shook hands, without any apparent reason, and smiled approvingly at each other. The lawyer being gone, Mr. Blemish retired to rest, and slept as men sleep whose consciences are at ease. When he rose in the morning, he indulged, as usual, in his shower bath, and, strengthened for the battle, issued forth to meet his foes.

Such foes! Such fierce, malignant foes! The meeting had been called in the commercial room of a great hotel; and the atmosphere of the room was surcharged with scowls. The creditors were broken into knots of three and four each, all of whom were recounting their special grievances with glib volubility. Black looks and savage growls fraternised in the cause against the common enemy. Although each sufferer put forward his case as the worst and blackest, there were no particular distinguishing features in them. All the creditors had believed Blemish to be a man of vast means; all had been eager to swell the amount of his indebtedness to them; and all discovered that they had been diddled. That was the word--Diddled. They had no pity for each other. A dreadful selfishness was rampant among them. It was all ME. He deceived ME: he told ME this: he led ME to believe that. It was more than human nature could stand. They lashed themselves into a fury. They ground their teeth, they clenched their fists, they anathematised the name of Blemish. That is, when Blemish was not present; when he made his appearance amongst them, the storm, if it had not passed over, was lulled. The great merchant had contrived to make himself look a shade paler than usual. When he entered the room he bowed gravely to the assembled throng, and said that it would perhaps be as well that they should at once proceed to business. The common sense of the proposal striking every one present, they seated themselves immediately round the long table, and waited in anxious expectation; Mr. Zachariah Blemish being at the head, supported on his right by his legal adviser, who had before him a formidable pile of papers. After a short pause the great merchant said, that no one regretted more than himself the occasion which had called them together. A sarcastic creditor begged Mr. Blemish's pardon: he (the sarcastic creditor) regretted it a great deal more than Mr. Blemish did or could. The interruption was received with approval by the few, with disapproval by the many--by the latter not out of sympathy for Mr. Blemish, but in consequence of their anxiety to hear what he had to say. That gentleman cast a reproachful glance at the sarcastic creditor, a glance which said, "*I* am the sufferer in this affair, if you please; be good enough to understand that;" and, having thus asserted himself, a victim, whose calamity deserved the respect of every right-minded man, Mr. Blemish proceeded to say that he hoped they would hear him and his legal adviser with patience. He felt how important it was that, at this serious crisis in his career, a proper humility should be exercised towards each other by all parties interested. And, taking into consideration this and the past teaching of his life--which he hoped had been strictly moral--he felt himself called upon, before laying the state of his affairs before the meeting, to pray (and here he raised his eyes devoutly to the ceiling) that their proceedings might be conducted with Christian toleration, and that wisdom would descend upon and guide their deliberations. After giving utterance to this pious expression of his wishes, he closed his eyes, and, slightly raising his hands, appeared to pray for a few moments; and having (like a clergyman bestowing a benediction upon his flock) invoked the blessing of Providence upon his creditors, he motioned to his lawyer, who, shuffling his papers in a business-like manner, opened the ball in a dry matter-of-fact voice.

It was not his business, the lawyer said, to make remarks which would not be considered pertinent to the subject. He believed that the position in which Mr. Zachariah Blemish found himself, commanded the sympathy of every section of the community. (Most of the creditors looked extremely dubious.) Mr. Blemish, a gentleman, a merchant, and a Christian, by his conduct, earned the esteem of all whom he had come in contact, and he trusted to be always able to retain that esteem. His connection with various movements which had for their object the improvement of his fellow man generally--he might mention, among others, the Moral Boys' Bootblacking Reformatory and the Murray Cod Association (Pooh! pooh! from the sarcastic creditor, of which the lawyer took not the slightest notice)--his connection with such associations was enough to prove the kind of man he was. But the profession of which he (the speaker) was a member, could not unfortunately, while in the performance of its duties, take into consideration anything which touched the sympathies. At the present moment he felt this most keenly--for he deeply sympathised with Mr. Blemish's position. But confining himself to hard matter-of-fact, he could not but see that his client had done everything for the best, and that it was only the force of circumstances that had brought him to this pass. Mr. Blemish had struggled for a long time against reverses--against falling markets, against losses by defaulting debtors--but he was unable to hold out any longer. It might be asked, why he had not placed himself in the hands of his creditors before his position had become so desperate as it was now. For it was desperate; there was no denying it. The answer was simple, and easily to be understood. There were in the room many creditors who were merchants. Those men knew how the slightest rumour affected credit, and it was for their sake, as much as for his own, that he had exercised a wise and judicious reticence as to his affairs. Mr. Blemish was always in hopes of being able to redeem his position. There was no chance of effecting this object if his credit were impaired; and so Mr. Blemish carried on business until he was compelled to succumb. He would not detain them any longer with remarks and explanations, but would at once proceed to figures.

Which he did; disclosing in the process a very disastrous state of affairs indeed. Mr. Blemish owed over a hundred thousand pounds, and his assets, in round numbers, showed a total of some thirty odd thousand. But in those assets there were debts that were bad; some very doubtful; many which it would take considerable trouble and expense to collect. Having fully explained everything, the lawyer sat down with the concluding remark, that Mr. Blemish placed himself unreservedly in the hands of his creditors.

First, a long pause ensued. Then, as if set in motion by a suddenly-loosed spring, everybody spoke at once. One asked the meaning of this: another the meaning of that. Indeed, they asked so many questions at once, that the unfortunate Mr. Blemish raised hands deprecatingly. When the meeting, in obedience to this deprecating motion, became a little less noisy, Mr. Blemish suggested that, perhaps, it would be as well that he should retire. They would be able to discuss more freely in his absence. One of the creditors, a man with pimples covering his face, said it was a very sensible suggestion, and that as many unpleasant things might possibly be said which Mr. Blemish would not like to hear, the moral merchant would act wisely by retiring. When he had closed the door behind him, Babel was let loose. The creditors stormed, and fumed, and threatened all manner of things. Some suggested that he should be arrested; others that he should be forced into the Insolvency Court, where vengeance could be wreaked upon him. There were many shades of opinion represented. All the creditors were not violent and unreasonable. There was the meek creditor, who put in mild suggestions, and who was quite ready to vote with the majority, and retire into private life afterwards,--a sort of man who could be induced to sign any document, one way or another, with less than half an ounce of persuasion. There was the sarcastic creditor, with whom everything was absurd, ridiculous, nonsensical; he was so persistent in "pooh-poohing" every suggestion, that he soon made himself the most unpopular creditor in the room. There was the creditor who swore frightful oaths, who banged the table, who got red in the face; and who suggested that the insolvent should first have his nose pulled, and then be kicked down stairs. There was the foreign creditor, who fumed in imperfect English, declaring that the insolvent was "von dam rascal," and vowing in incomprehensible lingo, that Blemish had swindled him, "picked my pocket, sare," of fourteen hundred pounds not more than a month ago. There was the silent creditor, who did not speak, but was ready to accept any cash composition, however small; he sat quite still, did the silent creditor, for he intended to call a meeting of *his* creditors the very next week, and he was taking mental notes of the behaviour of those present to whom he was indebted. There was the turbulent creditor, who would not be quiet, but who was starting up every other minute with some red-hot impracticable suggestion. And there was the friendly creditor (who had been quietly assured by Blemish's lawyer that he should be paid in full), pouring oil upon the troubled waters, and using all his powers of persuasion to allay the torrent of angry feeling.

When the storm subsided, the pimply-faced man was voted to the chair, and the conversation became more reasonable. A great many present, while regretting the state of affairs, thought it would be a pity to put the estate into the Insolvency Court, where it would be eaten up with expenses. It might serve the purpose of unpleasantly exposing Mr. Blemish; but the dividend would be much decreased. Half a loaf was better than no bread. The meek creditor agreed that it would be unwise to put the estate into the Insolvency Court. Mr. Blemish owed him two thousand pounds, and he would like to get as much as he could for it. The friendly creditor judiciously favoured this current of opinion; and he said, that it would perhaps be as well to ask Mr. Blemish if he had any proposition to make. Of course, why had they not thought of that before? Mr. Blemish was at once called in, and in reply to their questions, he said that there were three courses open to the creditors. The first was, that the estate should be wound up in the Insolvency Court; he knew, and they all knew, what would be the result of that proceeding--a long delay, and a loss of fifty per cent, on the realisation of the estate. But, if they resolved upon this, he would at once file his schedule; he was entirely in their hands. The second course was, that the creditors should accept an assignment in satisfaction of their claims; the estate, judiciously administered, might turn out better than he expected. The third course was, their acceptance of a proposal which he was happy to say he was in a position to make--for he was not without friends. He had not passed his long career in vain. There were many gentlemen who were ready to assist him in his hour of need; and it was their kindness and faith in his integrity which enabled him to offer to his creditors four shillings and ninepence in the pound, payable half in cash, one-fourth at six months, and one-fourth at twelve months, by guaranteed bills. If this were accepted, he could still carry on business, and if prosperity crowned his efforts, he would make it his special aim to pay all his creditors twenty shillings in the pound. When Mr. Blemish had made his statement, he was requested again to retire, and the debate was resumed. But most of the creditors, as prudent businessmen, felt that to accept the four and ninepence in the pound was the best they could do; and it was ultimately proposed that Mr. Blemish should be asked if he would increase his offer to five shillings. No, Mr. Blemish said, sadly; he could not do it; threepence in the pound extra would amount to more than his friends were willing to advance. A great deal of discussion and temporising ensued; until at last Mr. Blemish, on his own responsibility, increased the offer to four shillings and tenpence halfpenny. The meeting was adjourned till the following day, when the composition was accepted. The deeds of release were drawn up in a singularly short space of time (in truth they had been prepared before the meeting, a blank being left for the composition sum), the money was paid, the bills were accepted and endorsed; and Mr. Zachariah Blemish was a free man, purged of every worldly debt.

Purged of every worldly debt. Happy man! Mr. Zachariah Blemish held his head very high indeed that afternoon, for he did not owe a shilling in the world. Positively, not a shilling, if we except his butcher and baker, and other domestic purveyors. There is not the slightest doubt that he did not even owe a shilling to those worthy gentlemen to whom he had referred as being willing to assist him in his hour of need, and who had such faith in his integrity. Strange, inexplicable mystery!

It was, doubtless, the high exultation produced by his being free from the thraldom of debt that induced him to stroll into a jeweller's shop, and to purchase a diamond bracelet for a hundred guineas--purchase it, and pay for it, too! This he intended as a present to his wife, to mark the commencement of his new career. It was a white day for him, and he celebrated it accordingly. What a sacrifice for a beggared man to make! A diamond bracelet for his wife on the day of his ruin! A model of a husband!

Sitting that evening in his arm-chair, near the window overlooking his garden of roses, Mr. Zachariah Blemish said to his wife--

"Mrs. Blemish, I think of building another wing to the house. The architect has told me that it will not cost more than a couple of thousand pounds. It will include a billiard-room, and a new dining-room, which will be a great convenience. We are a little bit cramped in our old one."

Marvel of marvels! What a man of faith was here! No sooner down than he was up again, challenging the world to come on!

The next day his office was opened, and his clerks returned their stools at their desks, and went on with their journalising and their posting. The swing-door recommenced its life of toil, and wailed, and squeaked as before. And Mr. Zachariah Blemish moved amongst his fellow-men, with his usual affability. His linen was as spotless and as snowy as ever; his face was still smooth, and fat, and ruddy. And his reputation--let the truth be told--his reputation, in the eyes of the world, was as spotless as his linen. If there was any difference in the behaviour of his fellow-citizens towards him, it was that they cringed and bowed to him a shade more sycophantishly than before.

Great was Blemish, the Moral Merchant!

CHAPTER XXII
ALICE AND GRIF MEET FRIENDS
UPON THE ROAD

With a dreadful fear at her heart, and her whole frame quivering under the pressure of a terrible excitement, Alice, with Grif by her side, walked swiftly on towards North Melbourne. There lay the road to the open country, away from the sea. The fatigue Alice had undergone the previous day seemed to have had no effect upon her. Poor Milly's death, and the letter which she still unconsciously held crushed in her hand, had strung her nerves to the highest pitch of tension. Poor Milly's death! As she thought of it, her eyes filled with pitiful tears. Her husband's danger! She shuddered at that; and she hurried on the faster. She heard a voice crying, "On! on! and save him! Delay not; you may be in time!" There are periods in life when the mind is so enthralled by one all-engrossing idea, that the body is unconsciously strengthened to bear strains, that, if thought of, would appear impossible. Delicate as Alice was, she had within her now the strength of twenty women. Her first great fear had destroyed all sense of fatigue. Alice could not think of physical possibilities in presence of her devoted determination to save her husband. She *must* save him. "On, on!" the voice cried to her. "Delay not a moment. Your husband's and your father's safety are in your keeping." Oh, pitiful heaven! if she should be too late. Despair almost seized her at the thought. She possessed but a few shillings, the remains of the money Richard had left her. She yearned for means to take her to her father's Station; and she looked round imploringly, as if she fancied that some good Samaritan knowing her anxious misery, might come forward, purse in hand, to aid her.

"Have you any money, Grif?" she asked.

"Yes," replied Grif.

"How much?"

"Fourteen bob."

She had about the same amount. It would be sufficient to pay for riding a quarter of the distance, perhaps, and then--why, then she would be worse off than now. Her money gone, where could she obtain the means of completing her journey? No: they must walk, and their little money must be kept for food. The letter mentioned the date when her father was to complete his purchase of the Station. She rapidly ran over in her mind the intervening days, and she knew that she could accomplish the journey in time, if no accident happened to her, and if her strength held out.

"Are you tired, Grif?"

"No," he answered, stoutly.

"How many miles can we walk in a day?"

"Twenty, perhaps, Ally; but, lord! it'll kill you."

"I can bear anything now. I don't feel the least bit weak. You don't mind coming with me, Grif?"

"Mind! I'll walk my feet off, and not stop then, Ally, if you tell me to go on."

Their road lay past the burial-ground where Grif had buried his dog Rough. He cast a wistful glance in the direction of the grave, and vindictive feelings towards the Tenderhearted Oysterman burned powerfully within him. All through the piece the Oysterman had been his enemy. "But I'll be even with him yet," Grif muttered, "I'll cry quits with him one day." Grif was possessed with the firm conviction that the time would come when he would be revenged--fully revenged--upon the Tenderhearted Oysterman, and the thought brought much satisfaction with it.

They walked on for many hours, stopping only once for rest and refreshment. Alice had impressed upon Grif the necessity of economy, and their purchases during the day comprised but a small loaf, some tea and sugar, and a tin can. There were many people on the road, but each traveller appeared so wrapped up in his own concerns as not to have even a glance of wonder for so strange a couple as Alice and Grif. They chose tracks some little distance from the main road, so as to escape observation as much as possible. About mid-day they came to a refreshment-tent, where many a thirsty wayfarer was solacing himself with long drinks of cider and lemonade. They were crossing at the back of this tent, while a woman was drawing water from a well. Coming close to her, Alice saw that she was a Negress--an old woman, whose hair was turning white. When Alice asked her for a draught of water, the old woman said, "Certainly my dear;" and, regarding Alice's slender form with compassion, she invited her into the tent. Alice thankfully accepted the invitation, and seated herself upon a stool in the back division of the tent. This portion was used as a bedroom. It contained a very clean-looking bed, made upon canvas, which was tacked to posts of strong "quartering," driven into the ground; a snow-white quilt was spread over the bed. The walls of the room which were simply of calico, lined with green baize, were embellished with two or three religious pictures, pinned or pasted on to the baize.

"You look tired, my dear," said the old woman.

"I am not very tired," said Alice. "I must not be tired; for we have a long distance to walk."

"You are very young, to be walking in the hot sun such a day as this," said the woman.

Alice answered, "Yes; but I have no choice." She spoke hesitatingly, for she had a dread of being questioned. In the secret she had to keep, in the task she had to perform, lay her father's safety and her husband's honour. If others knew what she knew, the peril of both of those who were dear to her would be greater. She almost fainted with terror when the Negress raised the calico door in the centre of the tent, and gently called "Moses!" At her call there entered a Negro, whose hair, also, was almost white.

"Don't be alarmed, my dear," said the old woman; "it is only my husband."

Alice looked up, and saw a face of singular kindness. The eyes of the Negro beamed with benevolence. No one who saw him could doubt that, black as he was, he was a man in whose breast resided humanity's best virtues. The old woman said a few words to him in an undertone, and Moses returned to the store, and brought in lemonade and other refreshments, and laid them before Alice. He handed her a glass of lemonade; it looked deliciously cool, but Alice was compelled to refuse it. The instinctive delicacy of the Negro served him here. He did not ask Alice the reason of her refusal: he knew that she would not drink it because she could not afford to pay for it.

"This is not for payment, young lady," he said. "You are my wife's guest, and you will hurt her if you do not drink."

She did not answer; the Negro's kind action and gentle voice overpowered her, and she could not speak. She raised the lemonade to her hot lips, and felt as if she were drinking in fresh life.

"You, also," said Moses to Grif, who had been attentively watchful; and he handed the lad the jug of lemonade. Grif, without demur, took a long draught, and wiped his lips upon the cuff of his ragged jacket. Then he smiled gravely at Moses, who smiled gravely at him in return. Moses the Negro lived in Grif's remembrance for ever afterwards, and, indeed, he deserves to be kindly remembered by many whose skins are fairer than his own.

Alice would have departed immediately after this, but the old woman would not allow them to leave without having eaten something. She insisted, too, on bathing Alice's feet. Alice almost wept at the kind treatment of the good old Negress; but she needed all her fortitude for her task, and she repressed her tears. She rested for half-an-hour, and then rose, refreshed and inexpressibly grateful, and kissed and blessed the old woman as she bade her good-bye. Many a thankful look did both Alice and Grif cast back at the woman, who stood at the door of her refreshment-tent and watched them until they were out of sight. They did not walk many miles further that day. Grif, with a peculiar instinct, discovered a sheltered nook where they could camp for the night. He had been thoughtful enough to fill his tin can with water from the old woman's well, and he soon kindled a fire and made tea. After drinking some, Alice, thoroughly wearied, fell asleep, while Grif, stretched upon the ground a short distance off, watched and slumbered by turns. It was a beautifully clear night--such a night as is only seen during the Australian summer. The soft wind swept gently over the sleeping girl, and the heavens seemed to look down upon her with kindliness.

She rose with the first flush of morning, and, strong in her purpose, set out again upon her journey. She struggled on bravely, but she was a weak, delicate girl, and the fatigue she had already undergone was telling sadly upon her. Her limbs were weary, and her feet were very sore; and towards the afternoon a deathly feeling overpowered her. Her strength was giving way. The hot glare of the sun was too much for her to bear, and she sank at the foot of a tree in an almost fainting state. Grif, with a swelling heart, could scarcely keep from crying as he looked at her white face.

"I must rest a little, Grif," Alice said, faintly. "Can you get some water?"

Grif raced down a hollow, where he expected to find a creek; a creek there was, sure enough, but not a drop of moisture in it. Its bed was choked with stones, and dead leaves and branches, and hard mud. He clambered up again, and set off in another direction, and met the same bad fortune. He ran back to Alice, and looked round despairingly as he saw the expression of suffering in her face. There was not a tent near them for miles, and every water hole was dried up. But a hundred yards or so before him was a bullock-dray, toiling painfully along--so painfully, that its wheels squeaked and groaned, as if for pity.

"Stop here half a minute, Ally," Grif said. "I'll get some from the bullock-driver."

And, running off, he soon overtook the dray, and, almost breathless, begged for water.

"A nice thing to ask for!" grumbled the driver. "Look at my bullocks. Water! why, it's worth more than champagne, such a day as this."

"I don't want it for myself," pleaded Grif; "but she'll die if you don't give me a little."

"Who will die if I don't give her a little?"

"My sister," said Grif, boldly. "She's been walkin' all day, and she's dead beat."

The man cast a queer look at Grif, and, stopping his bullocks, accompanied the lad to where Alice was lying. She had fainted.

"Poor lass!" said the bullock-driver, and, stooping, he raised her head upon his knee, and sprinkled her face with the water he had brought with him. Presently she opened her eyes, and gratefully drank from the tin cup he held to her lips.

"Thank you," she said. "I feel much better. I think I can walk on now."

But, when she rose to her feet, she staggered against the tree.

"You're not strong enough to walk," said the bullock-driver, who had been regarding her with compassionate curiosity. "Which way are you going?"

Learning that their road lay for some distance in the same direction, he offered her a ride upon his dray. The offer was thankfully accepted, and the bullock-driver arranged a comfortable place for Alice to lie in, and assisted her to the top of the dray. Then he cracked his whip, and the bullocks strained at their harness, and the dray creaked slowly onwards. Alice closed her eyes, and yielded herself to the peaceful influences that surrounded her. The awning over the dray protected her from the sun; the grateful shade, the buzz of insect life, even the gentle jolting of the dray and the faint crack of the driver's whip, all invited repose. And the sweet sense of rest that fell upon her brought with it a balm to her bruised spirit. There was good in the world for her still. She had experienced it even in the short time she had been upon her journey. Yesterday, that kind Negro couple--to-day, this bullock-driver, who ministered unselfishly to her wants. These kind friends were surely sent to help her in the accomplishment of her task--they were omens for good. She lay, with hands clasped, prayerfully, and the weary look faded from her face, and hope rested there instead. And thus she fell asleep, peacefully.

Meantime, Grif and the bullock-driver walked side by side. They did not exchange many words at first. They were studying each other. Grif's face and dress and general manner were evidently puzzles to his new friend.

"You're a rum one," the bullock-driver said to Grif.

Grif acquiesced so readily and quietly, that the puzzle became still more puzzling.

"You told me she was your sister," the driver said, nodding his head towards the dray, where Alice lay sleeping. Grif looked a little dubiously into the face of his companion.

"Is she your sister?"

"Yes," answered Grif, unhesitatingly.

"Are you in the habit of telling fibs, young man?"

Grif did not reply. He was very grateful for the kindness the man had shown to Alice, and, for her sake, he did not wish to anger him. The driver did not pursue his inquiries, but contented himself with drawing Grif out upon other matters. Grif, glad of any diversion in the conversation, made himself so amusing, that they soon became good friends. When evening came, Grif helped to unyoke the oxen, which, with bells round their necks, were allowed to wander in the bush in search of food. Then they collected some brushwood, and kindled a fire. Tea being made, Alice was roused to partake of it. Rest and soothing thought had brought back somewhat of freshness to her fair young face; and when she stood before the bullock-driver and thanked him, he lifted his cap with the air of a gentleman, and bowed. Tea being over, he said,--

"You thanked me just now. I do not know why. It is I who should be thankful, for it is a long time since I sat down to tea in a lady's company. You will excuse me saying that I look upon this adventure as one of the strangest I have ever met with. It is not from any impertinent curiosity, but from a sincere desire to serve you, that I am emboldened to ask why so young a lady as yourself should be compelled (for I suppose you do not do it from choice) to undergo such a fatigue?"

He paused as if expecting Alice to speak, but she did not reply.

"You may trust me," he continued; "for, although I am a bullock-driver, I am a gentleman."

"I am sure of that, sir," said Alice; "your kindness is a sufficient proof."

"That may or may not be. I have lived long enough to have learnt to distrust most things; especially smooth professions. But as bullock-driving is scarcely a gentlemanly occupation, I could have forgiven you for doubting that I am a gentleman. You are a lady; I can see that. You are not this lad's sister!"

"Poor Grif!" said Alice, laying her hand upon his head. "He is not my brother, but he is my very dear friend."

Grif nodded, and that peculiar brightness came into his eyes which dwelt there whenever Alice spoke of him as her friend. The circumstance of his being detected in telling a lie was of the most trifling matter.

"It is really so strange for a gentleman to be a bullock-driver, and I have seen altogether so many queer things in these colonies, that I can easily imagine a set of circumstances (although, of course, I should most probably not guess the truth) which might place a lady in your position. You will excuse me for speaking thus, will you not?"

"Yes."

"I should like to win your confidence. If my family were to learn that I am a bullock-driver, I think they would go insane, some of them, at the degradation. My parents are at home; they mourned me as dead some years since; and I am dead--to them. Are your parents living? Forgive me," he said, quickly, as her face flushed with pain; "I did not mean to hurt you. I will ask you nothing further. But I *should* like to serve you, for your face reminds me of a sister whom I loved, and who died young."

"I think I could trust you, sir," said Alice; "but it would serve no good purpose, for you could not assist me. I will tell you, in return for your generous speech, that both my father and my husband are living; that it is in connection with them that I am travelling with this poor lad for a companion; and that my poverty compels me to walk. Let this suffice you, I pray."

"It shall suffice me. I will not attempt to trespass upon your confidence."

"Do not think any wrong of me, sir. I am unfortunate and unhappy, but it is through no fault of mine."

"I can readily believe it. And now we will change the subject."

They sat talking in the quiet night for an hour or two. Then the shafts of the dray were roofed and hung round with the tarpaulin, and a bed of dried leaves was made for Alice. Before retiring she beckoned Grif, and they strolled a short distance from the bullock-driver, as he lay smoking his pipe. The cool air was delicious after the dreadful heat of the day. Notwithstanding her one great grief, there was a feeling of devout thankfulness at Alice's heart.

"God is very good, Grif," she said, looking up at the solemn splendour of the stars.

Grif, who always listened to Alice with a feeling almost of veneration, could not find words to reply. He also looked up at heaven's bright beauty, and pondered. If God was so good, why was Alice so unfortunate? Why was she not happy? *She* was good, he knew that. If God was so good, why had Rough been poisoned, why was Little Peter torn from him, why had Milly died, why were they enduring such misery to prevent the doing of a dreadful deed? Of himself, he was doubtful. He might be really bad, and there was a doubt in his mind whether he deserved any better lot. But there was no doubt in his mind as regarded Alice. She had never done any wrong--never, never! If God was so good, why was Alice so unhappy? He would have liked to run away from her and hide himself in the wood, for he was afraid that she would read his thoughts, which he knew would be displeasing to her. She did read his thoughts; she saw the conflict in his mind; and she took his hand and held it fast in hers.

"God *is* very good, my dear," she said, earnestly.

"Yes," the boy replied, slowly; "I s'pose He is if you say so, Ally."

"You must not suppose it, Grif; you must believe it."

"I will believe anythin' you tell me, Ally." Blind yet noble faith! Blind, from the very circumstances of his birth and education; noble, because it was founded upon the rock of a good woman's goodness.

"I want you to believe it, not to please me, Grif," Alice said, "but because it is so. If we suffer in this world, we shall be recompensed for it by-and-by."

"That's good. It's what the preacher chap said when I was in quod; only he told me it different like. I didn't believe him. But I do you. And yet he wouldn't give me nothin' when I was starvin'!"

"See, now, how good God is," said Alice; "how He has sent us friends when we most needed them. Those good people yesterday--"

"That was a queer move, that was, for niggers," mused Grif. "They're the right sort, though. They oughtn't to be black; 'taint right. I've heerd of Black Moses often, but I never sor him before yesterday."

"May God bless and prosper them! And our last friend, too. I think I should have died if this kind man had not assisted us."

"He's a good sort of a cove, for a bullock-driver, and no mistake," said Grif.

"Do you ever pray, Grif?"

"No; never knowed how to."

"Kneel down with me, dear Grif, and thank the Lord for the good He has sent to us. When I think that, but for the simple act of kindness of that good man, I might be lying helpless, unable to pursue my journey, my heart is full of gratitude."

They knelt down together, and Alice said a simple prayer, Grif repeating it after her. When they rose, Alice said,--

"If I am in time to save my husband, I shall bless you all my life, Grif."

"You've got no call to, Ally," said Grif, half crying. "I'm not a bit of good, I ain't, and never shall be!"

"You are a dear true-hearted lad, and Heaven will reward you." And stooping hurriedly, she kissed Grif's cheek, and went to her bed of dry leaves.

Never before had Grif experienced such a delicious sensation as stole over him at that moment. He trembled with an exquisite pang of wondering happiness, and wrapping himself in a blanket which the bullock-driver had lent him, he lay awake for an hour, nursing the cheek which Alice had kissed, and which was wet with happy tears!

CHAPTER XXIII
THE STORY OF SILVER-HEADED JACK

It was the fourth day of their journey. Grif was trudging along by the side of the weary bullocks, and Alice was sitting upon the dray, under the friendly shade of the tarpaulin. The road seemed very long to Alice, who was pining for the end of her journey; she was sick almost to death. She had dreamed the previous night that she saw her husband with a knife in his hand, standing over her father: rushing forward, with a cry of terror, to arrest his arm, she awoke in an agony of fear and trembling. Thank God! it was but a dream. But if she should be too late! The thought brought such horror with it that she moaned, and pressed her nails into her tender palms, and felt no pain but that of her mental misery. How she envied the travellers on the coach, as it dashed along, with its six horses, at the rate of ten miles an hour--dashed along over the rough roads, winding its way through the forest of trees, until it disappeared from her sight, taking with it, as it seemed, all she had of hope, and leaving her helpless in her despair! The bullock-driver saw her distress; but he could not help her with money to enable her to travel more swiftly, for, indeed, he was poorer than herself. He was expressing his regret to her that they would have to part on the following morning, as their roads would then diverge.

"I cannot tell you," he said, "how grieved I am that I have not been overtaken by a friend who is travelling your road, and who could have taken you to within twenty miles of your journey's end. He ought to have been up with me this morning; and now it is nearly time to camp, and I don't hear any signs of him. He doesn't travel at this snail's pace, which I see is making you unhappy. He goes along bravely, does Old Jamie."

"I am very grateful to you," said Alice; "indeed, I cannot say how grateful, for you have been a friend to me when I most needed it. I am quite strong now, and shall be able to walk well in the morning. If I can ever repay you--"

"Tut! tut!" interrupted the bullock-driver. "Repay me! It is I who am debtor, not you. I was growing into a brute, and you have made me human again. I have almost made up my mind to go home, and confess what a bad boy I have been. They did love me, although I was a scamp! Thank you for that look. It is like wine to a man's tired spirit. Many of my old friends will jeer when they find I have come home worse off than when I left. No matter; I can't expect it all sweet. But that's not to the point, now. I wish there were fairies in the Australian woods, and that some gentle sprites would harness themselves to my friend's waggon, and drag it here with a whisk! But there are no fairies in these Antipodean wilds--nothing but dried-up creeks and leafless trees and ugly rocks; the fairies are too wise to make their haunts here. Queen Mab might do something with her team of little atomies. I would like to know of what use her whip of cricket's bone would be to me or old Jamie, and what kind of spring she had to her waggon! Hark!" he exclaimed, as a sound of tinkling bells fell on the ear. "By Jove! Queen Mab has done the trick! If that isn't Old Jamie, I'm a Dutchman!"

And, almost as he spoke, there came into sight a magnificent team of six dark bays, harnessed to an American waggon. They were splendid animals, and were dressed in handsome substantial harness. The waggon was piled with cases and barrels, and the driver, an elderly man whose face might have been carved out of leather--it was so brown, and looked so tough--was sitting in front, cracking a long whip, and shouting to his horses.

"Hi! there! hi! Get along, Truelove! Now, then, Silver! Pull it up!"

Whereupon the bullock-driver sent the cracker on *his* whip flying in the air, till it tickled the noses of the leading bullocks, and he cried,--

"Hi! there! hi! Get along Strawberry! Now, then, Lazybones! Pull it up!"

"Pull it up!" echoed the teamster, scornfully. "You may well say, pull it up. I'll pull you up, if you block the road in that way. Make room for a gentleman, if you please. Why, I should be ashamed of myself for a lumbering lazy rascal, if I was you. Here am I, started two days after you, tripping up your heels in less time than it takes to say Jack Robinson! Well, if ever I take to bullock-driving, may I be--"

But here he made a full stop, and turned as red as a peony, for he caught sight of Alice in the bullock dray.

"Almost committed myself," he whispered to the bullock-driver, as they shook hands. "I didn't know you had a woman with you."

"She is a lady, Jamie," said the bullock-driver. "I am so glad you have come up, you can't tell. She is going your road, and you'll have to take her on, to-morrow morning."

"All right. If you say so, so it is. It's time we camped. I hurried on to catch you up, so that we might camp together. And who is this?" he asked, pointing to Grif, whose hitherto forlorn appearance was not improved by the dusty road. Not that it gave Grif any concern; his torn clothes, his dirty skin, his almost shoeless feet, mattered not to him. He had no thought of himself.

"This," said the bullock-driver, putting his hand on Grif's head, and looking kindly into Grif's face. "This is one of the anomalies of human nature. I don't know if the family to which he belongs is a numerous one, but if it is"--he paused, and his look changed to one of pity--"if it is, and if the other members of the family are made of the same stuff, they deserve better than this," and he touched Grif's rags, thoughtfully and tenderly.

There must have been a sort of freemasonry between Old Jamie and his friend; for, ambiguous as was the bullock-driver's speech, the old waggoner understood it. He patted Grif kindly on the shoulder, and they then made preparations for camping.

They had a pleasant party that evening. Old Jamie and Alice were friends at once, and Alice's sorrow was lessened thereby.

"Would you believe, miss," said Jamie, when tea was over; "that this obstinate acquaintance of mine--"

"Friend, Jamie, friend," said the bullock-driver.

"Well, friend, then, as the honourable member for Bullock-dray allows me to call him--that he obstinately refuses, from a feeling of pride, to go home to his family, who would kill the fatted calf the moment they caught sight of his old phiz; and persists in remaining here in these antipodes, wasting his miserable existence as a bullock-driver?"

"Don't call names, Jamie," said the bullock-driver, "or I'll have your words taken down. Besides, how could you spare me? You know you have told me I'm the only scamp on the road you care to smoke a pipe with."

"I can spare you well enough," said Old Jamie, stoutly. "You are as vain as my black cockatoo, who gives himself airs because he belongs to the upper ten thousand of his tribe. I'll tell you what keeps him in the colony, miss, when he has no business to be here. It is pride. He wouldn't mind going home if he had twenty thousand pounds in the bank; he wouldn't make so many bones about it. I know lots of people who are pining to go home, but whose pride won't let them go; they came out here to grow rich, and because they haven't grown rich they think it a reproach on them."

"There, there, Jamie," interrupted the bullock-driver; "I will almost promise to go home if you will do one thing."

"What's that?"

"Tell us a story. You have been in the colony long enough to write a book."

"I have that; but writing's not much in my line. I can talk, though, any amount, as you have just heard. But what does the lady say?"

"I should much like to hear you," said Alice.

"And my shock-headed friend?"

Grif grinned, and said he was agreeable to listen; he was very fond of stories, he was.

"Fire away, now," said the bullock-driver. "Something that occurred to yourself; no fibs, mind."

"Very well. Did you remark," he said, addressing Alice, "that when I spoke to my horses, I called one of them Truelove, and one of them Silver? I did not christen them by those names without a reason; and, to prove this, I will, if you please, tell you a real, right-down, veritable, true story, about a mate of mine, called

SILVER-HEADED JACK."

"I have seen so many strange things since I have been in the Colony, and have seen the Colony itself pass through so many wonderful phases, that I sometimes grow bewildered when I think of them, and am apt to confuse one thing with another. When I am walking through Melbourne streets, my memory often carries me back to the time, and that not very long ago, when what are now magnificent, broad thoroughfares, lined with substantial buildings, were but tangled bush, in which one might lose oneself without much trouble. No fairy story can excel, in its imaginative details, the rapid and wondrous changes that have passed over Victoria since the gold discovery. Where banks transact that business which enables them to pay twenty per cent.; where merchants trade and negotiate for shipments from all parts of the world; where copies of London and Paris swells promenade; and where fashion parades from morning to night--the Aboriginal stalked but yesterday in all his dirty savagery. You might have seen plenty of them, a dozen years ago, with their boomerangs and their dirty blankets (a luxury which all did not possess), and their black eyes glittering from beneath their dark hair; you may live in Melbourne now for years, and not see a single memento of the original possessor of the soil. They are fast dying out, and by-and-by they will live only in the traditions of the country. I could tell you some stories about them that would make you whistle--I beg your pardon; I forgot that I was speaking to a lady. What I am going to tell you now is the story of Silver-headed Jack.

"He was a mate of mine on the Echuca gold-diggings. Not silver-headed at that time, for he had the glossiest curls I ever saw. There were three of us together: myself, Silver-headed Jack, and Serious Muggins. Serious

Muggins was not his proper name, you know, but the diggers have a knack of christening each other anew when they come together, and a name once bestowed sticks to a fellow all over the Colony. Serious Muggins had come out with Silver-headed Jack, and had got the title because he never smiled. He and Jack had been friends and companions at home, as you will find out presently. They were both about the same age, and of the same build; but you could not well imagine a greater contrast between any two men, than the contrast between Serious Muggins and Silver-headed Jack.

"Silver-headed Jack was always smiling; Serious Muggins was always frowning. If you could have transferred the smile from the face of Silver-headed Jack to that of Serious Muggins, I believe that Muggins would have been by far the handsomer man of the two; as it was, he was by far the uglier. For face is nothing; what tells, is the expression that lights it up. If you'll excuse my being poetical, I should say that the face of Silver-headed Jack was like a bright day, and the face of Serious Muggins like a dark night.

"Well, we worked together on the Echuca for nearly six months; and if bad luck ever haunted one and stuck to one, and worried one, and wouldn't go away from one, bad luck did all that to us. I said there were three of us in a party--myself, Silver-headed Jack, and Serious Muggins; it was a mistake of mine, for there were four of us--myself, Silver-headed Jack, Serious Muggins, and Bad Luck. We never sat down to a meal, but Bad Luck sat down with us, and didn't leave us enough to eat. We never marked out a claim, but Bad Luck got to the bottom before us, and took away the gold. We were among the first at a rush to a new flat, and we had marked out our claim, and had stuck our picks in it, when Bad Luck whispered to us that we were out of the line of the gold-lead. So we shifted our pegs, and another party took possession of our claim. We were only a few yards away from each other, and we came upon the gold gutter at the same time. The other party got an ounce of gold to the dish--we got a speck; and when I washed out the 'prospect,' I looked up and saw Bad Luck grinning at us. If it had been a man, we would have stood up and took our revenge. As it was a spirit, we could only swear at it. Which we did--with a will!

"'Floored again,' said Silver-headed Jack, as we sat down at night to our mutton and tea and damper, and not much of those; 'I wonder if we *shall* ever get a rise? Lizzie will die an old maid, and I shall die an old bachelor, if luck doesn't change.'

"'Or she will be tired of waiting,' said Serious Muggins, 'and marry some one else.'

"'She will never do that, as you know very well,' returned Jack; 'when I write home, I will tell her what you say.'

"Serious Muggins did not reply; but a darker shade stole over his countenance.

"You may guess from this that Silver-headed Jack was in love. He had come away from home, betrothed to a young girl, whose face, judging from the picture he had of her, was just the face that any one might fall in love with, and be proud of. Now, let me tell you what I learned at that time, from my own observation. Serious Muggins and Silver-headed Jack had come out from the same village, had been schoolmates and companions all their lives, and were both in love with the same girl. Jack made no secret of his attachment; his friend tried to keep *his* locked up in his breast.

"Yet I believe that if ever there was a man madly in love, and if ever there was a man madly jealous of the love he coveted, and which was given to another, that man was Serious Muggins. He had so possessed himself of the love he bore to her, that his lips would quiver, and every feature in his face would twitch, when he saw (as he saw daily) Silver-headed Jack take her letters from his pocket, and read them; and often, when Jack read aloud little scraps from them, he would go out of the tent abruptly, and make himself mad with drink at some grog-shanty. Silver-headed Jack could not help seeing this and taking notice of it, but he did not put the same construction upon it as I did.

"'Poor fellow!' he would say upon such occasions. 'You see, Jamie, he was in love with her too, but she wouldn't have anything to say to him. I don't wonder it preys upon him; I know it would drive me mad, if I was to lose her. It is her love for me, and the thought of our being together by-and-by, that keeps me good. God bless her!'

"I couldn't help admiring the young fellow, and wishing him success. At the time that this took place I was between forty and fifty years of age. Twenty years before that, I was in love, too, and with a woman that I thought then, and think now, the best, the purest in the world. I came out to the colony to make a home for her--that was before the gold was discovered. I was unfortunate; it is now a generation since I have heard of her. I was not fit for her--I know that now; she was too good for me. But if heart-photographs could be taken, she would be seen on mine; and the memory of her dwells within me like a star that will light my soul to heaven!

"I never liked Serious Muggins. I always believed that if he could do Silver-headed Jack an ill turn, he would not scruple to do it; and I had observed that the effects of our ill-luck were different upon the two. Serious Muggins actually seemed pleased that we were not successful. You see, he might have argued within himself, that a rich claim would bring Silver-headed Jack nearer to the woman he himself loved. He was like the dog in the manger, I had reason to suspect him; for just before the time came for us to part company, this occurred that I am going to tell you.

"We were working a claim that was just turning out 'tucker.' There were three 'drives' in it, and the last day I worked in them I noticed that the pillars of earth which were left to support the roof were firm and secure. The following morning Serious Muggins had a spell below, and when he came up, Silver-headed Jack took his turn at the bottom. He had not been down a quarter of an hour, when I heard a great thud beneath me, and then a scream. I was working at the windlass, and Serious Muggins was chopping down a tree, a little distance off, for firewood. I cooēēd[6] to him, and he came running to me with a face so scared, that I couldn't help noticing it."

Footnote 6: A peculiar cry which men in Australia use as a signal.

"'What's the matter?' he asked, trembling all over.

"'God knows,' I replied, preparing to go down; 'but I expect some part of the claim has fallen in. Lower me gently, and be careful to do exactly what I tell you, when I am at the bottom.'

"'Is Jack below?' he asked, eagerly.

"'You know he is,' I replied, shortly. 'Lower away.'

"By this time two or three other diggers had strolled to the spot, and they lent a hand. When my head was even with the top of the claim, I looked up, and the only thing that struck my notice, was the white face of Serious Muggins, with a wild, triumphant, yet half-frightened look in his eyes. I took a step in the drive in which Silver-headed Jack had been working, and called out to him. I was dreadfully frightened at receiving no answer, and creeping along slowly and cautiously, I found that one of the pillars had given way, and that Silver-headed Jack had been knocked down senseless by the falling earth. Only a part of his body was buried--his head was free. We dug him out after a little trouble, and got him safely up. Five minutes afterwards, the whole claim tumbled in. Jack was not much hurt. Beyond the shaking, and a few bruises, he had nothing the matter with him. We took away the windlass and our tools, and knocked off work for the day.

"'It is strange,' said Silver-headed Jack, as he lay resting on his back, on the bed; 'I never touched the pillars. I was picking away at the bottom, when, without the slightest warning, the earth tumbled in. Did you notice anything, when you were down this morning?' he asked of Serious Muggins, who was busy making an Irish stew for tea.

"'No,' was the reply.

"'Did you touch any of the pillars?' I asked.

"'No.'

"'I can't make it out,' I said; 'there has been no rain, and I will take my oath that when I was down yesterday, the claim was safe.'

"'I thought so, too, when I was last down,' said Serious Muggins, 'but we were both mistaken, it appears.'

"'I was not mistaken,' I said, in a pointed manner, 'and as I don't quite like the look of things, I believe it will be best for us to part. We have had nothing but bad luck since we have been together. We can't have much worse when we are away from each other, and we may have better. So to-morrow morning, my lads, we'll dissolve partnership.'

"A curious thing happened that night. We all slept in one tent. It was a pretty large one. Well, I woke up in the middle of the night, and, opening my eyes, I saw Serious Muggins sitting up in his bed, and kissing a picture. I thought I saw him crying, too. I must have turned in my bed; for Muggins threw a quick look at me, and hurriedly put out the light. I thought a good deal of this before I fell asleep again. I did not know that he had a picture he set so much store on, and I settled in my mind that it was the picture of Jack's Lizzie that Muggins was kissing, and which he must have taken from under Jack's pillow. Although I suspected Muggins, I couldn't help pitying him.

"In the morning, we dissolved partnership. I would have liked Silver-headed Jack for a mate, but he thought it a point of honour not to part from Serious Muggins. Jack did not entertain any suspicions of foul play, and I did not think I was justified in telling him my suspicions, for, after all, I might have been wrong. It was a pretty common thing for claims to tumble in for all manner of causes. So we parted, and I went to another diggings.

"It was eighteen months before I saw either of them again. I heard of them at odd times as being now at one place and now at another, but I did not fall in with them. For my own part, during this time, I was always able to make wages, and was always in hopes of making a rich 'find.' I should think a gold digger's life is very much like a gambler's. There is the same feverish excitement about it, and although you may go on losing and losing, and wasting your time, there is always the chance of a run of luck setting in with the very next deal of the cards. At a new rush, for instance, while you are sinking your claim, you are always speculating as to what it will turn out; and when you go to sleep, you will dream, perhaps, that you have found a nugget as big as your head. Such nuggets have been found, you know. Men at starvation point one day, may be tolerably rich the next. I once gave up a claim in disgust, after working at it for two months. Three miners took it up a few days afterwards, and went home with twelve hundred pounds a piece for a month's work. If I had driven my pick two inches further, I should have come upon as rich a patch of gold as was ever found. During those eighteen months that I did not see Silver-headed Jack or Serious Muggins, I had only two mates. You will stare when I tell you that one of them was a woman! and a jolly digger she was! She did as much work at the windlass as a man. Her husband was my mate, first; but he was seized with a paralytic stroke, and was in bed for a twelve-month. So his wife, like a noble-minded woman as she was, worked for him by day, and nursed him by night. But he got worse instead of better, and she was advised to take him down to the Melbourne Hospital, if she wanted to save his life. When this occurred, I shifted my quarters, and fell in with my old mates. They were still working together; but they hadn't been much more fortunate than they were when we were all mates. They had a quartz claim, now, though, which they thought was going to turn out splendidly. But a great change had come over Silver-headed Jack. He had not heard of his Lizzie for six months, and he was fretting for means to take him home, to find out the cause of her not writing. In those six months he had grown a dozen years older. I don't think Serious Muggins was very pleased to see me, but Silver-headed Jack was, and he offered me a share in the claim--a sixth it was--if I would join them. It was a pretty fair offer, for the claim was nearly down to the reef, so I accepted it. Serious Muggins would have objected, I dare say, if he could have done so without being suspected of animosity; but the claim wanted a second man at the windlass, and he knew I was a good miner, so he was forced to put up with me. Well, one day, about three weeks after I joined them, we put in a blast and fired it; and when the smoke cleared away, and Jack got to the bottom of the claim, he sent up a bucket of quartz, in which we could see a good many specks of gold. We had struck the reef, and it promised to turn out well. It turned out a good deal better than we expected. The quartz was about three feet thick, and we calculated that it would run at least six ounces to the ton. We came upon a very rich patch, too--so rich, that I almost danced with delight when I handled the golden-veined lumps of stone. We raised about forty tons of quartz, and made arrangements for having it crushed at a machine that stood hard by. We took some of it to the machine in sacks, and put it, with our own hands, under the iron stampers. We didn't leave the machine until the whole of it was crushed. The first night we were all together watching the heavy iron stampers, beating down with their one-two-three-four time, and wondering what sort of a cake of gold the forty tons would turn out. I said that I thought there would be at least four hundred ounces.

"'That will give me five hundred pounds for my share,' said Silver-headed Jack. 'I shall put a good wages-man in the claim, and go home to find out why Lizzie has not written to me. I can't help thinking there is some underhand work going on.'

"'Psha!' said Serious Muggins. 'She's tired of waiting, and has married some one else. You don't think a girl will wait for a man until she grows to be an old woman, do you?'

"'I don't know what girls will or will not do,' said Silver-headed Jack; 'but I know that my Lizzie would wait for me all her life. I am almost frightened to go home, for fear of hearing that something has happened to her. The world wouldn't be worth living in without her.'

"'Have you written to her?' I asked.

"'Regularly. Only think of my working all these years, and never till now having the means to send for her, and after all not to know if she is dead or alive! Jamie,' he said to me, 'if I was to hear that she was dead, I'm sure I should go mad, or something dreadful would happen to me. You can't think how I've set my heart on my Lizzie!'

"The crushing of that forty tons of quartz took nearly four days and four nights. They couldn't crush them as fast as they do now. Quartz crushing used to cost six pounds a ton, at that time; now you can get it done for a pound. Well, it was all passed through the machine, and Jack and I were watching the washing out of the quicksilver. Serious Muggins had gone to the post, to see if there were any letters (for the mail was expected) and he was to get us some supper ready by the time we came home with the gold. You may guess we kept a pretty sharp look-out upon the machine men, as they did their work; for it would have been the easiest thing in the world for them to have slipped a few pounds weight of the gold and quicksilver on one side, without our being a bit the wiser for it. There was nearly half a bucketful of the mixture. This was poured, about half a pint at a time, into a large chamois leather skin. The skin is porous, and, upon being tightly squeezed, allows a large portion of the pure quicksilver to ooze out, retaining the gold, coated, of course, with quicksilver. It was not until the men came near the bottom of the bucket that we found how rich was the quartz that had been crushed. The first few skinfuls of quicksilver escaped through the chamois leather like silver-water, and there was but little gold left; but, when we came near the bottom of the bucket, we jumped for joy at finding it was nearly all gold. After all the quicksilver was passed through the leather, the amalgam was put into a large retort, and screwed down. The retort was then put into the furnace. When it was red-hot, the quicksilver began to rise in the iron tube, which is joined to the top of the retort, and came showering down into the pail of water beneath, like a rain of silver stars. I was glad when the shower lessened; for I was half frightened that the gold was being spirited away. Then the retort was taken out of the furnace, and opened, and there lay the beautiful gold, changing, in the process of cooling, into all the colours of the rainbow. I wonder if a miser, in counting his hoardings, experiences the same kind of pleasure that I experienced, when I saw that splendid cake of gold! If he does, his rusty old heart must be lighted up by a very delightful feeling. The cake weighed six hundred and twenty ounces, so that the quartz had averaged nearly sixteen ounces of gold to the ton. Not so bad that, eh? Silver-headed Jack wrapped up the precious golden saucer in his pocket-handkerchief--it was a pretty good weight, nearly half-a-hundredweight--and we made our way to the tent. I had my revolver cocked, in case of any accident, I can tell you. When we got to the tent, Serious Muggins was waiting for us. Jack opened his handkerchief, and looked at the gold triumphantly. As for me, I was running over with delight.

"'Got you at last, you beauty!' I exclaimed. 'Oh, you sly coquette! What coaxing you want before you give yourself up! Jacob didn't work harder or more patiently for Laban's daughter than we have worked for you. Only think, Jack, of this bright beauty hiding herself in the caverns of the earth, and refusing to show herself until we plucked her out of her miserable home! Can you imagine a bright-eyed damsel, Jack, sinking into the earth, and we diving after her, until we catch her in the rock which prevents her escape? Oh, you beauty; I could kiss you!'

"You see, I *am* a bit of a poet.

"'I will kiss you,' said Jack, lifting the cake of gold to his lips, 'for you bring me nearer to my Lizzie. Hallo! Muggins! what's the matter?'

"'I've got bad news for you, Jack,' said Muggins, who had been shifting uneasily about.

"'What news?' asked Jack, dropping the gold, and turning quite pale.

"'About Lizzie.'

"'Well, man, go on.'

"'She's dead, Jack,' said Muggins, looking as white as Jack himself. 'The mail's in.'

"'How do you know she is dead?' I asked.

"'I have received letters from home.'

"Jack didn't say a word, but dropped into his seat, trembling, and covered his face. I beckoned to Serious Muggins, and we stole out of the tent; I thought it was best to let Jack fight with his grief alone. I knew what a blow this was to him. He had not been working for himself, but for his Lizzie; and just at the moment of success, to hear that she was dead--it was terrible! He was in a dreadful bad way about it. As I sat outside the tent, smoking, I heard him talking to himself, strangely. We had left the cake of gold upon the table.

"'You glittering devil,' I heard him say, 'why did you lure me away from my Lizzie? If it hadn't been for you, I should never have left home, and we should have been together now. What would it have mattered if we had been poor? Why did I fly from happiness to you, you false, cruel devil?'

"I wouldn't have him disturbed the whole of that night. I knew that all the talking in the world wouldn't ease him. But when I saw him in the morning, I rubbed my eyes, and thought that I could not be awake. He was sitting upon the bench, with his face resting in his hands, staring fixedly at the cake of gold. He had evidently not moved from his seat during the whole night, and during the night his hair had turned as white as silver! That was how he got to be called Silver-headed Jack. I tried to rouse him, but the answers he gave me were so vague and wandering, that I was afraid he had gone mad. I saw at once that he was very ill, so I ran for a doctor, who told me that my mate had gone in strong for the brain fever. Sure enough, he had, too. We thought he would never have come out of it, and it's my belief to this day, that he never would, if one of the strangest things hadn't happened! I should say it was six weeks after Jack had been struck down. I had nursed him all the time (he wouldn't let Serious Muggins come near him), and the doctor said he couldn't last another week. How poor Jack raved while in that fever! I wonder that my hair didn't turn white through the frights he gave me! He used to fancy Lizzie was in the tent with him, and he talked to her so naturally, sometimes waiting for her answers, that often during his pauses, I turned my head, half expecting to see Lizzie's white shade at my shoulder. I was sitting at the door of the tent one evening, listening to Jack's mutterings, for his tongue never seemed to stop. I was very troubled; you see I liked Jack amazingly, and I pitied him, and could sympathise with him, for, as I told you, I had been in love myself. Of course, my pipe was in my mouth. What should we do without tobacco, I wonder! Do you know, I think tobacco prevents a good deal of mischief. What used we to say at school?--'And Satan finds some mischief still, for idle hands to do.' But a man isn't idle when he has a pipe in his mouth; it is occupation for him. And you may laugh at me, if you please; it is elevating too. Men don't plan murder when they have pipes in their mouths. They've got something else to do; they've got to smoke and think--and thinking, when you're smoking, is generally good thinking. I could philosophize on this for an hour, but it's time I finished my story. I will say, however, that I look upon tobacco as a real good friend.

"Well, on this evening, I was sitting at the door of the tent, when who should I see coming along the gully where our tent was pitched, but a woman. Our tent was nearly at the foot of the gully, and, of course, there was a hill shelving into it. I saw the woman at the first point of sight on that hill, and it almost seemed as if she came out of the sunlight. There were half-a-dozen tents scattered about, and she stopped at one of them and asked something. Imagine my surprise when I saw the digger to whom she had spoken point to our tent, and when I saw her walking quickly towards me! She was a pretty, modest-looking lassie, and had a quiet, self-possessed air about her, which took me mightily. I was thinking over in my mind all sorts of things as to her, when she came up. My hair stood on end, and my knees began to shake, for I had seen the picture Silver-headed Jack set such great store on, and this lassie's face so resembled it, that I thought I was looking at a ghost. I believe, if I hadn't been so completely dumbfoundered, I should have run away.

"'Does John Staveley live here?' asked my ghost.

"John Staveley was Silver-headed Jack's proper name.

"'He's living here, miss,' said I, 'and he's dying here.'

"'My God!' she exclaimed, and as she staggered, I caught her in my arms. 'Don't tell me that!'

"'Who are you?' I asked.

"'My name is Elizabeth Truelove,' she answered.

"'Jack's Lizzie?' I cried.

"'Yes,' she said. 'Don't tell me that he's dying.'

"'He's dying because he heard that you were dead,' I said. 'You aren't dead, are you?'

"'No,' she said, holding out her hand. A true woman's lovable little hand--real pleasant flesh and blood.

"'I think I can see through it,' I said, when I was convinced she wasn't a ghost. 'Jack's very ill. If anybody can save him, you can. But don't be frightened when you see him. He is much changed. His hair turned snow-white the night he heard you were dead. I've been his nurse till now. You may as well go in and take my place.'

"She glided past me, and I walked away. I went straight to where I knew I should find Serious Muggins. He was in a concert-room, drinking with a lot of diggers. I went up to him quite coolly and slapped his face. He started to his feet, and asked me what I meant by it?

"'You're a lying scoundrel,' I said; 'and if you don't understand what I meant by the first tap, I'll give you another.' And I gave him another--a pretty smart one, this time.

"He was bound to fight, you see. We went outside, and the diggers made a ring.

"'Now, mates,' I said, as I was tucking up my sleeves: he had stripped off his shirt. 'You all know me pretty well. I have never done a dirty action in my life, and I never mean to do one. This fellow has done the meanest thing I ever heard of. When I have polished him off, I'll tell you what it is; and then, if you don't think I've done right, you can throw me in the creek, if you like.'

"Serious Muggins fought like a devil. I must do him the justice to say that he was, physically, a brave man. But he had been drinking for a good many weeks, and that told on him. I don't think I should have licked him but for that. As it was, after an hour's hard fighting, when I was pretty well done myself, he threw up his arms. Then, I told the diggers the trick he had played Silver-headed Jack, and how the woman he had said was dead was nursing my mate at the moment I was speaking. If Muggins hadn't been lying nearly lifeless on the ground, they'd have tarred and feathered him. As it was, they declared they would do so the next day. But the next day he was gone, and I never heard anything more of him. He left a rich claim behind him, and it was out of his share of that claim I bought my first team.

"When I got back to the tent, there was Lizzie Truelove nursing poor Jack as tenderly--as a woman, I was going to say. That would have been a nice bull, wouldn't it? Do you know, that although she hadn't been in the tent two hours, it had got quite a different look in that short time. What a little treasure that woman is! It did me good to look at her! It appears that Muggins had intercepted all the letters; and Lizzie, uneasy at not hearing from Jack, and being sure of his constancy, had come out by herself, to learn what had become of him. That was faithful love, wasn't it? I don't think I've any occasion to tell you that Jack got well. He did get well, and he married his Lizzie after all. He gave up his own name, and took hers when they were married. But although he calls himself John Truelove, everybody else calls him Silver-headed Jack."

CHAPTER XXIV
MRS. NICHOLAS NUTTALL TAKES POSSESSION

Mrs. Nicholas Nuttall was in a high state of glorification. It wanted but a few days to Christmas, and she and her family were on a visit to their rich squatter relative. The promise that Alice's father had extracted from his brother Nicholas had been strictly kept. Nicholas had not told his wife that his brother had been a married man. He had entered into the compact with a considerable degree of satisfaction, for apart from the sympathy he felt for his brother's unhappiness, he derived a malicious pleasure in the knowledge that he had a secret which he was bound not to reveal to Mrs. Nuttall, and which she would take pleasure in hearing. It was shortly after he had taken upon himself the charge of Little Peter, that Matthew Nuttall told his brother the story of his life. They were riding over the vast tract of land of which he was the possessor, and Nicholas was admiring the noble expanse of table-land before them. The world was prospering with Matthew; wealth was absolutely growing for him; his flocks were increasing, his rights and freeholds were daily rising in value. With an eager desire for possession, he had bought property all around him, until he had land enough for a kingdom. Some such thought as this stirred him to remark to his brother, that it was a noble estate.

"Grand," Nicholas acquiesced; "they have no thought of such wealth on the other side of the world."

"No," Matthew said, "your plodders in time-worn cities are but slightly acquainted with the wealth of our new world. When I complete my last purchase--I have the money ready in the house, and the deeds will be signed in a few days--Highlay Station will be the most valuable in the colonies. I always had an ambition to become the largest squatter in Australia."

"And you have gained it?"

"And I have gained it." The pride died out of his voice as he uttered the words. He had gained his ambition, but it brought no sweetness with it.

"It is a great thing to say that one has gained his ambition," mused Nicholas. "Not one man in a hundred thousand can say as much."

They rode on in silence for a little while, and presently they entered a wood, where the land was more broken.

"What singular trees!" Nicholas said, pointing to a group of dwarf trees, whose trunks appeared to be suffering from gout.

"That is the Monkey-Bread tree," Matthew replied. "In the proper season--three or four months from now--you would be glad to meet with a group of them, if you were lost in the bush. The fruit of the tree grows to a large size, and is very refreshing to a hungry man."

"And these?" asked Nicholas, pointing to a group, about twenty feet in height, whose green laurel-shaped leaves and delicate red blossoms were an agreeable relief to the sombre growth around them.

Matthew stopped, and dismounting, fastened his horse's bridle to a branch of a small oak; then he threw himself upon the ground, and looked up at the blue clouds through the delicately-coloured blossoms.

"This is our Christmas-tree," he said to Nicholas, who had followed his example. "The last time I saw it in flower was in company with my daughter."

He spoke with bitter effort, and Nicholas held his breath.

"It will relieve me to speak of her, Nicholas," he continued. "She is my only child, and I may never see her again. Do not interrupt me. I may never see her again; and I doubt, even if I saw her before me now, whether I would speak to her and forgive her. It is the curse of my hard nature, and I cannot control it."

"What is her name, Mat?"

"Alice."

Since he saw her last, her name, until now, had never passed his lips. The sound of it brought tender memories to him. Since the night on which he had spoken with Alice upon the sea shore, he had not seen or heard of her. All that there was of human love in his nature he had once delighted to lavish upon her; and now that his resentment at her marriage with Richard Handfield had had time to cool, he half repented of his harshness. It might have been, as he said, that, had she written to him, or directly asked his help, he would still have shut his heart against her. But her very silence pleaded for her. Like a smouldering fire, with no breeze to fan it into flame, his anger was dying out. It was but one Christmas since that his home was lighted by his daughter's smiles, and made happy by her presence. She was a light-hearted girl then; and he remembered his neighbours' looks of hearty admiration as she played the hostess at the Christmas gathering. He remembered the pride which had filled his heart at the thought that that fair and graceful girl was his daughter; he remembered that Christmas-- but one year back--as the pleasantest time in his life. Now, what was he? A lonely, miserable man. He knew that one word from him would alter all this--would bring happiness to his heart, love to his home. He had but to say to his daughter "Come," and she would have flown to his arms, and be once more what she had hitherto been, the light of his life. But he could not bring himself to speak that word. It was true what he had said--his hard nature was his curse. If a reconciliation could be brought about without any prompting from him, he might accept it; but after saying that he would not forgive her, to hold out the hand of forgiveness, voluntarily!--no, he would not so humiliate himself. And yet it seemed that the more she humbled herself to him, the harder he grew. She had pleaded eloquently enough, Heaven knows! on the sad night that they two stood together for the last time. The sound of the soft lapping of the sea upon the sands came often to his ears, and often in the night there would come upon his inner sense of sight a vision of white crested waves, with blue depths beyond, and stars shining in them. And never did this memory assert itself without bringing with it the image of his daughter, wrestling with her misery as she wrestled with it that night, with clasped hands, and drooping head, and pleading voice.

With these memories stirring within him, he told his story, pausing often in the narration, and when he had concluded, Nicholas, who had listened in pitying silence, said,--

"Can I do nothing, Mat?"

"Nothing."

"Yet you love her so--and would be so happy if things were once more as they used to be--as they ought to be. Think! let me go to her, and bring her to you."

"No! I forbid it, distinctly. If that were done as from me--and it could not be done otherwise now--I believe it would quite harden me. Let matters rest."

He spoke decidedly, and mounting his horse, led the way back to the house at a sharp trot.

Mrs. Nicholas Nuttall was in her glory. Her arrival at the Station had filled her with lofty aspirations. Immediately she set her foot upon it, she, as it were, mentally took possession. The sight of the broad-stretching pasture-land, dotted with sheep and cattle, afforded her ineffable satisfaction. At length, she could see realised the dream of her life. But two nights previously, she had lulled herself to sleep by chattering of her ambition.

"Nicholas, my dear," she said; "I like the look of this place so much, that I think I shall make up my mind to stop."

Accustomed as Nicholas was to the vagaries of his better half, he could not refrain from saying, "But we are only here on a visit, Maria."

"Precisely so, Mr. Nuttall. I do not need you to tell me that. But do you think that life has not its duties?"

"What on earth do you mean?" asked Nicholas.

"Ah! You may well ask, Nicholas, for you have not been troubled much. But I am thankful to think that I have borne with patience and resignation the trials you have put upon me. I have borne them," said the little woman, heroically, "as a wife should. Have I not, Nicholas?"

Although he was aware that acquiescence would amount to a tacit admission that he was a domestic tyrant, and although he was aware that such an admission on his part was neither more nor less than an act of dastardly cowardice--yet for the sake of peace, Nicholas said, "Yes, you have been a very good wife, Maria." He would dearly like to have added, "or would have been, if you hadn't nagged so!" But he dared not utter such words.

"Yes, life has its duties," pursued Mrs. Nuttall; "none should know that better than a wife and a mother."

For the life of him, Nicholas could not help adding: "Except a husband and a father, my dear." And then he shrank within himself, as though he felt (the candle being out, he could not see) the look which Mrs. Nuttall threw upon his end of the bolster.

"Your coarse jokes are more fitted for a tap-room, than for this chamber," Mrs. Nuttall uttered disdainfully, and was silent for so long a time that Nicholas thought she had abandoned the conversation; but presently she said aloud, so suddenly as to make Nicholas jump: "And one of the first duties of life is money."

Nicholas pricked up his ears.

"Money is, undoubtedly, one of the first," she continued. "Position is important, but I think Money is before it. Besides, Money gives Position. Therefore, I think I shall stop here."

"At Position, my dear?"

Mrs. Nuttall did not condescend to reply, and Nicholas waited patiently, knowing that his wife would soon explain herself.

"I am thankful--truly thankful--that I see my child provided for. She will be spared such trials as her mother has gone through; and, as a mother who knows what she has suffered, I rejoice. How much is your brother to give for his new Station, Nicholas?"

"Twenty-two thousand pounds, Maria."

"Very good. Although, if my advice was asked, I should say, 'Put your money out at interest where there is no risk, and where you can always clap your hands upon it.' But, of course, my advice is not asked. And he is to pay down in cash--how much, my dear?"

"Ten thousand pounds."

"Very respectable! There is nothing that looks so respectable as being able to pay down, say, ten thousand pounds, when you are called upon. It is but justice to say, that it reflects distinction upon the name of Nuttall, to pay down ten thousand pounds in cash; and (putting out the question that I might express myself differently if my advice was asked) I really have not much objection to the money being laid out this way."

"It wouldn't much matter if you had, Maria. Mat knows whether an investment is good or not, and generally takes his own advice."

"Precisely so. Things are not far advanced enough for me to go to your brother, and to say, 'Brother-in-law, I do not think this is a judicious investment; let the money remain out at interest, until something better offers.' Things are not far advanced enough for that yet. When the proper time comes, I shall, of course, do so if I think it necessary."

"You don't mean to say, seriously, Maria, that you believe Mat would care a farthing rushlight for your advice on any of his speculations?"

"Setting aside the vulgar expression of a farthing rushlight--although you might remember, Nicholas, that we are in a country where such things are not known--I do mean to say that, when the proper time comes for me to interfere, I have no doubt that my brother-in-law will pay me more respect than you have ever done, and that he will place a proper value upon my judgment. For, I say to myself, To whom does my brother-in-law's money belong? Clearly, not to himself. If he had a family of his own, it would belong to them. But he has no family of his own, and, therefore, it belongs to us, as the next of kin. Is not that the proper phrase, Nicholas? Marian shall not be in a hurry to marry. With her prospects, she may pick and choose from the highest in the land. Ah! If I had had such prospects when I was a girl--You have no occasion to kick me, Nicholas; I will not submit to such conduct, sir!"

"I didn't kick you," said Nicholas: "I only turned round."

"Another sign of good manners! Turn round, indeed! But you shall not put me out of temper to-night, Nicholas. I shall go to sleep with the happy consciousness that I have done my duty to my family, and that, by my efforts, they are at length provided for."

CHAPTER XXV
MRS. NICHOLAS NUTTALL RECEIVES VISITORS

Having completely made up her mind as to her right of possession, Mrs. Nicholas Nuttall conducted herself in a manner befitting her high position. Not only did it behove her to assert her superiority by means of silks and satins and grand airs, but it behoved her also to be practical. For she had settled it with herself that the property must be improved and looked after. Nicholas was certainly not fit to manage the Station: therefore she must manage it herself. There was no telling how soon she might be called upon to undertake the responsibility: her brother-in-law's constitution was evidently broken; already he was beginning to stoop, and he seemed to have grown a dozen years older in the few months she had known him. Then, he was so reckless--galloping about, here, there, and everywhere on wild horses; an accident so easily occurs! "I should never forgive myself," thought the estimable lady, "if anything were to happen--if his horse were to tumble over a fence, for instance, or into a ditch, or the dear man were to be gored by a bull--I should never forgive myself if I were not in a position to manage the estate properly. To do this, I must obtain information." In pursuance of this resolution, she set about, with praiseworthy assiduity, obtaining information: as to when was the lambing season; as to the rate of increase; as to supposing you had twenty-thousand sheep this year how many would you be likely to have next; as to how much wool you could get off a sheep's back, and whether the poor things were not cold when they were sheared; as to the increase of oxen; as to the value of hides and tallow; as to the wild horses; and so on. Armed with little bits of information, she would lock herself in her bed-room, and make calculations, the usual result of which was that the property had been dreadfully mismanaged, and that when her brother-in-law broke his collar-bone, poor fellow! or was found gored to death by mad bulls, or "went off" in some other way--there were so many dreadful chances to contemplate!--Nicholas, under her management, should become a millionaire in a very short time. Thus it came about that Nicholas found in the drawers scraps of paper covered with figures and strange remarks in his wife's handwriting, as thus: "Calculated at 100 per cent, increase, first year, 100,000 sheep; second year, 200,000; third year, 400,000; fourth year, 800,000; fifth year, 1,600,000; sixth year, 3,200,000; seventh year, 6,400,000; eighth year, 12,800,000--that will do--stop there--no, say another year--ninth year, 25,600,000--one year more, positively the last, because we shall be growing old--tenth year, 51,200,000--*that* will do! 51,200,000 sheep at ❦❦1 each, fifty one millions, two hundred thousand pounds: ask Nicholas how much a year that would be in the funds." And in the night, Mrs. Nuttall would keep poor Nicholas awake with questions about interest, and puzzling sums in multiplication and division. She was satisfied that she understood everything, and was mastering everything, but the land question. That bothered her dreadfully. She drove Nicholas almost crazy about it; the land question, she read in the newspapers, vitally affected the squatters. Therefore, as a future squatter-ess, it was of vital interest to her. At length, one night, she settled the question.

"And who is it that is kicking up all this bother?" she asked. "There's somebody at the bottom of it, of course. Tell me immediately who it is." She made this demand in a tone which implied that she was prepared to wither them, directly they were made known to her.

"It's the people," said Nicholas.

"Oh! The people!" she exclaimed, sarcastically. "And pray what do they want?"

"They want to unlock the lands," murmured Nicholas.

"Unlock the lands!" she exclaimed. "Never! While we have the key--we *have* got it, I suppose, somewhere--and while I have a voice in the matter, they shall never be unlocked. A nice thing, indeed!"

Then she dismissed the matter from her mind, and fell-to calculating again.

One day the worthy lady was taking her afternoon walk, with a green silk bonnet upon her head, and a white silk parasol in her hand-- which articles of feminine vanity, be it observed, were the objects of much admiration and envy on the part of a Native, known as Old Man Tommy, who, basking in the sun, was feasting his eyes upon them. Old Man Tommy was an institution on Highlay Station. He was tolerated because he was harmless and old, and because when he was drunk he told stories of distant places, where he could find gold in "big bits;" indeed, he often brought to a neighbouring store small nuggets of gold, averaging a few penny-weights, which he exchanged for rum. When he was in his drunken humours the men about the Station would try to extract from the old man some information as to the exact locality of his gold region; but the Native was too cunning for them. All they could obtain from him was a comprehensive waving of his arms northwards, and the words: "There! Plenty gold! Big lumps! Me King Tommy! All mine!" On this afternoon he lay, sober for a wonder, looking admiringly at Mrs. Nuttall's bonnet and parasol. She was not at all offended at his admiration. It is surprising how lenient we can be to the defects or failings of those who minister to our vanity! In Mrs. Nuttall's eyes, the savage was a very shrewd and estimable person, and she strolled by him two or three times, as if unconscious of him, but really to reward him for his good taste. While she was thus occupied, Marian ran up to her, almost breathless, and cried,--

"Oh, mamma! such a dreadful thing has happened! A stockman's wife has lost three children--such dear children! We noticed them yesterday, you know. The men have been out all night looking for them, but have not found them. The poor woman is in such a dreadful way! She says they have lost themselves in the bush, and will starve to death. And I have got a message for you, and one for Old Man Tommy--"

"Me, Old Man Tommy," said the Native, rising, and throwing his dirty blanket over his shoulders.

The girl started back, half frightened.

"You no frightened Old Man Tommy!" he said. "What you want?"

"You go--find children--lost in bush; you go--join them." And Marian pointed to a little knot of men in the distance.

"Ah!" grunted Old Man Tommy. "Piccaninny lost in bush. Me go find him." And he was walking away, when artful cupidity caused him to turn back.

"You give Old Man Tommy white money, him find piccaninny!"

"Oh, mamma!" exclaimed Marian, "give him some money. He will be sure to track them! Uncle said so."

"I'm sure I shall do nothing of the sort," said Mrs. Nuttall, indignantly. "Give money to a savage, indeed!"

"Me take hat," said Old Man Tommy, looking covetously at Mrs. Nuttall's green silk bonnet. Mrs. Nuttall started back.

"There, mamma!" cried Marian. "If you don't give him money, he will take your new bonnet."

Old Man Tommy's eyes twinkled, for he understood every word that was said. Mrs. Nuttall, to preserve her bonnet, took out her purse, and extracted a shilling.

"There, bad man!" she said, dropping the coin into his skinny palm. "Now, you go."

Old Man Tommy grinned, and with a leap, he raced off at full speed.

"He is a disgrace to the station," said Mrs. Nuttall, her opinion of the savage being entirely altered, "and when we come into possession--"

"*We* come into possession, mamma!"

"Yes, my dear. We are your uncle's only relatives, and of course, shall come into the property. When we come into possession, that savage, whose personal appearance is positively indecent, shall not be allowed to remain here a day."

"I am glad he is gone with them," said Marian. "All the men on the Station have joined in the search, and I heard one of them say that Old Man Tommy could smell footsteps--"

"All he is fit for!" exclaimed Mrs. Nuttall.

"And would be certain to discover the tracks of the poor children. And they think Little Peter is lost as well, for they cannot find him anywhere. Uncle's gone, and papa, too."

"Mercy on me! Your papa gone! What does he know about the bush!"

"I don't know, mamma. He and uncle kissed me, and told me to tell you not to be frightened--"

"Frightened! at what, I should like to know?"

"As, perhaps, they would not come home until to-morrow."

"Good gracious, Marian! You don't mean to say that we shall be left alone all the night?"

"Yes, mamma, uncle said it was very likely; and we are to see that the windows and doors are locked. I hope we shall *not* be left alone, mamma; for if they come back, they will have found the dear children, and I shall be so pleased."

"Well," said Mrs. Nuttall, as they walked to the house, "how your papa, at his time of life, can go poking about in the bush all the night, after a pack of children, is beyond my comprehension! But he always was a mystery to me, Marian. When you marry, I hope you will get a husband you can understand. Your father will come back with rheumatics, as sure as his name's Nicholas!"

There was, however, nothing for it but resignation, and Mrs. Nuttall made herself as comfortable as she could, under the circumstances. Excepting herself and Marian, there was nobody in the house but the cook, whose husband had also joined the search party.

"The natural anxiety of a wife," said Mrs. Nuttall, when the candles had been lighted, "entirely destroys any idea of sleep. Suppose we have a game of cribbage, Marian."

Now, it must be confessed that cribbage was a game of which Mrs. Nuttall was profoundly ignorant. She knew that there were so many cards to be dealt to each; that two cards were to be thrown out by each for crib; and that there was a board with holes in it, and pegs to stick into the holes. She had also (without knowing exactly how they were to be applied) certain vague notions of "fifteen two," and "one for his nob." Her knowledge of the mysteries of cribbage extended no further. And it was a proof of the wonderful confidence the little woman had in herself, that, in an off-hand way, she should suggest cribbage as a means of passing the time, just as though she were mistress of the game.

They played for about an hour. It was nearly ten o'clock, and Mrs. Nuttall was growing fidgety.

"There!" she said, throwing up her cards; "I'll not play any more. You're so stupid, Marian, that you can't win a game. How *could* your papa be so foolish as to leave us alone! Oh, dear me! Don't you hear some one moving in the house?"

"No, mamma," said Marian. "You are getting quite nervous."

"Nervous, miss!" exclaimed Mrs. Nuttall, packing the cards. "I am surprised at you! Why, you are as bad as your papa! Me nervous, indeed! I should like--"

The sentence was not completed. The cards dropped from her hands, and she fell back, trembling, in her chair. For at the door stood the apparition of a man, his face covered with black crape. Marian screamed and rushed into her mother's arms, where she lay almost senseless from terror.

"Don't be frightened, ladies," said the apparition; "don't be frightened. Strike me petrified! but I'm as gentle as a dove, and wouldn't hurt a chicken! Only don't you scream again, or we'll have to gag your pretty mouths. Come in, Jim; the garrison's deserted."

At this invitation, another apparition, his face also covered with black crape, entered the room. Mrs. Nuttall's heart beat fast with fear, but she had courage enough to say,--

"Oh, please, good gentlemen--" when the second apparition interrupted her.

"None of that gammon. We're not good gentlemen--we're bushrangers. Is there anyone in the house besides yourselves?"

"No, sir," said the trembling woman, contradictorily; "only the cook."

"Where are all the men? Come--answer quickly."

As well as she was able, Mrs. Nuttall explained the cause of the men's absence.

"That's lucky for them," said Jim Pizey, "and lucky for us, too. Children lost, eh! Whose children?"

"A stockman's, sir, and Little Peter."

"Little Peter! What! a pale little sickly kid, with a white face and no flesh. Grif's Little Peter! How did he come here?"

"I don't know, sir."

"You do know!" exclaimed the Tenderhearted Oysterman, fiercely. "And if you don't tell--"

How Mrs. Nuttall kept herself from swooning dead away was a mystery to her for ever afterwards. The Oysterman had laid his hand savagely upon her shoulder, when Marian interposed, and in a trembling voice told the story of Grif and Little Peter, and of how Grif had begged her uncle to take care of Little Peter, and would not come to Highlay Station himself because he had made a promise to a lady who had been kind to him.

"And didn't say who the lady was, eh?" asked the Tenderhearted Oysterman.

"No, sir."

"I wonder what the old bloke would have said if he had known that lady was his own daughter!" exclaimed the Oysterman.

As Mrs. Nicholas Nuttall heard this, and learnt for the first time that her brother-in-law had a daughter, all her dreams of future greatness faded away, and the fifty-one millions of sheep vanished into thin air. Notwithstanding her terror, she felt indignant that Mathew should dare to have a daughter (who would naturally come into the property), and not mention the fact to her.

"That's enough of that, Oysterman," said Jim Pizey; "we can't stop listening to women's yarns. We're safe enough for the next hour or two. We'll turn the place upside down in that time. Let there be a good watch kept outside. The first thing we'll do will be to have something to eat. Now, just you look here," he said, addressing Mrs. Nuttall, who betrayed symptoms of becoming hysterical; "we ain't going to have any of your nonsense--none of your screaming, or anything of that sort. We won't hurt you, if you're quiet. Do you hear? Get us something to eat--the best in the house--and some brandy. Make us a cup of tea, too. I should like to drink a cup of tea made by a lady."

That Mrs. Nuttall should come to this! But she made the tea, and placed meat and bread upon the table, and waited upon the bushrangers, too, while they ate and drank.

The fancy entered their heads that they would have music with their meal, and they ordered Marian to play to them. When they had finished eating and drinking, the Tenderhearted Oysterman said,

"You shan't say you played for us for nothing. Here, put this round your neck." And he flung to her Little Peter's stone heart, which he had found in the bag of gold he had taken from the Welshman after the murder. "Put it round your neck, I say," he cried, as the girl shrank into a corner, "or I'll do it for you!"

The trembling girl put the heart round her neck; and then Jim Pizey, jumping up, said,--

"Now, boys, no idling! To work--to work! Come, old woman, just show us over the house. Where's the old bloke's private room?"

But before Mrs. Nuttall could reply, a whistle was heard.

"Strike me dead!" cried the Oysterman. "That's Ralph's signal. The men are coming back." At that moment a shot was fired outside, and was followed by a scream of pain. "Look here!" he said, rapidly to the women; "if you stir from this spot, by the living Lord, I'll shoot you! Stay you here, and don't move, for your lives!"

More shots were heard; and, cursing fiercely, the bushrangers hurried from the room, locking the door upon the terrified women.

CHAPTER XXVI
A NIGHT OF ADVENTURES

Alice and Grif were within a few miles of Highlay Station. That morning, Old Jamie, having brought them to the road that led to their journey's end, had bidden them good-bye and God speed! They had walked during the day, and they were now resting in a clump of bush. Alice was very pale and thin, while poor Grif was absolutely clothed with rags. He looked dusty and tired; as indeed he was, for he had consistently declined to avail himself of the waggoner's invitation to ride, and had walked the whole of the way. His feet were bare, and he was suffering from the first symptoms of an attack of slow Australian fever; his skin was hot and blazing, and his white tongue clung to the roof of his mouth, and almost choked him. But he did not complain. He had sworn to Alice that he would be faithful and true to her, and he would keep his word. As they trudged along, side by side, that day, the devoted faithfulness of the lad sank deeper than it had ever yet done into Alice's mind. Much as she knew of his devotion and his suffering, much reason as she had to thank and bless him for the help he had given her, for the fealty he had shown to her, she did not know all. She did not know that the soles of his feet were one mass of blisters; she did not know that every time he put his feet to the ground and raised them again, burning pains quivered through him. But not a groan escaped him--he returned Alice's looks cheerfully and smilingly, and bore his agony without a murmur.

He had made a great impression upon the goodhearted waggoner. Old Jamie had received a hint from his friend the bullock-driver that Alice desired to keep her story to herself; he respected her wish, and did not distress her with questions. But he talked a great deal with Grif, and learned to his surprise that Grif and Alice were not in any way related, and that they had known each other for only a few months. He failed to detect any selfish motive for Grif's service to her, and he was a witness to the boy's heroic suffering. Ignorant as he was of their story, the strange companionship was a puzzle beyond his comprehension. "You love her?" he once asked of Grif, receiving in reply an affirmative nod. "Why?" "Because she's good," Grif replied. "There never was nobody 'arf as good as Ally." That was the substance of all he was able to extract from Grif, and with that he was fain to be satisfied.

The night before they parted from Old Jamie, Alice could not sleep. The near approach of the end of her task rendered her restless, and she lay until past midnight on her soft bed of leaves, kept awake by anxious thought. Unable to bear the torture any longer, she rose and walked softly about the woods. The influence of the quiet night did her good, and she rested against a tree, with a more composed mind. She had not so rested for more than two or three minutes before a voice broke upon her ear. Nervous and worn as she was, she trembled with alarm, but only for a moment, for she recognised the voice as Grif's, and remembered that he was sleeping near the spot. She inclined her head, and listened. "You'll take care on him, sir," she heard him say. "I can't go--I can't leave *her*. I shan't like to part with Little Peter, but it'll be for his good. I ain't got any grub to give him, sir. Don't say no, sir! Take Little Peter, and not me, and I'll do any thin'--anythin' but go away from where *she* is!" She knew, as she heard these words, muttered at intervals, that he referred to her when he said that he could not go away from where *she* was. "Good-bye, Little Peter; you'll never be hungry no more!" he sighed, and then Alice heard a sudden movement, as if he were sitting up. "I remember every word," he continued. "If ever you want me to do anythin'--never mind what it is, so long as I know I'm a doing of it for you--I'll do it, true and faithful, I will, so 'elp me G--! And I *will*; I'm her friend--that's what I am--I'm her friend, till I die!' She said so herself." Alarmed at the earnestness of his voice, Alice stole towards Grif's sleeping-place. As her eyes rested upon him, he sank down, and buried his face in the earth. His arms were stretched over his head; she laid her soft fingers upon his hard hand, and felt that it was burning. Presently he spoke again, but did not move his face. "He swore he'd kill Rough, and he's done it. But I'll be even with him one of these days! Little Peter! Rough's dead. Ain't you sorry?" He waited as if for an answer. "The Tenderhearted Oysterman's pizened him. Say, Damn him!" He waited again for an answer, and then he said, "That's right. Now, come, and bury him." A long pause ensued--a pause occupied, in the boy's fancy, by a walk on a dismal, rainy night, through miserable streets, towards a burial-ground. "Ashes to ashes!" he murmured. "Good-bye, Rough. Dear old Rough! Poor old Rough!" And with the last remembrance of his faithful dumb companion lingering in his mind, Grif's sleep became more peaceful, and he did not speak again. Alice sat by his side for an hour and more, and then retired to her bed, filled with a tender compassion.

The next morning Old Jamie bade them goodbye, and shook Grif's hand heartily. During the day Alice had been much occupied thinking over

Grif's feverish mutterings the previous night, and now, as they sat together near to her father's homestead, near, perhaps, to lasting misery or lasting happiness, she noticed Grif's burning skin and the brilliancy of his eyes.

"I have overtaxed you, my poor Grif," she said. "How tired you must be!"

"I'm all right, Ally," said the boy. "Never you mind me. So long as you are in time to do what you want, and can see your father, I don't care a bit."

"We are not far off. And now that we are so near, I am full of fears. Yet I should not be so, for Heaven has surely watched over us. What good friends we have met upon the way! How thankful I am! God bless the good men who helped us on the road!"

"Yes," said Grif, reflectively; "they was very good coves, they was. I'm thinkin', Ally, that a good deal of what the preacher chap said to me was right. Not all of it, you know, but some. He told me, when I was in quod, that men was charitable and good; and they must be, a good many on 'em. Look at them two coves, the bullock-driver and the wagginer. They'd got no call to help us. It didn't do 'em a bit of good, as I sees, for they didn't get nothin' out of us. Then there's this blanket the wagginer give us. I never got no one to give me a blanket before."

And Grif rested his aching head in the palm of his hand, and mused over this exceptional circumstance in his career. Alice noticed the action, and noticed also that it was prompted partly by physical suffering.

"You are in pain!" Alice cried, anxiously, as Grif, with difficulty, repressed a groan.

"Don't you bother about me," Grif said, stoutly. "I've got a little bit of a headache, that's all. I'll be all right in a minute."

"I am afraid you have a touch of fever," Alice said, "and I cannot help you now. By-and-by, when my task is done, I may be able to nurse you. If all goes well--"

"It *shall* go well, Ally," Grif said, dreamily. "It shall go well--you'll be all right, Ally, you will--you see if you won't!"

"If all goes well, Grif, I shall be able to nurse you; for to-morrow, please God! we shall be at rest."

"Yes--to-morrow, please God! we shall be at rest," Grif repeated softly.

"I knew last night that you were ill," she said.

"How?" he asked. "I didn't say anythin', did I?"

"Not when you were awake."

He looked at her, not comprehending her meaning.

"I was sitting by you when you were asleep, Grif."

A sudden moisture came into his eyes, and he repeated her words in a broken voice. "You sat by me when I was asleep! For how long, Ally?"

"For an hour, nearly, Grif."

He touched the skirt of her dress with his hand, without her observing him, and placed his fingers to his lips.

"And you were talking of a great many things I did not understand. I knew you were not well by the way you were talking in your sleep. Is Little Peter one of your friends? I heard you speak of him."

"I spoke of Little Peter, did I, Ally? Perhaps I shall see him to-morrow. I wonder if he'll remember me, and be glad to see me!"

Alice thought he was wandering in his mind, and she took his hand in hers.

"I ought to have told you before, Ally," Grif continued. "I know your father; I've seed him three times. Once, that night you gave me the letter, by the sea, you know; twice, when Mr. Blemish set me up as a moral shoeblack" (a sharp pang darted through him as he remembered that he had broken the pledge of honesty he had given to Alice); "three times, when he came upon me and Little Peter when we was sittin' under a hedge. He was very kind that time to me, Ally. He wanted me and Little Peter to go on to his Station, but I said I couldn't go, and asked him to take Little Peter alone. And he did--as much to please the lady as anythin' else."

"The lady!" Alice echoed.

"There was a lady with him, a young lady. She called him uncle. And they took Little Peter away with them, and I've never seen him since."

So, little by little, he told the whole story; how he had always felt as if Little Peter were his brother; how he used to steal for him when he was hungry: how, when he turned honest, Little Peter often had nothing to eat; and how sorry he was to part with Little Peter, and how glad to know that the lad would never be hungry any more. Grif cried as he spoke, and the pain in his heart was greater than the pain in his body.

"You did not speak to my father about me, Grif--you did not mention me in any way?"

"'Tain't likely, Ally. If he'd a' known that you and a poor beggar like me was friends, it wouldn't have done you much good. He knows pretty well what sort of life I've led."

"There are good and bad in the world, dear Grif. It is not your fault that your life has not been cast in pleasant places, nor amongst good people."

"They're a bad lot I've been amongst. That's the reason I'm so bad, I s'pose."

"Ah, dear Grif," said Alice tenderly; "if all were like you--"

"They'd be precious queer, Ally, if they was all like me. It's a good job for them that isn't! I oughtn't to have been born, that's where it is! I wish I never had been. I wouldn't if I could have helped it."

"Hush! you must not speak like that."

"I can't help it, Ally," said the boy fretfully. "If they'd come to me and said, 'Now, will you be born or not?' I should have said, 'No, I won't!'"

"It is by God's will that we are here," said Alice, with tearful eyes. "There is a better world than this."

"Is there, Ally?" asked Grif, eagerly. "Is there? The preacher cove said there was, but I didn't believe him, he spoke so hard-like. It didn't sound good the way he said it. It set me agin it."

"Yes, dear Grif, another world where sin and sorrow are not known."

"I wouldn't mind goin' there," said Grif, musingly, "if it's all right. I'd rather be out of it, though, if it's like this one--that is, unless I was a swell. I wonder if my dawg Rough's there! I should like to see old Rough agin. But lord! I don't expect they'd have me among 'em. I'm a regular bad 'un, I am!"

"There is One above us, my dear," said Alice, resting her hand lightly on the boy's shoulder, "who knows your heart, and will reward you for your goodness. If you have erred, it is through no fault of yours."

"Not as I knows on. I never bothered about nothin' else but my grub. I'm not so bad as Jim Pizey or the Tenderhearted Oysterman. He's a orfle bad 'un, is the Oysterman--ten times worse nor me! He'd steal a sixpence out of a blind man's tray!"

"I pray that our journey may end happily," said Alice, "for your sake as well as mine. You are my brother, now and always. I am so tired, Grif, that I must rest for a couple of hours; then we will go on to my father's house."

"All right, Ally. I'll watch, and call you."

And spreading the blanket over Alice, Grif retired a short distance, and lay down. He meant to keep awake, but he was overpowered by fatigue, and presently he dozed off, and then slept soundly.

What was this creeping stealthily through the bush? The form of a man, with haggard, almost despairing face; with beating heart, with hands that trembled with a convulsive agony. The form of Richard Handfield!

He had escaped from his vile associates. Strict as was the watch they had kept upon him, he had eluded them; he had made no idle efforts to escape; he had bided his time, and he was free. But of what use was his freedom to him? He had joined them for the settled purpose of obtaining some information, some evidence, that would render clear his innocence of the horrible charge which he knew men and the law were bringing against him. If he could have done that, he would have been contented. But he had not been able to obtain the slightest evidence to assist him; and hope, for a time, entirely deserted him, when he discovered that they all knew that the Oysterman himself had done the deed, and had laid the trap to catch him. Richard, for the sake of his own personal safety, was compelled to join in admiration of the devilish cunning which had thrown the suspicion of guilt upon himself. He had unconsciously strengthened the spring of the trap in which he had been caught; for, say the entire gang were taken, would not their vindictiveness lead them to bear false evidence against him? What else could he expect from such as they? They all hated him, they all suspected him; and he knew that they only admitted him as a comrade because of his intimate knowledge of Highlay Station, and of the house in which was concealed the purchase-money of the property which Mathew Nuttall coveted. That obtained, they would not care what became of him; nor did he, either, but for one consideration, care what became of himself. But for that one consideration, he would have bidden good-bye to life--he would have had courage for that, coward as he was--and would have allowed the waters of pitiless circumstance to have engulfed him for ever. That consideration was Alice. That she, knowing his weak, vacillating nature, should be led to believe from his silence that he was guilty, was the worst torture of all to him. He wanted to see her, to assure her of his innocence; then, let come what might, he would meet it with some sort of weak fortitude at all events. And he would save Alice's father if he could; he would do that one right deed for Alice's sake. So, matching his cunning with theirs, he had escaped from the villains that day; and now he was making his way to a hut, where he knew two stockmen dwelt, to give the alarm. He had not eaten food since the morning; he had a few shillings in his pocket, but he had not dared to diverge from his course to purchase bread. He halted for a moment, faint and weary, his heart racked with a terrible despair. He had brought it all on himself, he knew, by his unmanliness. Who was he that he should pass his time in repining as he had done? What better man was he than other men, that he should expect life to be made especially smooth for him? But he had expected this, and had wrecked his happiness by murmuring at the fancied hardships by which he had been afflicted. He thought of Alice waiting in Melbourne--waiting and hoping in vain--but still loving him, still believing in him. "I am unworthy of her," he groaned; "and have been from the first, utterly unworthy. No man ever had such a blessing as she would have been to me, if I had not been mad. Oh, bright Heaven!" he cried; "place it in my power to see her, and tell her of my innocence before I die!" He crept on in the direction of the stockmen's hut. At every step he took he halted, his heart in his ears; for he knew well that if he were caught by the gang, life was over with him. He was thoroughly acquainted with the locality. "They may lose some time hunting for me," he thought; "and I may gain a few minutes by that means." The moments were too precious to waste in repining. He had a purpose to accomplish--to fail in its accomplishment would be worse than death. And a moment might win it or mar it. Life had never before been so bitter and so sweet to him as it was at this time: bitter in the irrevocable past, with its load of shame and humiliation; sweet in the possible future in the thought that he might save the woman who had sacrificed all for him from the agony of believing him guilty. He dashed the bitter tears from his eyes, and crept along. But a few yards--for he saw a human form upon the ground. Who could it be? He crept onwards, and bending over it--Great Heavens! Was he dreaming, or was it a phantasm of Death? The earth and sky, blended together, swam in his fading sight. Then, he saw nothing but the white face of his wife, and he sank down beside it. He lost consciousness for a few moments, and when he recovered, he rose and looked about him with the air of one waking from a bewildering dream. Hush! she was speaking in her sleep. He knelt by her side, and listened. He heard his name and her father's mingled strangely together. He heard her entreat him not to--Horror!--was it Murder of which she spoke? He seized her by the arm, and cried, "Alice! Alice! awake!" With a scream of terror she awoke, and seeing her husband before her, she called him by the dearest of names, and blessing God for bringing him to her, she fell upon his breast weeping. For a brief space only did she allow herself such happiness. The full memory of her mission rushed upon her, and she extricated herself from his arms, and asked, "Oh, Richard, answer me quickly--am I too late?"

Too late for what? He did not speak the words, but she saw them expressed in his face. She saw, accompanying them, a look of such terrible despair, that her senses would have left her if her strong purpose had not upheld her.

"Tell me,--quickly, or I shall die," she said in a voice which, although it was no louder than a whisper, sounded on his ears like a knell; "am I too late?"

"Too late for what?" he was constrained to ask.

"To save my father!"

A sigh of exquisite relief escaped him. He thought it was of another danger she was about to speak. The change of expression in his countenance was a sufficient answer, and for a few brief moments she was silent, almost overcome with grateful thought.

"I am bewildered," Richard said, pressing his hands across his face. "What brought you here?"

"I came to save my father--to save you."

"Then you know--"

"All."

"All!" echoed Richard, shrinking from her. "Do not shrink from me, dear," she said. "Yes, I know all about my father's danger and yours. Do not look upon me so strangely, Richard. Is it not happiness that we have met before any evil is done? Be thankful for his sake, for yours, for mine."

He did not reply, but he came closer to her, and then she told him rapidly what had occurred to her since he left Melbourne. In as few words as she could relate the story, she told him of Milly's death, of the letter the poor girl had given her, and of the horror which possessed her when she read of the plot Jim Pizey and his comrades had laid to trap her husband--

Richard stopped her there. "Anything about a murder?" he asked. "No," she answered; "only mention of the circumstance that they had set a trap for him and had caught him."

That gleam of hope vanished as soon as it had shone upon his troubled soul. He pressed his hand to his heart, and motioned her to proceed.

She told him how she and Grif had started to walk from Melbourne half-an-hour after poor Milly died--every word she uttered of this part of her story struck him as if it were a dagger's point; she told him of Grif's goodness to her--(the lad had awoke, and was standing by them, listening to Alice with rapt attention, and when she mentioned his name she took his hand and kissed it); of the kind friends they had met upon the road; of their walking a long distance that day, and of their stopping providentially to rest for a while before proceeding to her father's house; all this she told him almost breathlessly. But he saw what she made no mention of; he saw in her care-worn face the anxiety and grief she had suffered for him--he saw in her patient, uncomplaining eyes, the perfect purity of her love--he saw in her soiled and ragged clothes the wondrous evidence of a holy self-sacrifice-

-and he fell upon his knees, and, burying his face in her dress, he sobbed like a little child.

"Oh, my dear! my dear!" he cried. "How unworthy I am of your love!"

"Not unworthy, Richard," she said happy in the thought that his nature was not hardened; "unfortunate, not unworthy. We have gone through terrible storms, dear, but they will pass away presently. Surely we have suffered enough!" But there was no sound of complaining in her voice as she raised her streaming eyes to heaven.

He kept his face buried in her dress, and the memory of their last parting, when he knelt before her as he was kneeling before her now, and when she blessed him with her hands upon his head, came to his mind. How low had he fallen since that time!

"There is a more terrible storm for you to bear than any you have yet borne," he said. "There is a greater peril before us than any we have yet encountered."

Her face was hidden from him, but he held her hand in his, and it suddenly turned cold. Her fingers tightened upon his, and she asked, "What is it? What storm? What peril?"

"I had a mate, a Welshman, a man with a soul as innocent as a child's--with a heart as tender as a woman's. I was growing to love him. I had another mate, a villain, who stepped between us and told to each of us such lying stories of the other, that we quarrelled, and almost fought. All the gold-diggers knew that we were at enmity with each other. They all knew that if there were any true cause for our quarrel, poor Tom would be found to be in the right, I in the wrong. They knew him to be good and gentle-hearted. They knew me to be proud and selfish. They loved him. They despised me. We lived in a tent together, and slept beneath the same roof. One night I came home, filled with bitter feelings, which I had been expressing in company. I was stung almost to madness by what my villain-mate told me Tom had said of me. I never stopped to think, I never stopped to ask, but I let my passion have full sway. When I came home, determined to quarrel, pledged to do so, proud fool as I am! because I had said as much out-of-doors--Tom met my passion with sweetness, and forced me to talk of the cause of our falling-out. Then we discovered that our false mate had been lying to both of us, to make us enemies for some purpose of his own, which I did not know then, but know now. We shook hands, and were friends again; we laid out plans for the future--for your happiness and mine chiefly, for Tom taught me my duty that night. We went to bed, and in the morning Tom was found dead, murdered with my knife! That and the other awful evidence of my own ungovernable passion were against me, and I was obliged, or thought I was obliged, to fly for my life; the gold-diggers swore they would lynch me if they caught me. So I fled in the company of the villains from whom I have but this day escaped. The false mate who set Tom and me quarrelling was the Tenderhearted Oysterman, disguised so that I could not recognise him--and the murder of the Welshman with my knife was the means they took of compelling me to join them. I escaped from them to-day--to warn your father and save him, if possible. That is why I am here. After that I do not know what will become of me. As I hope for mercy, I have told you the truth!"

When he had spoken the words: "Tom was found dead, murdered with my knife," Richard, whose face was still half-hidden in his wife's dress, felt her limbs tremble, although no sound escaped her. At that sign, he rose abruptly, and he spoke the last words of his confession, "As I hope for mercy, I have told you the truth!" with his back turned to her. The moment's pause that ensued seemed to him an hour; the stars paled out of the skies, and a thick darkness fell upon him and shut out the sight of everything but his own deep misery; then a great tremor of happiness came upon him, for he felt his wife's arms about his neck and heard her voice whispering in his ear: "I know you have, my love. Did you think I could believe you otherwise than unfortunate? More now than ever must we be brave, must we be firm; not only life and happiness, but honour is at stake. Courage, love! courage! Think! Is there no way to prove your innocence of this dreadful charge? The letter I have is something."

"It is something," he said; "but oh Alice, my dear, in the harsh judgments of men, with all-cruel circumstance against me, it will be but poor testimony in my favour. All the gang know he committed the crime. If I had a witness, one who had heard the villain confess, as he confessed to me, laughing the while, that he stole my knife, and with it did the deed, for the purpose of trapping me--if I had such a witness, my innocence would be established. Oh, Alice, if I had such a witness--for your sake, my love! my darling! whom I have surrounded with shame and misery--"

"Hush! my dear! Heaven will send such a witness! I know it! I feel it!"

"I scarcely dare hope it," he said; "it is known to none but to the four men in the gang. And they will not tell, for their own sakes."

"I will appeal to them--implore them. I have a message to the man Pizey from poor Milly. I will see him, and beg of him, for her sake, to clear you from the charge."

"You do not know them; pity never enters their hearts. There are four of them: Jim Pizey, the Tenderhearted Oysterman, Ned Rutt, as cold-blooded a villain as ever stepped, and Grif's father."

Richard said this last in a whisper, so that Grif should not hear. He looked at the lad, who was still standing by them in an attentive attitude.

"Is he with them?" asked Alice, with a pitying glance to Grif, who was now turning slowly away.

"Yes, and as bad as the rest. But Alice, we have tarried too long already. We must not waste another minute."

"Yes, we must go," Alice said, preparing to move. "You know the way, Richard. Take comfort, dear! All will turn out well--I feel it will. Where's Grif?"

Grif was gone. They called him, and searched for him in vain. They could find no trace of him.

"He was here but a moment ago!" Alice said, in deep distress. "Perhaps he thinks you are not pleased to find me with him. He is keenly sensitive."

"And I have spoken unkindly to him, and he remembers it," said Richard, to whom every memory of the past brought with it a sting of self-reproach. "If I can make it up to him, I will. He will find us, I have no doubt. We dare not linger now, Alice. The stockmen's hut is in the hollow. We must go there at once, and give the alarm. Come--there may be death to your father in every moment's delay!"

Keenly anxious as Alice was because of Grif's unaccountable disappearance, she felt how precious was time for the safety of her father: his life might depend upon their speed. They moved carefully away from the track, and walked through the bush as quickly as possible.

"There are few except myself who would be able to find their way here," said Richard. "But you remember, Alice, I was always fond of roaming about the Station. You would scarcely believe how near to this spot is your father's house. It is only two miles, as the crow flies--I could walk straight to it, in less than half-an-hour. Hark! We are disturbing the crows! I used to call this Crow's Hollow. See, we are in a hollow, completely hidden by the ranges and the thick timber. It is a melancholy-looking place."

It was in truth a dismal spot, and Alice shuddered as she heard the harsh cawing of the birds. Suddenly she stopped.

"Richard," she said, "do you hear nothing?"

He listened, and shook his head.

"Nothing but the crows," he said.

"It's not a crow, Richard. Listen again. Can I be mistaken? A child's voice, singing!"

And hurrying swiftly in the direction of the sound, they came upon a strange sight. Two boy-children were lying, as if dead, upon the ground, clasped in each other's arms, and one, a little girl, was covering them with her frock, which she had taken off for that purpose. She was the eldest of the three, and yet could scarcely be eight years of age. She was singing softly a child's ditty. A few yards from her was a pale-faced boy, looking vacantly before him. It was Little Peter, who with the other three children had been wandering in the bush for two days. They had set out for a long walk on the first day, taking two or three slices of bread and butter with them, and had lost their way. When the night came, they were near a cavern, the mouth of which was nearly choked up with stones and rotten underwood. They peeped through the crevices, and as it looked like a house inside, they crept in, and tried to go to sleep. But they had not been long in the cave before they heard a great flapping, and something rushed by, sending a cold wind to their faces. They were nearly frightened out of their lives, but they did not dare to move; every other minute came the flapping and cold wind. They thought the place was haunted, and they shut their eyes tight, and pressed their fingers in their ears, and lay trembling with their faces touching each other; they found much comfort in that! The bravest of the party was the little girl, sister to Johnny and Billy. These three were the Stockman's children. The girl, although she was mortally afraid, kept her fears to herself, and sang little songs to her companions during the whole night. And so they lay, with their faces touching each other, until the morning came. For a good many minutes they were frightened to look around, but when they did muster up courage, they found that there were a great number of bats inside the cavern, and that it was the flapping of their wings that had frightened them so. The floor of the cavern was strewn with the bones and dried-up skins of bats. The children were glad to get out into the bright light, and they washed their faces and dried them on the little girl's frock. Then they began to feel hungry, but all their bread and butter was eaten. They did not know where they were, and they wandered about the whole of the day, crying, and growing more and more faint, until night came again; they would not go into the cavern to sleep, so the girl had made her two brothers a bed of leaves, and was trying to sing them to sleep, when Alice and Richard discovered them. The child stopped in the middle of her song, and running to Alice, with a cry of joy, said,--

"If you please we have been lost in the bush, and Johnny and Billy, and Little Peter, and me, we've had nothing to eat, and we're so hungry! Please take us home?" The children clustered around her, and she was stooping to kiss them, when a groan from Richard caused her to look up.

"Alice!" he cried, seizing her arm with such force as to cause her pain. "See! We are discovered!"

Lights were moving in the bush, and the voices of men, calling to each other, were heard.

"It is Jim Pizey and the rest, looking for me," he whispered, hoarsely, and trembling with fear--for her, not for himself. "If they find us, it is all over with us. They swore to kill me, if I attempted to escape; and you--Oh, Alice! say that you forgive me for the peril to which I have exposed you!"

"I do forgive you, Richard!" Alice said, kissing him. "Have you any weapon?"

He produced a revolver, loaded.

"Is it useless trying to escape?" she asked.

"Quite. See--they are spreading themselves out. We are lost. They have no pity, those men. Oh my God!" he cried, in an anguish. "This is worse than all!"

"If those men be the men you fear, Richard," said Alice, rapidly, her limbs trembling, and a nameless horror resting in her eyes, "swear that you will kill me! Swear it, as you hope for mercy--as you hope to meet me in heaven, when all our misery is ended!"

"I swear it, Alice!"

"My poor husband!--my dear love!" and she pressed him to her breast. "Forgive us, O Lord, for what we are about to do!"

They stood hand in hand, their faces as the faces of the dead; while the children, clinging to Alice's dress, looked up at her in wondering fear.

Nearer and nearer came the lights, and louder grew the voices of the men.

"Here is a shoe!" one called out. "The children are somewhere near. We're on their track."

"It is my father's voice!" cried Alice, as the sound reached her ears. "Richard, we are saved! They are searching for the children we have found! Do you hear? We are saved! Father! this way! this way!"

But the last words died in her throat, and staggering forward, she fell into the arms of her father, who had hurried to the spot as she cried. He recognised his daughter, and a fear smote him, as she lay motionless in his arms, that she was dead. The remorse which fell upon him overcame his surprise at her appearance, and even made him look upon Richard without astonishment.

"She has fainted from fatigue, sir," said Richard; "she has been sorely tried."

"Why is she here?" asked Matthew Nuttall.

"She came from Melbourne, sir, to warn you of danger which threatens you, and to save me from disgrace; but for this latter, I fear she is too late. Your house, at this moment, is surrounded by bushrangers."

"Bushrangers!" cried Matthew Nuttall; "and there are only two women in the house!"

"We are stronger than the bushrangers," said Richard. "There are but four in their party. We have no time to lose. We must make for the place without delay. See, sir! Your daughter is recovering."

She opened her eyes, and looked wildly round. Seeing her father, her memory returned; and she slid from his arms, and falling upon her knees at his feet, she said, imploringly,--

"Forgive me, father!"

The sound of the soft lapping of the sea upon the sands fell upon his ears, but now there was a sweet music in the sound; and in the vision of white crested waves which came upon him again, the stars were shining in the blue depths with a glad light. Chastened and subdued, he raised his daughter to his breast and kissed her. The tears that welled into his eyes were tears of purification. His hard nature was softened by the perfect goodness of the pure and faithful woman! He held out his hand to Richard, who took it, and said--

"We dare not linger, sir. The bushrangers may be there before us."

"True!" replied Matthew Nuttall. "Keep a good look-out, men, and follow me. We'll take these villains, dead or alive! See to your pistols. Alice, keep behind with the children. Now then, On!"

CHAPTER XXVII
GRIF BEARS FALSE WITNESS

When Grif had fallen asleep an hour ago, overcome by fatigue, the fever which had made him shiver to his marrow seemed to have left him. Alice's words: "You are my brother, now and always," were like balm to his aching body, and caused him to forget his pain. "Her brother now and always!" he murmured to himself again and again, and sleep overtook him with a smile upon his lips. When he awoke he was not surprised to see Richard standing by Alice's side. It was a fitting continuation of the fancies that had been busy in his brain while he was dozing--fancies which took no defined mental shape, but pointed to a happy termination of Alice's troubles. So, he had stood quietly by the side of Alice and her husband, listening attentively to Richard's story, and taking no credit to himself for the part he had played in bringing husband and wife to each other's arms. As Richard spoke of Poor Welsh Tom, Grif thought, "I should like to know him; he's the right sort, he is," and when the despairing man came to the Welshman's murder, Grif felt as if he had lost a friend. It would be difficult to analyse the sensations that crowded upon Grif's mind as Richard proceeded with his story. All his pain came back to him intensified by the misery he felt was in store for Alice, unless her husband's innocence were established. Misery, not happiness, would be her portion if this were not accomplished. It must be done. But how! There were two reasons why it must be done--one infinitely less strong than the other, but having its weight nevertheless in the light of Grif's untrained intellect. The stronger reason was Alice's welfare; all considerations, but one, sank into utter insignificance, when her happiness was in question. The weaker reason sprang from his implacable hatred to the Tenderhearted Oysterman. And now the two dominant feelings which possessed him--the earnest desire to benefit Alice, and the intense desire to revenge himself upon the Tenderhearted Oysterman--seemed in some dim way to be connected. The very accomplishment of his desire to serve Alice must spring from the accomplishment of his desire to be revenged upon his enemy. That end he saw; but how about the means?

All this passed through Grif's mind while Richard was telling his story. The story being told, a despairing conviction stole upon Grif that Richard was lost, and with him, Alice. There was no way to prove Richard's innocence. As he thought this, he heard Richard's next words, "If I had a witness, one who heard the villain confess, as he confessed to me, laughing the while, that he stole my knife, and with it did the deed, for the purpose of trapping me--if I had such a witness, my innocence would be established." Then he heard Alice console her husband and say, "Heaven will send such a witness. I know it! I feel it!" As these words fell upon his ears, light dawned upon him, and a suddenly-formed, but fixed purpose, entered his mind. Watching his opportunity, he stole softly away--so softly that neither Alice nor Richard observed him. He heard Alice call to him, but he did not reply. He lingered for a little while, and was grateful to them for the trouble they took to find him. Alice was so close to him once that he was enabled to touch her; and for the second time that night he touched her dress with his hand, and then raised his hand to his lips. He kept it there for a few moments, thinking the while. "She wouldn't call me if she knew what I was goin' to do," he said. "Besides, she's got her husband now; she don't want me. What a artful trap they set to catch Dick Handfield! What oneners they are! But Grif'll show 'em!" And he walked off towards Matthew Nuttall's house, talking and communing with himself as he went.

"She wants a witness," he said. "She's got her husband, and she'd be all right if she had a witness. It's not a bit of good her comin' all the way up here, if she don't get a witness. What did Dick Handfield say? If he had a witness who could swear that he heard the Oysterman confess to stealin' his knife and murderin' the poor cove with it, his innocence would be proved! Yes, that was what he said. If he don't get that witness, he'll be took up for murder, and somethin' dreadful 'll happen to Ally. And if his innocence is proved, Ally will be happy all her life. That'd be very good, that would. 'Eaven will send the witness, Ally said. No, it won't. For I'll be the witness! And 'Eaven don't send me! Not a bit of it! Only think of the Oysterman laughin' all the while he told how he murdered poor Tom!" (Grif lingered lovingly over the memory of Welsh Tom, as if they had been friends.) "He's a rasper, is the Oysterman! But I'll be even with him. If I can get in with the gang--but they'd suspect me. I was moral when the Oysterman and Jim sor me in Melbourne--they won't believe I ain't moral now. How shall I manage it? I've got to be very careful with 'em. They're up to pretty nearly every move. I've got it!" he cried, after pondering for a few moments. "I'll say I've been sent up by Old Flick, to tell 'em that Dick Handfield's going to peach upon 'em. They'll b'lieve that! Dick Handfield's runnin' away to-day 'll make 'em believe it. They won't be up to that dodge. And I'll tell Jim Pizey that Milly's dead, and that she made me promise to come and see him at once, and arks him to take care of the baby. That's a artful move, that is, and no mistake! He liked Milly, did Jim, and he'll be sorry to hear she's dead." (Grif laughed and hugged himself as he thought of his scheme.) "And father's in the gang, too. I heard Dick tell Ally that; though he said it in a whisper, and didn't want me to hear. I ain't seen father since he shied that bottle at my head for stealin' pies. He said I'd disgraced him, and that he never was in quod for stealin' pies. He wouldn't mind if I'd been in quod for somethin' worse. I know what I'll do. I'll tell him I'm a regular plucky 'un, a regular bad 'un, up to anythin', and I'll get him to tell me all about the Oysterman's plot. Then I'll go and be a witness. Lord!" he mused, "what a queer move it is! They'll kill me when they find it out, but I don't care. It'll make Ally happy, and she'll like me all the better. Then there's the Oysterman! I'll cry quits with him, now, for pizenin' Rough! Won't he be savage!"

But any pleasure he might have derived from this last reflection was soon lost in the contemplation of his fixed purpose to serve Alice. Grif's love for her amounted almost to worship. When he told her that he would die for her, he meant, actually, that he would be glad to die, if, by his death, he could serve her. Born and reared in the midst of thieves and ruffians, no softening influence had fallen upon him until he had met Alice. She had been kind and gentle to him, who had never before received kind or gentle treatment. Accustomed from his birth to the association of men in whom brutality and selfishness were predominant, the picture of Alice's unselfish devotion caused him to reflect. It awoke the good principle within him, and she became at once his standard of perfection. "When she gave him her friendship, he felt that he was unworthy of it. Could he make himself worthy of it? No, he was sure he could not; he was so different to her, or, rather, she was so different to every one else. He was surrounded with evil associations, and he could not disentangle himself from them. Only once had he made an attempt to free himself, and that he did rather to please Alice than in the belief that he would be successful. Well, he had tried to be honest, and he had almost starved; he would have starved if he had persevered in his moral career--that he had settled satisfactorily with himself. It was clearly evident that honesty was not for such as he. It was not his fault that he had been born; it was not his fault that he was what he was; yet the world punished him for it. But Alice had pitied him because of his unfortunate position, and her sympathy fell upon his heart, like rain upon parched land. To the world, for its harshness, he returned defiance; to Alice, for her tenderness, he gave all he had to give of love.

"I wonder if they're at the house," Grif said, as he walked along. "If they are, I hope they won't hurt no one. He's a wicked devil, is Jim Pizey, though, and he'll be mad at Dick's runnin' away from 'em."

Soon he came to a fence, and, three or four hundred yards before him, he saw the Home Station. A fine house, built of stone, with a broad verandah in front, and surrounded with garden-grounds in beautiful order. Grif crept slowly along by the side of the fence, in the direction of the house.

"I can see lights movin' about," he muttered. "There's a man outside, walkin' up and down. He's got a gun in his hand, too. Yes, they're there, and he's keepin' watch. Everything very quiet."

By this time, Grif was within twenty yards of the house. He halted for a minute or two; he had crept very cautiously and carefully along in the shade of the fence, and had not been observed.

"I can't make it out," he said, conscious that he must not lose time, and puzzled at the almost deathlike stillness that prevailed; "Where are all the Station men? They can't have killed 'em. How awful quiet it is! Who's that keepin' watch?" he muttered, looking eagerly forward. "It ain't Jim Pizey, and it ain't the Oysterman. Why, it's father! I'll go right up to him."

And he walked away from the fence, towards the house. As he did so, he was seen by the sentinel, who gave a shrill whistle, and cried,--

"Stand!"

"It's all right," exclaimed Grif, recognising his father's voice; "Don't you know me?"

But the man did not distinguish what Grif said.

"Stand!" he cried again; "or I'll fire!"

"It's me, father!" cried Grif, running swiftly towards him. "Don't fire! It's me--Grif!"

He had scarcely uttered the words, when he was struck down by a bullet. Confused and dizzy, he struggled to his feet, pressing his hand to his side. In the midst of his confusion he became conscious of a terrible change in the aspect of the scene. A wild fury appeared to take possession of the place. As he looked round, dazed, he saw men running towards the house, and heard the sound of shots following each other rapidly.

"Who are you?" asked one of the men, seizing him roughly by the shoulder.

"Who am I?" the boy replied, looking about him in a bewilderment of deathly pain. The blood was flowing from his wound, staining the grass and flowers, and everything was fading from his sight, when he suddenly saw Alice. "Who am I?" he repeated. "Arks Ally! She knows. I'm Grif!"

And, with a wild shudder, he staggered forward and fell senseless at Alice's feet!

She threw herself beside him, and, tearing off a portion of her dress, she endeavoured to staunch his wound. By this time, the bushrangers were in full retreat, pursued by most of the men who had been engaged in the search for the children. Amongst those who stayed behind were Matthew Nuttall and his brother, and Richard Handfield. Nicholas had hurried into the house, to ascertain if his wife and daughter were safe; and he now returned with some brandy, which he put to Grif's lips. Richard, who had some little knowledge of surgery, examined the wound, and said,--

"He must not be moved, Alice. He cannot live many minutes."

"Do not say that!" cried Alice, weeping bitterly. "Oh, my poor Grif! He has died for me! My poor, dear Grif!"

The brandy which Grif tasted partially restored him. Opening his eyes, and looking with a loving tenderness upon Alice's face, he pressed her hand which held his, and said faintly,--

"All right, Ally. Don't you cry for me. I'm her friend," he muttered, "and her brother, too! She said so herself, she did."

"Are you in pain, dear Grif?" she asked.

"Not much. 'Tain't worth botherin' about. Where's father?" Turning, he saw Matthew Nuttall, and a look of recognition came into his eyes. Seeing that Grif wished to speak to him, he came closer to the dying lad. "Do you remember me, sir?" Grif asked wistfully.

"Yes."

"I want to tell you, sir, about them brushes and the boot-stand. You remember when Mr. Blemish set me up as a moral shoeblack? You was in the office, sir, at the time. I ain't ungrateful to Mr. Blemish; 'tain't likely I should be. But I couldn't get a livin', sir; everybody seemed to say to me, You got no business to be moral, you ain't! You ought to be ashamed of yourself for being moral, you ought! They was right, sir; it was out of my line, that's a fact. And one day, when I was very hungry, I sold them brushes and the stand to Old Flick for four bob. It was wrong of me, sir, but I couldn't help it--I was so hungry! Will you arks Mr. Blemish to forgive me, sir, and tell him he can get the brushes and stand back from Old Flick? Only he'll have to pay more nor four bob for 'em. Will you tell Mr. Blemish?" Matthew nodded in pitying silence. "Thank you, sir. Then I sor you the night you took care of Little Peter. You was very kind to me then, sir. I've often thought of it, and thanked you, when you didn't know nothin' about it." Grif had to stop many times from weakness. He looked at Alice, then at Matthew, and motioning him to lean forward, said in a whisper, "I had it in my mind, sir, to speak to you about her when you sor me and Little Peter under the hedge, but I didn't dare. I'm such a poor common beggar! But I know what good is, sir, I do. She's good;--ah! that she is! And she tried to make me good; but it was no go. You don't know what she's suffered, sir. I told you I'd made a promise, and couldn't break it. It was her I made the promise to, sir. And I've tried to be true and faithful to her, and I will--till I die!"

A gleam of satisfaction lit up Grif's face as Matthew Nuttall placed his hand on his daughter's arm, in sympathy with her grief.

"That's good, at all events," Grif said, softly to himself; "he ain't such a bad sort, after all." Then aloud, "I'd like to see Little Peter."

Little Peter was soon brought to Grif's side; he was tired and worn out with his day's wanderings, and he evinced no emotion at seeing Grif. But Grif did not look for any exhibition of gladness from the lad whom he had nursed and fed.

"How are you, Little Peter?" Grif asked, patting the boy's hand. "He looks well, sir. You're never hungry now, are you?"

"I was hungry to-day," Little Peter said.

"He was lost in the bush, Grif, with other children," Alice whispered, in explanation. "We found him very tired, and very hungry. He will be well to-morrow."

"You found him, Ally!" Grif said. "After I went away?"

"Yes. Why did you go away?"

"Never you mind. I didn't go away for no harm. The young lady who was with you that night, sir!" he said to Matthew Nuttall. "I think it was a good deal through her that you took care of Little Peter. Thank her for me, sir, please, when you see her."

"Thank her yourself, my lad," Matthew said, beckoning to Marian, who came forward, and stooped towards Grif. As she did so, Grif caught the stone heart which the Tenderhearted Oysterman had compelled her to place round her neck.

"It's like a dream," he said, holding the emblem in his hand; "everythin' seems to be comin' all at once. This heart--"

"One of the bad men who were here to-night made me place it round my neck," Marian said.

"This is Little Peter's heart," said Grif; "how did one of them get hold of it, I wonder?"

"Have you seen it before?" asked Richard.

"Yes, sir; it's Little Peter's heart, that is--I remember losin' it one night, but I don't know where. It belonged to Little Peter's mother. When she died in the horspital, she put it round his neck."

"His mother, then, must have been poor Tom's sister," Richard whispered to Alice. "I picked up the heart on the stairs when I wished you good-bye in Melbourne. The night before Tom died he saw it and recognised it. The Oysterman must have stolen it from Welsh Tom that dreadful night. It may be a clue to the proof of my innocence."

Alice pressed her husband's hand, and motioned him to look at Grif, over whose countenance a change was passing. Richard knelt and felt his pulse, and Alice took Grif's other hand in hers.

"Grif, my dear," she said, placing her lips close to his face, "you see that my father has forgiven me."

He nodded. Her lips to his ear, her hand clasping his, were heaven to him.

"It is you I thank for it, my dear," she continued. "I am in hopes that all will be well with us for the future, and that my trouble is nearly over."

"That's good!" he murmured.

"I tell you this, knowing you will be glad to hear it. I tell you this gratefully, thankfully, oh, my dear! because I owe it all to you!"

A smile of much sweetness rested on his lips. "I'm her brother, now, and always, that's what I am," he murmured.

"He is sinking fast, Alice," Richard whispered; "he cannot live much longer."

"What's that?" Grif exclaimed, in a loud voice, trying to raise himself; he had heard Richard's words. "I mustn't die yet. Don't let me die till I've said what I've got to say! Will anybody fetch a magistrate for a poor cove? I want a magistrate, that's what I want!"

"I am a magistrate," Matthew Nuttall said.

"That's the sort," Grif gasped out. "You hear what I've got to say, and put it down in writin'! I'm dyin', you know. Take her away first," and he relinquished Alice's hand. "Stand off a bit for a minute or two, Ally, and take him away with you." He pointed to Richard Handfield. The husband and wife fell back, in wonder; but, although she could not hear what he said, Alice followed, with her eyes, every movement of the dying lad.

"Now, then," said Grif, when Alice and her husband were out of hearing. "I've got something to say with my dyin' breath. Will what I say be evidence? I arks you as a magistrate, will what I say when I'm dyin' be evidence?"

"If you swear to it, my poor boy," replied Matthew Nuttall, gently.

"I'll swear to it! All right! I'll kiss the Bible on it. That's swearin', ain't it?"

"Yes," said Matthew, whispering to Nicholas, who ran into the house, and returned with a Bible and a writing-desk. While he was away, Grif turned his eyes to where Alice was standing, weeping, and he continued to gaze on her lovingly as he spoke.

"All right, Ally!" he muttered to himself. "I'll make you happy. You shall owe it every bit to me. You want a witness, that's what you want. I heerd you say so; everythin' might go wrong if you don't have a witness. And I'm a-goin' to be that witness, though 'Eaven didn't send me!"

"Now, my lad," said Matthew Nuttall. "What is it you want to say? Do not speak too fast, for you are very weak."

"Yes, I'm very weak. I'm a dyin', you know, and when I've said what I got to say, I shan't trouble nobody no more. Fust and foremost, then, them coves as stuck up your house was bushrangers. Put that down."

"That is down. I can write as you speak."

"Jim Pizey and the Tenderhearted Oysterman was two on 'em. I kiss the Bible, and I ses, I heerd the Tenderhearted Oysterman say as how he murdered a man--a Welshman--on the diggins', and as how he stole Dick Handfield's knife to kill him with, so that it'd look as if Dick had done it instead of him; and I kisses the Bible agin, and I ses as how all the gang knows it was the Tenderhearted Oysterman who done the murder, and not Dick Handfield."

"You heard the man you call the Tenderhearted Oysterman confess to the murder?"

"I heerd him say he done it himself, with Dick Handfield's knife. I kisses the Bible on it. You've got all that down?"

"It is all written, my lad!" said Matthew Nuttall, gravely.

"And I furthermore ses as how Jim Pizey and the Oysterman wanted Dick Handfield, when they was in Melbourne, to join them in robbin' Highlay Station--Everthin's goin' away! hold me up! Don't let me die till I'm done! The sky's a-comin' down upon me!"

The brandy was put to his lips, and he revived again; but the words now came very slowly from him.

"Where was I?" he asked.

"They wanted Dick Handfield to join them in robbing Highlay Station."

"Yes, that's it," said Grif, his voice falling to a whisper. "And as how Dick Handfield wouldn't. And as how they wanted to throw the murder on him, out of revenge."

"Have you finished?" asked Matthew Nuttall, as the boy paused.

"Yes--I forget all the rest," muttered Grif. "Where's Ally?"

"One moment! You swear to this?"

"I kisses the Bible on it."

"Can you sign your name?"

"I can't write. I can only read large letters on the walls."

"What is your name?"

"Grif."

"But your other name?"

"I never had no other. I'm Grif, that's what I am!

"Raise him, Nicholas, and let him put a cross here."

The boy was raised, and the pen being held in his almost nerveless fingers, he scrawled a cross.

"Tell Ally to come," he said, as they laid him down. Alice came, and knelt by him. He was happy now. The false evidence he had given seemed to him the only good thing he had ever done.

"It's all right, Ally," he gasped. She had to place her ear to his lips to catch his words. "You won't have no more trouble. I've never been no good all my life till now. I want to kiss Little Peter."

Little Peter was brought to him. "Poor Little Peter!" he said. "I'm goin' away, and before I go I want you to promise to be moral. You won't be no good unless you're moral. Say you'll be moral, Little Peter."

"I'll be moral," said Little Peter, mechanically.

Grif gazed at the lad lovingly, kissed him, and turned again to Alice.

"Ally, dear, you said there was another world. There is, isn't there?"

"Yes, Grif. You are going there, now."

"Shall I see you there, by-and-by?"

"We shall meet there, dear Grif," she answered, keeping back her tears.

"We shall meet there, we shall meet there!" he murmured, in a glad voice, and then was silent for a while. Presently he whispered,--

"You kissed me once; will you kiss me again?"

She placed her arms about him, and kissed his lips.

"It wasn't my fault that I wasn't no good. I only wanted my grub and a blanket. If any swell 'ad a-given 'em to me, it'd been all right. I tried to be moral, but I couldn't be. I wasn't cut out for it. Why, there's Milly!" and he suddenly raised himself, and a bright expression came over his face. Alice held him in her arms, and watched the fading light in his eyes.

"And there's Rough. Rough! Rough! And the old pie-woman, too!" he cried, as his arm stole round Alice's neck. "What was it Milly said the other night? Oh, I know! Forgive me, God!"

And with that supplication upon his lips, and with his head on Alice's breast, Grif closed his eyes upon the world!

Richard Handfield's innocence was proved without Grif s dying statement. The bushrangers were pursued; the Oysterman was shot dead, and the others were captured. When Jim Pizey was lying in prison, Alice visited him, and gave him Milly's message. In that poor girl's name, Alice implored him to confess who had killed the Welshman. His hard nature was softened by the thought of Alice's kindness to Milly, and by her promise to take care of Milly's baby; and, knowing that his career was over, he admitted that it was the Oysterman who had committed the murder with Richard Handfield's knife.

Here the story ends. If misfortune and poverty should come again to Richard, he would battle with them bravely, if only for the sake of the true woman who called him husband. But it is not likely he will be so tried, for Matthew Nuttall has been reconciled to him, and Richard and Alice live happily at Highlay.

Grif was buried near the Home Station. The husband and wife often visit his grave, and often speak of him, tenderly and lovingly, as of a dear and cherished friend!